SPECIMEN

I0588351

ISBN: 978-1-64456-773-9 [Hardcover]
ISBN: 978-1-64456-774-6 [paperback]
ISBN: 978-1-64456-775-3 [Kindle]
ISBN: 978-1-64456-776-0 [ePub]

Library of Congress Control Number: 2024920204

INDIES UNITED PUBLISHING HOUSE, LLC
P.O. BOX 3071
QUINCY, IL 62305-3071
indiesunited.net

Dedication

To Lee – my husband, soulmate, love of my life

And to my parents - my greatest inspirations and role models

"Life shrinks or expands in proportion to one's courage."

Anais Nin

Other Books by Lisa Towles:

Codex

Terror Bay

Salt Island (E&A Series)

The Ridders

Hot House (E&A Series)

Ninety-Five

The Unseen

Choke

And published under the name Lisa Polisar:

Escape: Dark Mystery Tales

The Ghost of Mary Prairie

Blackwater Tango

Knee Deep

Specimen

A Thriller

Lisa Towles

INDIES UNITED PUBLISHING HOUSE, LLC

Prologue

"Mmmmm."

"Is that you?" I asked, unsure. Her voice sounded dreamy. And who answers the phone that way?

Now an exhaustive sigh.

"Lise, answer me!"

"What was the question again?" I heard her footsteps on the other end, walking slowly, rhythmically on a hard surface.

"Where are you right now?"

"How is that relevant?" she clipped back. Salty. That sounded more like her.

"Because! I'm a–" My words caught in my throat. I wiped my eyes and coughed, hoping to swallow the feeling of horror. "I'm at your house, where-you-summoned-me, where your—" Breathe, Thea. "Why did you run?" My raspy voice ricocheted against the marble walls of the colossal foyer.

"I've got nothing to say."

"That's not an answer."

"Well ask me something easier then."

I had no time to pause and think, to consider a strategy or explain the shocking circumstances to the part of my brain grasping for reason.

"Why call me in the first place, then?"

The footsteps halted. I now heard the roar of cars on the other end of the phone; she was outside. I ran to one of the front windows. No sign of her platinum hair or Burberry trench.

"You're just leaving me here?? What about the police? Who does this?"

"Couldn't be helped." Her monotone told me she was dissociating from the situation, which might imply she was as upset as I was. Or maybe that was just a fairy tale.

"What do I tell them?" I whispered.

"Cops? Whatever you want. You know nothing so they won't waste time on you."

"Cut it out." I moved from the front windows back to the same spot inside the front door, where I'd placed the call. A safe distance from the kitchen. Then my emotions caved in, sobs rippling out through my nose and mouth. My eyes were a mess. I couldn't wipe the tears fast enough.

"Calm down, Thea."

"Calm down? Are you high? They're gonna ask me what I know about—"

"My dead mother? No kidding. Believe me, she's better off this way. We all are."

She'd said the words finally – *dead mother*. So I hadn't imagined it? Now I needed to close it up and get the hell out of here. "Lise, did you—"

A thud from the kitchen yanked my attention from my phone. I felt the vibration under my feet. Maybe Lise hadn't actually killed her. Maybe the killer was still here.

Chapter 1

Blood pooled under the mop of the woman's dark brown hair, her skin a horrid chalky color, gray almost, body awkwardly twisted like she'd been on her way somewhere and shocked by the thrust of something blunt and resolute intended to stop the beat of her heart, or at least her intentions. As to what—I hadn't gotten there yet. Was it a good day to die?

I stared down at her body from the kitchen doorway, one hand covering my mouth to quell the shaking in my soul. I knew her. How could this possibly be real?

The house was quiet except for the howl of wind, the Fenning's giant sycamore scraping the east side of the house like a demon's fingernail. Fitting.

Something made me turn, not a sound exactly, more like a sensation. I gazed at the upstairs landing that overlooked a foyer the size of a basketball court. A much better vantage point to say the least. I tore up the stairs and pancaked myself to the cold tiles. My erratic pulse banged in my ears. Tha-thump, tha-thump. Breathe, Thea. Breathe. Okay, my frantic brain re-engaged for the moment, I could see this was a much safer place to assess. The woman's lower half was visible from here on the marble floor beside the island – dark gray pants, expensive black heels, one of them on and the other three inches from her body exposing a bare, grayish foot. Lying on my stomach, pain jarred me from the phone in my pocket—glass on bone. I hadn't pulled it out yet or called for help because I needed time to gather my wits, I had no idea what I'd say and, more importantly, what if her killer was still here?

I used to think a day that began with a game of cards was destined to be good. With a father and grandfather in the Navy, of course I grew up playing cards. I could beat them both at cribbage by the time I was fifteen, or maybe they let me win. There was something about numbers that had always comforted me, like a tacit reminder of the ordered universe despite all the visual evidence of chaos. And cribbage was a game that valued numbers and pairs, and in my fragile heart that symmetry felt, somehow, like safety. Okay sure, life in the Marshall Islands was a little sheltered, but my dad wanted it that way. My mother disagreed and tried to move us all to San Francisco, where we'd have the support of her family along with the contemporary imprint of urban life. She won the battle but lost the war. My father remained five thousand miles away in Majuro Atoll, and after my brother Rudy died she and I built a new life in San Francisco's Mission District without them. The culture and beauty of my Islander roots lives in my heart forever but honestly failed to prepare me for the spectacle of Roberta Fenning's bludgeoned body. Could anything have?

Rudy died on his seventeenth birthday, my age now, which my mother said was like being erased by the universe and twice as bad as just losing him. Now we can't even celebrate his birthday without reliving the trauma of his loss. The closest thing I had to a brother now was Fergus Wilde, my best friend since the third grade.

"Stop dreaming and cut the deck," Fergus had said this morning while we drank coffee on the floor of my bedroom, preparing for another game of cribbage during the lazy, summer lull before college. And I had been daydreaming while he decided which cards to throw in the crib. Nothing I hated more than wasting time. And there was nothing I wanted more than to escape reality go back to the safety of that cribbage game right now.

My chin touching the cold floor of the Fenning's second floor landing, I couldn't make my lungs remember how to work. Sucking in air, I clawed the grout between the foyer's white marble tiles to steady myself. That same marble downstairs in the kitchen would now be permanently stained with Roberta Fenning's blood. Wait… why was there blood under my fingernails? I hadn't touched the body. Not even close. Had I?

I shouldn't even be here, I realized, gasping finally like a surfer reaching air after being held down by a set wave. My nose ran and the fluid mixed with tears sliding down my cheeks. I couldn't wipe it because whoever did this to her could still be in the house watching me right now. *Stay silent. Don't move.* Two questions: would I be next and, more importantly, why had Lise summoned me if she wasn't even here? I ignored the most obvious possibility because honestly it was too much weight on my heart. I needed to get the hell out of here before the police arrived. Had anyone even called them? Had Lise done that before she skipped out?

I went through it in my head to sort of rehearse. I entered with my own personal key to the Fenning estate, given to me by Lise Fenning, my other BFF. It's not that I lived here, necessarily, just that the house was huge and running to answer the door every time the bell chimed was apparently too extraordinary an effort on a regular basis. So they gave me one of the spare keys. Lise should have been here to meet me, and she was scheduled to be. I'd called out for her and at least expected Nanny, the live-in cook, to be in the kitchen where I always stopped in to say hi. She's nice, I liked her. Today the kitchen was completely closed up. No Nanny, no Roberta, only her discarded body staining the pristine tile with a pool of her blood.

What if they asked me if I knew her? I needed an answer ready for that. Yes, of course I knew her, I even liked her. She was my best friend's mother so I'd been to that house at least once a week for years. The words felt so strange in my mouth – *was, best friend*. Best friends didn't do what Lise has done. Roberta was the kind of woman, the kind of mother who cared about people and wanted to know them. She'd stop me in the hallway sometimes and grasp my shoulders, look in my eyes to not just ask how I was doing but see for herself. My God. Roberta.

I'd only stood in the doorway and honestly didn't take a single step into the kitchen. But when I crouched low, I caught sight of a pooling of blood in the back of her head, mostly dried now, and the ghastliest color I'd ever seen on another person. I tried to remember if she'd been sick lately, but she was fine the last time I saw her. My God, the blood. I knew that had to mean something about the timing of her attack, but my mind wasn't capable of critical thinking right now. I'm not sure why, but I'd snapped one quick photo of her lying there before charging up the grand staircase and dropping to the floor of the landing.

From this vantage point I could see into the kitchen, her lifeless legs visible and feet turned awkwardly inward. I might never be able to unsee the ghoulish cast to her skin, and the way rigor mortis had frozen her contorted fingers into these spectral claws belonging in a zombie movie. I felt sick and rolled onto my left side before vomiting, another assault on what had once been their pristine floor. How could this beautiful estate be habitable again after tonight? My fingertips gripped the edge of the staircase and pulled my body forward two inches, which gave me a bit more view. Some kind of leather strap stuck up beneath her on the side of the kitchen island, which I hadn't noticed before. Was it her handbag, and why hadn't I noticed it when I'd been in the kitchen?

My frantic brain began some basic calculations, starting with steps. An estimated thirty-seven to the lower landing and then roughly another twenty to the inner front door. Could I make it there before the killer spotted me? Wait a minute, I knew this house. There was a back bedroom. Lise and I removed part of the flooring once to access a support pole that weaved from the basement up to the second floor. If I could get to that closet, I might be able to use the pole to exit the house through the basement's bulkhead, which would be safer than ploughing out the front door for all of Sea Cliff to see. My wet, swollen eyes blinked through these new possibilities, fingernails clicking the white marble, performing a momentary risk assessment. Had the Fennings discovered our secret escape path and blocked off the closet? If someone *was* still in the house, this could be my only chance of making it out alive.

I tried texting Lise again. *Where the fuck are you?? Don't leave me here!*

I heard the clink of china from the kitchen, a saucer upended and see-sawing side to side before it came to rest.

OMG. My stomach tightened with an imaginary vice grip over my throat. That sound could mean Roberta was still alive. I pressed my hands over my mouth to suppress the urge to call out to her, because it could also mean that her killer was down there waiting for me.

Chapter 2

If there was somebody still here, they definitely heard me calling out to Lise when I arrived, or else throwing up on the landing. I crept out of view along the slippery tile, then hoisted myself toward the wall in the first corridor of bedrooms on the second floor of the palatial Fenning estate. The wind escalated to an all-out howl, adding to the macabre scene. My legs wobbled, too rubbery to even stand. Fine, I thought, re-adjusting my plan to crawl across the Berber carpet. It should be the last bedroom on the right, a guest room, and farthest from the front door, which right now was to my greatest advantage. Certain her killer was still downstairs, *get-the-fuck-out* was the only thought that fit in my head.

I flattened my feet to the carpet and reached up to grip the door handle, turning it clockwise. It opened to a large room, shades drawn, sheets covering the furniture. Why did rich people do this? Afraid of dust and air? I hurried toward the closet on a mission to find my secret escape hatch, but was halted by the shock of my unexpected reflection in a tall, vintage vanity mirror. Thea Riggs, seventeen years old and I honestly looked forty. Long, dark brown, soft wavy hair, tawny brown skin reflecting my mixed race heritage, puffy eyes and smudged makeup. Lord. Was this some stranger wearing my clothes? To the right of the vanity loomed a dark wood bookcase with what looked like first editions. I'd been reading adult classics like this since I was ten thanks to Grandma Irene, who exposed me to *Brave New World* and *Lady Chatterley's Lover* long before I was ready. Thank God for people like her. I dragged open the closet door. Peering down under the shoes I immediately smelled something musty. Yes! The mismatched blue rug Lise and I stuck under the rows of boots was still there. Listening behind me for any other sounds, I swept them carefully to the left and tugged one corner, peeling it up all the way. My shoulders relaxed a tiny bit seeing the reassuring hole in the floor, and the rusted pole in the middle of it. The opening was eighteen inches square – I knew because we'd measured it. Tetanus waiting to happen but there were no other options. What was worse, finding a dead body or getting blamed for it?

My phone buzzed. Fergus. Thank God.

Dude, where are you? It's movie night, he wrote.

Before Covid, I'd loved our movie nights, sitting in a cold theater crunching popcorn to some bedazzled scifi escape. For Fergus, it was more of an event because he was old enough to be out in the real world working, two jobs in fact—coffee barista at Peets, and bike courier delivering documents to medical companies. For me, it was post-graduation summer vacay, so leisure was my middle name for two sun-soaked months of the year.

Don't ask, I typed back, keeping one ear turned toward the hallway, still haunted by the clinking sounds in the kitchen. My traumatized brain imagined Mrs. Fenning's steps down the hall calling my full family name like she did sometimes—Thea Irene Kailani Riggs, always adding my middle names for a flourish. What if she really was still alive? But then her skin wouldn't have been blue and her hands like fossilized claws.

You're never late, Fergus typed with a sad-face emoji. *Where you at? Dying to talk to you today. Need to tell you more about that game...*

Fergus and his stupid internet games. I didn't even know what day it was at this point. Focus, stay frosty. I stuffed the phone in the back pocket of my jeans and crouched low into the closet. How had I done this before? Of course - I'd been smaller then.

The pipe vibrated from a tremor downstairs, my sweaty palms wrapped around it. I froze listening. One one-thousand, two one-thousand. I pulled my phone out again and shined the flashlight below. Their basement looked exactly the same as if no one had been down there in a decade. I had to assume the bulkhead was still operable and the doors still opened. If not, I was royally fucked. Lise, what have you done?

The sudden quiet didn't fool me. Someone or something had made that vibration, and the only other person in this house was dead. Could it be Nanny coming in to prep for tomorrow's meals? She would have seen Roberta's body in the middle of the floor and screamed. So if not Nanny, who else had a key? Had Lise come back, guilted by my text-whining? She'd be looking for me, but probably not in here. No one called. I was alone in the house with a dead woman. Hands and arms coiled around the pole now, my eyes welled up. The weight of sudden sobs shook my chest and I stayed there like that, letting the moment drown me, hoping my weight wouldn't dislodge the pipe from its brackets. Okay, let's do this, time to get out of here. I sniffed, blinked my eyes clear, and shimmied my way down inch by inch, happy that only the very top of it was rusted. I could see the floor. The pipe was ice cold. Just a few more feet to go.

Lise and I, even Emily, Lise's dead sister, used to go on nightly explorations of the estate when we were younger, wearing miner's caps we got from the Army Navy store. One time we made it as far back as the entrance to the tunnel before one of us, I forget who, heard a growling sound and we ran out screaming. God, I hadn't thought of that tunnel in ages. Was it actually real, and could it still be here? What were the chances that something had actually growled at us back then? More likely someone's stomach.

Now my right foot had fallen asleep, probably from being coiled around the pole and cutting off my circulation. I couldn't safely reach my phone from this position but I had to be just inches from the floor. Why did everything look darker down there now? I tried to remember what time I left the Mission tonight. Five, or was it more like five-thirty? I'd now been here over an hour. Okay, here we go. I inhaled and re-adjusted my grip on the steel support pole noticing how my hands were chafed and burning. I tried to pull myself down a few inches but something was caught, a part of my jeans had snagged something on the side of the pole. Shit.

I lifted my left knee, but it was on the right. My right leg felt tingly from the pins and needles in my foot and was spreading up my leg. God help me. And while I felt less and less control of my body, my mind couldn't pull itself away from the legal ramifications. I should be calling 911 right now, for Roberta, for the family. And to protect myself. So royally fucked.

Okay, one step at a time. I'd call 911, the police would show up and ask what the hell I was doing in the basement under the bedroom. I could say I'd heard a noise down here. And I had, hadn't I? No. The noise was somewhere else in the house; I'd just felt the vibration from something falling on the floor upstairs. Were they coming in my direction? Hard to tell, but there was no way I was calling 911. I was a person of color in an affluent neighborhood alone in a house with a dead woman. Of course I'd be blamed. I needed to get out of here, time was running out. Come on legs, here we goooooooo—oh no, no no no. I slid down, unable to slow myself until my elbow and ankle broke my fall on the concrete. Instant pain lit up my left side, and I swear I heard something crack. My whole left side ached up to my pelvic bone. Lying on my side, I couldn't feel anything. Please, God, don't let me die down here.

Chapter 3

At some point I'd blacked out, for how long I have no idea. My eyes opened and I smelled something damp, not water exactly. It smelled clean. There must be a washer and dryer down here. My mind ran through all kinds of scenarios, involving Lise coming back to rescue me, calling for me, apologizing, saying the whole thing was a big misunderstanding, her mother was fine and maybe they were hosting a murder mystery dinner party. But how could that be true when I'd seen her mother dead? Had she killed her and that's why she ran? My phone buzzed, Fergus again.

What's going on? Are you alright?

The pain in my elbow reminded me what happened. What a mess.

What are you doing right now?

Fleeing a crime scene, I typed back.

Ya right. Seriously?

More tears now, I couldn't stop them.

Do you need help?

That was what I loved most about Fergus. Always on my side no matter what, ready to drop everything and assist. It's not that he wasn't interested or curious about the crime scene, if it actually was one given my propensity for exaggeration. But like always, he was mature enough to prioritize my well-being first. If I didn't like girls so much, I'd marry that guy someday.

Hell, yes. I think I broke my ankle.

Where are you?

Lise's basement.

I knew what he'd be thinking. I also knew he'd be grabbing his wallet, keys, and running out the door. His apartment was three blocks from our house in the Mission district, but across town from Lise's estate in Sea Cliff. This time of night, rush hour...

I'm five minutes away. Coming right now. Do you need anything?

You're in Sea Cliff?

Went for a quick surf at Eagle's Point.

He was near China Beach just south of the Sea Cliff neighborhood and right around the corner. Miracle. *Text me when you're close,* I wrote. *And don't park right in front of the house.*

Why? Are you gonna tell me what's going on?

He'd find out soon enough.

I met Fergus when my mother and I first moved to San Francisco, me moping around Everett Middle School like a lost soul and Fergus trying to get thrown out of Mission Dolores Academy, the private Catholic school next door. He was older than me and funny. I liked him right away. We saw each other in the mornings, afternoons, started talking, and I took up the challenge of writing his ultimatum to his parents – he'd run away to LA if they didn't enroll him in Everett. It took two attempts but worked, to both of our advantage. BFFs.

I'm parked on the next street and standing behind a cluster of trees in the front yard of the house next to hers. I demand to know what's going on.

Demand. Funny. I hadn't moved from my spot on the basement floor, probably fifteen yards from the bulkhead doors with no confidence whatsoever that they'd even open. I hadn't heard any sounds or felt any vibrations in the past ten minutes, so I deemed it safe enough to make a phone call. I dialed Fergus and cleared my throat.

"Hey," I whispered.

"Are you okay? I can barely hear you."

"No dude, definitely not okay."

Pause. "I've got water, a first aid kit—"

"Head behind that huge elm tree in the front and follow the walkway around to the back of the house," I said slowly and clearly. "Stay behind the hedges." It was a stunning, large gray home with wrought iron railings, brick steps, manicured yard, and a rounded alcove protecting a slate blue front door. I loved this house. Until tonight.

"What's the point of that? They probably have security cameras all over the perimeter."

OMG. Cameras in the house.

"Stay on the line with me, it'll take me a minute," he said, out of breath so he must have started walking.

I heard him, and thought I responded but I suddenly felt so sleepy. That's when I noticed my lower leg felt cold. I must have moaned into the phone.

"Thea, are you hurt? Stay with me. Dammit say something."

His voice was strained and tight, my knight in shining armor. "I'm here," I said. "Sleepy. Check to see if there are any cars in the driveway."

"It's quiet out here tonight. Did you hit your head?" he asked.

I tried to recall what happened on my way down, but no I couldn't remember hitting my head. I told him so.

"Are you bleeding? I'm here by the way. Where are you?"

"Come around back and look for the bulkhead doors," I said. The winds hadn't let up, something about the architecture of the side yard and gardens. Lise, Emily, and I had used that to our advantage when sneaking in and out of the house. Carefree summer escapades that now felt bitter.

"I—" His voice sounded garbled.

"You cut out. Fergus? Are you there? Look for the bulkhead doors. That's the most efficient way in. And keep watch for—" I tried to think of another word for a killer, but my brain wasn't working.

"What are you doing in the basement?" His breathing was heavy. "Is Lise with you?"

"I'll explain when you get here, if you can even—"

The left door of the bulkhead popped open and Fergus climbed in, baseball hat on backyards, a six-foot-tall beanpole with beautiful dark eyes and a sideways smile. He scanned a flashlight across the main cavern of the basement. My heart relaxed a tiny bit.

"Over here."

He set a black backpack on the floor then reached down to grab my head and elevate it with his hands.

"Oh my God," I sighed, rising up to wrap my arms around his neck.

"Thea, you're bleeding," he said, shocked by the sight of me.

I hadn't seen the wound but I'd felt the sudden, numbing cold against my skin. Fergus flashed the beam on the floor and under my body. "Looks like you haven't lost too much blood so far." He pulled up my jeans from the bottom but they were too tight. "Sorry." He dragged a knife from his pocket and cut the seam, then tore open the edges to assess the wound.

"Is it bad?" I asked, with only half my attention on my wound and the other half behind me.

"Have you tried to walk on it?" When I shook my head, he hoisted me up to a standing position. "Hold this," he said, positioning my hand on a ceiling beam within reach. I watched the Eagle Scout wrap a blue bandana from his duffel bag and tie it around my busted ankle just above the bone.

"Ow ow ow ow too tight."

"Deal with it, we need to stop the bleeding. Here, hook your hand onto my shoulder and try to take a step."

I hopped on my left foot to get in position, one hand on the pipe, the other around his waist, and lowered my right foot toward the floor. I knew it wouldn't work—the foot and ankle were in the wrong position. Someone would need to set the bone for my broken ankle. Please not that.

He carried me piggy-back across the basement floor and deposited me on a hard, concrete step outside the bulkhead. He picked me up on the other side and set me far enough away to close the door again. Smart.

We headed back around the house, luckily downhill, but instead of following the perimeter, we took off through the lush gardens, me haphazardly dangling behind him. He had to pause every ten steps to hoist me back up and catch his breath, trying not to touch my butt in the process.

"Are we stopping in the trees?" I asked. "I need some water."

"I need some answers." Fergus stopped walking, pointed to a dark spot under some eucalyptus and lowered me to the ground. "What happened, Thea? Where the fuck is Lise?"

"Well," I laughed slightly, then immediately felt like crying. Again. "Those are two different questions."

Fergus crouched in front of me. "Start with the first."

I took a breath. The ground felt cold and solid. "Roberta's dead."

"Lise's mom? How? How do you know?"

I eyerolled and nodded my head. "I—saw her with my own eyes."

"Saw what exactly?"

"I heard something in the kitchen. That's why I booked it down to the basement. I wasn't sure I was alone in the house. In fact, I'm pretty sure someone else is still in there." Those images of her would haunt me forever.

Fergus frowned, moving his head side to side. "You're saying you saw an actual—"

"Her body? Yes, on the kitchen floor."

"And the police are where exactly?"

"Donut shops? How the fuck should I know?"

"T, seriously. You didn't call them?"

"No, I didn't call them! Are you insane?"

"Thea, listen to me. You have to clear your name and do it like right now."

"Roberta's a millionaire and I'm just some waif who's friends with her daughter. They're not gonna believe me if I tell them I was summoned to the—"

"W-w-w-wait a minute. Summoned? By who? Lise?" he asked.

I pulled the phone out of my pocket and opened to the chat thread. But something else caught my eye—a new chat I hadn't seen before. Please let it be from Lise. No, a number I didn't recognize. It was 8:49 p.m. This new chat came in five minutes ago, probably when we were exiting the basement.

"T, are you listening? Who summoned you?" he demanded. "Lise?"

"Um…yeah…wait a—"

"What are you doing?" Irritation grated his voice. I'd led him along and now he needed answers. Unfortunately, I didn't have any, and now I had even more questions.

I looked up. "We're screwed."

"You mean more than we were a minute ago?"

I handed him the phone.

"I saw you," Fergus read the text aloud, brows narrowing. "I know what you did tonight, and unless you're headed to the police to turn yourself in, I own you now." He looked up. "Jesus, who's that from?"

Somehow hearing it in Fergus' voice made it seem more real. "I'm dead."

Chapter 4

An ambulance siren wailed as it grew closer to us. Then a car drove past the house very slowly with the driver's side window down. I saw the driver and he was looking at his phone. Food delivery, most likely, searching for an address.

"What the actual fuck, T?"

"You need to get out of here, now. I can't walk…so—"

"What, you mean leave you here? No way. Especially not now. Get real."

"Fergus, you're hysterical, calm down. Where's your car?" I asked, keeping his attention focused on something logical. I knew how his brain worked, and knew how immobilized it could get by emotions.

"Around the corner."

"You go and bring it around—"

"I am not leaving you here after seeing that text. Tell me what happened. Now, Thea. What did you do?"

"Do?" I stared at him for a long moment. "What do you mean by that? Nothing happened. Lise texted me to meet her here. No one came to the door so I used my key, and—"

"You've got a key to the Fenning estate," he said, as a statement, lips pressed together. "Interesting."

"Shut up. Yeah, so I went in, called for Lise. No one answered, so I went in the kitchen to look for Nanny."

"Isn't Lise a little old for a nanny?" he asked.

"Her name's Nanette. She's the cook. Anyway, she's always here. But tonight she wasn't, and Roberta was lying on the floor."

"Dead?" he asked, stupidly.

I sighed and closed my eyes. "She looked...her skin, Fergus...oh my God."

"But definitely dead, right?"

"Blood on the floor under her head, I saw it."

"Please I beg you, tell me you didn't—"

"No, I didn't touch anything!" I shot back, but remembered what looked like blood under my fingernails. How had that gotten there? I'd blacked out before in tense situations. Had I actually touched her? It was overload to even consider that now. "I ran up to the landing for safety, and then heard something in the kitchen and got scared, so I went down to the basement."

I didn't bother telling Fergus about the pole, because he and Lise hated each other, and any closeness I reported about she and I would only activate him even more. I had one singular goal right now: to get off this street and out of this neighborhood.

Fergus sucked air into his lungs and leaned his head up. "Okay, stay here, going to get my car. And don't answer that text."

My throbbing ankle was starting to swell; a pounding in my temples swayed my balance when I tried to stand. So, I stayed there on the cold ground, letting the feel of the earth under my butt and hips ground me. 29-28-27-26. I liked counting backwards for some reason. It gave me time for my nervous system to adjust to whatever fucked-up situation I found myself in. It was working. The air smelled fresh and felt cold in my lungs. A nicer thought than who had seen me in the Fenning house tonight.

Fergus blinked his low beams on the curb past the outcrop of trees. There'd be no time to park and retrieve me. I had to get out to that car. I remembered, oddly, the last cribbage game we'd played, and how he brutally beat me by about forty points. It wasn't a wonderful morning that day—it was a normal morning for us that felt so far away right now. I hated the idea of the streetlight shining down on his car, but there was no other way. The house across the street was dark with no cars in the driveway. The neighbors must be at one of their gala fundraisers, or whatever Sea Cliff billionaires do this time of night. As for me, I hope I live to see tomorrow.

One of my secret talents, along with being able to perfectly simulate a terrier's bark, was my Hollywood-grade zombie walk carefully cultivated from ten seasons of *The Walking Dead*. Eyes on the car, why did Fergus have his father's Lexus tonight? Never mind that. Now or never. I took the first step toward the street, one foot walking normally and my left dragging because any weight on my ankle felt like three hundred volts of electricity. Oh God, I can't. I stopped in the middle of the street, hands on my knees. I set my left foot on the ground. The pain made my mouth froth, so gross. Fergus climbed over the seats to open the passenger door, then got out and ran around to my side.

"Hop on your right foot if it's too painful, but hurry the fuck up."

"Then come out and carry me, why don't you."

He did, scooping me up and setting me gently in the passenger seat. Oh my God, the lumbar support of the Lexus. I let my hips sink into the thick cushion while Fergus closed my door, whipped around to the driver's side, then tore down California Street like a bullet.

"Slow down! You're jostling my leg."

"Why didn't I put you in the back? Dammit. That leg should be elevated."

"I'd just get blood on the seat. Where are we going?"

"Sorry." He slowed the engine a bit. "Cal Pacific Medical Center's the closest. You've gotta get that—"

I turned my torso and grabbed his elbow, resting my head on the seat. "You can't take me there, to any hospital for that matter. It's too conspicuous, especially after—"

"Fleeing a crime scene?"

"I was gonna say after that text message, but yeah, that too I guess."

Big sigh. "Who do you suggest to set your ankle then? Don't ask me to do it. I can't." We'd gone through Pacific Heights and were on the edge of Chinatown now. Fergus slowed the car to twenty mph and rolled past the Courtyard Marriott on Van Ness then turned right at Mel's Diner and live-parked. I saw someone exiting the main entrance.

"Was that—" I whipped my head back toward the hotel.

"Yeah, odd. I think that was Kitty," he said, like Kitty didn't belong in the Courtyard Marriott. He didn't.

I knew we were both thinking the same thing, wondering if he'd seen us. Kitty, that's all we needed right now. "Back up." I rolled down my window and scanned the hotel's entrance.

"You sure you're ready to deal with him tonight?"

"Hell no, but I think he saw me so we can't pretend like we didn't see him. You slowed the car, Fergus, almost like you were meeting him." I checked his eyes. "Had you planned to--"

"Don't go turning on me now." He sighed. "The last time we saw Kit, he killed a guy."

I remembered. I'd done my best to forget the whole ordeal and honestly had bigger problems right now. The most likely person to have sent me that threatening text message was Roberta Fenning's killer, and they *were* still in the house when I got there. Question is, how did they have my mobile number?

I felt lightheaded and everything got very still, almost like the world stopped spinning on its axis. My heart pounded, blood pulsing through my injured body. I kept blinking, wondering if by doing so I could start the world up again. Was it all supposed to be this way, the tangled strands of life all scary and desperate? I thought of our aimless card games. I heard Bunny Wailer in my head and pictured the palm trees lining our forbidden stretch of beach in Majuro. But my Marshall Islands were a lifetime away from this moment. Fergus was right. A night with Kit Fury meant we could end up in jail, homeless, or dead.

Chapter 5

Kit Fury randomly standing in front of an upscale hotel reminded me that there are no accidents. His reddish hair was trimmed straight across his tall forehead, then vertically down to his ears, which made him look even more stark. His light-skinned, freckled face smiled with a bashful wave as he approached, the feigned sheepishness you see from the world's most violent offenders. Fergus and I watched him idly from the car, imagining our futures going up in flames.

"Hey," Kit said approaching the passenger window. Great.

I rolled it down. He leaned low and put his elbows on the door frame. I backed away, cringing. He saw this.

"My man," Kit said thrusting out his arm to shake Fergus' in their secret bro handshake. Slaps, slides, knuckles. Lord.

Fergus played along. "S'up bro. We're on the clock here, only got a minute."

"I know." Kit nodded, mostly at me, a smile always ready on that face. Even without teeth showing, Kit had a way of smiling with just his eyes, or the corner of his mouth. What kind of smile—well, that was another story.

I know? What the hell did that mean? Was he the one who'd sent me that text? Did he somehow know what happened at the Fenning estate?

"C'mere cupcake." Kit nestled his ginger-scratch crewcut, five o'clock shadow, and cigarette stench into my shoulder. "Your hair's like its own zip code. How long is it now?" he asked reaching out to touch it. I might just cut it all off now.

He was right, it was long, so long I'd taken to wearing it in a twisted up-do that my mother said looked like I was wearing a basket on my head. I didn't care what Kit thought of my hair. He looked heavier than last time we saw him, pasty complexion, perpetually sweating, those eyes always scheming.

"Hey," I managed, turning my head to plead telepathically with Fergus. Please, anything.

"Yeah, um, Thea's got a bum ankle and we need to get that looked at."

"No hospital," I added, brows raised as a challenge.

A devious grin spread across Kit's mouth and his eyes narrowed, head cocked to the side. "Cupcake been doing something she shouldn't, I think. Yo, let me in. I got a hookup for you."

I nodded at Fergus and he unlocked the back door. Kit climbed in. Immediately, the atmosphere felt charged, like it always felt around him, a walking vortex of chaos.

"Hookup meaning, what, an unlicensed doctor writing scripts for meth-heads out the back of a dirty van?" I said to Kit facing forward. "I have bones that need to be set and a wound that needs cleaning. And it hurts like hell."

Kit stayed quiet, forcing me to turn and look back where he sat arms crossed with a wounded expression.

"What?"

"Truth? I know someone."

"I need a doctor, Kit, now."

"It's ten minutes from here."

"Where?" Fergus asked from the driver's seat.

"Chinatown."

I'd already pulled Waze up on my phone. "Twenty-three minutes from here, according to Waze."

"What's in Chinatown?" Fergus again. I loved how he audited everything Kit said. But Kit must have known that approaching our car tonight, knowing baggage from our last encounter was of course coloring our opinion of him now. Or forever.

"You gotta wait," he teased. "But ohhh, it's worth the wait."

"Cut the crap, Kitty. I'm in pain up here. Who's the doctor?"

"Geez, girl," he whined.

"Call him now." I turned to scare him with my eyes. He'd told me before what beautiful I eyes I had. Fine, I'd weaponize them. "Do it! Make sure he's available and expecting us—"

"Or we're not going anywhere," Fergus added.

I just loved when we finished each other's thoughts. My perfect BFF, better than Lise at least.

No one talked for a while, as Fergus combed his father's Lexus down California and Bush Streets in Laurel Heights, passing the edges of Japantown and Tenderloin. Hardly any cars on the road this time of night, we still weren't moving more than twenty mph. It's San Francisco. I numbed out on the city lights, distracting myself from the gnawing pain in my ankle, a new hurt rocking my elbow, and the knot in my stomach about the body I'd left behind. Meanwhile, Kitty called a guy named Dr. Lee and arranged for us to be at his place. He said we were ten minutes away.

"Turn here," Kit said. "Take your first right and look for a parking spot.

"In Chinatown? Sure. Should take about forty-five—"

"Right there, bro." Kit tapped Fergus' shoulder and pointed in front of his face, dirt under his fingernail. Eww. I didn't even want to think about where that finger had been.

"Fergus parallel-parking his father's Lexus—that's what'll take forty-five minutes."

"Shut it," he said. I could have turned back to Kit and shared the comedic moment with him, but after what he'd put us through, I wasn't giving him anything and God it felt good to disappoint him.

"You guys go wherever you're going. I can't walk," I said.

"It's right here." Kit smiled, pointing at the yellow Tin How Temple sign with red Chinese characters, above which read Sue Hing

Benevolent Society.

"What am I looking at?" Fergus stared out the window.

Kit reached up and manually rotated Fergus's head twenty-degrees left. A white piece of letter-sized paper was taped to the exterior brick wall.

"That's the lightning bolt!" Fergus turned to me, eyes wide. "That game I've been telling you about. That's it!"

"A lightning bolt game, okay." I rolled my eyes, suddenly annoyed by everything.

Kit had gotten out and held his camera at the page, which must have had a QR code at the bottom.

"Ask Kit where his doctor's at," I told Fergus. He did, and Kit pointed across the street, where I saw an Icicle Bakery flanked by two acupuncturists. Oh God, not needles.

"See that red sign?" Kit asked.

"Every sign on the street is red."

"Zhao Acupuncture. Dr. Lee's on the second floor."

"Kit, come on! I need a doctor, as in medical doctor."

"Ye of little faith. Dr Lee *is* a medical doctor."

"Working in an acupuncture clinic?"

Kit sighed, arms outstretched, head to the sky. "Yeah. He's both."

"Take me there first, then you and Fergus can talk about lightning bolts."

I opened the passenger door and inched my legs into the correct position to step onto the curb without falling. Everything hurt—ankle, elbow, my lower back and hips suddenly, pain cascading down. Kit tried, but Fergus elbowed him out of the way and picked me up to carry me to the second floor of the clinic. Funny, those two fighting over me. Another day, it might have been cute.

Waverly Place was thick with walkers in both directions, on the curb, in the street, dodging cars, old, young. The rectangular building had three stories of apartments above the lower storefront, offset by zigzagging exterior staircases. The interior smelled like licorice, with something bitter and pungent on the nose. Fergus carried me carefully up a narrow, dark staircase to the second floor, my bad ankle throbbing, the good one dragging the wall.

"Thank you," I whispered, so glad it was his and not Kit's arms around me. I felt so fragile right now.

"Well don't you two look snugly. Door number 2," Kit said in his game show voice two steps behind us. Sure enough, the signage read *Dr. Louis Lee, MD, DOM.*

My mom had been to acupuncturists before, so I knew DOM meant Doctor of Oriental Medicine, which required eight years of training, most of which had to be completed in China. That in combo with an MD meant this guy was an expert. I hated needles but it was better than a hospital.

"Yes, yes, come in. You must be Miss Riggs."

I liked the man's accent. His trustworthy face was a relief after looking at Kit. When did he have time to call the doctor and let him know we were coming? Fergus deposited me in the lobby, where I balanced on one foot.

"Hold onto me, it's just ten steps to the left," the doctor said, then looked back at Fergus. "Come back for her in one hour."

"Do you always keep late hours like this?" I asked.

I felt the man's chin nod up and down as he led us along a carpeted hallway.

"All the worst things in life happen after dark."

"And that's where you come in?"

"Apparently so."

Chapter 6

Okay, I admit Dr. Lee seemed promising so far. But he came from Kit Fury, so any such referral was doomed for disaster.

The doctor seemed competent but was about forty years younger than I expected. My dad loved the original Kung Fu TV show and I pictured every acupuncturist looking like Lo Si, The Ancient. It was one of the only good memories I had of my dad and I.

Dr. Lee helped me onto an exam table, then ripped my already torn pants hem up to my knee.

"Hey! What are you doing?"

"Don't worry," he grinned. "We have pins."

In a quick, gentle manner he looked at my tongue and put each of his fingers on both of my wrists, pressing firmly, then lightly, gazing up like he was taking cues from the ceiling tiles.

The windows must be single pane with old seals because I could hear everything on the street below. Ambulance sirens, a man laughing, a stringed instrument playing a sad melody, firecracker poppers, and church bells from what had to be Old Saint Mary Cathedral. A few minutes later, a man sang Happy Birthday as he walked under the windows. My birthday was in six weeks, and my mother had already been asking me about gifts. I still hadn't answered her. Then again, she should know why.

I think I slept, and woke at one point smelling alcohol from when he was cleaning my wounds, and another time with needles in my head, arm, leg, and foot. A white panic clawed up my body about what those two were doing right now. Fergus had a backbone, he just didn't use it enough. And Kit seemed to have this otherworldly hold over him, bewitching him to do things he'd normally never do. As for me, I'd watched Kit strangle someone to death and that forever put him in another category.

Dr. Lee left and returned a few times. Not being able to walk easily was going to be a serious logistical challenge. Especially now.

"Miss Riggs, time to go," he said, clapped twice and stepped back to appraise me. "How do you feel?"

"Better than an hour ago, actually. How is it?"

"How is what?" he asked.

"My ankle."

The man shrugged. "Sprained. It's a typical sprain. It will heal better now."

"Shouldn't I wrap it in a bandage or something?"

"Do not make it easy for the joint to be weak. Walk gently and elevate it when you're not mobile."

When wasn't I mobile? "How much do I owe you?"

At the door, he put up his palms. "No charge. Any friend of Kit's is—"

"Oh no, I insist. Besides, I'm not a friend of Kit's."

He lowered his head to peer at me. "That's fine. Seventy dollars, discounted, and that includes one follow-up."

Seventy. Gulp. I still hadn't gotten paid for my last tutoring gig. "Thank you." I handed him the credit card my mother co-signed with a specific agreement not to exceed $100 in charges per month. Seemed reasonable. Except now I'd just gone over.

Waverly Place was deserted now except for that same lonely string player, dark enough to see the Chinese lanterns aglow like hanging fortune cookies of hope. The image struck me and I cried a little, reflecting on the day's drama and how Roberta Fenning would never again see this kind of magic. Not in this life anyway.

With no cast, not even an ace bandage, I practiced walking up and down the sidewalk in front of Tin How Temple to test my ankle. It almost felt okay enough for weight-bearing. The temple was so unassuming on the outside, but something luminescent shone back from that piece of paper tacked to the bricks where Kit and Fergus were buzzing around earlier. I glanced at it before but nothing glowed. I moved directly in front of it. Yeah—definitely glowing.

We'd done a project like this right before graduation, where we used glow powder to make luminescent paper. The one in front of me was a plain sheet with an image of a man on a surfboard riding down one of the zigzags of a lightning bolt, a QR code below it. Fergus tried the code with his phone earlier and said the URL was broken. I tried it and got the same 404 error. Standing here in the dark three inches from it, I could see there was a border behind the QR code, a green-glow and, when I moved closer, it had a mini-QR code embedded in that border. Whoa. But the page made no mention of a game of any kind. In fact, there was no text at all on it, just a broken QR with a hidden QR within it. Kit and Fergus where are you?

My jaw clamped shut as I pressed Fergus' mobile number, picturing them drunk, laughing on a bar floor, or snorting crack off some woman's ass. With Kit there was no telling what principles Fergus might be violating, though I'd only been gone an hour. Now he wasn't answering and my mind was spinning. Had Kit really been just randomly standing in front of that hotel when we happened to drive by? What if it wasn't random? What if he was a part of this somehow? Did he know the Fennings, or was he friends with any of Lise's friends?

Some old, or maybe young, part of me felt a ping of sadness in my chest. I'd already been abandoned once today by my "best friend" Lise. Thinking back now, she and her mother never got along well. Could something have happened, could Lise have snapped? Could she be capable of murder? I don't know if it was scarier to know or not know.

Are you just gonna leave me here? I texted Fergus. My phone rang a second later.

"T, listen."

Fergus only used 'listen' when he knew he was in trouble. Kit mumbled in the background. "Gimme gimme gimme the phone. Lemme talk to her."

"Dude, shut it," Fergus clapped back.

"What, she doesn't like games?" Kit was drunk. "Thea don't like no games, okay."

"Kitty, calm down. You don't even know her. She loves games. She's surprisingly competitive, actually."

"Surprisingly, that's a big word," I said.

I was booking an Uber home while I listened to their foolish banter.

"She's beaten me at cribbage the past two…thre—"

"Every?" I said.

"Cribbage?" Kit said, taking the phone from Fergus.

"Cards, dude," Fergus replied.

"Well, good," Kit said. "Skill up, you're gonna need it."

"Why? What do you mean?" I asked.

"Because I think your dead lady's just become part of the game we're playing."

Chapter 7

I barely breathed. Two old men walked arm in arm down Clay Street as Kit's words bounced around in my head.

"Let me talk to Fergus," I blurted, ignoring Kit's comment for the moment.

"Hey," Fergus said, his voice low.

"You told him about Roberta?" I couldn't fathom his breach of trust. I was two seconds from deciding to not even tell them about the hidden QR code.

"I know I know, I'm sorry."

I could tell he meant it. He didn't seem drunk; I knew what that sounded like.

"This is all freaking me out. I had to talk about it and get another perspective about what the fuck we should do."

"We should call the police," I said calmly, matter-of-factly, not quite sure where the words came from.

"Wait, now you wanna call the police? What changed your mind, and tell them what exactly?"

Everything I'd ever watched or read about crime detection always ended badly for suspects who withheld information. Being a person of color, I didn't trust that law enforcement would ever give me a fair chance or the benefit of the doubt, but right now I needed every advantage I could get. I moved back to the sheet of paper and held my phone up to the tiny QR code, used my fingers to zoom in, and held my camera on it long enough to bring up a webpage. I'd check it later.

"I'll tell them I was summoned to the house, which is true. Nobody answered, also true, and that's unusual and I'm worried about Lise's safety. You can request a wellness check and the PD will go by the house and ring the bell."

I heard him breathing through the phone, deliberating. "That's sort of true, I guess," he said. "So not telling them—"

"Fuck no. They'll figure it out eventually anyway. Won't they? Where are you guys?"

"Around the corner upstairs in Kit's apartment."

I remembered Kit telling us he scored a sweet deal in Chinatown. We'll see what his version of sweet looks like.

"Fine. Meet me outside, and I'll cancel my Uber." I stepped carefully to the corner, right foot, then left. A dull throb started in my ankle, reminding me it was too soon to walk. But I'd had soccer injuries before and knew it would stiffen if I didn't keep moving it. I continued on to the next corner. It was warmer than usual, early summer but summers were cold here according to Mark Twain anyway. I watched Fergus fidget as I approached, hands in pockets, then out, then clasped behind his back. Why was he nervous?

"Dr. Lee fixed you up good, yeah?"

I had way bigger problems than a busted ankle. "What did Kit mean?" I asked. "About Roberta."

Fergus hung his head like I'd caught him in a lie. Had I? "It's this game, T. I've been trying to tell you about it for two weeks, and you always seem so annoyed when I bring it up."

"How about now?" I said tipping my head to the side, snarkier than I intended.

He grabbed my shoulder and pulled me into the building where high eaves in the shape of a pagoda hung overhead. "The QR code I tried earlier didn't work because it only works for seven minutes a day."

"Seven, okay. I'm sure there's a reason for that."

"Yeah, well, there may be, but I know next to nothing about the bigger picture at this point. All I can say is that the QR code worked a few minutes ago and Kit showed me what to do."

"This ought to be good," I said, all the while watching Fergus' face change — jaw low, eyes wide, lips barely touching.

"It showed a picture. We ran that picture through an app called Outguess that takes a picture embedded with secret text and reveals the text."

How would they even know to do that? "Steganography," I said like it was obvious, hiding information in other artifacts. I loved the idea of it but had never actually seen it at work.

Eyeroll. "Of course you'd know what that is," he said. "I'd never heard of it."

"What was the text?" I asked. This was already taking too long and I couldn't be less interested in this game.

"Six letters." He paused, like he did when we were playing chess and he'd just put me in check, waiting for my response.

"What was the picture?" I asked. "Just curious."

"A pig, like a random, unedited internet photo of someone's pet pig."

I thought about what Kit said, Roberta being part of the game, maybe a tie-in to her address. GPS coordinates were structured with degrees, minutes, and seconds—two sets of each. I must have been nodding.

"You got it?" He peered at me.

"The letters on the pig image could have been GPS coordinates to the Fenning estate."

"Kinda random. What made you think of that?"

I pulled out my phone and looked at the page that the QR code brought up. Bingo. I held it out. "See? GPS coordinates of 130 Sea Cliff Ave." I opened another browser window so he could see the mini-QR code embedded in the border.

"Oh man, that's dope."

"Yeah, and not only that, it's glowing, so you can only see it at night," I said.

"I didn't see it glow…because it was still a little light out. Okay. I think the real QR only works for seven minutes a day but the mini-version works all the time, because the game rewards those who pay attention to detail."

I tried and failed to contain my eyeroll. None of this made any sense. How would a rich woman Roberta's age be involved in a game like this?

In the minutes we stood there, the sky darkened and the air seemed to chill under the hanging Chinese lanterns now in full view between Broadway and Bush. I was forever mystified by the amazing mishmash of architecture in San Francisco, especially compared to the Marshall Islands. The very top of the Café Maiko building in Chinatown on the corner of Grant and Waverly had sculptures and paintings of Chinese figures in a palette of blues and blacks. I could barely take my eyes off it. Fergus motioned me inside to Kit's apartment, but I'd taken all the risks I was going to today.

"Come on, Thea. You're smart. Kit has information about this game that we need. Let's learn as much as we can about it."

"I don't care what he knows," I hissed. "I don't trust him, and neither should you."

Fergus had this way of opening his eyes wide and blinking when he was deciding something. Another tell, and I knew them all, which brought me endless satisfaction. I agreed, finally, to go upstairs and hear what Kit had to say, but insisted on being taken home after that. I needed to check in with my mother and tell her…well, I don't know yet what I would tell her. I'd think of something.

Fergus offered to carry me up the stairs but I remembered what Dr. Lee said about not encouraging the joint to be weak. I can do this, I thought, one step at a time.

Kit Fury could just as easily have Persian rugs and a butler named Jeeves bringing round tea service as an empty crack den with no furniture. More stairs, we were now above a Lee's Donuts and the air was thick with yeast and cinnamon. Could be worse, honestly. I was already hungry.

The rugs in here didn't look like they came from Goodwill. A collection of black and yellow abstract paintings hung over several pieces of furniture, obviously from the same collection. I kept the scowl glued to my lips, not intending to give Kit anything.

"He's in here," Fergus motioned me toward the living room, where the windows showed an awesome view of Coit Tower. Drug money had to be funding this place.

"Bougie," I mumbled and sank onto a low, upholstered foot stool. It was meant as a dig.

Kit stood behind one of the armchairs, hands gripping the padded leather. "The couch is more comfortable," he goaded.

"I won't be here long," I shot back. He wanted me to sit on the couch and look comfortable in his home as if I was accepting his gift of hospitality. This was the world he ran in, a continuous currency of leverage and favors. No thanks.

"Don't get salty with me, cupcake, not in my house. The door's right there if you wanna go."

"I do want to go. Fergus dragged me up here."

He didn't scare me. Justified or not, Kit viewed me as the gatekeeper of Fergus, and he needed Fergus or guys like him to serve as ego-boosters, attendants, servicers. I'd lived in the Mission long enough to have seen glimpses of this underworld. Probably more than a seventeen-year-old should.

I met him in the moment, staring back with fire from my eyes. Fergus told me once that Kitty thought I was exotic, ever curious about my mixed Latino and Pacific Islander ancestry. And now I couldn't wait to shut him down again. "I paid for Dr. Lee myself." It was meant to be cruel. Kit got scary calm, slowly bringing his thumb and forefinger to the bridge of his nose. Was he suppressing emotion, or maybe he was about to strangle me. I'd seen it before.

He raised his chin. "You wanna tell me what the fuck you were doing at 130 Sea Cliff tonight?"

Fergus entered and sat on the corner of the sofa nearest to me.

"I was summoned there to meet my friend. Why do you ask?"

Kit and Fergus exchanged looks. That scared me.

"What? Aren't you supposed to be telling us about some game?"

Kit shrugged, then rubbed his face with opened palms. His forehead looked sweaty, more than usual. "As of tonight, the game's changed again. So, we need someone better than me to explain it now."

Chapter 8

The game's changed again. What did that even mean? Puzzle games like this always felt so manipulative. Was the goal to make players feel like a rat on a wheel, round and round going nowhere fast? Or was there a deeper agenda?

In the thirty minutes since leaving the clinic, I'd lost every ounce of the relaxation from Dr. Lee's magic needles, agitation buzzing again in my hands and chest. Now the donut smell was making me gag. How long had it been since I'd left the Fenning estate? About two hours, maybe a little more. I consumed as much of CSI, NCIS, and other cop dramas as I could, so I remembered the TV-version of forensic science related to stages of death. Every minute past Roberta Fenning's time of death would mean something to the investigation of what happened to her. I started pacing to keep my ankle from seizing up and realized Kit had pads under his beautiful rugs. What would he surprise me with next?

He took the chair opposite me and dragged it forward. "Do you remember Cicada?" he asked, reading my mind.

"Cicada 3301? That was a long time ago," I said, too young to play it back then but I certainly knew about it. Everyone my age did.

What I didn't tell him was that Rudy, four years older than me, had played it for a while. And now he was dead. I stared back at him, jaw clenched.

"What'd I say?"

"It was an internet puzzle game that the CIA used to recruit operatives."

Kit nodded, brow raised.

"There was a movie about it. I never watched it," I lied, still walking on his cushy rug. "And it nearly broke the internet every time game admins posted a clue, pulling every nerd out of their basements to run around to random buildings in the middle of the night."

"This game is similar," Kit said. "It posts clues around the world that have pictures and links and riddles. The more clues you solve, you progress in levels. Fergus, what level are you on?"

Chuckle. "Two. You?"

"Three. Anyway, there are these *keys* or totems, like animals and artifacts, that have special meaning." Kit glanced back at Fergus and they stayed there in some sort of silent conversation. "You can use them to earn more points and get more clues."

"To solve what, exactly?" I asked. "What's this game called?"

"DSC, and so far no one knows what that stands for."

"Why does any of this matter right now?"

Kit sighed. "You know why. You found it yourself. One of the clues today had GPS coordinates to your dead lady's house."

I knew Roberta. I'd talked to her, sat with her, drank iced tea on their back patio in the summer, hot chocolate during the holidays. She worked hard and was no-nonsense. "It doesn't make sense."

"Maybe not," Kit replied. "But one way or another, your friend Roberta is part of this game."

Fergus faced me. "And since you found her body, now you are too."

It felt like all the air got sucked out of the room. It seemed obvious now. "I've got to call the police. I can't *not* do this. I fou—" My words caught in my throat. "I found her body!"

Fergus came to me and put his hands on my shoulders. "But you left evidence all over that house, including blood from what you told me. Right? We gotta think this through."

"Okay." I realized only then that I hadn't been walking on my ankle, I was pacing like a caged lion. I collapsed on the stool, looking up at Fergus, hoping he might think of something, Kit staring at us back and forth all the while. "And the wellness check won't work."

"Why not?" Fergus asked.

"Because she's dead!" Kit and I said it at the same time, an odd synchronicity. "I don't know. I just don't—"

"We need a house cleaner," Kit suggested, an evil glint in his eye.

"You mean like hotel housekeeping?" Fergus asked. Poor Fergus.

"Um, that's not what he means," I whispered, suddenly feeling sick. I wanted to retrace my steps to identify when I'd slipped into another vortex.

"I'm serious and it might be the best solution right now."

"Come on, Kit," I said gently. "You know that song always ends the same way. I-know-a-guy-who-knows-a-guy always results in prison or death. Besides, there's no time for that."

"I can get someone there in fifteen minutes." Kit disappeared, then I heard the refrigerator door and a bottle opener. He came back with a beer and stood in the doorway.

Fergus raised his palms.

"Sorry bro, help yourself." He turned back to me and Fergus didn't move. "Here's how it would go down. Cleaner goes in first, we'll tell him everywhere you went in the house, he sanitizes it, leaves, *then* you call the police. Then it's safe, and you tell them what you told us earlier, that you were summoned, and you're worried about your friend."

I lowered my head into my hands. "How's he gonna get in? It's not some little beach shack. It's a fucking mansion in Sea Cliff."

"I have another idea." Fergus this time. He looked at Kit. "Can you submit pictures to the game? Like for points?"

Kit looked dreamily at the ceiling. "Of keys you mean?" He nodded slowly. "I think I remember reading about it, yeah. Octopus, cards, the number seven—" Kit looked at me. "Sevens are wild in this game for some reason."

"Let me guess, no one knows why."

"What if we submit a picture into the key folder...of Roberta?"

Fergus suggested.

"Her dead body?" I shrieked, losing it. "Are you completely loco?"

"Kind of like gaming the game?" Kit moved toward Fergus, making a conspiratorial huddle inside the front door. I could seriously just jump out the window right now, the way they do in movies. I probably wouldn't feel a thing.

"I could check the Subreddit," Kit mumbled, "see if anyone's submitted photos before, and maybe someone will talk to us."

"There's no time, guys. Let's go ahead with the cleaner idea. Were you serious about that?" I got up from the stool and faced off with Kit, eye-to-eye. I was almost as tall as him. "You know someone you could call right now, just give them an address and directions and no questions asked?"

He shrugged and nodded, like it was the equivalent of ordering Grubhub.

"Who is it?"

"Less you know, the better."

I nodded; he was probably right. I went to Fergus and hugged him, letting him hold me for an extra second because I needed it, because he needed it, and because this crazy fucking world needed to stop temporarily. I didn't care that Kit Fury was watching our private moment, or how he interpreted it. I breathed into Fergus' shoulder and he held the back of my head. That one gesture made me somehow feel like I might live through this night.

"Alright, do it," I said, turning back to Kit. "Fergus knows everywhere I went in the house, and he knows how to get in through the basement. I'm going home to see my mom before she calls in a missing persons on me."

"Leave the Fenning estate to us," Fergus said.

"Fine. I hate my life right now."

The whole ride home from the back of an Uber, I wished Fergus was with me. I texted him to tell him I'd gotten sick on the upper landing, which meant even more DNA evidence that would have to be sanitized, along with the foyer, kitchen, back bedroom and basement. I couldn't stop looking at my phone with this shoe-drop dread waiting for the next text message to arrive. Who sent it, how did they know what happened, and know about my actions unless they were watching my every move? How could they have been?

And the idea of Lise was unraveling me more by the minute. She knew what was going on, but she wouldn't talk to me. She couldn't have killed her, could she? If Lise was hiding out right now, there had to be a reason, and I was probably the only one qualified to find out.

My Uber driver turned his radio to a hip-hop station, sounded like 106.1 FM. I used the time to think of what to tell my mother, opting for a gutless alternative to the truth.

Hi Mom, Lise and I are at the movies, spontaneous decision and sorry I didn't tell you earlier. Don't wait up. I'll poke my head in when I get home.

What are you seeing?

Shit. I had no idea what movies were even playing right now, or where they were playing.

We're at The Roxie. Lise wanted to see some dreary Russian film with subtitles. Seemed like a safe plan.

Sounds like her. Have fun.

Love you, I typed back. I wondered, as my fingers thumbed the words, whether it was actually still true. Were there any seventeen-year-olds on the planet who loved their parents, loved the incarceration of their rules and curfews, the judgment, suspicion and jail? How could I?

On the surface, I'd just bought myself a couple of hours with my mother's blessing. Unfortunately, she was smarter than the average mother and knew all my tricks. That was the toxic cycle of lying, wasn't it? You needed another lie to protect the first, and so on. And right now, I had no strength or fortitude to even get through the day let alone extra logistical details. I could spill everything to her, and I know she'd make me call the police. Maybe that was the answer—wait till we'd called the police, then tell her.

"I leaned toward the Uber driver. "Actually, could we make a change? Instead of the Mission could you bring me to Fort Point?"

Chapter 9

"Here?"

My driver, who introduced himself as "thirty-something-Bharat", rolled down the 25-degree decline to the parking lot. 10:35 p.m. He pulled into a spot and did what everyone did when they got here—gaped wide-eyed at the iconic spectacle of the Golden Gate Bridge, typically veiled in fog. I got out and just stood there for a few moments sucking the cold, salty air into my lungs. The up-spray from the waves showered my face and moistened my hair. My driver had rolled down the window to badger me with questions.

"I can't just leave you here alone in the dark. I'd be happy to wait with you until your ride shows up," he said.

My ride? What ride? Did I really look that helpless? "I'll be fine," I said. "This place helps me think."

It was true. I'd come here with Fergus many times in winter, usually January, when the winds were offshore and the waves were clean and head-high. A typical surf session for him was two hours, which meant I could stand here on this platform watching how the sea and fog rolled in and out. Even an hour of that made any problem feel smaller. The Presidio behind me, Alcatraz and Angel Island ahead, I drank it all in.

Growing up in the Marshall Islands smack dab in the West-Central Pacific, I had a deep ancestral connection to the sea. It made me sad, looking out now under the scant stars, to think that my dad might be staring out there too from the trunk of an overgrown mangrove at Laura Beach under this same sky, four thousand miles away. Was he wondering about me, wondering about my mom? No. He was probably blaming himself for raising me incorrectly to want to leave our idyllic atoll, and now being blamed by the rest of the family. It hadn't occurred to me until now that our decision could create hardship for him. Wish you were here, Dad. You'd know what to do.

Thirty-something Bharat drove off finally, leaving me alone in the dark parking lot. I felt it, too, as the gate was about to close for the night. I moved near the edge of the concrete platform and stared down into the dark soup, waves thrashing against piles of treacherous black rocks, the angry mist soaking my skin. I lifted my eyes to the bridge tower at the same time the foghorn sounded, guiding ships to safety. Maybe that horn was meant for me, too. To an onlooker, I probably looked like I was about to jump down into the black, glistening rocks. I heard something in between waves, a mumbling sound near me.

I turned my head to the right and saw a lone white van parked on the narrow slip of shoulder, partially concealed by overhung Eucalyptus branches. I could smell what they were smoking in there. I'd probably end up with a contact high, maybe I needed it. Three male voices argued back and forth in a low murmur.

"...game, I know, everyone at work's playing it," one of them said.

Next I heard code, codes, or coding, something about Python, so they might be software developers working at one of the tech companies in San Francisco. After a few more waves, I caught the words 'wild seven'. That was it. Had to be DSC again.

Normal Thea would have considered all the statistics of sex-trafficked teens, especially my age and non-white in an urban area. And it's not that I didn't care about my safety. But I wasn't normal-Thea right now and hadn't been since seeing Roberta dead in her house. Something inside had changed. I needed answers and I had a feeling that stupid game was the only way I was gonna find them.

Options: An approach might seem like there was something I wanted or needed from them, or worse: something I was offering. I suspected they were too high to make any moves, so it was to my advantage to pique their interest by showing some of my own.

I left my prime viewing spot and walked to the end of the lot, heading halfway up the hill toward the van.

"Hey," I shouted over the roar of the surf.

Scrambling sounds from inside resulted in four bare legs hanging off the sideboard with the door fully opened. Their heads angled out, looking for me behind the trees.

"You guys are playing it too?" I said. "Cool."

That was the bait. Now I'd see if they were interested enough to come to me. According to Fergus and Kit, success with the game came from knowing things, information as a commodity that led to more information from cryptic clues. I honestly had as much interest in an internet game as a trip to Disneyland right now—the furthest thing from my mind the summer before college. If Kit was right, and Roberta was either part of this game or died because of it, that now meant I was part of it, too.

"Where is she?" one of them whispered. "You wanna party?" another called out.

I took a few tentative steps toward the van, not my best idea ever. When I was within a couple of yards, I saw a third guy sitting on the rear bumper, the other two on the side.

"Always happy to share with a fellow traveler."

I could see them clearly now, three skinny guys, no shirts, probably no more than a few years older than me. I flashed my palm. "I'm cool. I heard you say wild seven. You playing that new game everyone's talking about?"

Another guy hopped onto the pavement and slid into a pair of sneakers. He had a shirt on and seemed a little older. "Wouldn't say playing exactly," the first guy said, and cracked himself up. "More like getting nowhere."

"What level are you on?" the athletic guy asked me.

"Oh, I'm just learning. I don't know that much about it." I tried not to laugh at the sound of my genius, stroking the male ego.

"Milo's on Level 3."

"Bro, shut the fuck up."

"What's the issue, man? She doesn't know anything about it anyway."

I stared out through the trees at Alcatraz, amused by their posturing. "How many levels are there?" I asked in my bimbo voice, turning to face them.

I heard mumbling in the van from the other two, Athletic Guy hissing commands.

"No."

"Why not?"

"Because…"

"My friend's on Level 2 but he just got something today," I said. "I don't know what. Maybe that means Level 3? I'm not sure."

"There are 7 levels," Athletic explained. "It used to be called SC or Sevens Club. Then one of the first players to reach Level 7 died suddenly, by odd circumstances. So people started calling it Dead Sevens Club."

DSC. "It sounds dangerous," I said, goading them again. "Does anyone know how the guy died?"

"He was found dead on the floor of his kitchen."

Chapter 10

It was dark but I could see the stranger's hard stare as he enunciated the word kitchen. Did he too know about Roberta and my connection to her? Could there be a connection between the two deaths? Worse yet, could he be the author of my mysterious text? My being here was a terrible idea. A day late and a dollar short as usual.

My stomach churned. Now suddenly I didn't want to be here, but the Uber driver had already gone. I came here for some peace and quiet, and now this stupid game was around every corner. Fine, I'd use this to get out of here. I held my head low and mumbled something, visibly upset, desperately hoping they didn't follow me.

"Hey, I didn't mean to upset you. I guess I thought you wanted to know what we know."

"No worries," I said, walking past the van up the hill. "My ride's coming. I just wanted to catch a glimpse of the bridge and watch the waves for a bit. See ya."

I trudged up the steep incline to the Fort Point entrance without any thought to how I was gonna get home, the boys arguing and mumbling behind me about driving me away. Ankle throbbing, I was careful to step slowly tp distribute my weight evenly. My phone vibrated and I shuddered, quickly developing a fear response from that innocuous little chime. Lise? No. It was Fergus.

The problem, of course, in trusting someone like Kit Fury with the fate of my future was that you never really knew which Kit you were getting. Our last encounter with him started in a teen dance club and ended in an alley behind the historic Warfield Theater, a man lying strangled on the ground, and Kit bloody and stumbling around, yelling his head off. Fergus and I ran toward Civic Center BART Station and hadn't talked to Kit since, a year ago, until tonight.

Hey, Fergus wrote, which meant to call him. But I wasn't calling. I needed to be all eyes and ears to make sure I wasn't being followed. Come on, Thea, just a little further to the top.

What's up? I typed back. *Is it done?*

Yes. No. Sort of.

Fuckers. I shook my head and slid the phone back in my pocket. Avoidance was a powerful tool, and right now I just couldn't cope. At the top of the hill, I caught sight of my Uber driver leaning his elbow out the window like a fucking tour guide and waving. Another stalker? Please no.

"I saw you were limping when I dropped you off," he shouted from across the street. "I thought you might need a ride somewhere, or medical attention or something."

Bharat, my humanitarian driver. He reminded me of the tennis pro on *Red Oaks*. From here, I had a full view of the bridge, the ghostly fog coiled up to its waist, with only the top showing. Stunning. The Fort Point gate was about to close, and the pothead van was still in there. Maybe they had a special arrangement.

Fine, I could use another ally right now. I thanked the Uber driving, saying I needed to make a call first.

I moved ten feet away from his car to call Fergus. "What does yes and no mean?" I asked without saying hello. "Where are you guys right now?"

"We never left. Kit mobilized his friend and—"

"Did he get in? Did he do it? And before you tell me to chill out, don't. I'm on the verge of a freaking breakdown over here."

"I know. I'll tell you everything." He paused—a bad sign.

"Now, Fergus!"

"Okay okay. Yes, he got in the house, yes he, um, I guess the word is sanitized it."

"But what? Was he seen?" When I asked that, it seemed like my driver was listening to my conversation. God, what if he was recording me?

"No."

"Did he get out safely?"

Fergus mumbled something to Kit, then came back on the line. "He's out."

"So? What's the issue?"

"There was no body on the kitchen floor."

I couldn't breathe, just like on the upper landing of the Fenning estate when I stared down at Roberta's dark hair and blue skin, which had now miraculously vanished. What the fuck was going on here? I did Kit's move, thumb and index finger on the bridge of my nose to keep from crying. It wasn't working. The air turned colder and the wind came back up. I wasn't sure when exactly I hung up the phone, but I did.

Kit's apartment wasn't gonna work for me right now. We needed somewhere else to talk, somewhere safe, private, and on neutral ground. I thought of my friend Janelle, who co-owned Linnea Caffe on 18th Street, because it had a room in the back, and a basement that she let me crash in sometimes, if I was willing to unpack coffee sleeves or unwrap cups. Sometimes she stayed open late working on bookkeeping, but more often opened super-early. Probably closed this time of night.

Meet me at Vesuvius, they're open for another two hours. I typed the text because honestly I didn't trust what came out of my mouth right now. I climbed in the backseat of Bharat's black Toyota and told him to head to North Beach.

"On my way, Miss. Your trusted chariot," he said in a cheery voice.

The car smelled strange; I couldn't put my finger on it. Not good, not bad, but something. Herbs, that's it. It smelled like basil, also dill. I wasn't asking about it because honestly I had too many threads in my head already. I just didn't have the space to add something about his wife's grocery business, or buying food for a soup kitchen. Though he seemed like the type. He was delightfully quiet, thank goodness. This gave me a little bit of space to watch a creepy cluster of clouds glide across the night sky over the water. Now we were headed inland to North Beach to what I'd always thought of as one of the most clandestine bars in the city.

Vesuvio, in the two hundred block of Columbus between Grant and Kearney, was so jam-packed with clutter, colors, mosaics, textures, that it was impossible to actually see anything in there. That's what I wanted—gather the intel I needed and pretend to disappear. I got there first, using my 5'8" height to look like I was old enough to be in a bar, and ordered a Coke but probably could have gotten away with a Negro Modelo. I hid on the second floor under slanted eaves in a hobbit corner. It was so cramped you were forced to crouch low and lean your heads in to hear each other. You could plan a robbery in here, talk at a normal volume, and no one would ever know. At this point anything was possible.

I heard Kit down in the entry, as usual talking too loud. Fergus came up first, leaving Kit to stop at the bar. Normally he wouldn't do that, opting to supervise Kit and make sure he didn't start a fight or stick his hand down some woman's shirt.

"Hey, hey." He leaned in and gave me a quick hug.

"That's two hugs in the same day."

"You okay with that?" he asked.

"Let's not make a habit of it."

He released his grasp and sat beside me.

"Where's the body?" I asked, zeroing in on the most important detail. "Was there any evidence she had been there? Like…"

He knew I meant blood, but he shook his head. "Nothing. I don't suppose you took any pictures, did you?"

"Oh my God," I whispered, my hand involuntarily covering my mouth. "Yes! I almost forgot. I took one from the doorway of the kitchen, which sort of shows that I never actually went into the kitchen itself."

"Lemme see the picture. Hurry up, Kit's coming. Don't show it to him. Do you hear me?"

"I hear you." I fumbled to pull my phone out of my too-small pocket, Kit suddenly looming over us like a giant. He stood at the table with two beers, noticing Fergus and I were seated on the same side of the table. Was that a mopey look on his face? Ohhh, I love it. Jealous, territorial, whatever it was, I'd have a field day with his neurotic baggage. Our eyes on him, I slid my phone into Fergus' hand under the table and took his. He put my phone, posing as his, on the table as he sipped the beer Kit brought him, looking for the image of Roberta Fenning's dead body on her kitchen floor. I made sure not to look at his face when he saw it, not only for discretion but because it was all so horrible. I sipped my Coke, now wishing it was a vodka martini.

"Dark beer," Kit said, looking at my glass with a raised brow.

I didn't correct him. "Not sure what you're concluding from that, but you should know that I also drink black coffee." I watched his eyes as I said it, feeling the unspoken vibe of resentment (mine) and shame (his) between us. I just prayed he didn't bring up The Warfield tonight.

"She's also seventeen," Fergus said to Kit, who closed his eyes and smiled.

"So, T. What are we doing here?" Kit asked, as Fergus and I switched phones again under the table.

"I like this place because during the week no one comes here, or not upstairs anyway. I need to know what your cleaner found." I paused, sipped, nodded, waiting for Kit to bring up the topic of compensation.

On the street, in his world, information was a hot commodity. He'd sent someone to the Fenning estate tonight on my behalf to remove evidence of my presence on a night that mattered—to Roberta Fenning anyway. Now I was gonna owe him, and I was ready with my payment. The only complication was if Kit already knew what I was about to share.

Chapter 11

I felt scandalous sitting here at Vesuvio instead of next door at City Lights Books, my usual haunt. A multimedia collage of Frida Kahlo with a string of little red lights stared back from the wall. I took in her grim, beautiful face and signature eyebrows. But they had no answers for me tonight. Would anyone?

"You already know," Kit said.

"No body?"

"No body."

"Did your man also clean the kitchen?"

"Nah, he didn't touch that. Just the areas we discussed. All of them, including the basement, entry, landing, back bedroom, and the outside doors."

I drummed my fingers on the ancient table going through it in my mind. The amount of time that had elapsed between my exit and Kit's cleaner couldn't have been more than three hours. Someone could have come in the service entrance, where Nanny usually entered, which was two rooms away from the kitchen, and the easiest path. The benefit of that plan was the gated side yard with overhanging trees, which was protected enough to allow for removing a body in broad daylight. And, of course, the killer could have done it if they were still in the house.

"Is it possible she wasn't dead when you saw her?" Kit asked.

"Dude, I saw blood under her head. Besides, she was blue," I said, praying Fergus didn't mention the picture. "Her skin...I can't get that color out of my mind. I'd never seen it before."

Fergus puckered his lips. "So, someone removed the body before we got there, probably leaving their own forensic evidence at the scene," he said.

"Well you obviously won't need to report anything to the police," Kit added. "Because there's no need now."

"But—"

"What are you gonna tell them?" Kit was pushing, red-faced, and I knew why.

I shrugged. "Then why was the estate's address a clue in that game?"

Fergus and Kit looked at each other, each waiting for the other to answer.

"Something about that house has a connection to it, one way or another," I said. "How are you guys doing with it? Any progress to report?"

Kit sat back and crossed his arms. "With the game? The QR code in the latest clue isn't active yet."

"What, are you supposed to check it every five minutes or something? Like people have nothing better to do?"

"I think there's an algorithm that dictates when the QR works every day," Fergus said, "only for seven minutes at a time and always a different time of day. I haven't figured it out yet."

"You can set your Reddit notifications so you get a ping when people log a comment or respond to a thread," Kit said.

I sipped my Coke and reached down to rub my ankle, so bored by their gaming geekdom.

"Also, YouTube has some stuff on it posted by Cicada conspiracy theorists."

"Conspiracy? What are they saying?" I asked, trying to figure out the right time to drop the intel I'd gotten from the surfer potheads.

Kit leaned in on his elbows. "Not sure it's really a conspiracy and it has nothing to do with Cicada 3301—"

"Except that all the same people who played that are playing this game," Fergus added. "And there's definitely some traction with this one so far."

Kit nodded and took a thoughtful sip. "So, the theory floating around is that somehow this game is connected to a series of unsolved murders that happened ten years ago."

I instinctively looked around the room behind me. "Here?" I asked.

"South City," he said.

I knew very little about South San Francisco other than a friend who lived in Dogpatch, which wasn't even near there.

"The Wharf, a luxury condo complex at the Shipyard, was the site of some killings years ago, and after the first two, their—"

"First two?" I asked. "How many were there? People living in the same complex?"

"That's the thing," Kit said. "Seven people died under suspicious circumstances. The building owner disappeared after the first two deaths."

None of us spoke or moved.

"Seven people died over what period of time?" I asked, wondering if this tied in with what I'd learned at Fort Point. I knew I was irritating him with all my questions but I couldn't help it. Fergus sat calmly beside me taking it in.

"Six months or so. Anyway, the owner's first name was Edgar, and for a while the internet was flooded with Where's Edgar memes. So, when the news picked it up, they started calling it the Edgar Heights Murders because The Wharf, the condo complex where it all took place, is in Bayview Heights."

"Where's Edgar," I mumbled. Where had I heard that phrase before? I was too young when those headlines were circulating, but I'd heard it, or maybe seen it, somewhere. A bumper sticker maybe? But where?

"Did they ever find the guy?" Fergus asked. "The owner of that complex?"

"They brought him back and arrested him but eventually determined he had nothing to do with the murders."

Fergus shook his head. "The conspiracy is, what, that this game has something to do with the Edgar Heights murders?"

"Why though?" I asked. "What's the connection?"

Kit put his palms up, and I reminded myself to check Reddit later for *Where's Edgar* activity.

"Well, I might know something, but not sure it has anything to do with seven unsolved murders." Could this be related to the kitchen floor murder I learned about from the surfer potheads? I stopped and considered this, again looking around the empty upper floor. The details of those murders must be public knowledge by now. Hearing them suddenly made me wonder about Roberta. Would her murder get swallowed up by the media and churned out as some internet meme, with me along with it? Now my stomach growled. "Well, I think I know why the game is called DSC at least."

"If you do, it's not common knowledge," Fergus said.

"There are seven levels and the game used to be called Sevens Club with all kinds of ways for the number seven to be used for points. Then, the first player to reach Level 7 died suddenly, and by odd circumstances, as I was told. So, players started calling the game 'Dead' Sevens Club after that. DSC. Then the clues got harder to prevent anyone from getting to that high level again."

Kit's mouth contracted and he picked at his fingernails. "Where'd you pick that up?" he asked jerking his chin up. Of course he'd be annoyed. I'd gotten this information first.

"Basic eavesdropping. I heard a bunch of stoners talking about it at the beach." That was mostly true.

"How'd the guy die?" Fergus asked. "What were the suspicious circumstances?"

"I didn't get that far," I lied, but I knew for sure that he died in a kitchen, just like Roberta Fenning had. So, maybe there was a connection to those earlier unsolved murders after all. I tried a redirect. "What happens when the QR code is activated? How will you know, and how will you be able to see it?" I asked.

"I've got a business associate tracking that for me," Kit said. "They're checking every five minutes."

"But once it's active, you need to drive across town to find it? And you have to do all that in seven minutes?" I laughed. "Don't these people have, like, jobs or something?"

"No, no," Kit said. "I know where it's at. The last one was in Chinatown, you saw that one. This next one's in Bayview."

"Hunter's Point. Great." Fergus, this time, commenting on the neighborhood. He was such a wuss. But I had a different thought.

"Bayview?" I asked Kit. "Where exactly?"

He picked up his phone. "Lemme find it. You're thinking it's the Shipyard, where the Edgar Heights murders took place?"

"Exactly. Just seems like a coincidence, don't you think?"

"It's not the same address but it's…" He paused and expanded the map showing on his phone. "Interesting. It's right across the street from the lobby of The Wharf."

"Why don't we go there?" Fergus suggested. "Then we're on-site and we can look around while we're waiting for the QR to activate."

"Have at it," I said yawning. "I've had enough for one day. Besides, I've got tutoring tomorrow."

"She's a calculus tutor," Fergus bragged. That was cute, though I'm sure Kit would just use that information to come up with some new quip about me for next time.

Fergus let me out of the booth and we all stood just as a new text popped into my phone. Shit, the *I own you now* guy. I widened my eyes at Fergus, then looked down again.

"It's my mom. Don't get me started," I said for Kit's benefit.

Friends close; enemies closer.

Not bad advice, all things considered. I hugged Fergus and met Kit's watery blue eyes while I considered this. "Thank you," I said directly to him, and in that moment anyway I meant it. "For the rescue tonight. Didn't turn out like any of us planned, but I appreciate it."

He recoiled an inch with surprise, offering me his sweaty hand, which I shook knowing I would probably need him again.

Chapter 12

After midnight, San Francisco's night life was just getting started, even on a week night. It was one of the things I loved about this city, but there were so many. A cluster of young guys stumbled down the sidewalk shouting at a nerdy student with a backpack, reminding me that I was supposed to be headed to San Francisco State in the fall. Although I'd already gotten my acceptance letter into the School of Mathematics, I had a feeling that wasn't my destiny.

I'd planned to book another Uber from the alley next to Vesuvio, but I spotted Bharat's shiny black Toyota SUV live-parked across the street. Either this guy was stalking me, he was being paid by someone to keep tabs on me, he was lonely, or he was a kind soul looking to keep me safe from the predators of the world. So far, I was going with the stalker theory because anything else seemed too unbelievable. Still, with lack of any other options, he was here and I needed a ride - again. Fuck.

I crossed the street coming up from behind the car, and knocked lightly on the back window, still deciding whether I believed in fairy tales. He turned and smiled, motioning me in with his hand.

I got in, gave him my address in the Mission, then posed those three possibilities to him.

He let out a big belly laugh. "Me, I'm a driver," he said, heading down Columbus. "I don't know why, but I like driving people around. You know, helping them get where they need to go. There's something sort of Zen about it."

"Right now, I need to go home. But I'm not helpless, just so you know."

"Well, obviously. You're limping around on a sprained ankle, for one thing."

I eyed my mother sleeping in the living room chair through the front window when I came up the front stairs. Despite my urge to have her look at my ankle, I didn't wake her. She was a pediatric nurse and would be able to tell me how effective Dr. Lee's care had been, but she'd also pump me for information about where I'd been all day and night. I had no energy left for lying tonight. I collapsed on top of my mattress in my clothes, shoes and all, and felt myself drifting off. Five minutes later, my eyes sprang open in a panic with a shuddering realization: I had to do something about that picture. Tomorrow.

I felt my mother kiss my head before she left for work the next morning. I had tutoring sessions scheduled from 10-4 at various private residences in Berkeley Hills. That meant getting over the Bay Bridge just after rush hour, ugh. Sometimes Fergus drove me; sometimes he even let me drive his father's car, but in a pinch I'd bring my bike on BART and walk it up the crazy, steep hills.

Bharat gave me his mobile number before I left last night, and since Fergus may have stayed in the city at Kit's, that seemed as good a plan as any at this point. I texted my new personal driver, eating a bowl of Cheerios in our sunny kitchen while I waited for an answer. The swoosh of cars out front drowned the cheeps of birds from the backyard. I stood at the sink eating, watching a hummingbird buzz up to the window, then to the lemon tree out back, then again to the window as if she was watching me and had a message. I'd take advice from anyone at this point.

I sat with a cup of my mother's strong coffee just staring at my phone, considering the gravity of having the last ever picture of Roberta Fenning and different possibilities of what to do with it.

Would my secret texter also know that I'd snapped a picture with my phone? Was that the meaning behind his message? Unless a camera in the foyer recorded my movements and that's what the texter meant. *I know what you did.* Time to get rid of that picture.

My primary email was a Gmail account. I had an iCloud account I never used. I had a separate email through the tutoring company I worked for. I don't think I'd ever used it, nor did anyone know about it. But maybe a better idea was my brand new SF State email address. The account was active because I'd already checked my access and there was a welcome email. But no one knew about it so far, not my mom, Lise, or Fergus, which made it a perfect choice. I could email the photo there, password-protect the attachment or, even better, store it in a private Google Drive folder then password-protect the whole folder. I could email myself a link to that folder, which only I could access with my Google password.

I did the multiple file transfers from my phone, opened Google Drive to set up the password encryption, and tested access. Then as a double-check, I logged onto my laptop and tested access there. The encryption was set, I could log in, and the file opened. Next, I deleted the email I'd sent to myself, put it in my spam folder, and went back to my phone to delete the image from my photos. Now my photograph of Roberta Fenning's dead body only existed in the spam folder of my Gmail account and in an encrypted Google Drive link. Other than the Recently Deleted/Recover process, which had never worked for me, my secret was safe. For now.

Bharat said he'd pick me up at nine. I just needed to find a way to explain him to Fergus. I pulled my secret journal out from the back of my dresser and made some notes from last night, including what happened with the white van and the conversation at Vesuvio. If only I'd gotten a plate number. When Bharat showed up, I brought it with me to continue writing.

"Good morning!" he bellowed, too loud, too chipper. Ouch. I climbed in the back. He passed a crumpled bag through the seats and pulled a medium cup of something from his cup holder.

A blueberry muffin and a latte. "You brought me coffee? And breakfast?" I nearly cried at the unexpected kindness. The coffee was too creamy and sweet for my taste but I guzzled half of it down, hoping the jolt of caffeine might dislodge the image of that photograph from my frazzled brain.

"I'm sure you don't eat right. No one your age does."

"How will I pay you if you're off the Uber clock?" I asked him.

"I like cash," he said. "Ten dollars a day and, if I'm free, I'll take you wherever you want to go."

I liked his East Indian accent and his friendliness was a respite. "Why, though? Why would you drive me around when you could be making more money from Uber clients?"

Long, theatrical sigh. I could tell this guy was funny. "Uber passengers never talk to me. I'm a social person. I like conversation."

And the no-talking was exactly what I liked about Uber drivers.

"Okay, so let's say that's part of my price. Ten dollars and friendly conversation. Deal?"

I nodded, making idle conversation but mostly concentrating on my journal, realizing that what I'd written so far had created a complication for myself if anyone found it and connected it to me. I always thought of those things too late.

Luckily my four tutoring clients were in the same grade, same school, and from the same neighborhood. The bad part was that the Berkeley Hills were vertical. My ankle was getting better but wasn't a hundred-percent. Sipping the last of the froth, I thanked Bharat and nibbled at the muffin while limping down the walkway of the first student's house, making sure my weight was properly distributed on both feet.

All told, I felt uncomfortable about being in the Fenning mansion at all last night. Though the body had disappeared, that still didn't erase the image of Roberta's bloody corpse on the kitchen floor, the fact that Lise lured me there and then took off, or the fact that Nanny hadn't showed up. She was always there in that kitchen, apron permanently affixed to her waist, hands dusted with flour. She wasn't much older than me but she always seemed older, and I don't think I'd ever been to the house when she wasn't there. Had she been the one to move the body? She was average height and build, but didn't seem vigorous enough to pull a dead body across a long stretch of floor.

Now that I'd gotten text number two from my secret blackmailer, his prompt seemed almost tailor-made to my white van buddies. Not sure if they qualified as friends or enemies, but either way it seemed like a good reason to make another visit there tonight, if nothing else to get more information out of them. They were playing the game and obviously knew things about it that Fergus and Kit didn't. And when it came to Kit, leverage was vital. But what did I have to offer them in return? I'd better think of something. I looked again at my stalker's original text, mentioning the police and the fact that he 'owned me now'. I wasn't afraid yet knew that was one of my biggest flaws, as Fergus constantly reminded me. If this person wanted to hold Roberta's death over my head, what power did they have now that the body was gone? Or had they been the one to move her?

I was dying to know what happened last night at The Wharf, if they found what the QR code led to…and if they located it in a hidden QR code like last time. I tried not to bother Fergus when he was working. His primary job at Peets was busy and stressful; his other job as a corporate courier was an opportunity for him to ride his bike, which he loved. Today was Thursday so that meant Peets. I couldn't help it—I texted him.

Hey good morning.

Is it still morning? I've been running around for the past four hours. U ok?

Just teaching math to people who hate it. Have time to tell me what happened last night?

Give me twenty minutes to clock out. Then I head to my other job and can call you on the way.

KK

Chapter 13

I walked down the Arlington Avenue hill toward John Hinkel Park catching sight of a lone, west-facing bench with a perfect view of Berkeley's architectural mishmash. Modern, Craftsman, Tudor, words I knew from HGTV, my mom's favorite chill-out channel.

My phone rang.

"Hey, hey." Fergus.

"Hey."

"Where you at?" he asked.

"Still in Berkeley. I'm done."

"Wish I could come get you but I'm headed to job number two."

"I know, I'll be okay," I said, leaving out the fact that I'd somehow scored my own private Uber driver. "How was Peets today?"

"Impossible to concentrate on spilled coffee and muffin shortages after how we spent the past twenty-four hours."

Yeah, I could certainly relate. "What happened with Kit last night after I left? Did you go to The Wharf?"

"Yeah."

"And?"

All I heard was heavy breathing on the other end as he pedaled through town. "Um, it's hard to explain when I'm dodging traffic, but there was a page with a picture of a part of an octopus, with some text below it about creepy octopus behavior."

"This was part of the game?" I asked, picturing his description tacked to a building. I wondered if it had the secret QR code again.

"It's one of the keys. Keys are like, I don't know, mascots, sort of. There are things like a deck of cards, an octopus, a guy surfing down a lightning bolt. And if you find pictures of them near the sites of where the clues are posted, you can upload them to a folder on Reddit and submit them to the game admins. If they accept it, it'll be posted publicly and you'll get points."

His voice was tight, tone tense. Why was he using discretion while on a bike? Almost like sharing this detail was some kind of code breach. "What do you do with those points when you get them?" I asked, staying on the concrete details.

"How do I know? I haven't gotten that far." Now the tone turned defensive.

"So, what are you supposed to do with the picture and text?"

"Same answer. I'm not far enough along to know yet."

The whole thing sounded so stupid. I tried to keep the eyeroll out of my voice. "Is Kit?" I asked.

"Thea, do you think we had a sleepover at his house last night or something?"

This didn't sound like my best friend. "Dude, are you okay? You sound edgy today."

"I'm fine," he said, but I knew he wasn't.

"Can you send me a picture of it? I wanna take a look. Shoot, that's right, you said the website is only up for like seven minutes."

"That's true but…" He let his voice trail off.

"Ahhhh, someone thought of something."

Now he snickered. "I'll send it at the next stop sign. You might see something I missed. I've tried everything."

"I'm in. We never had our movie night this week. You up for it tonight?" I asked, hoping he'd say yes so I could feel a tiny bit of normalcy.

"I can't tonight, I'm helping my dad with something. Tomorrow?"

"Sure," I said, hiding my disappointment, hiding my certainty that something was wrong and my theory that someone had gotten to him.

Fergus' dad was a trial lawyer who didn't have time to eat more than once a day, let alone spend time with his only son. So, I didn't believe they were spending time together tonight like he said. I can't remember when he'd lied to me before. Was he seeing Kit to play the game, or did he have a date? Now I was getting paranoid. While I waited for that picture at a bus stop in Berkeley, my ankle throbbed reminding me I hadn't elevated it today. I tried Bharat, first via text and then phone. He didn't answer, but his text came in ten seconds later, my own private driver. Probably a serial killer, with my luck.

Hello! I'm in El Cerrito, he wrote. I loved his flair. *Where are you?*

At a bus stop in Berkeley Hills near campus, heading back to the Mission.

Text me your cross streets and I'll see you in twenty minutes.
Thank God.

I stayed on the bus stop bench waving off two buses, grateful that I'd have Bharat's comfortable seat to hopefully elevate my leg. I'd seriously need to ice it, and probably show it to my mom when she got home from work. Then I remembered this was her long day; she didn't get off work till eleven. Funny how I'd hardly eaten in the past two days and still was barely hungry. I could feel that my stomach was empty but no appetite. Stress and anxiety had taken its place.

Kit's comment about the game having changed again kept nagging at me. What did that mean? Fergus would know, but since I'd be home alone tonight I'd finally have time to do some Reddit research on DSC, look up *Where's Edgar* and see if there was anything on game structure changes. For some reason, I felt pulled by the story of the Edgar Heights murders. Sometimes my pulls meant something.

Bharat's SUV rolled around the corner. I climbed in the back and asked his permission to put my foot up.

He turned and put his arm on the back of the seat. "You need more than a footrest. You need a doctor. I should have taken you to the hospital last night. Shame on me."

"Oh no, nothing like that. I just need to put ice on it when I go home. Thank you so much for the lift."

"My pleasure, Thea. So, what shall we talk about tonight?" he asked, rubbing his palms together.

I remembered my contractual obligation for conversation, but I was dying to study the picture Fergus had just texted me. I tried to come up with a topic, then I thought of the game. Why not?

"There was something I was wanting to ask you about, Bharat."

He glanced back with a wide grin. "Excellent."

"Give me a second here, I want to ask you about a website." I glanced down at my phone, opened Fergus' text, then the image, and saw the octopus arm with suckers on it, with the text on the bottom. Nothing looked odd or out of the ordinary. I zoomed in on different parts of it. I bet if I ran the image through a standard filter, like the ones on Instagram, it might bring out highlights or shadows and show something more, like hidden text or another QR code.

"Have you heard of this new game everyone's playing? I don't know how old you are but do you have kids?"

"That's three questions, actually. I'm thirty-one, have twin seven-year-old boys, and I'm literally drowning in games. Mario Kart, Animal Crossing, Zelda…where do I start?"

"Oh, I meant online games, adult games."

He checked my face in the rearview and tipped his head. "Now when you say adult do you mean—"

"No not porn or anything like that. An adult internet game. What did you do for work, Bharat, before you drove for Uber?"

"Not before, still now. I'm a software engineer, a contractor. I do short-term gigs. Right now, I'm a front-end app developer for a startup. The pay is good and I can make my own hours. Usually, I work nights and drive during the day, with the exception of last night."

Oh my God, what were the chances of that? He could know about DSC. While I took in this new information, I looked down at my phone and, in the shadow of a building, I saw something in Fergus' photo—a small, dark blue smudge in the middle of the blue octopus arm. I zoomed in on the dark color. Numbers? No, something else. I zoomed out a bit. Was it a URL? No, an IP address, which was the address of a particular computer device. I knew I could use dnstracker.org to look up the owner of the computer but, wait, there was another dark smudge on another of the octopus arms, which had previously looked like a blue smudge. Tricky. The other instance, when I zoomed in this time, was a tinyurl. I copied the address into a browser and it brought up Google Earth. Bharat was waiting.

"Okay, um, did you ever play that Cicada 3301 game several years ago?"

"I know about it, I read about it, saw the movie, but never played it. I read it was a purported CIA training program, also possibly cult recruitment, honestly that was enough to scare me away."

I liked Bharat, and felt safe enough with him, but was still deciding whether I believed anything he'd told me so far. We'd just crossed over the Bay Bridge and were heading down Seventh Street toward the Mission.

"Really? But so many smart people were playing it," I said. "You really didn't try to solve any of the clues?"

"No, but I know someone who did; he got through the first two, I think. I just thought it seemed like a mouse with a spinning wheel."

That was exactly how I'd felt about DSC. That meant Bharat was a kindred spirit. He glanced in the rearview. "Why do you ask? Did you play it? I heard the 2014 game still hasn't been solved."

"No, I was too young back then, but there's a game out there now that I keep hearing about."

"Do tell."

I looked behind me out the right window. Something about the Subway signage on the bottom floor of Hotel Isabel tugged at my attention. A young woman with platinum blonde hair. Omg, Lise! "Bharat, stop please. I need to get out. That's my friend, I've been looking for her for days. Can you pull—"

"Yes of course, give me a minute to put my turn signal on so I don't crash us into another moving car." He pulled to the curb. My eyes hadn't left the back of the woman's head. I was only eighty-percent certain it was her, but it looked like her hair, her walk, and an old cap she sometimes wore when she wanted to disappear. Finally I was about to get some answers. I got you now, Lise.

Chapter 14

Bharat pulled over but refused to drive away, vowing to wait at least a few minutes. I climbed out and handed him the ten-dollar bill I'd pulled out of my wallet per our agreement, jogged down the street after her, surprised that my ankle felt okay. I could still see her, the hat and her tall stature, which collectively distinguished her from any crowd. Where the hell was she going? My phone rang. Bharat.

"Sorry to have run off like that," I said quietly into the phone, not losing sight of her.

"Are you going to approach her and ask her to stop, or do you want me to sort of…"

"Tail her? Would you do that?"

"She didn't just rob a bank or anything, did she?"

I just loved this guy. "No, she's avoiding me," I said, leaving out the part about her possibly having killed her mother.

"Fine, get in. I'm still right behind you. Luckily I have tinted windows."

"You can charge me extra for this."

"We'll work something out."

Why was Bharat willing to get involved in this tangled plot? He seemed not only accommodating but looking for adventure. Maybe he too was running from something. What a pair.

Twenty steps back to his car, I kept my eyes fixed on Lise while Bharat maneuvered into the right lane with flashers on. A great idea. He stayed back at least a half a block from her. She was walking quickly with purpose, heading straight ahead, not looking around. She knew where she was going. But where? Straight down Seventh Street, crossing Langton, and waiting calmly for a car to pass before she entered the crosswalk. What I didn't yet understand was a) why wasn't she trying to conceal herself, and b) why whatever she was doing needed to be a secret.

"Can you get my granola bars in the backseat?" Bharat asked.

"This is probably not what you envisioned doing when you left your house today."

"Nonsense! Chasing down a mystery woman is nothing less than invigorating. I'm hungry, that's all," he laughed.

I felt a box under the passenger seat, pulled it out, removed a Raspberry Nutri-Grain bar, unwrapped it, and handed it to him.

"Thank you, my dear." He spoke like he was much older. He bit off the entire top half. "Now," he said chewing, "are you going to tell me what's really going on here? What did this woman do?"

I told him something, but not the truth because Bharat was still a stranger, and there was no telling what he was really up to. I said the woman's name was Jane, I'm sure he didn't believe me, and that she invited me to a party, didn't show up, and there was a sick woman lying on the floor. I thought she was dead at first—a story with some elements of truth in it. Bharat chewed the granola bar, drank from his water bottle, and nodded as he listened to my tale.

"And your friend, Jane," he said with affect, "hasn't spoken with you since? Why is that such a big deal?"

"I need to know that our mutual friend is okay. I can't reach her either." Shit. Now I'd told him two lies. I knew what a runaway train this could be.

"Look look look." Bharat pointed ahead. Lise slowed her walking speed and entered a building on the corner of Seventh Street and Folsom, a tall, vertical, blue building that looked like it could be a residence. "This is like Sherlock Holmes. The woman entered the building at," he looked at his watch, "4:25 p.m." He turned and smiled again like an excited child chosen for an important task. Everyone had always told me as a child that I was seven-going-on-thirty. Bharat was the opposite.

My phone buzzed, and something fluttered in my chest, thinking it was Fergus, that it had been all in my head that he too was avoiding me. But it was from my mystery blackmailer. Oh. no.

"You're watching for her, right?" Bharat asked.

"With every cell in my body."

He touched his large belly and laughed. OMG too funny, almost enough to make me forget.

You have a beautiful cat, the text read.

Cat. Now he's been to my house. My mother? No, she's working late tonight. Unless he went there before she left. OMG, I felt sick.

"Hey Bharat, my mom needs me. I just got a text. Do you feel like watching for my friend Jane while I go home and come right back? It's in the Mission, just a couple blocks from here."

"Yeah, yeah, go, I'll stay right here. And if she leaves I shall follow her. You have my number. Call me when you need to, but call instead of texting so I can keep my eyes on our subject. Ha ha!"

With that personality, he should be hosting a game show.

To save my ankle, I hopped a city bus I knew would be going right by my street. I was home in five minutes. There was a note on the kitchen table in my mother's handwriting. "Your teacher came by, the one you're working with on that photo imaging project, said he can't meet at noon tomorrow but can do one. He said you'd know where. Handsome, too. Can't wait to hear about your project." She drew her signature large heart with a smaller heart in the middle and the letter M.

My knees buckled as I collapsed in one of the kitchen chairs. Sasha rubbed her silky fur against my other leg, reminding me of the note. I picked her up and held her, moving my fingers around her little body.

"You okay, my sweetheart?" I held her face in front of mine. She jumped down and I eyed some leftover food in her dish. I pressed the number to my mom's mobile, knowing she wouldn't answer. It rang twice, then dragging sounds in the background.

"Mom? Are you there?"

"Hey, just changing clothes. How's it going? Did you see my note?"

I gulped. "Did he come to the door or something?"

I could hear some kind of announcement in the background, paging a doctor to the ER. Long exhale. "I was watering the plants on the front porch and the door was open when I was in the bathroom. I came out and a man was standing in the entry."

"Oh okay," I said, trying to sound casual.

"Photo imaging project? What the hell is that? A math project, I would have believed that. What are you doing, Thea? That man was in our house."

"I'm sorry he scared you mom. I need to—"

"Me? I can take care of myself. It's you I'm worried about." She paused. I pictured her sitting on the locker room bench, rubbing her temples the way she did when we argued. "What's going on with you? I've hardly seen you since graduation. You're like a stranger lately. And what the hell does photo imaging project mean?"

"I have no idea but I'll look into it. I'm sorry. I've gotta go." I disconnected, then texted her an apology and said I'd call her later. Lame, but my hands were shaking and I was too afraid to think straight. Photo imaging could only mean the photo I'd taken of Roberta. That visitor had to be my text-stalker. And now he'd been to my house. Had he gone there hoping to find the house empty so he could look for it?

I checked every room and every window to secure the place, re-hydrated, and changed into surveillance attire. Black leggings, black overshirt, tennis shoes, and a black baseball cap. I smeared some of my mom's Biofreeze on my ankle, ate leftover rice and beans from the fridge, then drank cold coffee straight out of the carafe for another caffeine hit. Savage.

I texted Fergus while elevating my leg. *The "friends close enemies closer" guy has been to my house!*

Jesus, T, are you there now? I hope you're not alone. Where's your mom at?

Working. She saw him, left me a note about him. Said he was handsome, ffs.

OMG.

He wants the picture.

Of RF? Shit.

I assume so, he made up this story for my mom that he was my teacher and we were working on a photo imaging project together.

Let's not text, Fergus wrote. *Can you call me? Where are you right now?*

About to get on a bus.

Where are you headed?

Chasing Lise.

Chapter 15

Our blue and white house on Lexington was about nine miles from Ocean Beach and walking distance from Linnea Caffe, one of the Mission's hidden gems. I changed my mind about the bus and booked an Uber instead. Sitting outside on the front steps reminded me that I loved this neighborhood, and this city. A park nearby, close to everything, where life literally never stops. The farthest thing from a remote island and I liked it that way. I watched a throng of girls my age walk past the house, talking, laughing, barely noticing me. I moved here almost eight years ago and that never changed – still the same smart, nerdy loner.

I never minded being an outsider because the idea of being an insider terrified me. I didn't look like the Latino girls in my neighborhood, or the students I went to school with. But I didn't look Islander either.

I rose to recheck the lock on the front door and a voice startled me.

"Miss Riggs?"

I turned and shoved my keys in a small backpack I'd brought

with me.

"Thea Riggs?"

I stared back at a female police officer standing outside an SFPD squad car that had rolled down my street when I turned my back. Fit body, sculpted cheekbones, gorgeous. Breathe, Thea. "Um…yes?"

"I'm Officer Maddox with the San Francisco Police Department. I'd like to ask you a few questions."

If my heart pounded any harder, I'd end up on a slab in the morgue tonight. "Sure," I said, trying to sound casual. How many times had she seen behavior like this? I was sifting through all the strands in my head, quickly deciding what to say, not say, how to say it, when the best thing to do, as Fergus always told me, was to shut up and listen.

"Mind if we step inside?" she asked.

I pointed behind her to my Uber, which was parking on the opposite curb. "That's my ride," I explained. Please don't drag me down to the police station, please please please.

The woman pulled out a notebook, a mini-pen stuck in the coil binding, and wrote something. I motioned with my index finger to the Uber driver, hoping he wouldn't drive off thinking I was a murder suspect. Maybe I was.

"Do you know a Roberta Fenning?" the officer asked.

I nodded. "She's my best friend's mother."

"She's been reported by the family as missing and I'm tracking down anyone who may have seen her before she disappeared."

Yes, of course she was missing. She's dead. The officer wanted to know if I *knew* she was missing or not. I felt faint, suddenly, but didn't want to grab the staircase railing because it would speak to my state of mind. My grandmother, Irene, always says, *Tell the truth, Thea.*

"I haven't been able to reach my friend, her daughter, in almost two days. I was starting to get worried." At least that part was true.

"What's your friend's name?" she asked, writing.

"Lise. Lise Fenning."

"When did you last speak with Roberta?"

It was a perfect question, because now I wouldn't need to lie to a police officer. She said *speak with.* "About two weeks ago. I came over to study with Lise and her mother was just getting back from some trip."

Writing. "You spoke with her that night?" she asked, glancing up to appraise me.

"I said hi." I knew I was giving her short answers but I wasn't stupid. I'd grown up watching what can happen during encounters like this.

"Do you know where she had traveled from?"

I didn't. "No." She wasn't making much eye contact with me. That had to mean she wanted me to trust her. I didn't, of course. Or maybe she wasn't even a real cop. I moved slowly down the stairs to make a motion to my Uber driver, if nothing else to remind the police officer that I was about to leave. I so desperately wanted to ask her how she got my name and address, but I suspected it came from Handsome, who'd apparently been watching me the whole time I was at the Fenning estate. What else had he told them about me?

The Uber driver, not Bharat this time, tapped his fat fingers on the steering wheel. Officer Maddox was writing something on a business card. Her personal cell number? Or was that just wishful thinking? Something in the center of my body throbbed, I could feel the pulse making my hands hot. I wondered if her first name was on that card, if she was married, and I'm not even *out* yet. God help me.

The police officer's name was Eve Maddox. I always liked the name Eve. She let me go but still hadn't driven away as my Uber headed down Lexington to 19th Street. Finally in the back of an Uber where I wasn't obligated to talk, I called Fergus. I rolled down a back window to create a sound buffer.

He picked up on the first ring.

"Hey," I said. "Are you on your bike?"

"No."

"Are you…with Kit?"

Pause. "Why would you ask that?"

Man. Something was seriously up with him. "Because you were with him last night."

"So, you thought—"

"Oh my God, Fergus. What's the issue? You're acting so weird lately. My life is literally falling apart at the seams right now. Oh, did I forget to mention that I just got interrogated by the police outside my house?"

"What? Why? What did they ask you?"

I didn't answer, still fuming.

He cleared his throat. "I'm not with Kit, but I do need to show you something, and I can't text it. Can you meet me at my house right now?"

"No, Fergus, I can't." It came out whinier than I intended. "I'm meeting someone on 7th Street because we're looking for Lise." Shit. Now I'd have to tell him about Bharat.

"Who?"

"Just someone who's helping me."

I tried to imagine what he was doing on the other end. Was he in a store checking out, pulling cash from his wallet and that's why he was pausing? Or was he editing his thoughts and pacing before answering me? This isn't the Fergus I know.

"Where'd you see her? I thought she'd been MIA for two days."

"I know, that's why when I saw her I had to follow her. I can meet you later if you're gonna be home." I said it more as a question, desperate suddenly to calm my anxiety and look in his eyes. Only then would I be able to see what was going on. Maybe.

"That's fine. I should be home within the hour. I'm doing a pickup at some mental hospital."

"Mental hospital? Are any of those still around?"

"San Rafael."

"You took BART and the 130 bus?" I laughed. Fergus hated taking the bus. It was one of his many quirks.

"Yeah, put my bike on the bike rack, such a pain. See you later," he said, and hung up, also very unlike him. Something was going on. I had to find out what.

Bharat's SUV was parked in the same place. I'd had my other driver drop me off at the end of that block to keep me out of view. I don't know why I tipped him extra. Maybe because I felt guilty for exposing him to my police inquiry.

Bharat's car was no longer running. I could see twenty feet away that the car was empty. I backtracked to the corner and stood under the cover of a large, green awning.

It's Thea. Where are you? I texted Bharat. *I'm back and on the corner. Did you see her?*

Y, he typed. A single letter. He was probably following her in the building.

Using my camera app, I aimed my phone at the building and zoomed in as far as I could.

She left that building and turned right on Folsom. She's in a red brick building now with a Cobaltic sign out front. He texted me a picture of Lise walking into the Cobaltic building. I'd never heard of it but guessed it was some kind of tech company.

How long has she been I there? I asked him.

Twenty minutes. Feed meter pls.

Now that I presumed I wasn't being watched, at least not by Lise, I bought gum at a Dollar Store and used the spare quarters for Bharat's meter. I followed 7th to Folsom on foot and peered around the corner, noticing only now that I'd barely thought about my ankle this morning. It must be healing; thank you Dr. Lee. I kept questioning why I felt so safe around Bharat and why I wasn't more suspicious of his constant availability. When I closed my eyes and thought of my brother Rudy, I could picture him smiling – at me, at the sky, the sea, everything. Like his very bone structure was designed for that pose. Bharat's face seemed the same way to me. There was something undeniably Rudy-like about it. So maybe Rudy had sent him here to help his troubled sister.

Are you IN the building?

No, of course not, he typed back. *It's an office. I'd need a story.*

I can help you with that. Do you have AirPods or ear buds on you?

Y.

Put them in, call me, and I'll guide you through it.

Through what exactly?

I'd already looked up Cobaltic and saw that they were a technology consulting firm. I was walking toward him.

They're consultants. You're gonna go in and say you're thinking about hiring them.

I don't know if I'm up to this. Where are you right now? he wrote back.

"Here," I said, a foot in front of him.

Chapter 16

Bharat closed his eyes and gasped. "You startled me."

I couldn't help asking. "Why are you willing to help me like this?" I squared off with him, knowing it sounded like an interrogation. "You've been driving me around for days, charging me next to nothing and you're always available when I need you."

"Would you believe I'm in a sort of transition and bored? Whether you believe me or not, it's the truth. Besides, you seem like a good cause."

I'd never thought of myself as a cause before but I liked his answer. Now it was me with my eyes glued to the Cobaltic building, where Lise had apparently entered nearly an hour ago. The earlier wind had died down and dark clouds had slithered in creating a dark canopy overhead. Bharat looked nervous beside me as I hammered him with questions.

"What does she look like?" he asked of Lise.

"A blonde bombshell. Like Cara Delevingne with platinum blonde hair."

"And what exactly am I—"

I put my hand on his shoulder without moving my eyes from the door. "Tell them you're a small business owner who's just been acquired by a larger company, and you need serious IT help."

"An acquisition..." He sounded dreamy. "That's genius, in a way. How do you even know about that?"

"I watch Billions," I said, though I'd only watched a few episodes.

"You'll be listening so you can advise me?"

"Affirmative."

"Like Cyrano de Bergerac?"

I'd read the play my junior year. "Yes, but your nose is fine, believe me. Now go."

He took two steps then turned back and smiled. "Does she work here?"

"Oh my God, Bharat, please. Just go. I don't know if she works here."

"I thought you said she was your bff."

He was right to ask, and maybe I didn't really know Lise at all.

"Wait," Bharat said. "My phone's ringing."

Lord. "Dude, that's me calling you. Answer, turn the volume all the way up, and stick your phone in your pocket with your ear piece in."

I looked down and saw an incoming text notification on my phone now. My blackmailer. I was able to read it without actually touching the message, so it wouldn't show that it had been seen. It read, *They're expecting you.* Shit.

"Oh, yes, of course. Right." And in an instant, I watched my hapless driver transform from a sweaty bundle of nerves to a soldier poised for battle. He opened the door, took off across the street, grabbed the front door handle of Cobaltic and charged in with gusto. Right on, I thought, deciding that nothing good could come from telling him about the text, even if it was true. He was nervous enough.

"Can I help you, sir?" I heard a woman say. Bharat was in. I hoped he was looking around for Lise. What could she be doing there?

"Thank you, yes. I'm a business owner in desperate need of IT support and a friend referred me to your firm. Is that your area of expertise?" I said to Bharat, realizing that was probably too many words for him to remember all at once.

He recited them word for word, no mistakes. An instant operative.

"Certainly," the woman said. "I can see if someone's available to learn more about your needs."

"Thank you," he said, and I could see he was texting me by the moving dots.

I don't see her. Keep your eyes open outside.

Roger that, I wrote back, grateful in this moment for his help. I felt even more destabilized today after the note from my mother, the text about my cat, and of course Officer Eve Maddox. Sure, Roberta's death could have been staged, but for whose benefit? Lise had summoned me, but maybe that was all a setup. Was someone else supposed to be there too? My desperate heart clung to a tiny thread. Maybe Roberta was only missing and not dead.

I had Bharat on speaker now, listening to him reiterate his initial question to someone else. They were asking him what type of business he was in.

"Digital marketing," I said into the phone, which he repeated. He must have his phone on his lap because he was texting me again.

She's here. She just came down the main staircase and turned a corner. Seems like she works here.

"We're good, Bharat. Get out of there before she sees you," I said. "I know she doesn't know you but she could have seen you talking to me. Tell them you've got an urgent call with your banker and you'll be back in touch in the morning. I'll meet you at your car." I disconnected the call and walked back to 7th Street hiding myself under the storefront awnings.

The late afternoon sun spilled a vertical orange stripe down the front of the building across the street. Stunning. I snapped a picture and heard footsteps running on the sidewalk. I turned, my heart thudding out of my chest. Bharat was coming toward me out of breath.

"Slow down," I said, reaching out for him. He passed me running to his car then climbed in the driver's side. I got in beside him. I had tissues in my backpack. I handed him one and he mopped his forehead with it.

"Are you okay? What the hell happened in there?"

He took a minute to catch his breath. "Nothing. Okay something, but really nothing. I was talking to one of the consultants, a young guy with a weird name. I forget what it is now. Anyway, I saw a flash of light, and when I turned my head it was your blonde bombshell. Boy is she ever one. She was coming down the stairs like a freaking starlet. Then she turned the corner."

"So, you ogled a beautiful woman. What's the big deal? She eats it up, believe me."

Bharat stared back.

"What's the matter? I won't tell your wife."

"The consultant saw me," he said, eyes wide. "I mean, he knew I wasn't just ogling her."

"How do you know that?"

"He raised his eyes and gestured to someone behind me after he saw me glance at her. I honestly didn't know I'd even get out of that place." He mopped his face with the wet tissue. "Thea, what the fuck have you gotten yourself into? And me? Because whatever you told me before…"

"What I said before wasn't a lie," I said. "I just…didn't tell you everything. Maybe for your own protection."

He didn't ask for the rest of the story and I wasn't ready to volunteer it right now either. I had Bharat drop me at Fergus' house. I'd planned to get down to Fort Point again after dark, to plug the stoners for more information about the game.

The whole ride there I kept checking my phone, completely paranoid now about the next message from my blackmailer. He was getting closer. He'd gone to my house. Now he was monitoring me. Fucker. And as for my mom, I had no clue what to tell her about her visitor today. I'd triple-checked that the photograph I took of Roberta Fenning wouldn't be visible, or at least readily, in their two locations of my spam folder and on Google Drive. But I thought of one additional precaution—I could rename the file as something else, like "Work Shoes" and continue storing it in my spam folder. That way, if anyone did a search on Roberta Fenning in my Gmail folders, they'd come up empty.

Bharat pulled up in front of Fergus' house and turned off the motor. "Well, what a day."

"You look like you're about to collapse. I guess I should

probably stop calling you, yeah? I'm sorry for putting you in danger."

"No don't be silly. A stiff drink and I'll be good as new." He snickered. "Right, maybe two drinks then. You're too young to join me, but I'll see you soon, Miss Thea. I'm sure."

I had no idea whether Bharat would help me again or not, but I now knew for certain that Lise had a whole other part of her life I knew nothing about. I felt in my bones that somehow it had something to do with DSC. She'd never mentioned it before, and she used to tell me everything.

I don't think Fergus ever trusted my friendship with her, probably thinking that Lise thought of me as some token person of color that gave her circle of friends more diversity. After all, I was headed to a state university and Lise, well, she'd be at Yale in a few months followed by a Director-level position in her uncle's venture capital firm in New York. High and low.

Fergus' parents were in bed when I got to their house at the designated time. I knocked on the glass of their living room window. He let me in, motioning me to his room in the basement, where we could talk. I checked his eyes when I got to the bottom of the stairs and saw something I'd never seen in there before. No hug, no offer of something to drink, and he didn't check in on my ankle, which was also strange. Okay, I needed to be able to adapt to these changing conditions and get whatever information I could out of him before he became officially compromised and no longer reliable. I was capable of this; I could keep moving in this direction, pretending not to feel rejected, heartbroken and disappointed. Besides, there were so many things to discuss.

He plopped down on his bed. I wheeled his desk chair so I could rest my ankle on an empty spot in his bookcase.

"How's that feeling today?" he asked finally, polite but distant.

"Sore, but not terrible," I said.

He pulled his fists up to his eyes and rubbed them. Was he crying? "What's going on, Fergus? I know you're fucking lying about something. I can feel it."

"I'm not supposed to tell you. I swore I wouldn't." He lowered his fists and stared back unblinking. "They threatened me."

"Who?"

He propped himself up with pillows and wiped his face. "I never went to work today, to either of my jobs."

"You were with Kit, weren't you?"

"Yeah."

I knew it. "Doing what? Playing that stupid game? Well, I was playing it too. I found some things in your octopus picture. Clue number two, remember?"

Fergus's face was frozen.

"Spill it, for fuck's sake!"

"You're part of the game. You, Thea. You're in it now."

I shook my head, pulling strands of hair out of my eyes. "In. What does that even mean?"

"Remember I was telling you how you could submit artifacts? Pictures, NFTs, videos, signage? If what you submit is accepted by the admins, it's stored permanently in a Reddit folder where everyone can see, use, study, and interpret it."

"You're scaring me. What the fuck was uploaded? Did you submit something?"

"Of course I didn't. But someone did. A picture—"

I jumped up. "No no no no no!" My hands were shaking. "There's no way it could be that."

He angled his head low, eyes wide. "What?"

"Yes, I did take a picture, but since I last saw you, I found an ingenious way to hide it so no one will ever find it. Not in my phone, my email, anywhere. It's safe." I was proud of myself for being so clever, but Fergus' grave look scared me and sapped my joy.

"What now?"

"Thea, it's a picture of you at the Fenning estate. The night Roberta Fenning was murdered."

Chapter 17

Hearing the words spoken out loud made it even more ominous. A trembling started in my hands; it spread to my chest; my ears felt hot and tingly. I leaned down to grasp my knees, weakened by the sound of my life crashing down around me. I had no idea what these words really meant but watching Fergus' horrified expression unglued me. How had he gotten sucked into this vortex? Because of me, that's how. Fat tears spilled down my cheeks. I wrapped my arms around my body.

The low lighting in this basement made the moment worse. It was one of those vintage, awful fluorescent things that never got upgraded because why would you bother? When Fergus moved here from his upstairs bedroom, it was because it had more space, was more private, and because his capitalist parents wanted to charge him rent. Hard to believe.

I sucked air in and out to get oxygen to my brain, because that was the only thing in life I'd ever been able to truly count on. I slipped off my shoes and paced, barefoot on the cold floor. I kept my thoughts on concrete questions. Would the picture have a time stamp on it somewhere in the metadata that could prove I was there? I stopped pacing, leaned down and put my head between my knees again.

"T, calm down."

"It could have been my mad texter, the guy, or girl, I guess, blackmailing me because they apparently saw me go to the Fenning estate the other night and obviously had me on camera." I rose.

"Well, the Fennings obviously have a security camera. Your texter must have access to it, or else hacked into it."

"Was the picture blurry?" I asked.

He was rubbing his face. "Yeah, actually. Why?"

"Because it was probably a still photo captured from video footage inside the house. Can I see it? I mean, does it look like me enough to be, you know—"

"Legally incriminating?" Fergus asked, son of a trial lawyer. "I'd say sort of. Lemme show you." He pulled out his phone and I watched him open the Reddit app, log into his profile, and thumb through topics and subreddits.

"How many gaming categories does Reddit have?" I asked.

"There's a main topic called gaming and about a hundred subreddits," he mumbled, still scrolling. "Then also subreddit gaming communities including ARGs." He looked up.

"Alternate reality games?" I asked. "Or do you mean AR/VR?"

"No, AR is something else. Pokémon Go is AR. You were right the first time. Alternate Reality Games use the real world and a physical place as the platform but with multimedia storytelling to influence game direction, player-influence--"

"Adding in their hidden URLs in the comments," I said, "which are usually a one-way door to a dark hell."

He was nodding.

"And Cicada's one of them."

"One of the most famous and widely played. Cicada was a game and a puzzle."

"And a hoax," I added.

"That's not proven, but possibly."

"I remember I Love Bees, that Microsoft spinoff of Halo." I was surprised I remembered.

"Exactly." We stopped there and seemed to land together in the same moment, feeling the same gravity pulling us down. Lower, and lower.

"Is my life in danger?" I asked him. "I'm obviously being targeted."

"At this point, let's assume yes."

I only realized now that this basement had no windows. That had to be a code violation, especially in San Francisco. I wished I had my journal with me because I had an idea.

I still had to deal with my guilt over not telling Fergus about Bharat, not to mention Cobaltic. Fergus had a household arrangement that allowed him to take one of his parents' cars after they were asleep, "until such time as that decision proves foolish," he told me. That meant we might be allowed to take his father's car for a trip to Fort Point. Worth asking, anyway.

"Where?" he eyerolled, already poised to say no.

"Field trip."

He lifted his brows, which I knew meant he wouldn't take me unless I told him.

"Fort Point."

It was dark out, so we obviously wouldn't be surfing. No questions asked, he grabbed a set of keys in the kitchen, and we slipped out through the garage. I climbed in the driver's side.

"No way."

"Come on, you've let me drive this before. I have my license."

"You drove it in the parking lot of Target, at midnight, and yes you have a license but no driving experience. Besides, it's dark out."

"All the better," I argued, happy for a somewhat lighter subject for a change. "The roads will be empty."

He shooed me with his hand. I climbed over the gear shaft to the passenger side.

"What's at Fort Point?" He took too long to ask. Normally the reason for the field trip would have weighed in on his decision.

"Not what. Who."

I tried to enjoy our leisurely twenty-mile-per-hour ride in the right lane, reminded of the pace of Majuro Atoll. I loved the throb of San Francisco at night though, such a stark contrast. A flyer tacked to a telephone pole caught my eye. Somewhere on Valencia, the word *wipeout* reminded me of the Wipeout Bar & Grill on Pier 39. The white van stoners had to be surfers. Why else would they park on the water? They were watching the surf during the day, assessing the swell, wind, and the hundred other variables that go into a decision about where to paddle out. Fergus was a surfer. He'd surfed Fort Point before, but not since last winter. I remember him telling me that Fort Point "turns on" in January. It was almost July now, and summer surf in northern California was usually only rideable near Santa Cruz.

"What's going on inside that head?" Fergus asked me, my nose pressed against the window.

"Was I snoring? Or humming again?"

"You were smiling. What's your idea?"

"Surfers."

By some strange coincidence, my watch read exactly 10:50 p.m., the same time I arrived here last night. Grandma Irene always said coincidences happened when the universe was trying to tell you something. I admit synchronicities implied some evidence of alignment. And with all the tangled questions in my head, that felt good. I was here again, same time, same place.

Sure enough, the beat-up van was parked on the narrow shoulder going down from Presidio to the Fort Point National Historic Site parking lot. I suspected they parked on the shoulder because it was a discreet place to smoke weed, not that San Francisco even cared anymore. They'd make their way to the water eventually. I had Fergus pull into the same spot where Bharat dropped me off last night. I stood facing the water with my arms crossed, feet spread apart. It was cold and I was wearing shorts again. Seriously? Fergus closed the driver's side door and leaned on the front of the car in perfect view of the rest of the parking lot. Sure enough, the van crawled down the same spot three spaces away. I gave Fergus the lowdown on last night's exchange.

"One of them had a super loud voice," I said of the van bros. "Another was always shushing him. The one I called Athletic was the one who told me about the dead seven."

"The what?"

"The player who died after reaching Level 7 of the Dead Sevens Club game."

The van reeked like they were growing it inside. They parked longways so they could slide open the side door and zone out to the sound of waves. Very island-life.

Fergus did his protective deal and stood beside me shoulder to shoulder. "How do you wanna play it?" he asked.

"Start talking about surfing, loud enough for them to hear."

"What about surfing? Like a surf spot?"

"Yeah."

"Have you ever surfed Mavericks?" I asked Fergus, then whispered for him to repeat the word.

"Mavericks? Hell no, I'm not that good. The right facing wave looks interesting, but I'm not— No. No way."

I nodded an affirmation and we resumed our nighttime surf watch in silence. I heard them mumbling. "…brought her boyfriend with her tonight." Great, so they did remember me. And they thought I was straight. Hilarious. All the better.

"T, what are we doing here? It's fucking freezing out."

I moved closer, sliding my arm around his waist and resting my head on his chest so he could hear me whisper. "I wanna ask them if they know anything about any of the game admins, and see if they heard anything about my picture that was uploaded. I'd also like to ask if they've ever heard of Roberta."

"How do you plan on doing that?"

"Very carefully."

Chapter 18

A door, then footsteps pulled my attention from the water. It was Athletic, walking alone in bare feet, baggy jeans, and a hoodie, holding a jay between his fingers.

"Hey," he said. "Back again?"

"How's it going?" I asked.

"You seemed pretty upset last night when you left. Sorry about that."

Earnest, good looking, and wondering if I'd noticed that. Now wasn't the time to talk about my sexuality. "Yeah, I'm okay." I looked at the ground. "Honestly so many things about this game are upsetting."

The guy looked intermittently at Fergus but said nothing to him. I prayed Fergus wouldn't do the posturing thing that men found so irresistible. "Like what?" the guy asked.

"Someone uploaded something to the game that has to do with me. I need to find out who the admins are so I can request it be taken down."

"They don't do that," the guy explained, one step closer. "Least I don't think they do. Was it published in the key folder?"

I looked at Fergus, who shook his head. "It's in a sub of the main, called Mascots."

Athletic took a few tokes, didn't offer us any, which was interesting. "What is it, a naked picture or something? Sex?"

I shook my head. "Nothing like that."

"Who would have a picture of you besides you?" the guy asked looking at Fergus.

"I didn't take it," he said.

I shrugged. "Someone who's trying to—" Fergus elbowed me.

Another powerful wave crashed into the rocks, making it too loud to talk. Nature asserting itself, or maybe, like Grandma Irene says, pulling you inside yourself to seek your truth. Scary thing is, truth was getting harder and harder to recognize.

"I might know someone," Athletic said. "My brother's an ARG game developer."

"Awww no way. What a great job," Fergus said, gushing. "I mean, what does he do exactly?"

"He's a writer. They hired him to flesh out the storytelling part of the game."

"Has he ever worked on DSC?" I cut in.

"Yeah, but early days, a long time ago. They were getting some traction, then they closed up for a few years to regroup. When they started putting out clues again, they'd designed a slick website, a YouTube channel, Twitter account."

I went through these new details. "Regroup, you mean, after that guy you told me about died?" I asked, careful with my execution of what I knew would be a hard question. This would tell the guy that I'd shared his report with Fergus, whom he just met.

First he stared back like I'd broken some sort of code, took another toke, and eyed Fergus. The two others from the van wailed at something on their phones, I saw the lights from them. I looked up.

"Reels, TikTok live. If I left them alone there, they'd never come out."

"When you're not surfing, you mean?" Fergus this time.

"Not much surf in summer," the guy said.

"Not up here there isn't." Fergus grinned. "Did you catch that last swell down south? I got the tail end of it at Waddell, but the wind came up right after I got there."

The guy nodded and his face lit up. "I was at Ano the day before, and it was great," he said.

Anu Nuevo State Park. I'd been there to walk and take pictures, but the surf was way too big for me. This was good, surfing as the equalizer. Now might be the right time to share my truth. Here goes stage two.

"Look," I said. "Sorry to interrupt you but I've got a serious problem and need your help. I'm Thea, by the way. This is Fergus, my best friend in the world," I added, making our relationship status clear.

"Brody," the guy said with a half-hearted wave. "So, what's the deal?"

I wondered, in that moment, if this guy Brody could be one of the game admins, or maybe their weed smoking was a cover and they were hackers trying to crack the DSC database.

I looked back at the morons in the van, glancing at Fergus to be my safety barometer. None of this felt right, but these dudes were playing the game and might have more information than we did. Plus, the 55-degree-wind and spitting surf were chilling me to the bone. Now or never. "Remember the pig image from the first DSC clue?" I asked. "You're past that level, yeah?"

"I remember," Brody said. "The geek squad—" he gestured toward the van—"said there were GPS coordinates embedded in the image. We never got around to tracing it." He lowered his head and peered at me. "I take it you did?"

I nodded. "They're the coordinates to a house where a woman died a few nights ago." I wrapped my arms around my body and shivered.

Brody blinked back at us, nodding. "How did you find out?"

I breathed in the cold air, as a way of answering him.

"You were there?" he asked.

Fergus put his arm around my shoulders. "You don't have to do this, you know."

"Yes, Fergus, I do," crying again. Dammit. "I'm sorry. I'm a wreck right now. But I need to find out what the fuck is happening, and why I'm involved in it. It seemed so random at first," I said with my eyes on the cloudy sky. "But I'm starting to think nothing about this game is random."

"Yeah, she was there," Fergus answered. "But not for the reason you think."

My brows wrinkled at Brody. "Wait, you didn't think... did you? I knew her. She was my best friend's...well, my best girlfriend's mother. I went there to see her, she wasn't there, and I found her mother." My voice caught in my throat. I stared at Brody, eyes wide. Breathe. "I found her dead on her kitchen floor, just like the Dead Seven you told me about."

"Whoa." He took a few steps back. "Kind of a coincidence."

"Yeah, well, I don't believe in coincidences, generally speaking."

"There's more," Fergus said. "The body's missing, and someone got access to the camera footage, which shows Thea in the house that night. They pulled a still photo from that feed and uploaded it to Reddit."

"Where?" Brody asked.

"The DSC Keys folder."

"Wait. The body's missing? But you said you saw it when you went there."

"I did," I said. Shit. Now we were gonna have to tell him about Kit and his cleaner. I leaned down to touch my knees and stayed there a few seconds.

"So, how do you know the body's missing, then?"

Fergus' warm hand rested on the middle of my back. "Thea was questioned by the police yesterday about the woman, her name's Roberta, but they said she was missing. Not dead. So, obviously, the body disappeared from the kitchen or the police would have found it."

"Gotcha. Where's the picture?" Brody asked.

Fergus rolled up his sleeves. "You got a laptop?"

We followed Brody to the white van. "Thank you," I whispered in his ear. It was a great save to tell him about Officer Maddox. Anything to avoid talking about Kit.

Brody informed his crew of our question. I heard fumbling around, the clanking of something metal, a "Bro, find my glasses." It smelled like weed and Cheetos. Brody returned with a MacBook; Fergus disappeared and came back a moment later with a mostly dry surf towel he set on the trunk of his father's Lexus away from the

89

water. "Up here."

Brody opened the cover, upped the brightness setting all the way then logged into his Reddit account. He spun the screen toward Fergus to let him drive. We huddled over the laptop, Fergus between Brody and I. I watched him click through the different DSC folders to find Keys. He leaned into the screen, head down. No one moved or spoke. My heart pounded, feeling another oh shit moment coming.

"Thea," he said, pointing.

"What? Is it there?"

Fergus stepped back motioning Brody to the screen. "Here's the original picture that someone uploaded. There, see, under the railing?"

It was me, flat on the floor of the Fenning's upper landing overlooking the foyer, eyes wide. From the screen resolution, my face looked white, large dark eyes and two outcrops of my crazy, wavy, Moana-hair.

"That's you?" Brody asked. "Would've been a good hiding place, if you weren't being filmed that is."

"I was up there looking down at part of the body in the kitchen. I was hiding because I heard a noise in the kitchen and felt sure her killer was still there."

Fergus closed that photo and opened another from the same folder.

"Hold on," I said, peering at the screen. "Now there are two photos? Seriously—"

"No, you're fine. It's just a prank. Look." He'd opened the second picture, which was a magnified version of the first photo, honing in on my face. Great. Except someone had added long, black rabbit ears on top of my head with the caption, "#blackearedrabbit."

"What does—what—I don't—" I lowered my head onto the car hood and banged it three times. "Now what?" I pulled my hair out of the messy bun, if nothing else to do something with my anxious hands. Plus, it might keep me warm.

Reading my mind, Brody went to the van again and came back with an oversized flannel shirt. He held it out to Fergus first, said, "Do you mind…?"

"Sure," Fergus said, as Brody passed the shirt to me.

"Thanks, I'm freezing." It almost fit twice around my body. I was pleasantly surprised to find it smelling like laundry detergent. Small miracle. "Okay. So…not only did I come face-to-face with a dead woman but my doing so has inspired a new social media hashtag? Is that what you're telling me?" I asked into the dark night.

Brody and Fergus seemed to be in some silent conversation. I leaned against the car pulling my arms through the sleeves of the shirt and rubbing the tops of my legs.

"You got nothing to worry about, right? You didn't kill her," Brody said, but it sounded like a question, like he needed confirmation.

"No, of course I didn't," I said, enunciating each syllable.

"Now someone's created a black-eared rabbit subreddit." Fergus turned to make sure I heard him. I'd heard him alright. He opened the new subcommunity, where someone had added the new black-eared rabbit version of me with some accompanying text: *Found this on a related sub, see below. Anyone else thinkin this rabbit is gonna be part of the next clue? #whoisblackearedrabbit*

"I feel sick."

Chapter 19

We exchanged mobile numbers and split up. Fergus knew what needed to happen next.

At the top of the Marine Drive incline, I saw a familiar car parked behind the Fort Point sign.

"Hold on." I opened the door.

"Thea! The car's moving. What the fuck?"

"Just pull over. I'll be right back."

"Oooookay." Fergus parked, rolled down his window, elbow out, glaring at the car across the street on Lincoln.

"Please, no posturing tonight. I honestly can't take it."

"Who is that guy?"

I climbed out of the Lexus and walked over to Bharat's opened driver's side window. I stood back with my arms crossed, secretly so happy to see him I couldn't feign anger. "What are you doing here, Bharat? Are you following me?"

He hung his head. "Yes, I am very sorry. I was curious how you've been doing and I...well, tailed you. Please don't have me arrested for stalking."

I shook my head. "I won't. I'm with Fergus."

"Ohhhhh!"

"Cut it out, he's just a friend. We're going somewhere to talk. You're a part of this now, I guess, so you might as well join us."

"Your faith in me is less than reassuring. Are you sure I won't be a, how do you say, third wheel?"

"It's fine." I walked off. "Follow us. I'll—I don't know. I'll explain it somehow."

"At your service."

Fergus drove. We didn't talk, allowing my mind to wonder what time it was in my Marshall Islands, and what my mother and I had left behind. Four years older than me and already graduated from college, Fergus was far more attuned to city life than I was. His family emigrated from Majuro Atoll two generations ago. His grandparents still live there. He told me he had two cousins working at a resort on Bikendrik Island, Majuro's private island boutique hideaway. Maybe I'd always feel like a transplant. After seven years I still hadn't quite adapted to the sophistication and complexity of San Francisco. One block here had a greater density of people and activity than I could have ever imagined.

"What's going on, T? You don't look so hot."

"I feel dizzy," I admitted, remembering I'd also felt dizzy this morning. "That guy's gonna follow us."

"Okay," he said, surprising me again. "Where's the huddle?"

"Your basement? No. My house? Certainly no."

"Why not?"

"Honestly, I'm afraid to go there. My blackmailer was there today, petting my cat, charming my mother. I'm surprised he didn't ransack the place but that might be next."

"Has he contacted you again?" he asked.

I pulled out my phone with a sigh of dread. "No. How about the playground?"

"We can see who's there, but yeah, might be a good idea."

I motioned for Bharat to follow us and he gave me a smiley thumbs-up. "Okay, so his name is Bharat and he's harmless."

"Homeless?"

"No, harmless!"

"Where'd you meet him?" The question shot out like a bullet.

"He's been my Uber driver for the past couple of days. He was worried about me when he dropped me off at Vesuvio because he said I looked injured, and he waited for me. I don't know, he just felt trustworthy and, really, I've been on the verge of a breakdown. So, he seemed like—"

"A helper?"

"Yeah. Naïve I know."

"I get it. But why are we talking to him now?"

I gulped and closed my eyes. "I sort of told him some of—"

"Are you completely crazy? This is big leagues now. Somebody died, T, and it might be because of a game that now seems to be targeting you. Plus, how do we know he's not part of it?"

"I know, I know. I haven't told him everything. But when he was driving me home, we saw Lise walking down the street. We followed her, and he agreed to go into the building to try to get information about her."

"Whoa. Where was this?"

"Folsom, a consulting firm called Cobaltic."

"She was in the building?"

My phone chimed. Bharat. "Hey Bharat." I put him on speaker. "Hold on, getting you on Bluetooth."

"Helloooo travelers! My name is Bharat and I'm an alcoholic."

Fergus and I turned heads. "Um…"

"I'm joking."

"What a thing to joke about," Fergus said.

"Oh, it's no joke, I really am. And I'm in a lovely 12-step program with a sponsor who looks like Jennifer Lopez. God works in mysterious ways."

Fergus and I cracked up.

"Hey, Bharat," Fergus said. "Thea brought me up to date on your —"

"Sorry to interrupt but we're getting close to where we saw your friend Lise earlier. Cobaltic is on Folsom. Do we want to check it out while we're skirting the edge of that neighborhood?"

"Not a bad idea," Fergus said to me.

"Sounds good, Bharat, I'll show him where it is. Stay behind us."

"Righty-oh. Over and out."

"He's hilarious," Fergus said. "What's his story?"

"He's a software developer who contracts out to different companies."

"And drives for Uber?" he asked. "Like why? He's probably making a hundred and eighty thou."

"He said he's married with two little boys, but he seems to have a lot more availability than new fathers would have…"

"You're thinking…divorced?"

"I'm thinking helping me was maybe better than going home to an empty house." Made me sad to say it.

We weaved in and out of traffic on 101 near the Civic Center. I didn't see Bharat behind us. I texted him.

"Is he still back here?"

"No. Wait, there he is. Slow down a little so he can catch up."

"I just remembered something my dad keeps in his trunk. Did you say Lise is working at that place, whatever it's called?"

"It seems like that but who knows what the hell she's doing there. I really have no idea what she's up to. What are you thinking?"

"Night vision binocs."

"Ooooh, aren't you fancy. Could be good, but it's a business. Not sure why anyone would be working there this late."

"Depends on what they consider work."

We parked on Folsom diagonally across the street from Cobaltic so we could see the back of the bus stop. Bharat parked behind us and jumped in the backseat with his usual flourish.

"Hello, beautiful people!" He put his hands on Fergus' shoulders. "I've heard all about you, young man."

"Um…thank you?"

"Sorry, I'm out of my mind tonight." He moved to the middle of the backseat so he could see both of us. "I notice there's a light on upstairs in that building. Kind of late, don't you think?"

"We were just thinking the same thing," I said.

Fergus grabbed the gear out of the trunk and brought a black case to the front seat.

"Night vision goggles," Bharat said. "Tech saves the day again, eh?"

I could tell Fergus was already tiring of Bharat's over-personality. "They're new and I've never used them before." Fergus held them out to Bharat, who took off the lens cap.

"Do you see her car parked anywhere on the street?"

I snickered. "She doesn't drive."

"She has a *dri-ver*," Fergus mocked. "Probably named Jeeves or Nigel or something."

"It might help to note that Fergus hates Lise."

"I see," Bharat said, "no doubt that's because her attention takes you away from him. Yes?"

"Just watch the building, Bharat."

"Yes sir. Ma'am. Whatever."

Fergus checked something on his phone, which reminded me to avoid mine for fear of any further threatening messages. "So, how'd you do at The Wharf the other night?" I asked him, all of us watching the Cobaltic building.

"Nothing more to report, really. The QR turned on between 11:07 and 11:14 p.m. and showed the blue octopus photo that I sent you. Kit and I didn't have time to look into it further. So, I guess that's a no." He faced me. "Did you find something?"

I nodded. "You know the mini-QR code that I found from the clue in Chinatown?"

"You found another one? Damn, I looked for that," Fergus said, disappointed he'd missed it again, but I knew he liked the competition. Or maybe he was just glad I was finally playing. I told him about the tinyurl that led to Google Earth. "But without any specific coordinates, I'm not sure what to do with that."

I turned away from the building to pull the strap from my backpack out from under me. When I did, something light-colored caught my attention. Oh my God.

Chapter 20

That platinum blonde hair, even under a wool cap, glowed for a second too long, and my tired eyes landed on her pressed against a brick building fifteen feet from Fergus' car—staring me down. For a second I didn't move or breathe. Lise lowered her head to ensure eye contact, then placed a finger over her lips, pulled it away with a summoning motion, and pointed ahead down Folsom.

"I'll be right back, I want to check something out." I jumped from the car before anyone could protest. I stayed out of plain view and hurried to the end of the block, following my notorious friend, starving for answers. I stayed on Folsom spotting her about thirty feet ahead, crossed 7th Street and turned right on Langton. Lise stood by a tree next to a white building monikered The Bike Connection. Part of me wanted to run up to her and embrace her, the other half strangle her. The craziness of the past few days had lifted a veil, in a way, allowing me to see her as a skinny, introverted billionaire misfit surrounded by designer clothes and invitations. Without any of those trappings, she was just a girl, like me, looking for the path that was also looking for her.

She saw this change in me. I saw the recognition in her face, her dark eyes recalibrating to a new set of assumptions for whatever manipulation she'd planned for me. Where were the thousand questions I'd been storing up for the next time I saw her, the anger and the betrayal that had shaken my core that terrible night? Right now, what I felt was sadness—for both of us.

She obviously had to know I wasn't here alone, right? Maybe she'd already taken that into account. Or maybe she'd been following us the whole time. Lise moved in her slow, swan-like glide from under the tree to a spot against the white brick building. She'd had walking lessons from some old pageant-meister, speaking and diction classes, can you imagine? People are starving all over the world and Lise needed to walk and speak like an aristocrat.

She had on black jeans and a blue bomber jacket, with her fashion signature visible—gold nail polish. I always thought it was tacky, but the fashionistas who shadowed icons like her used her design whims as inspiration for TikTok videos and Pinterest boards. Her family lineage followed the Balenciaga dynasty so, naturally, fashion-forward was part of her DNA. I moved toward the ice queen one step at a time. She watched me, unmoved. One of us had to speak at some point. Who would do it first?

As if the universe willed this moment to happen, the street grew quiet, no cars, no foot traffic.

"I don't bite," she said softly, always adhering to the same controlled Contessa-voice regardless of the situation. I can't image what her orgasms sounded like, if she even had them.

"Don't you?" I asked. "Do you work there?"

"Where?"

"Okay." I nodded. "That's how you're playing it?"

"I'm not playing anything. I miss my friend and needed to talk to you. I saw you, you saw me, here we are."

"Here I am. So, talk," I said.

No response, just the blinking of those cold, calculating eyes.

"You didn't need to talk to me the night your mother died? Did it occur to you that I might need to talk to you?"

Don't cry right now, don't cry. Too late. I tried to sniff away the tears but it didn't work. This person didn't look or feel like my friend Lise. Maybe she wasn't anymore.

"What are you doing?" I asked, trying a different approach.

"What do you mean?"

"Out here," I extended my arm. "In Soma at fucking midnight, on the street, hiding behind buildings. Do you work at that place, Cobaltic? Are you a technology consultant now? What, are you also married with three children? Maybe married to more than one person?"

The calm face changed. She moistened her lips, ripped the cap off her head, and used her gold fingers to tousle her hair. Long sigh. Then she bent low to stretch her back. "So that was your man in there yesterday? You sent a spy to tail me. Why?"

"Lise, I've been looking for you for days! I saw you walking down the street, nonchalantly as if I hadn't been calling and texting you frantic and scared to freaking death. What have you done, Lise? What have you done?" My tears turned to sobs, and in an instant I was a complete mess. I no longer cared. "You called me," I said in a quieter voice.

She moved three steps closer; I didn't want her to but I was cornered between her and the building. I imagined Fergus and Bharat were around the corner watching the whole thing.

"You summoned me. And then you left. What the fuck is that about, Lise?" My tears, now my sobs should have been anger, or outrage. But I could feel old wounding. When Lise abandoned me the night her mother was killed, I think that abandonment triggered the memory of Rudy, when I was suddenly alone in the world without him. Maybe Lise had never really cared about me in the first place.

"Come on, Thea," she said, drawing out the word.

"Answer the question!" My voice pierced the silence. "Are you even capable of telling the truth?"

"Yes," she said, a quick, tight-lipped answer.

"Are you capable of murder?"

"Don't do this. Not here."

"What did you mean when you said she'd be better off dead?"

"I was—"

"What happened to the body, Lise? It's gone, isn't it? Gone from the kitchen floor."

This surprised her, I could tell by a slight rise in her brows and forehead muscles. No cars, no sirens, dogs, wind, human voices or cell phone rings interrupted the silence of that moment. We stared in a face-off. Again, I wondered who would break the silence.

"Did you kill her? Did you kill your mother?"

"I'm asking you the same thing, Thea."

The scream of rubber tires snapped my head to the left. A muscle car screeched around the corner of 8th Street and onto Folsom, tearing past us at probably ninety miles an hour leaving a cloud of fumes half a block long. When I turned back, Lise had moved to the side of the building, crouched holding her knees and speaking into her watch. I knew she sometimes wore a Smartwatch, but this didn't look like any Smartwatch I'd ever seen. It was a James Bond moment that I wasn't supposed to see. Her face contracted as I trained my eyes on her. She knew I'd seen. Who was she communicating with?

"I want to apologize," she rose. "Please, Thea, give me a chance to explain."

I came closer, my back to the street now and not believing a word of it. I wondered when my two bumbling knights might get here, and at this point if they'd be able to find me.

"I need to tell you something."

I was watching her talk, watching the emotions she was controlling on her face.

"Nanny's dead. They found her in the backyard, probably heading out to her car. She'd had a heart attack."

Nanny, the Fenning's cook, dying of a heart attack? Not likely, though I'd been wondering why she never came to the door that fateful night, why she wasn't in the kitchen, and where she'd been when Roberta was murdered in cold blood. Now I had my answer, or maybe *an* answer. She saw something she shouldn't have, and they killed her to cover their tracks. I put my hand over my mouth to stop myself from screaming. Sure, I knew Nanny, I knew her well, we'd talked in Spanish about the estate, the Fenning family's curious eating preferences, and I'd started teaching her some words in Ebon, the local name for Marshallese. She could cook, too, for a girl not much older than me. Her *arroz con pollo* was to die for. Maybe in more ways than one. The night air blowing my hair around, I found myself more interested in Lise's motivations for lying to me.

"I want to give you something." It was barely more than a whisper. I had to move closer to hear her. Give me something, like a poisoned chocolate? I listened to the sounds in my periphery but I came to her, now just a few steps away. Her ridiculous fingernails were folding something of the same color, gold. She unfurled its length and coiled it twice around her hands, with a heavy pendant dangling beneath. Oh my God, her locket.

"Lise, what are you doing? You've had that since—"

"Since Emily died. It was hers. And I want you to have it."

New tears formed in my eyes at the mention of Lise's younger sister who died two years ago in a random shooting. Was there really any such thing?

"Please. My life is a mess. I don't trust it will be safe with me any longer. Will you take it, for Emily's sake?"

Safe, interesting word coming from her lips. "I'll keep it for you for a while, that's all."

Now I was just inches from the ice queen, her face a chiseled masterpiece frozen in time. In a thick, liquid moment, she held out the locket in a big circle, motioning for me to lower my head like I was being awarded a medal. *For Emily.* Oh my God, Em. Where are you when I need you?

I brought my neck down a few inches and felt the trace of Lise's hands on the back of my head as she set the locket on my neck, then she jerked her hands away quickly. I couldn't see them, or her suddenly. "I can't breathe. What the—"

Chapter 21

"We had an agreement. You're not to hurt her."

Her voice was muffled by the scratchy sack someone dragged over my head. So that's why she apologized, wow. Doesn't work that way, Lise.

A set of meaty hands had grabbed my shoulders, the man directly behind me keeping me from running away by using his right arm for a head lock. We were closer to the back of the lot now, out of view of the main street. I felt oddly calm, my mind reverting to my personal trainer sessions at Golds Gym where we did hamstring-strengthening, setting fitness intentions, and self-defense. One of the moves I learned involved leaning forward, tucking my knee to my chin, then jabbing my foot simultaneously back and up. Though not necessarily intended for self-defense, I could see the logic in using this move as a sudden thrust in the right context. It was a longshot.

The back of my head brushed the man's throat, which meant I'd need to aim high, very high. They were arguing now, him shouting something about Lise not calling the shots anymore. I didn't recognize his voice. I squirmed around to set my trap, forcing his arms to hold me closer, eventually putting me in a headlock. Perfect.

I crumpled forward and started coughing convulsively. "I can't breathe!"

"Let her go for God's sake!"

Right knee up and leaning on my bad ankle, I thrust my right foot back and upward as hard as I could, hoping to make contact with the man's most vulnerable part. I felt clothing and flesh on the other side of my foot. I'd made contact alright.

"Ohhhhhh—" The thick arms loosened from my body. The man toppled hitting the ground hard, moaning and rolling onto the sidewalk. Oh my God, please don't be dead, not another one. Amazed it actually worked, I couldn't stop myself from secretly laughing. I ripped off the hood, tucked it under my arm and ran back down the street toward the car, leaving Lise behind me draped over her downed operative.

I reached Fergus' car and started banging the trunk and windows. "Go go go go go!" I shouted and jumped in the back seat. Fergus turned around and saw the hood in my hand, then started the engine. Bharat climbed in the passenger seat and Fergus took off.

"Dude, please hurry up," I begged.

"It's a stop sign."

"Just go!"

"What happened?"

"What are we doing?" Bharat asked.

"Someone just tried to abduct me. With this." I held out the black hood and glanced behind me, knowing they were likely following. "I kicked a guy in the crotch."

"Ouch," Bharat winced. "Are you okay?"

"What guy?" Fergus now.

"I want to tail him," I said to Bharat. "Any chance you could keep an eye on Lise's movements? She was on the sidewalk around the corner from the bike shop with her thug."

"You're like a ninety-pound superhero," Bharat said, then instructed Fergus to pull over. "I'll let you know when I find her. She's hard to miss." He stepped out and gave me the V-sign with his fingers, which meant I'm watching you.

Fergus looked pissed, his mouth poised in a scowl. "Are you okay?"

It was the right question even though I knew he hated me right now. "I will be," I said, hoping.

Bharat took off toward Eighth Street to hopefully keep an eye on Lise and report back.

I got out of the backseat and took Bharat's spot in the front.

"What happened?" he asked.

"Lise baited me with a necklace she was trying to give me, then some guy jumped me from behind and put a hood on my head. Are you going? We need to tail that guy to find out who he is and where he was planning on taking me tonight."

He swallowed, otherwise unmoved, pulled the car from the curb watching me as I directed him to where my abductor was left lying helpless. "There he is! See him?"

"Thea—"

"Follow him, Fergus! I need to know who this guy is."

I knew what was coming. He didn't want to be here, doing this, in his father's car no less. He was approaching the block where my abductor was slowly getting up. The guy held onto a telephone pole with one hand and practiced walking. My God, how hard had I kicked him? The poor guy. "Is it true you can make a guy sterile by kicking him in the balls?" And why did I feel bad about it this?

"Thea! What-the-fuck-is going-on? I can't take this anymore, this constant life or death and endless chase." He slowed the car and breathed in and out. "Yes, you can make someone sterile from that." He sighed. "But it sounds like your response was entirely appropriate for the situation."

"The guy works for Lise. I'd just like to know in what capacity and what he was intending for me tonight."

"You're gonna find that out how exactly?"

"Just get close to him and leave that to me."

The man saw us, and did a good job dodging the car, until he turned onto Hallam Street, a dead end.

"I don't see him now," Fergus groaned. His voice sounded tired.

I hadn't taken my eyes off the road. Where the fuck did he go? "We might be at the end of the road, tonight anyway." I called Bharat. "Hey, any sign of her?"

"I don't think she sees me," Bharat whispered.

"Great, please stay on her a while longer. We'll stick around this neighborhood to see if my abductor comes back."

"Righty-oh, back to you shortly."

"Hang up." Fergus pulled over on a dark street, then turned off the engine.

I looked out and saw bushes. "Where are we?"

He scrolled through his phone contacts, pressed a number and waited.

"My man," someone said. I was sitting beside Fergus and heard Kit Fury's voice. Great.

"Can you talk?" Fergus asked him.

"What are you doing?" I hissed, grabbing his arm.

"Yeah, man, I'm chillin'," Kit said. "What's up?"

"Thea was almost abducted on the street just now. Someone put a hood over her head. We chased the guy but he got away."

Silence. "She there with you now?" Kit asked.

Fergus pressed the speaker button. "Hey," was all I could muster.

"What are you doin', girl?"

"Trying to make it to eighteen."

"What happened since I last saw you?" he asked.

"Nothing, other than someone going to my house and giving my mother some line of bullshit about a photography project."

More silence. Fergus and I both saw a shadow move behind a fence ahead to the right. I pointed. He started the car.

"Someone wants that picture," Kit said. He was right of course. "Sounds like they've leveled up."

"How would attempted abduction be considered leveling up?" I asked Fergus.

"On the street," Kit said, "risk is remunerated with respect. They're leveling up because they were willing to take the risk of abducting you. They're escalating, less afraid of the consequences, which indicates your abductors are getting paid more money for taking that risk. Either that or they're getting desperate."

"Kit, we need protection for her," Fergus said it as a command.

I grabbed Fergus' forearm and dug in my fingernails. "What are you doing?"

"Is that, like, a service you provide?" Fergus asked him.

"Yeah, in exchange for what?" I asked.

Fergus glared at me. "Thea, shut it. I'm trying to help you."

"I got you," Kit said gently. "I'll put someone on her. You won't even see him."

"On foot?" Fergus asked.

"Leave that to me. Where you at now?"

While Fergus gave him our location, the shadow I'd been watching moved. I climbed out of the car, hearing Fergus yelling at me after I slammed the door shut. I loved that, again saying no to someone trying to control me. There was no joy in the world that matched that feeling. Kit wanted to protect me only because it would mean Fergus would owe him a favor. Okay, sure, Fergus was trying to help, and I was in real danger tonight. Who knows where I might have ended up had I not remembered the back kick move and had the huevos to actually pull it off. I'd just proved that I could take care of myself. That was something at least.

The shadow was a dog chasing a cat into the bushes. I felt like running, like Lise did the night her mother died, and like I'd been doing pretty much my whole life. Only now could I see the pattern on this invisible threshold under a sheet of stars. Run back to the safety of Fergus' car, stand by to receive protection from one of Kit's paid goons, owe them unspeakable favors, or go it alone. I could vanish right now into the night and send Fergus text messages so he'd know I was okay. I could be my own protection, my own team. The idea of it felt like relief, in a way, when I considered the level of danger I'd put Bharat through in the past two days.

They nearly got me tonight; one more second and my abductor would have had his arms wrapped around my body and chucked me in the back of a van, and then who knows. Interrogation? Torture? Trafficking? I had to go it alone now, at least for a while to keep my friends out of danger, and because I needed the time and space to figure this out for myself. I knew it was cruel and selfish. These people cared about me. But I had to protect them against whatever I was searching for. I made one last call.

"Now where the hell are you?"

"Fergus, listen to me. Tell Kit to put his man on my mom, not me. She's the one I need to protect. They've been to the house already. They're gonna come back, maybe tonight, maybe tomorrow. Please. I'll do anything."

Silence. "What about you?"

"I'll be okay. Take care of yourself and go get some sleep. Your interview's tomorrow," I said, then hung up. He hated that. And I'll bet he'd forgotten about the interview. This one mattered because Fergus didn't want to be frothing lattes all day. He had a talent for digital marketing and was destined for great things. The door to adulthood was open to him and I would not let all my drama stand in his way.

I looked down at my phone. Why hadn't I heard from Bharat?

Chapter 22

Now nearly 1:00 a.m., I stayed in the shadows - in and out of clusters of trees, through unfenced yards, never more alone in my life. I walked all the way to Mission Playground, the park we'd planned to meet at later, scanning the tennis courts, basketball court, soccer pitch, and children's playground behind two apartment complexes on Guerrero. I found a worn belt swing and fell into it with my head leaning on one of the chains gazing at the sky. My first interruption was a text from Brody:

Is this you? Let me know you're okay.

The accompanying picture was—oh my God. As if taken from across the street with a screen magnifier, it was the bottom half of my body with a hood over my head and a man standing behind me. He was even taller than I expected. Fucking Lise. I'd only had the hood on for a minute. Was it only to take that photo?

Where did this come from? I typed back.

The s/reddit/blackearedrabbit subfolder. Is this you?

I now had my own folder in a SubReddit community. Despite the obvious street cred, I felt notorious. Obviously someone was tracking me. But how? *It was, but I'm fine. Is there a way you can tell who uploaded this to Reddit?*

IDK, I'll check around. We're down at Fort Point every night after dark if you need us. Stay safe.

I liked having a new friend, even though his report added to my overall sense of alarm. I sent the picture to Fergus with Brody's message.

Dissed by Lise. Lying to Fergus. Maybe this was a typical post-graduation breakdown. The new threads of my future pulling me from the comfy, idle cocoon of high school life, testing me but now adding loneliness and isolation to inspire change. I'd do anything for the safety of that cocoon again, if I could ever find it. Sheltered oblivion? Yes, please.

Like the universe knew what I needed, the playground was quiet tonight with only the swish of occasional cars, crickets, and night birds. I sucked in a few deep breaths to quiet my thoughts, and put my hand on my chest at one point so I could feel the evidence that I was really still alive. That was a close call tonight, way too close. People were trying to harm me. What really hurt was that Lise had been the decoy, distracting me with...wait, the locket! I'd almost forgotten.

My fingers fumbled to tug the long chain out of my shirt. Almost down to my waist, the pendant was heavy, and now hot from my skin. It was too dark to see it. The moon kept threatening to slide out from behind clouds, but for now I was nicely hidden in shadow, intending to keep it that way. I used my thumb and forefinger to examine what felt like a heavy, vintage piece of expensive jewelry. Family heirloom? It could be Emily's necklace, which Lise had started wearing after the funeral, or maybe it was something similar purchased for this occasion. At this point, anything was possible. In the few seconds I saw it in her hands, it seemed too shiny to be an antique. My fingers took in the unique, barrel-shape. There wasn't any kind of release mechanism so obviously not a locket. But then why create a barrel shape? She'd given this to me for a reason. Add that to my list of unanswered questions.

The moon emerged, spilling a blanket of light on some dry dirt that would turn to soft grass when the rains started in the Fall. I found a new spot on the ground against a chain link fence along the back perimeter, which gave me a more strategic view of any potential abductors. I recalled the feel of that black hood jammed down over my face and, for some reason, I wasn't afraid. I didn't feel traumatized by this close brush with whatever it might have been, because I'd escaped—without anyone else's help. I didn't fully recognize this new superhero, but all the better. I was gonna need it.

Pulling my brain into analysis-mode, I used the scrunchie perpetually affixed to my wrist and coiled my hair on top of my head, wondering what it might feel like to actually cut it all off. Roberta Fenning was in her late fifties and had obviously been involved in something other than real estate. Then again, maybe that depends on what you consider real estate. I'd read about laundering money through fake real estate transactions involving property that didn't really exist. She'd gotten rich when her billionaire husband died, but maybe all that money wasn't enough and she needed more. I know what I saw on that kitchen floor. Besides Roberta's body, there was blood, more than the kind of bleeding that happens when you slip and fall. Someone struck her in the head and she hit the floor, and there's almost no way that could have been accidental. Who murders a real estate agent? Someone who thinks she knows something about a criminal enterprise or a piece of property related to one. At the end of the day, her death meant that she was in somebody's way. And now it appeared they were coming for me. I had a few hours of darkness left in this secluded haven, but what I really needed was a computer.

I checked the bars on my iPhone, miraculous that it had any charge left at all. Problem was, turning up the brightness would burn battery and make me more visible. I went partial-brightness and brought up Roberta's real estate website and scrolled down. This told me nothing. What I needed was to find a list of her recent transactions, maybe focusing on international money laundering hotspots. Fergus and I read spy novels one after the other, then talked about them to see who figured out the plot first. The last one had a laundering scam involving properties in the Bahamas and the Cayman Islands. A Google search led me to MLS.com, where if I paid a fee I could access a list of sold properties and cross reference them with a particular agent of record. Too complex and too hard to do on a phone. But the San Francisco Public Library had laptops and they opened at nine o'clock.

The cold ground under my butt had turned damp. I dozed intermittently, dreaming of Grandma Irene's macadamia nut pie and how she always secretly made two and hid one in the pantry. Where are you, Tata? Can you hear me five thousand miles away on the other side of the sky? Are you making *Chukuchuk*, those coconut rice balls I can't get enough of? I'm so tired, I told her in our imaginary conversation. Of chasing answers, people, and the motivations they hide from the world. I don't know who I am or what I need right now. I'm lost, Tata.

Half awake, I fumbled with Lise's locket. I think I was holding it the wrong way when I was straightening back up to a sitting position and it broke—like the barrel shape completely broke in half. Shit. Here I was, thinking it could be worth a million dollars. Wait, there was something straight and flat on one of the broken sides, not jagged like I would have expected. It was smooth protruding out and seemed hollow inside. OMG, this could be a flash drive. I'd read about these, you could buy them on Etsy in the form on a vintage-looking locket. So, Lise gave me a jump drive before she tried to have me abducted. Why? Did she want me out of the way, or was she giving me a clue and that was that the only way she could get it to me?

I needed more than just a computer. I needed my own. On my way home, I made a mental list of research topics, among them the Where's Edgar hashtags on Reddit, discussions about DSC, Roberta Fenning's real estate transactions, and now the Reddit blackearedrabbit community. Not exactly how I planned on spending my last carefree summer.

Chapter 23

I wanted to stay off of main streets, so from Folsom I turned on 14th then Mission for a few blocks, then took 19th Street to San Carlos, the street behind Lexington. Not only my ankle throbbed now but also my right foot and knee, maybe because of how I'd been sitting on the ground. I knew if I didn't rest soon and elevate it, my mobility could be seriously impaired. That was the last thing I needed.

San Francisco backyards, at least in the Mission, were virtually nonexistent other than tiny dog-runs or open decks large enough for a two-seater and a tiny table. Thank God the Caruso's behind us never locked their back gate and it was still dark enough to move around freely. I was able to fit through crouching on all fours past their kitchen window. I jumped their back fence, then I entered our backyard. I could stand on the tall recycle bin to reach my bedroom window, which didn't have a lock on it. Small miracle.

I paused, first, to make sure no one was up and looking out their window. Crickets and cars but no one watching. Phase two was climbing in the window without letting Sasha out. It slid up two inches then stopped. I wedged my hands in to try pulling it up with my thumbs on the back side, come on, one more inch, now another.

One more and I was able to push my head through and used my shoulders and back to thrust up the hundred year old window enough to crawl in the gap.

I should have used my phone's flashlight to look around first. An intruder had been here, schmoozing my mother and hunting down that photo. And they were never gonna find it, bastards. After climbing in, I closed the window behind me and shoved my laptop and charger into my backpack. I didn't see Sasha and prayed she hadn't slipped out. Unfortunately, there was no time to do anything but get out of here and find a safer place. Funny, a safer place than home. Okay not that funny, actually. I heard a car out front. God, my mother. No, it was too early for her to get home from a double shift. I pictured Roberta's dead body, the image of her smashed skull and pool of blood on the floor as I crawled back out the window. I stopped, perched on the wobbly recycle bin, when my phone buzzed with email notification sounds. I never got emails this time of night.

I crept down into the backyard and hid in the Caruso's overgrown bushes to read it. An email…from my mother? She never emailed me. *Men came to the house*, she wrote, *they looked around, didn't take anything, but they broke Sasha's dish.* Mom said she was emailing me because she thought someone was monitoring my texts. Clever. I checked the timestamp—ten minutes ago. Night shift. I dialed her cell, please, please pick up.

"Thea? Jesus."

Thank God. I muffled my voice by talking into the sleeve of Brody's flannel shirt. "Mom? Are you okay? Are you at work?" I asked.

"Yes." I could barely hear her. "You got my note."

"Who was it? Do you mean that one guy, or someone else? What did they want?"

"Stay away from the house, Thea. For now, anyway." Her voice came out as a chilling monotone. My hands shook.

"Mom, what were they looking for, what did they ask you?"

Metal clanging sounds reminded me of the noises the lockers made in the nurse's lounge. She was getting off shift, preparing to go home. I heard my mother sigh, plopping down on one of the hard benches after being on her feet for an unthinkable sixteen hours of a once weekly double-shift. I knew she was doing this for me, so we'd have the money to have a good life in an expensive city with opportunities that didn't exist on a remote island. My heart was breaking right now.

"Thea, listen very closely. Whoever was here came here to hurt you. I felt it."

"Did they hurt you, Mom?" I tried to keep my voice steady. It wasn't working. "What did they do?"

"No, just talked, standing in a dark shadow in the living room. Threatening me. I was too afraid to turn on the light. What have you done?" she asked. "Have you taken something?"

"I didn't steal anything, if that's what you mean, no. I witnessed a crime. I took a picture of it and someone caught me on camera doing it. Now they're after me for that picture."

I heard her labored breathing in the phone, pictured her sitting in her navy-blue scrubs and black Dansko shoes on the locker room bench. "Where's the picture? You better give it to them, because I don't know what they'll do if you don't. And don't go home. It's not safe. Can you stay with—"

I cut her off before she said it. "Yeah. I'll be fine. But what about you?"

"I can stay here for a few days, since I'm working weird shifts anyway. I won't ask you for any more details over the phone, because frankly even this doesn't feel safe. I wish your father were here."

Wow, as if I needed another turning point. The world must be seriously fucked up if she mentioned my dad. "Please, don't get him involved," I begged her.

"Involved in what?"

It took me a minute to find the words, words that could explain what I'd stumbled onto. "A game. A deadly game."

After we hung up, I realized I'd forgotten to ask her about Grandma Irene's dish, which Sasha had been using for water ever since we got her. Had they broken it by accident, or smashed it in front of her as a symbol like they do in gangster movies? But my attention was frozen on a pair of eyes staring back at me in the darkness of the yard.

"Oohh!" I felt a jab in my left ankle as I tumbled off the recycle bin. A hand grabbed a wad of my hair and yanked. My head was forced backward in an unnatural angle; a leather-clad arm struggled to slide around my neck. It had to be Lise's thug. Had he followed me here? I jabbed my bony elbow into someone's chest but it barely made contact. Someone else, in front of me now, reached up toward my head. I tried kicking but kept getting air as my weight was lifted from behind. Not the hood. Please not that freaking hood again. They were smart. There was no way I could knee them this time if one of my legs, the one with the bad ankle no less, was out.

Long arms enveloped my chest and torso, obviously to distract me. They'd pricked me with something sharp behind the ankle bone where the skin was thin and vulnerable. These weren't the Kit-variety of thugs. These guys were pros. I had to keep the locket away from them, even though I wasn't certain they even knew about it. I used my elbow this time, jabbing it behind me. It seemed like it hit this new assailant in the sternum. He didn't make a noise in response but the surprise forced his body backward a few steps. With the same upper body motion I used to jump Caruso's fence, I hoisted myself back up on the recycle bin, thanking God that I'd left my bedroom window open a crack. I had to pretend to be trying to get into my bedroom, so when they pulled me out by my legs, they'd feel like they won the battle. I don't know how I knew so much about wartime tactics, but I trusted my inclination here. Who else could I trust but myself anyway?

I waited for some kind of drug to kick in and sedate me, though I had no idea what kinds of substances could be injected like this. So far I felt nothing.

I got high enough to raise one hand to the window, where I'd been gripping the coiled-up locket in my closed palm. I opened my hand to grasp the window sill and coughed three times to mask the sound of the metal locket hitting the floor behind my white bookcase. I just hoped Sasha didn't find it and drag it all over the house. One thing at a time. The locket was safe, at least for the moment. Why wasn't anyone behind me now?

I heard screeching tires out on the street so maybe they just took off. But then what was the point of their assault? Obviously to inject me with some unknown drug. I closed my eyes and body-scanned myself, but still felt nothing from that pin prick.

My phone vibrated, as usual the worst possible time to start a conversation. I pulled it out of my pocket slowly, keeping my eyes peeled for movement around the perimeter of the back yard. The same *Unknown* label caused instant tension in my body. There was no preview message showing so I had to touch it to open it.

They will kill you for that file.

My blackmailer's first message was menacing, bordering on threatening, and since then the tone had changed to warnings. Was this person my adversary, my attacker, or someone looking out for me? I'd thought, a few nights ago, about how they were tracking me. Was there a surveillance sensor on the bottom of my shoe? But I'd worn flipflops one night and tennis shoes the next. Was there a jacket I'd worn consistently since Roberta Fenning's death? No. What was one thing I'd had with me ever since? My phone.

Chapter 24

I had a burner phone stashed in my room in case I ever found a tracker on my main phone, though I knew my mother wasn't techie enough to do something like that. Fergus had one too, for emergencies, though I don't think he'd ever used it. Mine was out of charge anyway. I'd almost shimmied my way through the window again, when the static of a police radio crackled behind me and the glint of a flashlight. What now?

"Miss Riggs, is that you? Come down from there please."

It sounded like Officer Eve Maddox. Out of some sudden survivalist mechanism, I turned quickly and waved, smiled, and lip synched the words *Thank God* so she would think I was relieved. The light drew closer as I climbed down, making sure to stumble and fall to the ground, holding my ankle. Was I an actress now? When had I learned how to do this?

"Miss Riggs?"

"Yes, hello," I said in the professional voice I'd cultivated for college admissions interviews. I held onto a tree branch and stood. "I lost my house key and was climbing in the bedroom."

"That's a pretty foolish security risk leaving your window open like that," she said. "Not to mention preventable." She said it as a question, looking for further explanation. "And what are you doing climbing around in the dark? Someone could see you, call it in as an attempted robbery and get you arrested."

I'd already noticed that Officer Maddox looked like she could be biracial, like me, half Latina and half something else. Maybe in her case European, light brown skin and deep brown eyes, with a slender nose that made her bone structure even more striking. My brain scrambled to prepare the correct answer.

"Actually, the window doesn't close all the way. You know, lots of old homes in this neighborhood."

A pause and a half-smile. "I know. I grew up here," she said.

Oh my God my heart was pounding again. I could see her profile when she responded to a noise in the next yard. My assailants? No way, they wouldn't touch me if I was talking to a cop. I climbed down and met her in the back by the perimeter fence.

"Are you limping?"

"Just now, yeah. I must have twisted it climbing down from the bin."

Officer Maddox turned off the flashlight, hooked it on her belt, and crossed her arms. "Keeping pretty late hours. What are you doing out here this time of night?"

I imagined my brother Rudy's voice in my ear. *Tell the truth, Thea*, he always said. "My mother's working a night shift and I was at a friend's house studying." I shook my head. "I don't know what I did with my key."

"Are you in school?" Her voice didn't sound threatening; really more conversational. But I knew better.

"Not till the fall, but I'm doing some summer classes."

She was studying me—eye movements, twitches, deciding because she obviously thinks I'm lying. Rudy forgive me. These are extenuating circumstances.

"Why don't you proceed in the house through the back, and I'll meet you on the front porch. Do you need help getting up?"

"I got it, thank you." I pointed behind me. "You can go through the side yard, it's unlocked."

I climbed in after she disappeared behind the side fence and grabbed the edge of my bedroom bookcase. I crouched on the floor, my fingers feeling for the metal chain, then picked up the locket and put it around my neck again under my two shirts. I had to find another hiding place for it that wouldn't put anyone else at risk. The dark house scared me tonight, I guess the feeling that an intruder had been in here with my mother. That was way too close.

I unlocked and opened the front door.

"Miss Riggs, this is the second time this week I've been over here. Is there something going on you want to tell me about? If you need help…"

I tried not to laugh. Go to the police for help? Get real. "Thank you, Officer, I appreciate it. I'm just trying to get through a tough period and keep my head aimed forward. Know what I mean?"

She nodded and seemed taken aback by my comment. "Can I ask how old you are?"

"Almost eighteen." I'd wouldn't turn eighteen for months.

The officer nodded and turned away. "Next time I'm here, I'll want to talk to your mom. So, let's hope there's not a next time. Agreed?"

"Agreed, thank you."

My hands shook on the other side of the door. I stayed there leaning my back against it, catching my breath and reminding myself not to turn on the lights. Clearly I was being pursued by Roberta Fenning's killer and Lise was a part of that. Where the hell was the bodyguard Kit supposedly put on our house to protect my mother? I felt like strangling him, and instead plopped face-first on my bed and let my quiet sobs drain into my pink pillowcase. It smelled of the lavender laundry detergent my mother used. I had to assume my assailants watched that entire exchange and had eyes on the house right now. Maybe they'd assume the cop was still here. The glow of an iPhone or laptop could be seen outside, since it was still dark enough. Fine. I carried my laptop to the closet, sat on a pile of shoes and booted it up, remembering it only had about 15% charge. I'd charge it later. No, on second thought, I crawled out and plugged it in behind my nightstand, then resumed my hiding spot.

I wanted to check my Google Drive folder to make sure that photo was still there, but there wasn't time. I opened Duckduckgo, the search browser that ensured anonymity along with site encryption. There was a lot of debate about whether you could still be tracked there, but it felt like a safer option for tonight's research.

From the main browsing window, I logged onto the main Reddit site, keeping my back to the open closet so I could hear any sounds of an intruder. I had only a few precious minutes while my assailants regrouped with their next planned abduction attempt. I typed 'Where's Edgar' in the main search bar, which brought back a listing of conversations about the Eldenring Gaming Community. Nope. A few more combinations brought me to 'Where's Edgar DSC' and something shown as 'DSC/Edgar/WIE'. The WIE had to be Where is Edgar, and that it was connected to DSC seemed promising. But there was nothing in the list. I scrolled again, looking more closely at the results. There was one entry by someone called u/missing/WIE that had an embedded YouTube video about DSC. Great, I shared the link to my email so I could watch it later. But I needed more than that. Next, I typed in 'Edgar Heights Where's Edgar' and felt the vibration of a thump somewhere out back.

They're coming.

I quickly changed gears and booked an Uber, not through Bharat but through the app. I'd put Bharat in enough danger already. Ridiculous, really, to go through the trouble of Ubering to a spot five blocks away. But right now, I was a target and needed to stay out of sight. The Uber app showed a driver two minutes away. Perfect. I went to shut down my machine when I caught the title of a Reddit entry: 'Multiple Unsolved Murders Linked to Bayview Heights Property Manager.' That was it, Bayview. Edgar Heights. Finally, a lead.

I folded the laptop in my backpack and shoved the power cord in the front compartment. One of the quirks of this house was that the front door locked when you closed it, no key required. This would allow me a faster exit in case someone else was waiting for me out front. I peered out the living room window and saw nothing but the gray glow of early dawn. When had I last slept a full eight hours…in a bed? My pants were still damp from the moist dirt at the playground. I did a quick clothing change and left through the front door, down the stairs, and was planted safely in the back seat of an Uber in thirty seconds.

"Good morning," I said as a general greeting without knowing if my driver even spoke English.

"Linnea Caffe," my driver said reading from her phone. "You know they're not open yet." She looked even younger than me.

I nodded and I texted Janelle from the backseat. *Hey girl, it's Thea. Any chance you're open now? Could really use a place to think for an hour.*

Sleep when yr dead, right? Sure, come to the back and knock. I'll let you in.

I didn't bother booting up the laptop for a five-minute drive but did keep my eyes peeled. I wondered if Fergus made it to his interview and, after all this, if I still meant something to him.

"Here?" the driver asked, pulling in front of the modern, blue structure.

"Could you drive around the back?"

I gave her a 25% tip, the maximum, paying it forward because right now I needed all the good karma I could get. After two bold knocks, a windowless door opened to a somber Janelle, without her devilish grin or sly eyebrows. Her wide eyes told me it wasn't safe here. God, not again.

"Good morning," I said, somehow calmed by the sight of her signature pink hair.

She inched closer, holding onto the door. "Two guys just came by here, like a minute after your text came in. They showed a picture of you, asking if I'd seen you. They said they're canvassing the neighborhood because you might be in danger. They didn't look like cops."

I put my palm out and stepped back. "I'm so sorry to scare you, Janelle. No problem, I can go if you don't want to—"

"Go?" her face contracted. "They're looking for you. Get in here."

Oh, thank God. She grabbed me and put her arms around me and squeezed extra hard.

"Come in and wait for me in the basement."

Chapter 25

The building didn't have a basement. I must have looked confused.

"Behind you." She reached around me to open a door hidden by hanging aprons. Had she planned it that way? Were commercial properties here even zoned for basements? She flipped a light switch and I disappeared behind the door, extra careful down the steep, dark steps. I turned the corner to find a large rectangle with a concrete floor and low ceiling. With two walls stacked with unopened boxes, she'd obviously been using it as a storeroom. A fluorescent, flickering overhead added to the vibe.

"Sorry about the horror movie lighting," she said, and jogged back up the stairs, while I moved around the space searching for something to sit on.

Oddly, there was a full bathroom complete with a shower stall and a long counter. I set my backpack on a large box and crouched on the floor, drawing a few long breaths to steady myself. Canvassing the neighborhood…for me? My fingers searched for the metal chain around my neck and traced it to the pendant. Leverage.

"Sorry it's so damp down there," Janelle said, returning with a small bag in one hand and cardboard tray in the other. She handed both to me then sat on the same box I'd put my backpack on. She passed me a cup of coffee.

I shook my head. "You're the best. Thank you for this."

"Coffee, 'cause I'm your barista and I know how you like it."

"A damn good one, too." She'd also put a bottle of water on the tray. In the bag was a bear claw and a plain bagel. At this point I might have forgotten about food entirely if someone didn't bring it to me.

A clump of her pink hair fell over her narrowed eyes as she appraised me. "You gonna tell me what's going on, girl?" Janelle was Fergus' age, three years older than me, old enough to drink legally. She'd co-owned this business with her brother for the past two years. Talk about enterprising. "You look terrible," she added.

No wonder. "It's a long story. The less you know you the better, really."

She leaned back and put her hands behind her, obviously thinking about my answer. I liked the ballerina flats she always wore under long, colorful skirts. The effort towards style, in any form, was admirable whether it worked or not. And for her, it worked perfectly.

"Okay, so nobody knows about this basement except Jason," she said of her brother. "And he never comes down here, or not since we opened the place." She laughed. "So as far as I'm concerned, if you're in a jam right now, which you clearly are, you're welcome to stay here as long as you need." She pointed to a door. "Back entry. I'll give you a key."

I blinked, waiting for the entrepreneur to deliver her terms of this new arrangement.

"But you've gotta work for me."

I laughed. "I knew it. Upstairs?" I asked.

"Well, judging by the two visitors asking for you, that's not safe. But..." She twisted a stand of hair. "I've always wanted to make a habitable space down here." The sly smile and raised brow challenged me to improve the decor. I glassed the four walls. Not counting the bathroom, it was a pretty large space, almost as large as Fergus' basement bedroom a few blocks away.

"You got it." I sipped the mocha latte and closed my eyes. Delicious. "Right now, I need like an hour of laptop charge and wifi so I can do some quick research for a project I'm working on."

"Project, huh?" The smile disappeared. "Look, we're friends and I'll cover for you, but you better not be involved in anything against the law. This isn't just my business, you know. Jason put up all the original funding for it and I owe him bigtime."

I watched her, waiting, already fortified by the strong Sumatra beans she'd ground and probably just roasted. "Are you gonna tell him I'm here?" It was a reasonable question. I needed to know how private this space was going to be for me.

She got up from the box and stood at the bottom of the stairs, then shook her head. "If he comes down here and sees you, just tell him you volunteered to help me organize the stock."

I got up and gave her a quick hug. "You're the bomb."

"You already know the wifi password, power's over there. Just text me if you need anything." She pointed to the back wall and turned to head up the stairs, then and stopped to reach in her jeans pocket. "Here." She tossed me a key.

Before Janelle even got back upstairs, I'd plugged in my laptop. It remembered the password from when I'd been here studying for finals before graduation, back when I thought two idle months awaited me. As much as I wanted to know what was on that flash drive, I knew it likely had a tracker and would be able to detect the IP address and location of whoever retrieved it. So, I couldn't open it, not here anyway. Dammit.

I fingered through the full, opened boxes along one wall of the space taking an inventory of her stock, when I should have been taking an inventory of my relationships. Fergus had said the word helper, about Bharat. Now I apparently had another, neither of which offset the atmosphere of peril that had surrounded me since leaving the Fenning estate. Why was I always exhausted and out of breath now? Grandma Irene would no doubt ask me what I was running from, then give me her signature cockeyed smirk that always meant the same thing: myself.

I returned to the Duckduckgo window and started a new research thread: *Edgar Heights murders*. If that old investigation was in some way related to the Dead Sevens Club, that meant there may be eight or even nine murders associated with it now, when you included the guy who researched Level Seven in the game, which Brody told me about, and now Roberta. She might not have any connection. But if she didn't, why was the picture of me in *her house* now an important part of that game? I tried to ignore, for a moment, the fact that her killer was looking for me because, thanks to Janelle, I now had a safehouse. Every good fugitive had one, so I was in good company.

The musty air down here made me miss that dark playground, but it was the first time I'd felt safe enough to slow down and consider my next move. I put some cardboard on the floor and sat with my computer on my lap, coffee and snacks within reach.

A preliminary Google search showed headlines starting in late 2011, when the first victim from The Wharf was found. The police investigated it and got nowhere. A second victim was discovered the following February, after which the property owner, Edgar Rickart, was unavailable for comment, unresponsive to inquiries and then all-out missing. By March, the 'Where's Edgar' meme started and a third victim was found in the same complex, dead in his unit like the other two. Every month or so after that, another victim was found. How did residents continue living there when they were dropping like flies?

I'd gone through Janelle's excellent coffee and refilled the water bottle twice. The hydration filled cracks in my soul, but the caffeine made me even more jittery. I could keep going on this line of inquiry but I knew how my mind worked. A thread connecting them together would be nice. So far, there wasn't one. I needed a diversion to let all this new material set in.

I scoured the space for a box cutter or scissors, and found a Leatherman tool on the floor by the wall, which Janelle probably brought down here and then lost. She was flighty that way. Even still, she was in her early twenties and already a business owner, so right now she was my idol. I opened one box and that led to another, and another. I dragged the tiny blade down the seams, ripping apart the cardboard, quickly moving to the next. Swift, violent in a way. I was sweating by the time I reached the last one. Cups, lids, insulating sleeves, black plastic cutlery, small plates, and napkins. I opened the door to air out the mustiness.

This place needed shelving, a nice area rug, and some lighting to make it seem less like a dungeon. Exactly the project I needed.

I took a shower, soaping off days' worth of dirt, sweat, fear, and anxiety, drying off with a wad of paper towels. Like camping, right? Minus the fire, singing, marshmallows and fun. I sat with my knees to my chest, naked on the bathroom floor by the shower stall taking in the shudder of uncertainty. Why did I feel crippled by fear and yet utterly fearless other times? Was that normal? Moving here from Majuro, especially after losing Rudy, had been bewildering. Starting in a new school, middle school no less, forced me through that isolation. But now, targeted by a killer and nearly abducted, I'd never felt fear like this fear. For some reason, seeing my picture in that Reddit folder scared me worse than Roberta Fenning's body. There was no way I could do this alone. But until I could uncover what 'this' really was, I had to keep going. I was in the middle of something, deep enough to get lost, and now nothing else mattered but finding the truth. Finding the order that I knew would always come from chaos. And hopefully getting out in one piece.

When I left through the back door, I texted Janelle about some stuff I ordered for her space, which should arrive tomorrow. Thank God my mother sometimes made deposits in my bank account. I chose only items that were available for one-day shipping. In the meantime, I used the largest boxes as tables and stacked an assortment of everything neatly on top of each box for easy access. I was showered, caffeinated, hydrated, and fed. And it's not even 9:00 a.m.

Time for my next stop.

Chapter 26

The San Francisco Public Library on Larkin was a three-story work of art, complete with an atrium, art gallery, café, and a rare book room. It even smelled like an art gallery with the scent of oil paint. Their community tables had five-year-old desktop computers with updated software that could be signed out and used for up to two hours at a time. Linnea Caffe was on the 33 Ashbury/18th Street bus route, which rolled down Van Ness stopping a block from the library.

It was too warm for Brody's flannel shirt today, but I had it tied around my waist, because it felt lucky that I'd found his van that night at Fort Point. Without him, I never would have known the dark history of the Dead Sevens game and my accidental connection to it. I scored the coveted computer on the back wall, which had absolute privacy from onlookers. I logged on, looked left and right five times before pulling the locket out of my shirt, and broke apart the two halves of the vintage-looking pendant. In a sort of momentary vigil, I held it between my fingers, knowing there would be no way to unsee whatever horrors had been stored here. Truth or die, right? I inserted the end of the flash drive into a USB port on the front of the CPU under the desk. People used these clunky boxes instead of laptops, really? It seemed unthinkable. Nothing happened. I ejected the drive and tried again. While I waited, I picked up my phone to text Fergus about his interview, but there was a text I hadn't yet seen from Bharat. Finally. A set of four photographs popped up, which looked like Lise and a man I didn't recognize coming out of the Cobaltic building. The accompanying text from Bharat read: *Your friend Lise with the same man at 9:00 p.m. every night this week. Worried I haven't heard from you. Let me know yr okay.*

He hadn't heard from me. I'd already brought enough drama to his life. I checked the flash drive again, confirmed it was plugged in correctly, and again nothing was happening. I texted Fergus.

Hey, how was your interview?

OMG finally! Where are you hiding out? I drove past your house but didn't want to ring the bell in case you were asleep. Are you okay?

Found a safer place to hide out for a few days. So…how did it go?

They said I'm moving to the next level up and I should hear back in a week.

I added three fire emojis, and he sent back a love emoji. On any other day, that might have been enough to calm my heart.

The library's Windows machine was having a hard time reading the contents of the flash drive. Not surprising, all things considered. The red light on the drive was blinking, which meant it was in progress. I opened my Google Drive folder and entered my password to make sure *it* was still there, then opened what I'd renamed the Work Shoes folder. No, of course I wasn't going to open it here at the library, but that made me wonder if someone had installed a keystroke tracker on this computer. If so, they could easily follow where I'd stored the file, and might be able to reconstruct my password with a keylogger program like Revealer. I needed a Plan B.

Even so, that didn't answer the question of what was actually on the flash drive, how Lise got it, or why she gave it to me. Bharat's pictures of Lise could just be some guy she was dating. I'd have to— wait. The drive stopped blinking. I turned my head to glance out the window to my right.

I double-clicked the task bar icon for the flash drive and then again to open it. I tapped my fingertips on the desk while I waited close to a minute for the folder to open. Geez, how many files were on here? Or maybe it wasn't the number but the size of them. Video files were typically huge. Why did that make my stomach tighten? Okay, here we go. I pulled my chair closer to the screen and leaned my head down. There were seven videos and seventeen files in total, some image files with still photographs and three PDF documents. Someone had spent a lot of time on these uploads, not to mention the file architecture. Someone was sending Lise, or maybe ultimately me, a message.

My phone buzzed with a text from Janelle. *Hey, Joanna Gaines,* she wrote of my secret love of HGTV. *Your stuff is here from Wayfair. I assume I can just stick it in the basement and you'll do the rest?*

Affirmative, I wrote back with a smile emoji. Wait, no. I accidentally chose a rainbow emoji by mistake. Shit. Now would Janelle think I was gay?? Maybe she already knew? Funny how the mind manipulated the secret desires of the human heart. I hadn't even come out yet to Fergus, let alone my mom or anyone else. Maybe I still hadn't even acknowledged the truth of my sexuality to myself. Janelle sent back a thumbs-up emoji. I honestly didn't have time right now to confront this issue and decode the different possibilities of its meaning. Maybe Janelle had just learned something new about me. I'd deal with that later. For now, I refocused on the list of documents staring back. I changed the contents view to a list and went in order.

File 1 was an mp4 video file that opened with a short delay, then a viewing box popped up on my desktop, roughly 3x5 inches. I could see from the timeline slider that the whole video was two minutes long and this one had no audio. I pulled my earpiece from my backpack and connected it, just in case, turned the volume all the way up, and pressed play.

Roberta, her dark hair pulled back into a high ponytail, a silk scarf wrapped around the scrunchie for color. Stylish as always. My hands started sweating, please God, no. The scarf was navy blue and gold, a nice match for her professional pantsuit and crisp white blouse. She was standing outside against a gray, concrete wall with some kind of sign behind her, most of it blocked by her body. The camera was aimed on her talking to someone and smiling like she was comfortable with them, someone she'd spoken to before. Interesting that I couldn't see the other person—only their hands, a man's hands by the size of them, no rings, and folded in front of him, with his body hidden. Why would the videographer have included his hands only? Halfway through the video, she was still talking, head tipped to the side as she listened to her companion. But I was more interested in her mouth than the position of her head. The smile and the eyes had changed in response to what the other person was saying. Now her arms were crossed in front of her and it looked like she shivered.

At the very end, I watched the arms uncross, face tight, and she stretched out her palms as if to ask a question and the screen went black. My mind raced with infinite scenarios, all culminating in the truth of what I was undoubtedly about to witness. Did I have the strength to go on with this? I set my palms face down on my knees and took a breath, asking myself. What was the saying, in for a penny in for a pound?

Video 2 was ten seconds long. Instinct told me to squint my eyes, bracing. I clicked the play arrow. Roberta screaming, head shaking, someone's hand and a white cloth pressed to her mouth from behind, her eyes widened like unnatural globes. She was standing this time in a different place, a white, polished wall of shiny tile behind her with the camera farther away than last time. I recalled her kitchen and that unthinkable scene. What had she been wearing that night? I closed my eyes, which sometimes helped sharpen my thoughts. Gray pants, yes. Light gray pants, like the kind of dress pants she usually wore, a dark blouse, not black but dark blue maybe tucked in at the waist, and some kind of suit jacket that didn't specifically match the pants.

I wanted more than anything to be back in the cocoon of my new safehouse instead of a public library with a window behind me. This might be the last opportunity I'd have to see these files and bear witness to whatever tragedy befell my best friend's mother. Obvious now why someone would kill for these files, the questions nagging my brain were who had filmed these moments and the intended audience. By the distance and perspective, it obviously wasn't her assailant, but they had been in the room in close proximity. Did her assailant know he was being filmed? Had he commissioned it? Of course.

I was dying for something to drink and distracted by a sudden, throbbing pain in my ankle. Odd because I hadn't put weight on it in about thirty minutes. Actually, it was the pinprick from where I'd been injected three nights ago. Maybe they had injected me with a tracker. A new dread spilled over me. Were they sophisticated enough to have that technology in something that small? I'd have to deal with that later. It was now or never. Whoever knew I was seeing these files right now was likely on their way here. Precious minutes left. I opened Video 3.

Roberta with her white blouse unbuttoned partway, no jacket, half of her hair hanging loose from the container of her careful ponytail, mascara smudges on her reddened eyes, seated in chair in a darkened room with her hands and ankles bound. Her captor went through the trouble of untying the scarf from her hair, then using it to bind her wrists behind her back. My God, Roberta. Who did this to you?

Chapter 27

I had a feeling what I was about to see in the following videos, and there was no way I could get away from duplicating them and live to see another sunrise. A guy walked up to the study carrels and took one in the same row as mine. Probably a grad student. The next four files were photographs, jpegs with small file size, which probably meant low resolution. The megapixel standard with iPhones generally produced super sharp photographs in the range of 1600 x 1200 px at a bare minimum. I considered, before opening them, what would make a file size 95 x 95? Possibly by cropping a larger photo, or using outdated equipment. Assuming her assailant was using modern tech, I think cropping was the most possible reason.

Picture 1—A grainy, color photo of the inside of some kind of chateau, black ceiling, gold curtains, and a room filled with guests all clad in the same attire—black robes and old-fashioned looking gold theater masks. Holy shit, it was like that movie *Eyes Wide Shut*, which my mom wouldn't let me see but of course Fergus and I watched it anyway. The room felt cold suddenly, the scene also reminding me of a documentary I'd seen on a secret society where re-enactments of pagan rituals were performed with people watching silently, and guests being charged hundreds of thousands of dollars to participate, even just to watch. I tried to remember the name. *What had been cropped from this photo?*

Picture 2—Same scene but with flickering torches lit in the corners of a grand ballroom. This time a zoomed-in view of a long table surrounded by creepy robed guests, with tall men at each end holding long, pointed sticks. A woman, face turned downward and covered by her long, dark hair, stood in a white, see-through nightgown beside the middle of the table. It had to be Roberta. I could see where this was going. I glanced around scanning for a trash can in case I got sick.

Picture 3—Roberta lying naked face-up on the table, hands at her sides, with men on each side of her. One of them had what looked like her nightgown in one hand draped over his arm.

I resisted my paranoid urges to jerk my head left and right every time I opened another file. My ears as a barometer of safety told me no one had moved. It was early so only one other computer station was being used by the scruffy grad student with shoulder-length brown hair, partial beard, wearing army pants and a track suit jacket with white stripes down the arms. He didn't look familiar.

I opened Picture 4. Thank God for screen guards or I'd surely be tossed out of here for a porn violation. Same figure, who I was still assuming was Roberta. Wait. I glanced back at the flash drive folder; this picture was 4 but there was also a 4a and a 4b. I opened all three of them to see if they followed the same progression, and repositioned them on my screen in order.

Picture 4 followed number 3. Roberta's skin looked shiny. One of the robed men was leaning down and appeared to be rubbing something on it, like oil. Gross. Picture 4a showed another man, or maybe the same one, rubbing something gray on her belly. Gray? Sand? Her whole belly was covered and the black-gloved hands were spreading whatever it was upward toward her chest. I took special note of Roberta's face in these photos. It almost looked...serene. Obviously they'd drugged her to ensure her compliance with whatever ceremonial ritual was being performed. Picture 4b showed one of the men bent over her holding a small towel over her chest. What the fuck was going on here?

I closed the image files and sat back, rubbing my palms over my face. I needed to walk around and think, drink some coffee, feel fresh air on my face. There just wasn't time for those luxuries. Someone had stuck a Keep Calm Carry On sticker—I was so tired of that meme—on the back of the study carrel. Come on Thea, do what it says. Carry on. Deep breath. Okay, analyze this. It looked like something I'd read about a month ago when I was preparing my final World History paper on the historic oppression of women. I included a chapter on ancient purification rituals. Lustration—Greek or Roman, was a purification rite to cleanse a body of impure thoughts, pollution, germs, or demonic possession. Sometimes water was used, as well as oil...or *clay*. I hadn't used this in my paper because it was more than just women who were targeted for this ritual. Oil. Clay. Roberta Fenning was being ritually prepared for something by cleansing her and then washing it off with a towel. All I could think of was a human sacrifice, or something even more horrible. I'd feared, when I saw the long poles the robed men were holding, that she would be mutilated in some way, but her body on the kitchen floor had been intact other than the wound in the back of her head. Naturally there were no timestamps on these videos or image files, or maybe they'd been erased. So, when had all this happened, and why?

More photographs. One showed the same scene of robed onlookers encircling a round table where two people were having sex, naked but masked. The onlookers were also masked. Weren't they always with events like this? The richest and most powerful of society escaping lives of predictable boredom into elaborate games of depravity and intrigue. I opened Duckduckgo and searched for something called Rothschild surrealism, remembering the documentary I'd watched—a 1970's picture with hooded, masked attendees. What I remembered most about it was that the cost was something like $100k per attendee, even more if you were to participate first-hand in any of their activities.

The last of the still photographs looked similar to the previous image. I moved closer to the screen to get a better look, trying not to magnify anything. Interesting. Same circle of onlookers, but instead of a sex exhibition, it looked like the same two people standing within a circle drawn on the floor aiming guns at each other's heads.

Okay...... I sat back. That was my limit. I closed all the files, but then remembered there was another folder on the disk. Shit. Maybe one more quick look with my eyes squinted this time. There were three photos of the same scene in a sequence, all showing two men carrying the body of a woman, Roberta! I recognized the hair and gray pants. So, wait; they abducted her, interrogated her, brought her to this sick party, subjected her to torture, then re-dressed her in her original clothes and brought her home to her kitchen? Was she drugged the whole time? There was no way to determine whether she had drugs in her system at the time of her death...because her body was missing. I spent all my TV time watching crime dramas—urban murders, country murders. But these videos, these disturbing scenarios, defied the ordered predictability of human contact, at least what I'd seen in seventeen years. Surely whoever made and organized these files intended to show the truth of what happened to her. All that trouble, and I was no closer to determining her killer. And now a new, maybe the most obvious question knocked the inside of my head – why was I chosen to see these? Okay, one more time.

I noted that the guy in the track jacket in the carrel beside me was tapping one of his feet on the carpet. I felt the rhythmic vibration. He must be listening to music.

I opened the first folder and scanned through the videos I'd already seen. I must have missed one. Nope. I opened the second folder again and...wait, there was another video file I hadn't seen before because the window was too small. This one was forty-seven seconds long. I made sure my headphones were plugged into the port and pressed play.

The camera shot showed the bottom two-thirds of a tall man in dark pants and a light dress shirt with the sleeves rolled up, no jacket. Roberta was seated in the same chair as the interrogation video, but this time her bindings had been removed and she just sat there, wide-eyed, like she was waiting for directions. The sweat on her forehead glistened. She had a swelling under one eye. I came closer to the screen. Her left eye was red and swollen, and there was a darkened part of her left temple, which could be dried blood but the image was too small and grainy to be sure. She mumbled something inaudible, barely moving her lips.

"Why yes, of course you can go," said her captor. "Certainly, you can. As soon as you give us what we want. Go ahead, get up out

135

of the chair."

"If you can walk," another man said from out of view. I didn't recognize any of their voices.

She stood slowly, wobbled, and held onto the back of the chair.

"Where-is-he?" the man asked, after which Roberta slowly rotated her head left and right, eyes closed like she knew what was coming.

"I swear, I don't know. I haven't seen him in ten years." Her voice sounded like her, but without the normal energy and inflection. She was terrified of these men. Who could they be talking about? Roberta had two daughters—Emily, who died, and Lise. No sons, and her husband was also dead.

"Sir," the other man said.

"What?"

"She was seen with him a week ago. They were photographed coming out of the St. Regis. At five in the morning."

Chapter 28

The tall man took two steps toward Roberta, who had retreated back to the chair. She gripped the seat sobbing, rocking back and forth. "I don't know where he is! Do you hear me? I never know. He sends me a text once a month, when it's time, and I bring him the money."

"How much?" the tall man asked.

She shook her head slowly, like she'd asked herself the same question over and over. "It changes every time."

"That little shit." The other man again. "He's more resourceful than I would have thought."

The tall man crouched. Now I could see his face. Oh my God, he looked familiar, I just couldn't place him. A long, sculpted face, clean shaven, white guy with a tall forehead. Politician? Celebrity? I'd seen him somewhere, recently too I think. I paused the video, took a picture of the face with my phone, and emailed it to myself, moved it to my spam folder, then deleted it from my phone. I knew that face. I swear to God.

"Alright then." The man stood and stretched his back. "Where and when is next month's meeting?"

Roberta took a long breath and licked her lips. "Hyatt." With her head aimed low, she looked up at the man's face, gauging, preparing. The man took two steps toward her, a gun in his right hand. She closed her eyes and braced. He stretched his arm back, then brought the gun down on her left temple so hard they both fell to the floor. The man's right foot slipped, and Roberta's body lifted up from the chair, then slumped to the floor. I held one hand to my mouth. Even though this was taped, it felt different from scary footage I'd seen on TV or online. This was someone I knew, liked, admired even. I'd just witnessed her death. My nose was running and I had to wipe it on my sleeve. So gross. I removed the drive and clicked the bottom piece back into the locket pendant around my neck, wishing I could turn back time.

Still, something was off. When I'd seen her body in the kitchen, she was wearing gray pants and a blue shirt. Maybe they cleaned her up after that and changed her clothes. But what advantage could that have? And how did the oil and clay ritual fit in with everything else I'd seen?

Underneath my shirt, the locket was almost undetectable. I still had ten minutes left of computer time. I went back to Reddit, doing a more general search on Google. I didn't mind the bots and trackers compared with Duckduckgo, because this wasn't my personal computer. Anyone could be searching here. Besides, I'd signed into the library using my standard fake name—Kristin Miller.

A Reddit search for blackearedrabbit brought up the Reddit subcommunities. The rest of the search options included nature and wildlife sites. Come on… My next search was for Dead Sevens Club. Here I switched back to Duckduckgo because I remembered the camera in the front of the building. If I was seen walking into this library and one of the computers here showed a search history for DSC, that was too easy. I needed to be discreet—now more than ever.

The search results brought up all the Reddit activity, also Twitter, a Twitter group on DSC. Wait, what was that? The word mythology grabbed my attention. I leaned closer to the screen where the Google description read DSC Mythology Blog by XYC. I noticed the blog wasn't one of the free, open-source options with cross-platform social media sharing capabilities. This writer was using telegra.ph, a type of anonymous blog that didn't require setting up a user account or signing in through a social media account. Fergus and I talked once about co-writing a cribbage-themed blog but neither of us wanted to be directly associated with something so geeky. So, we looked into anonymous blogs. Most of them used paid-hosting models typically intended for corporate whistleblowers intending to publish controversial content anonymously. In this case, XYC could be a precocious thirteen-year-old, an elderly billionaire on his deathbed, a foreign corporation, or AI. There was no telling. What the hell, it's not my computer. I clicked the link and a short narrative came up on the main page:

You've heard things. And if you're really tapped in, you've seen things. Things you don't readily understand, but you want to. They pull you. Have you played the game yet, pressured by your drinking buddies or challenged by a whispering coworker? If you have, you know that once you step across that threshold, there are no answers to anything—only more questions. Even so, DSC has the power to quickly transform into a bottomless hunger you can't ever satisfy. So why do it then? Why will you open Pandora's Box again and again knowing its destructive power? For the same reason that I will: you're a searcher. So, let's get on with it then.

Three small horizontal lines in the upper right corner indicated a menu that contained five options: *Current, Archives, Secrets, Keys, Contact.* I wanted to actually read one of the posts to verify that I was in an authentic Dead Sevens space, but my time was running out. I clicked the Contact link, knowing this was an anonymous website and the likelihood of a response was about zero. *Hungry for more and not finding what you need here? Send me a message. If you don't, you might regret it.*

Arrogant, and probably psychotic as well. Fine, I'd send a message. I chose one that was sure to get a response, if the messages were actually routed to an email address that somebody maintained, which was questionable. It was more of a Comment box than a contact link, because there was no required email to send the message. Anyone could send anything here. Here goes nothing:

Black-eared rabbit seeks camouflage from predators.

I clicked the Submit button and sat back in the hard chair. Three seconds later, my phone buzzed with a text from an unknown number. It read *Ding dong.* Was that supposed to be a door bell?

What the hell? And without a moment of uncertainty, I knew that the person who maintained this blog was sitting in the study carrel on the other side of that wall. Holy shit. How could I know this? I just felt it. Grandma Irene always talked up the importance of intuition. I exhaled loud enough for him to hear me, but what was the point of concealing myself now? I rose, standing over the man wearing a black track suit.

"XYC I presume?" I said, studying the thin face, shoulder length brown hair and goatee.

"Black-eared. Pleased to make your acquaintance."

The weight of this realization forced me back down in my chair. We were the only ones using the computers right now, with no one else anywhere near us on this floor. The voice was raspy but cultured. And he'd sort of smiled at me.

"Did you follow me here?" I asked in my normal voice. I felt thoroughly defeated.

He made a pfffff sound with his lips. "Anyone could have. You took no precautions."

How did he know whether I had or not? Fuck this guy. "How did you know I'd come here today? I didn't even know myself. And how did you know I'd stumble onto your blog?"

"You did, didn't you? You rang, and I answered. Now what do you want?"

I leaned my elbows on the desk and rubbed my eyes. My back was killing me, and my ankle still felt tweaked. "You read my question."

He snickered but said nothing about my call for help.

"I've seen the what and the who," I said, still talking through the carrel walls. "I need the why...now. I need the mythology to understand what the fuck is going on."

The guy made sounds like he was packing up. I heard his chair scrape the thin layer of carpet on the floor. He rose, and with a role reversal, he was now standing over me, taller than he'd seemed. "What do you want? And it's a one-word answer. You either want out, or you want in. And for either one, you'll proceed at your own peril."

The potential for more danger didn't even scare me at this point. I knew what I wanted, and I was sure he knew it too. "Where are we headed?"

Chapter 29

Track Suit dropped his jacket and a wool cap over the wall of the carrel. "Put those on and meet me out front," he said in a hushed voice. "Blue car. Wait five minutes."

"Fine," I said, but it all felt like nonsense. The guy was full of himself, and arrogance repelled me. I liked how poetic his blog message was, but it said nothing of consequence about the Dead Sevens Club, the game, its tangled history, and his connection to it. We'd only just met and I was already bored. In or out...fine. I'll tolerate your Morpheus complex and go *in* to see what I can learn, and hopefully I'll live through the experience.

I didn't wear a watch, so I monitored the time from my phone. Another text came in, this time from my surfer friend, Brody. No message, just a Reddit link. God, not again. I didn't have time to sign out the library computer again, nor was there time for me to boot up the laptop in my backpack. I clicked it from my phone, hoping it recognized the library's wifi. Oh my God no.

I packed up and headed for the stairs, feeling lower than I had an hour ago. Shake it off, I narrated as I moved through the library. My limbs felt heavy, the tops of my shoulders tight, an ache in the back of my skull. I eyed the security guard and waited inside the doors, hoping he'd given me only a momentary glance. A blue Prius pulled up. Feeling the guard's eyes on me, I pushed open the doors. By the time I reached the car, the guy was peering at me under the sun visor. I got in the front seat, still deciding whether this man was trustworthy or not. I think he probably knew things that could help me right now, and I might have information of my own to trade. Just not sure how close he could get me to the answers I was looking for. Who killed Roberta Fenning, why, and how was I connected to that reason?

"Where are we going?" I asked. "Do you live in the city?"

He pulled away from the curb and headed down Grove Street. "That's two questions. I have an apartment here, yes, but that's not a smart place to go with someone who's currently wanted by the police." He turned and stared. "Not to mention everybody else."

My head jerked left. "What? How do you know that? I'm not *wanted* wanted, if that's what you think. Wanted means, like—"

"Miss Riggs. I'm not sure you entirely understand the position you're in right now."

Apparently I didn't, because unless he lived on Lexington Street, there was no way he could know that I'd been approached by Officer Eve Maddox.

"I do have information for you, but not here."

"Is your car bugged or something? Are you a person of interest to the police?" It was a jibe, I admit it. Yes, I was making fun of all his cloak and dagger crap and, honestly, I was tired of feeling like a pawn. He didn't answer me anyway. "Where are you taking me?"

"A hotel on Sutter, The Cartwright."

I watched the city flash by like a yellow blur, listening but not understanding. My brain was on overload. "You're renting a hotel room, what, so we can talk?"

"Money is no object, Miss Riggs. I have money. I've earned money, I grew up with money, I inherited money. It means very little to me. Right now, you are a target. By finding a secure place to exchange information, I'm preventing myself from becoming one as well."

"Who are you?"

"You can put your pack back there if you like," he said.

I felt out of control, like I might open the car door while it was still moving just let myself fall onto the street. I folded my hands to stop them from shaking. From anger, or was it fear?

"No thanks." I set it at my feet, then pulled out my phone and clicked the Reddit link that Brody sent me. "God, not again."

"What?" the guy said.

I tossed the phone back in my pack. "A friend's been sending me links from a subreddit called blackearedrabbit." I turned and stared.

"And that's you, obviously."

"You know about it?" I shot back, angered suddenly by his cool attitude. "How is it that you know so much about me and I've only just met you? Could someone please tell me why I'm the fucking last to know everything?"

"Where?" he asked.

I hung my head forward. "Where what?"

"Where was the latest picture taken?"

The one Brody just texted me was of me standing on a trashcan. "My house, the Mission."

"Who knew you were there?"

"An armed assailant who's been chasing me for the past two days, and the police officer who caught me coming out of my bedroom window. I don't think it was either of them."

"Why not?"

"They were too far away from me." I looked more closely at the photo. "This was obviously taken from a closer spot."

"Did you see anyone else there?" he asked.

I rolled my eyes as I clamped my seat belt and slumped down low. No I hadn't seen anyone else and I had no answers to any of these reasonable questions. I felt like disappearing. It was warm. The sun was out. This wasn't what post-graduation summer was supposed to feel like.

The room the man had rented at The Cartwright was what magazines called nicely-appointed, and cramped. I liked small spaces. They felt safer, and right now that had a special appeal. Sturdy furniture, though a bit too ornate for the twenty-first century. I went to the bathroom and washed my face and hands with bergamot-scented soap. At this point I'd take anything. I stood in the doorway and realized, only then, that there was just one bed in here and one chair. Seems sort of sparse for a nice hotel, though the room was small. But it was a strange setup for a conversation. And if he had something else in mind, I'd now successfully weaponized a Pilates kick.

The man stood at the desk and poured what looked like liquor into the cap of a shiny flask. "It's fifteen-year-old scotch. You're welcome to some." He took two swigs.

"No thanks."

"As you wish." He sat in a black, swivel chair at the desk and motioned me to sit on the bed. The whole scene felt so wrong and haphazard. I needed to get back to Janelle's. I needed to eat something.

"Introductions first, I think."

"Knock yourself out," I said. I didn't want to be here anyway.

"My name is Michael Horvath." He crossed his legs. "I'm a writer and a researcher, a lifelong gamer, and a bit of an expert on the Dead Sevens Club."

I nodded and raised my eyebrows, impressed, if it was true. "I know it's a game, I've been following—"

The man's hand went up. Talk to the hand. Such arrogance. "No, not the Reddit thread."

"That's not the game?"

"I'm talking about the first game. The first generation."

"There are generations? For fuck's sake."

"Miss Riggs, why are you involved in this?"

"I was gonna ask you the same thing. I went to the Fenning estate because I was invited by my best friend, Lise, Roberta's daughter. But she wasn't there. She'd given me a key a while ago, I used the key and went in. The house appeared empty. No Lise, no Nanny, she's the cook. I went toward the kitchen and saw Mrs. Fenning, Roberta, lying on the floor." I covered my eyes and sobbed for two seconds, the image still so fresh. "Dead."

"That's *how* you're involved. What I'd like to know is why."

"What do you mean, and why are you badgering me?"

"I don't mean to. I'm trying to get some answers, and hopefully give some to you as well."

"It was random, okay? Wrong place at the wrong time, I guess. Story of my life, right?"

"Not likely," he said, unmoved from his position in the chair. "Only rarely do I experience events that are purely random. Conversely, I see coincidence and synchronicity everywhere I look."

"What are you saying? What do you mean, that I'm to blame for her death?" More tears. I knew I was a wreck and now he'd look at me like a teenager.

He paused and breathed, still watching me. "That you were chosen."

I climbed off the bed, stepped in the bathroom and splashed water on my face again, this time letting it drip onto the floor. "Look," I said from the doorway. "I don't know what kind of tragic, human theater I've stumbled upon. Maybe I'm on a movie set. Have you ever watched *The Twilight Zone*? You're old, you've probably seen it. There was an episode about a guy named Arthur Curtis who thought he was going to work one day, and discovered he was on a movie set, and wasn't Arthur Curtis at all. His life wasn't his own and he'd lost his mind."

"You're still Thea Riggs," he said, leaning forward. "You're upset right now, anyone who saw what you've seen, who watched what you just watched, would be. Of course. But you're still living, breathing, and grounded in reality. Yes, something's going on here, and I'm going to help you figure it out."

I shook my head, not the least bit reassured by whatever sales pitch he'd prepared. There was no way he could have known about the videos I'd just watched...unless the flash drive came from him and he'd filmed them himself. And if that was the case, why?

Chapter 30

"Look, I don't have all night. I need to check in with Fergus, and besides—"

"He's probably calling you right now."

Still in the bathroom doorway, I glanced down at my phone on the bed, ringing. I raised my eyes to the ceiling and shook my head. "What is this, exactly? How could you know that?"

"Let's just say I have my sources. You are certainly a person of interest right now, Thea. More than just to me."

Janelle said two men were canvassing the street with a picture of me. She said they'd been wearing suits, which could mean they were feds. How could a seventeen-year-old, high school graduate get the attention of the federal government? I watched the incoming call, unmoved.

"Lemme guess," I said. "He's about to tell me he was questioned by the police, by my new best friend Officer Maddox. Great."

He outstretched his hands and closed his eyes momentarily. "Sit down, Thea. Please. There are things you need to know. You're smack in the middle of everything right now. It's in your best interest."

"I need to get back to—"

"The coffee shop?" he interrupted. "How will you get there? Your private Uber driver is working right now. Whoever you call will expose your location to those watching you."

I crossed my arms and peered at him, leaning a few inches further out the bathroom doorway. "Did you kill Roberta Fenning?" I asked him.

"No."

"But you were obviously there when she was killed."

"Interesting. Why obviously?"

"You could only have known about the videos on my flash drive, which I was watching on mute no less, if you'd filmed them yourself. The perspective was close up. You were in the room when she was being interrogated."

"The perspective was close, yes, you could say that. But I wasn't there."

I returned to the bed, my legs too tired and wobbly to continue standing, but perched on the edge allowing for a fast getaway if needed. "Who was the *he* they were talking about in the video? The man she was protecting."

This man, Michael Horvath, tented his fingers like a politician at the negotiating table. "Finally. The million-dollar question. First of all, she wasn't protecting him." I watched his slow, deliberate movements as he poured himself another capful from the flask. Seemed an inefficient way to get drunk if that was his goal. He swigged it, then set it back down on the desk. "She didn't know his name."

"I doubt that, but you do, and I'll bet you know where he is." I stretched out my arms. "You brought me here. So talk."

Commotion in the downstairs lobby echoed up from the street. The windows were closed but the curtains were open. I swung my legs over the bed and onto the other side to peer out, but saw nothing out there. I heard raised voices, then silence, then raised voices again. We both heard it. The world's going crazy.

Now my phone again. I checked, hoping it was Fergus. It was my blackmailer, or at least the same number as his last text. This one had no words, just an image—a night sky image of half of a mountain with white letters and the phrase *Trust No One*. An old X-Files meme, I recognized it because that was my one of my retro TV obsessions until I'd watched them all and ran out of seasons. Interesting timing of that message when I was sitting here with journalist, Michael Horvath, who I suspect had made a science out of DSC history.

"A member of your fan club?" he asked.

I didn't like his sarcasm or riddles but suspected this was the way people like him talk, the way they communicate without actually sharing anything. I set down the phone and stared at his face, giving him the impression of undivided attention, something I was barely capable of during normal circumstances.

He leaned forward, took a deep breath and slumped his shoulders as he exhaled. "Okay. Listen carefully. Once upon a time, there was a young boy whose parents died when he was seven. He was put in a foster home then raised, for a while anyway, by his maternal grandparents. Every summer, he went away to camp and bonded with the same group of boys who attended that camp every year. It became a tradition." He paused. "More than a tradition. A ritual."

The word made me sick, thinking of the masked party videos, with one naked person holding a gun to the other's head.

He was watching me closely but went on. "The group of boys became best friends, inseparable almost, though they only saw each other for two weeks a year. For the orphaned boy, they became a sort of family and vowed on their 21st birthdays to get a house together or all live together in the same apartment complex and play the same game they'd played every night at camp." He watched my eyes.

"Lemme guess. Dead Sevens?" I asked. "What was it, a board game or something?"

"No, something you'll appreciate. Cards."

So that meant, what, they were monitoring Fergus' basement, where we played cribbage? I laughed aloud but contained it. "How do you play?"

"Did you ever play crazy eights?"

"The stupidest game ever? One time Fergus and I played it for eleven straight hours and still nobody won. So pointless."

"Dead Sevens is like crazy eights, but instead of eights, sevens are wild. And instead of an eight getting to change the suit, drawing a seven means you're out."

149

I wondered if, in some contexts, *out* meant *dead.* "Wait a minute. You said apartment complex. Was that—"

He smiled.

"The Wharf?"

The man nodded, getting more animated. "That's right, you've been there for the second clue in the game. The Wharf, which used to be called..." He paused and made a circular motion with his hand.

"Was that the Edgar Heights apartments?"

"Right you are."

"When was this?" I asked.

"Ten years ago. This month, actually." He paused to get some water from the bathroom sink, and now it was him who stood in the doorway, watching me seated on the bed, his eyes goading me, egging me on to continue. The Wharf, Edgar Heights. Right.

"Roberta Fenning was a real estate broker, or agent, whatever she was. Did she get them the apartment?"

"Very good. You're half right. She brokered all of their apartments—there were seven, all arranged by the orphaned boy, the powerhouse. He was the organizer...well, at least of that. His name was—"

"Jeffrey Dade," I said dreamily, blurting two words that had never even entered my head, let alone my mouth, before, not consciously anyway. Horrified by the sound of it, sobs erupted in my face. Oh my God, really? Here? In front of this guy? Seriously just kill me now.

"So you know," the man said. He'd moved cautiously to the very edge of the bed and sat, not touching me but comforting me just the same with his quiet presence. I knew, then, that he wasn't intending to take anything from me but to give me something. Guidance. He was trying to help me.

"How did I know that? What's happening to me?" I asked, through labored breathing. I searched the databanks in my brain for any familiar reference to someone named Jeffrey Dade. There was nothing. "I have no idea who that even is. I've never heard that name before in my life. Yet...when you said orphaned boy, it's like..." I wiped my eyes with my hand. The tears kept coming. "I just knew. Somehow, I don't know. I just don't understand what's going on."

"It's alright."

"Something's happening to me—" I slapped my chest— "inside. I feel things. I know things, and I don't know why."

He gave a thoughtful exhale. "You're a part of this story, Thea. An important part. And the full extent of those details still hasn't revealed itself to either one of us."

Now I had a decision to make. *Trust no one.* Sure, sounded like good self-preservation, but I couldn't see the bigger picture from where I stood and I clearly needed help. "Someone's been sending me threatening text messages since the night I found her body." I spoke slowly and softly, so he'd know I was giving up something of value. We were sitting close now, close enough for me to scrutinize his eyes and facial expressions. He looked older up close, and a little sad. "At first I thought it might have been you."

"What do you think now?" he asked.

I shook my head, terrified of the implication. "Jeffrey Dade's been contacting me? I mean, how would he know me? How would he know my name and my mobile number?"

Michael Horvath shrugged. "Easy enough to find out, I should think. You were the best friend of Roberta's daughter, so your number and name would be easily accessible, and he saw Roberta every month."

"Do you think it's him? Why would I be a threat to him?"

"Is he threatening you?" he asked.

I thought about all the messages so far. "Actually, no. He's been giving me a head's up as things progress."

"So he's helping you then." He paused to consider this possibility. "Jeffrey Dade's an interesting...how shall I say it, specimen."

His face changed as he said it, clenching his teeth inside his closed mouth, eyes firm and hard. Specimen, okay. No idea what it meant but I made note of it.

"Not what I'd say is a typical sociopath," he went on, "but he's both refined and damaged, having been messed with his whole life. Who knows what that can do to the personality over time."

I considered this, still in awe of how I knew to blurt out the name Jeffrey Dade, especially if I'd never heard it before. "I feel like what happened to Roberta is somehow my fault, because of something I did or didn't do."

"You're confused and overwhelmed. That's what the brain does in a crisis. If there's no coherent, logical reason for an event, the brain invents one."

"What happened to them? At the Wharf?" I asked.

"Nothing at first. They all graduated from college and were having the time of their lives. They worked menial jobs during the day and came home every night, got high, and played Dead Sevens. It was idyllic for them, exploring San Francisco, and it worked, for everyone, for six months or so."

I was curious about the card game version of Dead Sevens, remembering our daily cribbage games before the whole world imploded. "Then what?"

"Roberta was not only the real estate agent, she was also the property manager of this complex. Jeffrey's an artist so he was home during the day, and that meant available to let her inside the apartments when they needed maintenance fixes. Eventually, how shall I say this, they started spending a lot of time together."

"Roberta and Jeffrey Dade. Wow," I thought back a moment. "If this was ten years ago, her husband had died a few years before that. But she must be so much older than him."

"You're making an assumption that I meant they were lovers. That assumption may not be correct. But please," he raised his palm. "Build it out."

"What do you mean?"

"Keep going, keep building your theory. You're getting something."

"You said Jeffrey Dade was a go-getter, right?"

"Exactly."

"And Roberta was a billionaire, from her husband's inheritance but she came from money too."

"I didn't know that," he admitted.

"So, Jeffrey started sleeping with Roberta to get access to her money."

He shrugged. "I'm not convinced that was necessarily the nature of their relationship. Some kind of connection though, yes. But—"

"What else would—"

A *pop-poppop* sounded from downstairs, obviously gunshots.

I lowered my head and crawled off the bed and onto the floor.

"What is it? What's going on?"

"Stay away from windows," Michael said. With swift practiced hands, he gathered up the flask, motioned for me to collect my backpack, and pointed at the door. "Meeting's over. Let's go."

Chapter 31

"What the hell was that?" I shouted, two paces behind Michael Horvath on the concrete stairs of the Cartwright heading down toward Sutter. My mind always focused on silly details in times like this. The smell of stale cigarette smoke, the uncarpeted steps, the spot of thinning hair at the top of Horvath's head. I guessed he was about forty-five.

He stopped and turned back. "Are you asking me if those shots were meant for us?"

"Were they meant for me?"

"Keep moving."

"Wait a—"

"Move. Now."

"How do you know the shooter won't be down here waiting for us?" My voice sounded whiny and afraid. This felt like the night I'd seen Roberta, like someone was out to get me because I'd seen something I shouldn't. Except tonight it was something else. Did they, whoever they were, know I was here? I'd do anything to be invisible right now.

"Here." He pointed, stopped at a door on the second level,

opened the hallway door an inch. "Come on. The housekeeping elevator's around the corner."

"Do you live here or something? How do you know that?" I asked, right behind him. But I knew the answer. This must be a safehouse he used for secret meetings. Why did he need such a place, though? He said journalist, but I already knew he wasn't the kind who writes for mainstream media outlets. This guy was a whistleblower, researching illicit activities and pulling up rocks to watch what scurried out. Maybe I was in good company.

Sure enough, the service elevator led to a dock in the back of the small hotel. The adjacent lot was empty with no gate, which gave us easy access to where he'd parked. Michael Horvath, I said his name to myself, knowing he'd probably just saved my life.

The man drove me to Janelle's and waited in the alley behind 7th Street, literally door to door service. Before the interruption, a lot had been said in that hotel room, a lot of history to sift through. And then hearing two gunshots two floors below us seemed a little too coincidental. He was right to get us out of there. I still didn't trust him though.

"What now?" I asked, hand on the door handle.

"Come back tomorrow for part two."

"Back there?" I asked. "I don't think your safehouse is very safe."

He smiled a little, eyes moved toward me. Was it out of respect, or fear of growing an emotional attachment? It had happened before, older men taking me under their wing, mentoring me, and suddenly they couldn't live without me. I was looking for no such entanglements right now, certainly not from a man. Officer Eve Maddox of the San Francisco Police Department? Well, that was another matter.

"I have another place where I conduct meetings. The Royale on Post Street."

"Nice." I'd been there once and sat on their iconic red sofas.

Now he turned. "Fake ID?"

"Yeah, I have one. Doesn't everyone my age?" I asked, though I'm tall so I usually didn't even need it.

The man let out a long sigh, then yawned. "I like your style, Thea Riggs. You don't care about frivolous things."

"If I did, what good would it do me?"

"Do you have a place to sleep here?" he asked. "Isn't this a coffee house?"

"I'll crash on the floor. The owner's letting me stay here if I organize her storeroom downstairs."

He handed me a business card. "Call me if you need help. And —"

"I know. Be a vampire. Only go out at night, stay in the shadows. I'm barely even alive right now anyway."

He turned and gazed earnestly. "I'll help you, if I can, get to the bottom of this. I can give you more of the backstory, but it's you who has to figure it out, to understand your connection to this mythology."

"Mythology," I repeated and snickered. "There is no *mythology*. It's a bunch of aimless bros who lived in an apartment complex together and sat around playing cards."

"You're not wrong, but the real story is an iceberg, and you're just seeing what's peeking above the water line. Truth is, all but one of those guys is dead. And the police still don't know who killed them."

"But you do?"

"Good night, Thea."

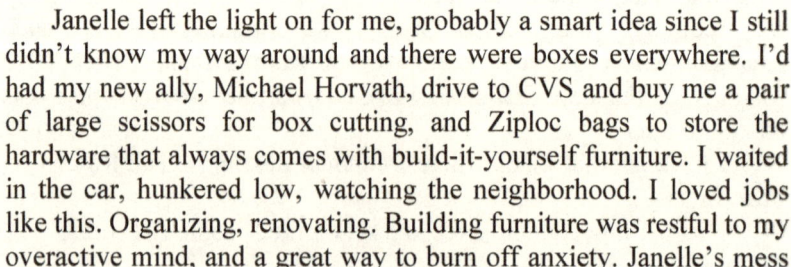

Janelle left the light on for me, probably a smart idea since I still didn't know my way around and there were boxes everywhere. I'd had my new ally, Michael Horvath, drive to CVS and buy me a pair of large scissors for box cutting, and Ziploc bags to store the hardware that always comes with build-it-yourself furniture. I waited in the car, hunkered low, watching the neighborhood. I loved jobs like this. Organizing, renovating. Building furniture was restful to my overactive mind, and a great way to burn off anxiety. Janelle's mess of a basement was about to get transformed.

I'd texted Fergus earlier to ask if he'd help me build these things. Two pairs of hands were always better than one. I plugged my phone into one of the two wall outlets and saw two texts that had come in on the drive over here.

Fergus: *I'm off tomorrow, can be there around 10. Ttyl.* Great. I'd text Janelle in the morning to make sure she was okay with this.

Then a second text which I'd missed before…from my mother. I let out a long sigh. My God, I'd totally forgotten about her. I set down my backpack, pulled out my water bottle and the two bags of pretzels he bought me at CVS, then settled on the floor in a dark corner.

I don't know where you are right now, she wrote. *I'm praying that you're out there somewhere in a safe place. Whatever you found, and whoever's looking for it, they ransacked the house. I've called the police who took a statement, and pictures. I'm not touching it. I'm staying at the Caruso's for tonight. The cop who came, a woman actually, said you need to contact them in the next 24 hours or they'll issue a warrant for your arrest. I know you didn't do this, but you have something that someone else wants. Just give it back or someone's going to get hurt. And I don't want that someone to be you.*

When I was little, in the islands, Rudy and I played hide and seek in the marshes. It was dark as death there at night, and our parents forbid us from going, even in daylight. So of course we had to play there. When you're a kid, danger is oxygen. While I read the text from my mother, something hard, like a tiny icicle, formed in the center of my chest. I think it had already been there and maybe it was just growing, emblematic of the climate of fear and anxiety that had taken over my life. Since that one fateful night.

In Majuro, even now in our house, I always had a thinking chair. A place to crash and lounge, dangle my feet over the edge, gaze at the ceiling, or out the window, and take a breather to process the chaos. There were no chairs in this basement but it was safe here and certainly quiet. My mother would be pleased. I decided this spot on the floor was my thinking chair. I closed my eyes to center myself. Breathing in, out. In, out.

My mother said to give it back to them or someone would get hurt. She was probably right. I knew how to access the picture I'd taken of Roberta Fenning lying on her kitchen floor, before her killer moved the body. But where would I take it, and who would I give it to? If I was gonna do that, I could get a message to Lise…through

Bharat who had been watching her for days now. I could tell her I had a photograph of her mother's body, and I was prepared to give it to whoever's been pursuing me. It wasn't a great idea but might be better than doing nothing. Proactive versus reactive.

My mother said I had to contact Officer Maddox within twenty-four hours to avoid getting arrested. But when did the clock start? I checked the timestamp on my mother's text message, 9:00 p.m. Fine. I'd call her tomorrow afternoon and arrange to meet and answer her questions.

And what about Michael Horvath? Where do I even start? I'd watched him, analyzed his movements, mannerisms, personality traits. He was smart, super-smart, and highly controlled. I'd met people like him before, people with military careers, high-intensity jobs in high-stakes professions. Michael Horvath was more than just a blogger, and was probably an operative, or at least a police informant. But I was too exhausted and hungry for anymore processing right now.

From my bedroom, I'd taken a few pairs of clean underwear and a beach towel. I took another quick shower, enjoying the upgrade from paper towels, and returned to the concrete thinking chair with my folded, wet towel under me. My outlook had improved by about 2%.

"What are you doing, Thea?" I said the words out loud so I could hear my voice. I was a fugitive, avoiding the police, living in a basement on water and pretzels, hiding from killers, and worse, hiding from myself. I got up and hung the wet towel over the shower stall and put my dirty clothes back on, then froze at the *bang-bang-bang* on the basement door.

Other than Fergus, nobody knew I was here.

Nobody except Michael Horvath.

Chapter 32

I moved to a spot just inside the windowless door, naturally no peek-hole, put my ear to it but heard nothing. Those knocks had been deliberate. But if these were the pursuers who ransacked our house and scared my mother, why alert me to their presence? No one knew about this place other than Janelle, Fergus, and now Michael Horvath.

"Fergus?" I said into the crack in the door.

"Yeah, I'm here with Kit. Let us in."

God, I so wasn't in the mood for Kitty tonight. Fergus, if he brought the cribbage board and a deck of cards, maybe. I unlocked and opened the door, and stood aside to let them in.

"Hey."

"Nice place," Kit said with a smirk. Asshole as always.

"Slightly bigger than Harry Potter's cupboard under the stairs." I turned and relocked the door after they entered, assessing their expressions. Fergus was slightly taller than Kit, slightly thinner, and in way better shape. "Miss you," I said, giving him a half-hug, then turned to Kit. "How's it going?"

"Better than you, apparently."

"Why do I smell—"

Fergus opened the door, picked up a pizza box and a six-pack of beer they'd left outside, and brought it in. "Hungry?"

"Starving. So sweet of you guys." And I was starving but company was the last thing I needed right now.

"Have you been crying?" Fergus asked me, touching my chin, and pulling it up so he could see my face.

"Dude, my life's falling apart. So like…yeah."

Fergus and Kit tracked each other in some silent conversation while I put the pizza on a box-table and brought in some paper towels from the bathroom. "Geez, you guys brought me pizza, beer. But how did you know I'd be here right now?" I froze and waited.

They looked at each other again like they were deciding something, Fergus doing that lip thing, where he curled them inward to keep from speaking his mind. "Is your laptop booted up?" Fergus asked.

I pointed to the backpack in the corner.

Fergus glanced at Kit, who nodded.

"Tell her," Fergus said.

"Fucking tell me what?"

"The black-eared rabbit sub-Reddit is tracking you," Kit said.

"What?"

"Sorry. I know that's bad news," Kit's face looked grim. Maybe not an asshole all the time then.

"So that means…what exactly? Are there a set of GPS coordinates that are constantly changing, or a map? Who's doing this, and how?" I asked. Not to mention why.

Fergus saw my phone plugged in on the other side of the room. He picked it up. "Why's there no password on here?" he asked.

"Burner."

"Good."

I stood beside Kit, watching Fergus swipe left, right, up, down, checking my settings.

"What are you doing?"

"Looking for trackers."

I thought about what might have been injected in my ankle but didn't feel like mentioning it now. Maybe because it was another symbol of vulnerability, another thing I couldn't face. Instead I pulled a beer out of the holder and used my shirt to twist off the cap.

"Are you eighteen yet?" Kit joked.

"No, so you've just committed a felony by giving alcohol to a minor." I wondered if that would violate the terms of his parole but maybe I shouldn't mention it. Instead, I took a long sip and held the cold, bubbly brew in my mouth before swallowing. The first sip was always delicious.

"It's a misdemeanor," he corrected me.

"Cool." Fergus set down the phone and plugged it in again. "I have good news and bad news."

"More bad news, excellent." For this, I sat on the floor and pulled open the Valencia Pizza and Pasta box. Fergus knew this was my favorite in the Mission, and right now I needed fortification.

"Good news, please," I said, closing my eyes after the first bite of their pesto pizza. Delicious.

"No tracker?" Kit asked him.

"Nope." Fergus looked at me. "So, the Reddit thread's tracking you but not through your phone."

I stopped chewing. "Guys, cut it out. This is like Jason Bourne shit now." I wiped my mouth on the back of my hand and stood up. "Look at me."

"We are," Fergus said.

"Is it, what, on me somewhere? Where?"

"You're gonna have to take off your clothes," Fergus said.

"All of them," Kit added. Eww.

I clanked the beer down on the concrete floor, rage buzzing in my palms. "For fuck's sake. I didn't think it could get any worse."

I went into the bathroom, pushed the door closed but not all the way, then started chucking out my clothes, one garment at a time. Hoodie, thin t-shirt, cami, bra, all lying in a pile now outside the bathroom door, my dirty clothes right next to the only good food I'd had in a week. I wriggled out of my jeans and felt like burning them, reminded of how much I hate skinny jeans. Underwear, tennis shoes, socks, hair tie.

"There. Happy?" I screeched in a half yell-half cry, leaning cross armed and butt-naked against the bathroom sink, door closed.

"In another context, this could—"

"Shut up, Kit," Fergus and I said in unison. I managed a snicker, somehow reassured by our deep connection, even now.

"What are you looking for?" I bellowed from behind the bathroom door, becoming more unglued by the second. "And how are you gonna find it if you don't know what it looks like?"

"Show it to her," I heard Fergus say.

"Show me what?"

Fumbling around, then a clicking sound, slow clicking then faster clicking, then footsteps. Kit stuck one hand behind the door. He was holding a small device about the size of a thermometer, made of black plastic. It had flashing lights on it.

"A bug sweeper. Where'd you get that?"

We'd watched them used on crime TV shows. I'd seen some tracking devices online that were as small as a pea, even smaller, that were used to track children at daycare, even older people who had a tendency to wander off. Someone could have stuck one in the hem of my shirt. But how could they have accessed it to do that? I searched my brain to rerun my movements over the past few days. I hadn't run into anyone, or been mugged, or drugged or lost consciousness. When could they have planted it? I turned and looked at my face in the mirror. I was sweating and my eyes lately looked permanently bloodshot. But nudity was a reminder of vulnerability, and the mirror was too unbearable. I twisted a lock of hair, the same lock all the time so I'd made it into a Shirley Temple banana curl. My hands fumbled with the chain around my—omg! The locket. Lise, how could you do this to me? I was stuck naked in a three by five foot room with a tracking device literally around my neck. It had to be in the locket. And I had to have stumbled upon some reality TV show. That was the only rational explanation.

"Kind of quiet in there," Kit said, and hadn't answered my question. "You doing okay?"

Fuck Kit and his smarmy innuendo, I knew what he meant by that. "Just waiting for you spy wannabes to finish your geek patrol so I can get dressed."

If I was being tracked, and the tracker wasn't in my phone or my clothes, the locket was the only other explanation, because I'd had it on for three days straight. Then again, they'd been tracking me before that.

Lise gave me her locket, placed it over my head to distract me from one of her minions as he put a bag over my head. So now I knew, through the process of elimination, where the tracker was, and I knew how I'd acquired it. The problem was, what I was gonna do about it here? I didn't want either of them to have to see what I saw on that flash drive. Plus, I'd pretty much incontrovertibly confirmed by now that the locket was worth killing for.

Chapter 33

I was dying to pull it apart and examine the top half, but could that trigger the device? Stop panicking Thea. Breathe and think logically.

- If it was smaller, I could wedge it into a bar of soap if the soap was soft and wet. Naturally, it wasn't.
- I could hide it in the cabinet under the sink, but what if the doors creaked and Kit and Fergus heard me? Would they scan under there anyway?
- A window to toss it outside? No windows down here. Great.

I turned on the faucet, locked the bathroom door and crouched low to see under the sink. Sure enough, there was a depression where I might be able to fit the tracker. If I could even get it out. It all felt so hopeless. There was no time for the careful planning required of something so perilous. I had no tools on me and only seconds left before one of them knocked on the door holding a pile of my clothes. With the faucet still on, I opened the locket paying close attention to the top side. I saw nothing in there. I set down the top on the sink and peered into the bottom half. I pulled out the flash drive and laid that on the sink next to the top. Ah, okay. Under the flash drive was something gold and round, which didn't look at all like the same metal of the locket design. Fuckers. I found you. That had to be it.

I knew Fergus and Kit weren't monitoring the tracker results on a laptop. So they might not know for a few hours what really happened. Thank God my fingernails were a little too long right now. I pulled off one earring and used the sharp end of the French wire to hook the edge of the device. I moved slowly to prevent it from flying across the room. One flick—nothing. Second try and...voila. It moved. By the third flick of the earring, I'd separated it from the locket and emptied it into the palm of my hand. Earring back in my ear, flash drive back in its frame, and the top and bottom pressed together, I pulled the chain back around my neck. In one swift movement, I tossed the tracker into the toilet and flushed.

"Can I have my clothes now please?" I opened the door a crack and stuck out my hand.

"Here." Fergus handed me my shirts, pants, and underwear. I grabbed them without looking out. It was awkward enough.

"Kit's gone?" I asked. He must have left when I flushed the toilet. "Business he had to attend to? Someone needed to be rubbed out, or driving drugs across state lines?"

"Another DSC clue goes live soon. He's gonna check it out and will let us know what he finds."

Clothes on again, I emerged from the bathroom. "So? Anything?" I asked from the doorway, feigning frustration even though once again I'd solved my own problem myself.

Fergus shook his head. "No signal on your clothes anyway. I'm sorry, I don't know how they're tracking you. I could run it over your skin, in case you'd been injected with something?"

"Don't be ridiculous," I said and pulled a beer out of the carton. I passed it to Fergus and he was giving me that look. "What?"

"Nothing. I don't know."

"So, Kit's like, what, exactly?" I planted myself near the pizza box and picked up another slice. Cold. I was no longer hungry anyway.

"He thinks he's trying to help." Fergus sat opposite me on the floor. I wished I could close my eyes and magically transport us to his basement with a cribbage board between us.

"Why do you look...sad right now?"

"You're in trouble, T." Fergus rose and started pacing, hands in his pockets, head low. I knew this body language. "I don't think you realize…"

"What, that every follower of the Dead Sevens game, or club, or whatever the fuck it is can now track my whereabouts? Yes, Fergus, you broke the news to me already."

"Where were you tonight?" he asked in full-fledged interrogation mode, like he expected me to lie, like I was planning to. There was no point anymore.

I took a long sip of the now room temperature beer. "What, you mean you weren't tracking me? Shocker."

"Wait a minute. I don't—"

"I met a man at the library. I went there this morning to do research, I found this guy's blog, I sent him a message to ask a question about it through the Contact link in the blog, and I got an email back five seconds later."

He cocked his head to the side, thinking. "He was at the library? Was he following you?"

"I guess so. He's a journalist who runs a DSC mythology blog. He's some kind of gaming expert or history buff or something."

His brows rose at the mention of gaming.

"His name is Michael Horvath, alright? I'm not holding anything back."

"I know."

"You know what?" I asked.

"I know you were with Michael Horvath."

"Fergus…what the actual fuck? Who is this guy?" I stood and now it was me pacing, in bare feet on the concrete floor. My feet had been freezing all day, and I only just realized it now. Was I so cut off from my body that I could feel discomfort for so long and it didn't register? Would I even feel a gunshot wound right now? More tears, which reminded me I hadn't had enough water today. "I can't—I can't." I stood in the very corner of the room, behind boxes like I was using them as a fort. "I knew you could all track me through the signal my tracker was putting out. Now you're telling me there's a camera on me 24/7??" They weren't words coming out of me now. They'd turned to something between sobs and wailing.

He approached me like you'd approach a rabid dog, two steps at a time. He moved boxes out of the way, but slowly, careful not to make too much noise. His hands pulled the last box away, then reached for my hand and walked me back to the pizza beer encampment. "Come on, right here. Sit on this box, it's warmer than concrete."

I crouched low and sort of crumbled into his lap. He held me. It was the first time I'd felt like a human being in I don't know how long. We felt so connected when I stopped crying, just breathing calmly, his hands stroking my head with a comforting touch I never knew he had. I wanted to tell him about Eve Maddox, about how I was starting to feel about her, and how I'd felt that way about other girls. If I was gonna come out to someone, I always knew it would be him. Tonight was clearly not the right night. As usual, things weren't lining up.

"Michael Horvath isn't just a journalist," he said.

"I know." I sat up and faced him.

"He's a conspiracy theorist and a whistleblower who's served time and started a corporate watchdog company called UnderTalk."

Not all that surprising. "What did you and Kit see on Reddit today about me?"

"The tracker, which you know about."

"What else?"

"A picture of you getting into Michael Horvath's car, and a link to an article about him. It said something about this consortium he's been tracking, and trying to expose for the past few years but gotten nowhere." Fergus checked my face. "Someone wrote into the thread that they think Horvath's using blackearedrabbit to try to flush them out."

"Me? Flush who out?"

He shook his head. "That's all I know for now."

"If Horvath's befriending me as an ally for the purpose of using me, why don't we use him instead? I'm supposed to see him again tomorrow to hear the rest of his story. I'll pump him for information and use it to my advantage."

"How?" he asked.

I told Fergus everything I'd seen in those videos down to each horrifying detail, relayed every blow by blow from my conversation with Horvath, including the mythology about Jeffrey Dade and The

Wharf, even showed him the locket and told him about the tracker, which I'd flushed. It felt so good to finally share the burden. But he'd also told me the cops showed up where he works and questioned him about me. That reminded me that I had to pay Eve Maddox a visit today, lest I ended up in jail. That was the last thing my mother needed to deal with right now.

"I'll get Horvath to tell me what to say to Jeffrey Dade in the text messages, make Dade feel like I'm *his* ally, get him to trust me and maybe meet with me."

"No, T, it's too dangerous. You know nothing about him, either of them."

But I did know something. Michael Horvath said Jeffrey Dade went missing after his friends were killed, but that he didn't believe he killed them.

"Are you tired?" he asked, surveying the room.

I laughed, like a head-back teeth-showing laugh. I was too tired to be tired. "What did you have in mind?"

In two hours, the pizza and beer were gone, all the boxes were opened, bookshelves assembled, and filled with neat rows and stacks of plates, cups, cupholders, stirrers, sugar, napkins, cutlery, paper signs, plastic signs, and a separate nook just for Janelle's marketing materials like business cards and brochures. Janelle was about to be the happiest business owner in San Francisco.

Chapter 34

There were several ways to do this. I decided to call and leave a message for Officer Eve Maddox. She called back twenty minutes later, I spoke politely with her, asked her what time she'd like me to come in and showed up on time at the Mission Police Station on Valencia Street. I'd already botched the first impression thing, but so far my do-over was off to a good start.

When it came to police interrogation, I'd done my research. As a non-white person born of Latino and Pacific Islander parents, I'd seen a hundred demonstrations of the dynamic between police and black and brown people. Even still, I had this sort of subversive way around authority that slipped out as my natural personality. It was somewhere between sarcasm and disdain with a tinge of comedy. Almost like peril activated my sense of humor. But this was totally not the time to look cool or prove myself. Fergus reinforced this on the way here too, that I was two steps from jail, and the cops were just looking for an excuse.

Officer Eve Maddox—so there was that, too. I hadn't told Fergus anything about her, or how I thought I felt about her. Would he figure it out because he knows me so well? Maybe. I might find out later that he already knows. Would it still count as coming out then?

"Miss Riggs, come with me please." A male officer, older, heavyset with thick glasses, escorted me through a set of glass doors, where I followed him to a large, empty room with a small table and two chairs. The building was sparse, with the same brick and dark green paint inside as the signage hanging above the exterior door. I'd seen interrogations like this on TV. My nerves were shot right now and my emotions were all over the place. Fergus had counseled me to conjure an image of something serene and comforting. That little grove of kukui nut trees on the southern edge of Laura Beach west of Majuro would be my focal point. Someone knocked and entered the room.

Whatever stories I'd told myself over the years, about whether I was actually gay or not, were irrelevant now. There was no question.

"Hello," I said without emotion.

Officer Maddox reached her hand out and I shook it, watching her take the chair across from me. Breathe, Thea.

"Remember me?" she asked in a taunting voice. I tried not to laugh because I could draw every detail of her face if I had to.

"Yes," I said. "It's nice to see you."

She smiled, and I think it was genuine surprise on her face. "Well, it's nice to see *you* actually. You've been living on the edge lately, haven't you?"

"Not by choice," I said, determined to give her honest answers. We'd see how far that got me.

"Why don't you explain to me what's been going on." Officer Maddox sat back and crossed her long legs. I guessed she was about thirty, and maybe five foot eight. Her features and skin tone suggested she might be mixed race. Her name, Maddox, sounded English. Focus, Thea. Fergus and I had rehearsed the answer to this question on the way here so I was ready.

"I went over to see my friend Lise Fenning because she invited me, but no one answered the doorbell. I waited a few minutes, then used my key to enter."

"Why'd you have a key to your friend's house?"

"I feed the cat when they're away," I answered quickly. Where had that come from? Lise was allergic to them. Even still, it was a logical reason.

"I didn't see anyone in the house but I heard a noise," I went on. "So I hid and then left out the basement."

"Why the basement?" she asked.

I paused like I was searching my memory. "I was afraid, for some reason. No one was home, that was unusual. Not Lise, not the cook, no one."

"So, you never saw your friend or her mother that night?"

"No." My response, my lie that is, was flawless. Not too abrupt but I answered quickly enough to make it seem like I hadn't edited my thoughts and I made eye contact. "Ever since then, someone's been following me. A man was at my house. He talked to my mother."

"About what?" she asked. Why wasn't she writing anything down in the notebook she brought with her? Because she didn't believe, that's why.

I shook my head. "Nonsense. About some project we were working on together, but I don't know who it was, and there is no project. Have you found anything that might help find Roberta?" I asked, turning the tables. That made me sound eager, nervous, but also that I cared about Roberta, which was true. "I'm feeling very targeted, actually, and I haven't done anything wrong. I just went to my friend's house. Now there are people after me and I don't feel safe." I'd chosen my words carefully. Her pen moved fast across a blank page in her notebook.

Officer Maddox sighed, deciding, I was sure, whether I was full of shit or not. I knew she didn't trust me. "Where's your mother right now?"

"At work this time of day. She's been staying at a neighbor's house the past two nights, after our house was broken into and pretty much trashed."

"Did your mother file a report?" she asked.

"Yes, she came here to the station to do it the next day, not that night. She was too afraid and exhausted from a double shift."

"What does she do?"

"Pediatric nurse at Cal Pacific."

Raised brows, more scribbling. "What do you think they were looking for?" she asked after setting her pen down.

I paused a second and shook my head. "I have no idea."

More writing. "What were you doing two nights ago when I saw you climbing out the window of your house?"

"Getting some clean underwear and my computer. I didn't feel comfortable staying there." I closed my eyes and shook my head. "I still don't." Okay, I was laying it on thick. But I needed to get out of here.

She left, I waited alone in that room for close to an hour before she came back in and stood in the open doorway. "Thank you, Miss Riggs, you can go."

I got up from the table. "Is Roberta okay? Did you find her?" I asked.

"Sorry, I can't comment on an open investigation."

It was only 9:30 a.m. and I'd already skated through a police interrogation and gotten texts from Bharat and Janelle. I asked Fergus to drive me home, search my house for intruders, and wait for me while I washed off the misery of the past two days. I heard him putting the house back together while I toweled off. Clean hair, clean clothes, fresh pot of coffee, and I felt like a million bucks.

"Cribbage?" he asked, shuffling cards at the kitchen table.

"No time," I said. "Aren't you working today?"

"It's Monday, no work till noon. I love Mondays."

"I think you're the only person who's ever said that." We sipped coffee and ate bowls of granola in silence. I'd had to reschedule four tutoring sessions, and my mother had emailed me about my upcoming orientation at San Francisco State. We'd planned to go together. We'd planned to do a lot of things that right now seemed less significant. College, somehow, felt like a door to a future that was no longer mine. I don't know how I felt about that.

"Did you hear from Janelle?" Fergus asked with his mouth full.

"Oh my God, dude," I giggled and showed him her text. "Twenty-five hearts and thirty gratitude emojis. We're both gonna have free coffee there for the rest of our lives."

"I love their What's Going On blend. It's not flavored but a tiny bit sweet. Perfect."

"I'll tell her you said so." My phone vibrated in front of us with a new text. My sunny mood sank when I saw the number. I slowly raised my eyes to Fergus.

"That's him?"

"Kompromat." My blackmailer. Fergus and I spent half of last summer reading spy books and learning lingo. *Kompromat* was used by Russian intelligence to control targets with potentially dangerous material. I was the target, and now that photo would be the death of me.

"You really don't think this is Michael Horvath?"

"One of these messages came in while I was talking to him at the library." I remembered our conversation at the Hotel Cartwright, still wondering about the shots fired downstairs in the lobby. Maybe it had nothing to do with us. "Besides, he already identified himself as Jeffrey Dade."

"Are you gonna read it?"

I picked up the phone, resenting the interruption of a perfectly, wonderfully normal morning. Long sigh. "It says *Go deeper.* I don't know what that means. I'm waiting to hear from Michael Horvath and—"

"Thea."

"What?"

"Do you think he's, Horvath I mean, using you to get to Dade, or to snuff out that organization he's been looking for?"

I disappeared into my room to grab socks and running shoes. "Why would he need me to do anything?" I yelled. "If he's such an accomplished operative, I'm just a bewildered, good-for-nothing kid."

Fergus scrunched up his face at me when I returned to the kitchen. "Not to me."

I tapped my chest with my fist. I knew he meant it, too. I grabbed my backpack and stood at the door. "I only just met Horvath. He seems genuine, but I have no idea what his real agenda is. I'll tell you this though. If he is intending to use me to get to that syndicate, or whatever they are, I'm gonna turn that on its side and use him so I get to them first."

"Dayum, girl."

"Fuck, yeah. I want my life back. I need to know what I've

stumbled onto. But more than that—"

"Roberta," he nodded, reading my mind.

"That, and I need to know how my investigation into her death has now become a new thread in the Dead Sevens game. I don't think it was random that I ended up on the landing of the Fenning estate right under one of their cameras."

He lowered his head and took a step closer. "You think it was all a setup to pull you in?"

"I'll get back to you on that."

Chapter 35

I could tell my mom wasn't here because her robe wasn't hanging from the hook on the back of our bathroom door. I loved that robe, all her robes actually. There was something clean and maternal, almost lemony about the way she smelled, the way her clothes smelled. I was dying to put on that robe, to remind myself that she had my back, that she was my protector no matter what happened, no matter how old I was. That I was safe as long as she was nearby. No robe today. Seemed symbolic.

On Mondays, she worked a half day because Sundays were always double shifts at the California Pacific Medical Center. Fergus dropped me off at the ER entrance so he could make a few deliveries before his noon shift started at Peets.

I stopped at the Starbuck's in the lobby, then took the elevator to the third floor. Right off the elevator, a man carrying a ginormous flower arrangement almost tanked into me.

"Whoa, sorry about that."

"No problem," I said, swerving to avoid a Bird of Paradise in my eye. It was a sign; I believed in signs.

I approached the desk of the third-floor nurse's station and saw someone I didn't recognize. "Is Nurse Carmen Riggs available? I'm her daughter."

The woman sitting at reception paged her, but I knew she wouldn't answer a page if she was with a patient. That was just her way. She also didn't keep her cell phone with her at all times, unlike 99% of the human population. It stayed in her locker because she felt cell phones depleted our quality of life.

I heard footsteps behind me and turned quickly. A bear hug smacked into me, thrusting my body into the edge of the reception desk. "Thank you, God," she said, squeezing me hard. She placed her hands on each side of my face and looked in my eyes, then touched my forehead with hers.

"I'm okay, Mom. See? I'm fine." I handed her a coffee.

She looked at the cup but didn't take it right away, just stayed there staring down at it. I knew then how this situation, a situation I caused, was unraveling her.

"Can we talk somewhere?" I asked.

She started down the hallway toward the double doors, beyond which were the Family Rooms. Comfortable sofas, matching rugs, relaxing art work. She picked one on the right, empty, and closed the door. I sensed I might be in for a second interrogation of the day. I told her the same story I'd told Officer Maddox, except lately the weight of my sexuality secret was becoming too heavy, along with all the other secrets I was holding. The conversation started out fine and quickly devolved into a shouting match about how I didn't care about college. She was right.

Michael Horvath's text came in while we were talking, actually shouting. Thank God I resisted the urge to pull it out and answer it because I think she would have strangled me. I kissed her cheek before walking out and closing the door behind me, knowing our little talk had probably done more harm than good. Hopefully I'd convinced her it was safe to go home at least, and sure I'd keep thinking about that looming orientation date coming up. But I can't go to college just to please my mother. I have to want it myself too.

Back at the hospital elevators, I checked my phone. The text read: *Flowers.* Just flowers and nothing else. What is this? I checked and it definitely came from Michael Horvath's cell phone number this time.

I wrote back two question marks and waited. No status dots, nothing to indicate that he was responding. Just flowers. Well, wasn't it a coincidence, then, that a guy carrying a huge flower bouquet almost crashed into me near the elevators? I went back in my mind to that moment, and it had almost seemed like he intended to crash into me. I checked again, but no follow up texts.

Okay. I retreated down the hallway and paused to look around the third floor. I tried to remember the delivery guy but I'd only seen his straight brown hair when I looked beyond the bouquet. I stopped back at the reception desk.

"Did you by chance just see a guy carrying a huge flower arrangement? He was here about fifteen minutes ago."

"I saw him get into the elevator. I think he thought this was the second floor."

"Thank you." Second floor. Right.

The door to the fire exit was across from reception. I opened it and tore down the stairs. The second floor looked the same as the third, but with white tile instead of carpet. I scanned the floor looking for flowers. Left corridor? No. Right corridor, also no. Another reception desk. This was already getting old.

"Did you see a guy carrying a huge flower arrangement a few minutes ago?" I asked a woman at the workstation on the left. It took her a few seconds to look up from her paperwork.

"Who are you?" she asked with irritation.

"Um, Thea Riggs. I'm looking for a—"

"For your flowers, yes. I heard you. A guy tried to deliver them here but I said I didn't know anyone by that name, and he—"

"Wait." I shook my head. "He said they were for me?"

"Well, yeah. Isn't that why you're looking for them?" She laughed, then looked at her computer.

"Did you see where he went?"

"Elevators. Down I think."

Now how could she know that he was going down if she was sitting behind a desk? Was everyone out to get me? Or maybe the elevator chimes were different for up versus down. And maybe I was literally losing my mind. I thanked her and waited at the elevators, heading back to the lobby.

The doors opened. The guy was standing in front of me.

"Ohh! I'm Thea Riggs. Are those flowers for me?"

"Full circle. I should've given them to you the first time. Sign here, please," the guy said, stepping back from the elevators against the wall. He had a clipboard with a pen. But when I picked it up, there wasn't a delivery manifest on it or an empty page where I would sign. It was a note folded in half with my name on it. I pretended to sign the sheet then carefully pulled the note off and stuck it up my sleeve.

"Thank you so much." I struggled my arms around the sprawling arrangement.

This time I went back up to the third floor and returned to the reception desk. "Could you let Nurse Carmen Riggs know that Thea left these for her?"

"Her lucky day, huh?"

When I got in the elevators again, alone this time, I opened the note. It read, "Drum Bridge, Japanese Tea Garden, 10:00 p.m."

I already knew the Tea Garden at Golden Gate Park closed at 5:45 because Fergus and I had gotten kicked out by security before. I also knew that after dark you could jump the gate on the Presidio side. They usually had a security guard roaming around. After my meeting with Officer Maddox this morning, I needed to be careful. Unfortunately, careful wasn't my best thing.

What was Michael Horvath doing that required such secrecy? I thought about going to The Cartwright again, but if he sent me this note through a flower delivery service, there had to be a reason. Things were escalating and I needed protection. Maybe he did, too.

There was a courtyard between the hospital's east and west wings with benches set along each side about ten feet apart. One of them was shaded by a tall tree. I sat and called Fergus.

"Dude, I know you're working, sorry. I have a quick question."

"I'm between jobs, actually. What's up?"

That meant he was leaving Peets to go to his delivery job. I told him about the flower delivery and the note.

"You're like living in a spy movie right now."

"I know, and not in a good way."

"Where are you meeting him?"

"Tea Garden at ten o'clock tonight. I was thinking that maybe I might need backup."

"Meaning me, or—"

"Actually, I was thinking Kit."

"You know he has a thing for you, right?"

"Eww." I shook it off. "This is a business transaction. Doesn't he perform services like this for hire? I'd like to hire him to give me back-up tonight, make sure I can get into the garden after dark, keep security from finding me, and help me get out of there in one piece."

"Yep. Sounds like a perfect job for Kit." There was a downward lilt to his voice, so I knew he didn't like it. I didn't either. "You want me to call him?"

I sighed. "I'll call him."

"I should tell you, Kit won't take money from you."

Long exhale. "What does that mean?"

"Think about it," Fergus said.

"Oh, like I'll owe him favors for the rest of my life instead?"

"Pretty much. That's how he rolls."

Fuck. That was the last thing I needed. "Let me think about this."

"Keep me posted."

Plan B was Bharat. I opened our last exchange. Shit. He'd sent me four texts, which I hadn't yet addressed. *Hey Bharat, I'm so sorry that I couldn't respond. I hope I didn't worry you. Are you busy tonight?*

I saw the little dots right away. Finally, someone responding to my texts. *Not too busy for you, Princess. More surveillance?*

No, tonight's assignment is a security detail. Up for it?

Hell, yes. Just say where and when.

Chapter 36

Another problem—my tutoring students. One of them had exams scheduled for next week, and the other two had IEPs and needed more, not less, help. At least I called their parents with a phony story that I'd been sick and hoped to be back to my normal schedule next week. Was there anyone I wouldn't lie to right now?

Relieved that I'd booked Bharat for later tonight, I retreated to Janelle's beautifully private basement to think. She long-hugged me on my way to her back room, which told me she was a) worried about me, and b) also worried about herself and the café. My hands stuffed with another drink tray and bag of food, I couldn't wait to see the newly-organized store room in daylight. At the bottom of the stairs, I found an old, leather club chair that looked too wide to even get down the narrow staircase, and a pull-out sofa bed made up with a comforter and pillows. She even brought a dinged-up bedside table with a drawer. Omg, Janelle. I knew these had probably come from Goodwill but I wanted to run upstairs and thank her all the same. Instead, I stood numbly at the bottom of the stairs. What the hell was I doing here?

The too-thin mattress was firm but not uncomfortable. Even the chair reclined, and she'd bought me a new yoga mat. I didn't know enough about yoga to do it on my own without a class or a video, but it was all an awesome surprise. After texting Janelle a hundred heart emojis, I propped myself up in bed with the pillows, laptop on my lap, fed, hydrated, and tried to enjoy the safe privacy. I knew it wouldn't last long.

I checked the Where's Edgar thread on Reddit. Another Dead Sevens clue had been dropped last night, like Fergus said. According to the thread stats, no one had solved it yet. I stared back at the blackearedrabbit thread, checked for new uploads, and paced the room a few times. Someone somewhere was watching me, but more than that—tracking and monitoring my movements. Kit and Fergus hadn't found the tracker on my clothes, but I'd found it—and flushed it. Should be clean now. Or was there another tracker somewhere? Time would tell.

Alright, here we go. I put my hands on the keyboard and double clicked #blackearedrabbit/r. Almost immediately, my phone buzzed. Saved by the bell. It was my blackmailer, whom Michael Horvath believed could be the elusive Jeffrey Dade. I read the text from my notification banner: *They have her.*

I called Fergus. "Hey, are you busy?" I asked from my newly-designed crash pad. I told him about Jeffrey's text.

"How do you know it's Jeffrey Dade, I mean for sure?" he asked. "Wouldn't the *he* be him? In which case he would have said *I*. And the *her* has to be Roberta, right? So that means they're storing her dead body somewhere? This is giving me a headache."

I couldn't remember the last time I hadn't had one. "Maybe Jeffrey's trying to tell me that there's another player I need to know about, and that player has Roberta."

"Maybe," he said. "I don't know. Normal logic doesn't apply here."

"Bharat's going with me tonight to Golden Gate Park," I said, knowing he'd be asking.

"Probably a better idea than Kit. Then again…"

I knew what he meant. Kit had weapons, he knew how to use them, and he also had other resources at his disposal that Bharat, a software engineer and Uber driver, probably didn't. "Hopefully it won't come to that," I said. "Michael Horvath said he has something he wants to give me. I'm leaving soon. Keep your phone on."

"Yep. Let me know what happens."

I checked the time. Bharat would be here in two minutes. Game on.

The night air felt damp and heavy, fog cloaking most of the bridge and the top of the water. It somehow made the scent of wisteria from the gardens behind me even stronger.

There were several ways into the Japanese Tea Garden. Shuttle, buses, but Fergus and I had always gone by way of the DeYoung Museum and walked the southern path past the music concourse. For tonight, especially if my pursuers knew Bharat's car, our best bet was street parking on 18th Avenue and walking down Park Presidio to the gardens. The gate was easy to climb over, and the gardens were pitch black under a cloudy sky.

"This is both good and bad," Bharat said. "Good because it's too dark to be seen, bad because I can't see."

His quips and constant commentary somehow made the whole situation a little less bleak, and his voice three feet behind me reminded me I wasn't completely alone out here. I followed the shape of the road as my eyes adjusted. "I see it," I said.

"The bridge? I can't see anything."

"About fifty feet ahead." I turned around. When he caught up to me, I set my hands on his blocky shoulders. "Stay here," I whispered. "I can only assume we're being watched right now. I want to be the only one seen on that bridge."

"Or under it," he suggested.

"Isn't there a creek down there?"

"There may be, but I know the banks on each side are a popular make-out spot."

I snickered. "I like that image a lot better than meth dealers. I'm off. Can you see me okay?"

"Starting to. I'll be twenty feet away if anything happens. What's going to happen again?"

I stopped and walked back to him. "It's a handoff. That's all."

"Godspeed, Princess." He grabbed and kissed my forehead.

"How exactly do you know about that make-out spot, Bharat?"

"That information's available on a need-to-know basis."

Thankfully I'd remembered to wear tennis shoes instead of my noisy flip flops. Per Bharat's suggestion, I checked out the area under the bridge: no one there so far. A security guard was supposed to monitor the grounds after closing time, but in all my visits here I'd never seen one.

Texting Bharat might be a bad idea because of the light from my phone. Had I been more organized, a walkie talkie two-way transceiver would have been handy. Fergus had one. Right now, my primary job was to be invisible. That meant standing on the top of the bridge was out of the question. I kept my eared tuned to detect either the sound or vibration of footsteps. So far, nothing, and it had to be just about ten o'clock. A compromise included a spot at the bottom of the bridge partially concealed by bamboo.

It was dark, I was on time and in position. Ready to roll. And nobody's here. WTF?

I moved under the bridge to warn Bharat about roaming security guards and returned to my spot.

The clip clop of heavy footsteps echoed from under the bridge. Someone was approaching from the west side at a steady clip, not trying to conceal their entrance either. That told me something. I peered out seeing the shape of a man, medium height. It didn't look like the size and shape of Michael Horvath. I could see his outline on the bridge, black leather jacket and a baseball cap. The man stood firm, looking at the sky, no doubt waiting for me. Could be Horvath, but my gut told me no. It was too dark to tell. I cleared my throat.

"I have something for you," a man said in a clear, neutral voice I didn't recognize. I so hoped Bharat was close enough to hear the exchange. Definitely not Horvath. Dammit.

"Who are you?" I asked.

"A messenger."

"Where's Horvath?"

"I don't know who that is. I was asked to make a drop, plain and simple."

"Asked or paid?"

"Irrelevant."

"Fine."

"What's your name?" the man asked. "To ensure security."

"Roberta," I blurted.

He didn't move at first, then slowly moved down the bridge and stood a foot from me holding a large manila envelope. He tossed it on the ground, then retreated into the thick darkness.

My heart drummed in my chest as I tried to steady my breathing. I hadn't picked up the envelope. Wait one more minute to be safe. His footsteps faded as I counted back from a hundred. I bent down and picked up the envelope, feeling the contents through the paper. It felt empty. Fitting. All this for nothing.

My phone rang.

"Hey." Bharat. Thank God. "Are you okay?"

"Yeah, let's get out of here."

We sat side-by-side in the front seat of Bharat's stealthy black car, engine off, watching our surroundings. He'd found a perfect spot for spectating. I told him about the exchange, and lowered my head onto his dash.

"I don't get it. Why did you tell him you were Roberta Fenning? I thought you said she was dead."

"It just came out." I stayed quiet while the thoughts congealed. There was still so much we didn't know, so many leaps.

"Who was that man?" he asked. "He wasn't your contact, right? Do you know him?"

I let Bharat continue with his questions while I moved deeper inside, as if my mind was a cave and there were answers beckoning me. My mother said assumptions get you in trouble. Grandma Irene, Tata, believed your body can know things long before your mind understands why. That's what was happening lately. I was *feeling* answers right now, but there was no proof. "The messenger didn't seem to know either me or Roberta," I said.

"Okay, but what does that mean?"

"I don't know why, but I think it means Michael Horvath is dead."

Chapter 37

I had no proof of this other than my intuition, but why else would someone show up instead of him? They could have only known about this appointment through Michael.

"Can you just drive, Bharat? Somewhere? Anywhere."

"Onward then."

I felt numb watching the fleeting specks of San Francisco's night life, like I was barely even part of this world anymore. The Thea Riggs I'd known all my life was slipping away. And Michael Horvath, my intrepid ally—I had no proof that he was dead of course, but I felt it.

I opened the envelope once we were on 101 North heading toward Marin. "Nothing written on the outside," I narrated, using the light from my phone. "The flap is closed only with the metal prongs, not glued shut."

"What does that tell you, my dear Watson?"

"This is not a murder mystery dinner theater," I sighed, sort of hoping he didn't hear the unfiltered protest. "People are dying."

"I meant no disrespect to anyone. Alive or dead."

"Sherlock Holmes does make it all a little less horrible, I admit."

"Haste," he explained. "That's a word they use in all the Granada episodes I've seen. Someone put this envelope together quickly. If you lick the flap—"

"Lick the flap? You mean run your tongue along the toxic chemicals? People do that?"

"If you do, that creates another layer of security for the contents, taking the recipient just a bit longer to access the contents. They didn't do that."

I turned the envelope in my hands while considering this, then unclasped the prongs and shined my phone light inside. There was a yellow-lined legal pad sheet folded in half. I pulled it out, unfolded it; something was written in very small script. I aimed my head down and recited the scrawled words:

They're after me
Not much time
Left something for you
Check school email

Interesting, since I hadn't given that email address to anybody. If this was Horvath, someone had obviously taken his phone, but allowed him one last indulgence to send a message before they killed him? Not likely. I read the message to Bharat.

"What do you want to do?" Bharat asked. "Can you check that email from home? Do they have trackers on your computer?"

I hadn't even thought of that, because I hadn't given Horvath my school email address. He didn't even know about school. "I can do it from another computer and wipe my browsing history afterward. If I had another computer."

"Mine's in back under my seat. Be my guest."

"You're a lifesaver, Bharat."

"I am rather wonderful, aren't I?"

I just loved this guy. Sure enough, I felt the handle of a messenger bag under the driver's seat in the back.

"The system password's JennyBenny, just like it sounds." He turned to me. "My kids."

"Okay. I need wifi."

"Hey Siri," he announced like a game show host. "Find me the closest restaurant that's open now."

I was already looking on my phone. "There's nothing up here," I said. "Burlingame has a Leann's Café open 24-hours, probably has wifi too."

"Opposite direction. How about—"

"Got it. Jack in the Box in San Rafael...well, near San Rafael. Open twenty-four-hours, and their website says they have wifi."

Amazing how enticing something like Jack in the Box seems when you have no other options. Bharat pulled into the empty lot, drove around the white and red building so we could see if lights were on inside, then rolled out to the street again to turn back into the drive-thru lane. A sign facing outward read, "Lobby Only". He stayed there reading the menu, then parked thirty feet away.

"You're seriously hungry?" I asked, surprised he could think about food.

He patted his belly. "As you can see, I'm always hungry. As for you, I'll bet you haven't had a square meal in—"

"I'm good. You know why I'm here."

"Yes indeed, but they'll be more likely to leave us alone out here if we've supported their business."

Okay, he had a point. While we waited for his four-course meal, I unzipped the laptop bag and opened his machine. The power button was in a strange place. "I'm impressed," I commented when it booted up quickly. That either meant he had a super-fast processor, or it could also mean he had almost nothing stored on it.

Bharat got out of the car to pick up the order, while I glassed the parking lot again. He returned with two white bags.

"If I searched through your browsing history right now, would I find—"

"What, porn? Are you kidding? I have a four and a seven-year-old. Besides, I'm not that type," he added.

I was in no position to judge him, or anyone else for that matter. I got out of the car and climbed in the backseat, where I had more room to stretch out with the laptop on my lap. His computer searched for the Jack in the Box wifi network. There, unsecured but better than nothing.

"Bharat, can I ask you something?"

"Other than my browsing history? Sure." He'd started in on a chicken sandwich and fries.

"I don't mean to snoop into your personal life, but I was wondering why you aren't home with your family."

He let out a long sigh. "It's a long story, Thea, and we're all escaping something. Aren't we?"

"Are you divorced?"

"Almost."

I knew it. "Sorry to hear that. Do you get to see your kids?"

"Yes, but only because my mother-in-law adores me. She's heartbroken that she raised such a shrew of a daughter."

"That bad?"

"Horrible. It was an arranged marriage, typical for my culture. On paper we were a wonderful match. She's terribly smart and terribly gorgeous." He sighed. "And funny! Seems perfect for me, right? Unfortunately, she's just not very nice. After the babies were born, she became even worse. And I became, I don't know, redundant." His voice trailed off, and he resumed his attack on the sandwich.

"I can't log in."

"What exactly are you logging into?"

"I'm going to SFSU in the fall, three weeks from now. They already set up our email accounts. It's not taking my password."

"Have you ever used it before?" he asked, and I remembered he's a software engineer.

"Yeah."

"Take your time and try it again."

I did, one character at a time. This time it worked. I opened the mail icon on the portal's homepage. It came up slowly. Three messages, two of them from the Office of Student Engagement, and one from an unknown source. It scared me I'd never told Michael Horvath anything about school—where I'd been accepted, when I was going, and certainly not my email address. How could he have known this? Because he was an intelligence operative. I clicked the email.

It was from a Google email account with a long string of numbers after the word Google. The subject was *Bread Crumbs*. Interesting symbolism. In the body of the email was *Ferry Building, Terminal 2, #1179, 19-44-38.*

Did the Ferry Building at the San Francisco Embarcadero even have lockers? If Horvath left me something, of course I'd send Kit. Not because he's expendable, necessarily, but because he's fearless and crazy. Another thing—Kit liked the appearance of being in charge. So he'd probably assign one of his underlings for the pickup. A leadership opportunity. I did a Google image search on Ferry Building lockers, nothing. But I found a YouTube video of someone surveying a row of lockers.

"Okay, I got something. There are lockers in Ferry Building Terminal 2, and looks like he gave me the locker number and combination."

"What are you picking up?"

"I have no idea. Wait, there's an attachment." Darkness filled my chest again, as I thought of those videos. Not again. I watched Bharat wipe his mouth with a napkin and crumple up his bags of sin. Alright, here we go. I double-clicked the attachment and a video player opened on Bharat's computer. "It's a video. You might want to see this," I said. It took a minute to load.

"Are you sure you want to open that?" he asked.

"I'm sure I don't, but he sent it to me for a reason."

"I'm coming back there, I want to see this." He got out, walked around the car, and climbed in beside me in the back.

I'd already briefed him on the last set of Michael Horvath videos from the library. I remembered the messenger at the tea garden. I looked up into Bharat's eyes. "Michael Horvath may have died because of this video," I said. The player still hadn't opened.

"Let's hope not."

We were sitting side-by-side in the backseat staring at the same screen holding his computer on my lap. It must have looked odd, the two of us. Even suspicious. I moved the touchpad; the player finally started rolling. I turned up the volume but realized there was no sound.

"What in holy hell is that?" he asked, leaning into the screen.

"A party," I explained. "Most of the other videos I saw were of this same party, or maybe the same type, but on a different night." I pointed to the screen. "Everyone here wears the same long, black robe and different masks."

"No one is without a mask?" he asked.

"No."

"Who are these people?"

Whoever was filming this, presumably Michael Horvath, paid close attention to certain elements, zooming in to show them in finer detail, like the long table Roberta Fenning had been lying on. I recited the details to Bharat as the film kept going.

"This must be something important," I said, the camera moving from a crowd of guests to another part of the large room—a line in the back with two people behind a long table. The camera zoomed in, but it didn't seem like the videographer was using much discretion. Maybe they were an invited guest?

"What are they doing? Let me get my reading glasses. Be right back." Bharat climbed out.

Five seconds later I heard, "Yes, Officer. Certainly."

Chapter 38

Fuck. Police? Bharat retrieved his license and registration for the officer with a cheerful vibe that was certain to fool no one.

"What are you doing out here in the middle of the night, sir?" the officer asked.

Bharat wove his string of bullshit mentioning the 24-hour wifi. I apparently had a paper due tomorrow for summer school, and our wifi crashed at home. Freaking genius, because now I'd be able to sit here working while he talked our way out of this.

I watched the images in the video player realizing what I was seeing finally: it was a close-up view of someone behind a desk holding a long, metal tool, about six inches, shiny chrome, and pushing it into the top of each person's hand, where it left a slight red mark. After which, the recipient received some sort of voucher. I'd had a glimpse of this in the library, the day I met Michael Horvath. The cameraman zoomed in on the voucher showing an image of... omg, a man on a surfboard riding a lightning bolt—the signature image of the Dead Sevens Game. What??

"How are you doing, sweetie?" Bharat. Now I was his daughter. God help me.

"Dad, don't call me that. I'm seventeen," I said with my grumbly teenager voice. Or was that my normal voice? The officer stepped closer and peered into the car. "It makes me sound like a toddler," I added.

I don't know why I expected a fat, balding officer to stride over to the car with a booming voice. This man looked more like someone I'd see at the gym. He was wearing a police jacket but not a full officer's uniform. Interesting. I made sure not to look directly up at him, because it occurred to me that maybe he wasn't a police officer after all.

I kept my eyes on the screen but my antenna up. I also checked all around the car—the lot was still empty. Bharat continued schmoozing until the cop walked back to his squad car and drove off. I video-called Fergus. I knew he had an early meeting. I also knew he kept his phone literally inches from his face at night.

"Mmm. What? You okay?" he mumbled.

"Sit up so you can watch something," I said.

"You're video calling me when I'm sleeping. You really want me to owe you one of these?" He used his elbows to prop up. "This is punishable by death."

"Sorry."

"You will be." I heard him rustling sheets and pillows. "Go ahead. What am I looking at? Where are you? At Janelle's?"

"Don't ask."

"All the better."

I positioned the phone facing my screen and started the video at the closeup of a robed figure pulling out his arm, getting his hand pricked with something, then the closeup of the voucher so Fergus could see the insignia."

"Holy shit play that back again." Fergus mumbled. I replayed it. "That's the—"

"I know. Keep watching and tell me what you see." I advanced the recording, which now had a highly-magnified closeup of the device that was being used to stamp people's hands, running in slo-mo. At one point it was frame-by-frame."

"Wait wait wait wait wait, back that up," he said. I did and ran that same segment again. "That looks like a skin sampling tool."

"Skin sampling." I whispered. "For—"

"DNA sampling." He was sitting up, eyes wide.

I stopped breathing for a moment, not like a puzzle piece fell into place, but like one piece of it suddenly morphed into a completely new puzzle. I realized we might be looking at everything the wrong way. Maybe Michael Horvath and Jeffrey Dade were just pawns in a larger scheme.

"Oh my God, Fergus."

"Run that last bit again," Fergus said. It showed a closeup of not the front, but of the side of the medical device—a metal, long-handled holder with a needle on the end.

"I see it," I said, something embossed in the metal. "It looks like the letters IG."

"Whoa."

"What?"

He was pulling a t-shirt over his head with one hand. "I might know what this is."

"You've seen the IG emblem before?" I asked.

"No. Not the emblem embossed on metal. But I recognize the letters together, and the type of letters too, the font they use for that brand."

"Where have you seen it?" I asked, watching Bharat return to the driver's seat and start the engine. "Fergus," I said, to Bharat pointing at my phone.

"Sangstrom Hughes," Fergus said.

"What is that?" I didn't recognize the name.

"You know my delivery job?"

"Delivering documents to law firms and stuff?"

"Also, medical supply companies, like Sangstrom Hughes." His eyes widened. "Which I think is a subsidiary of IG."

I brought Bharat up to speed, then my phone buzzed with a text...my blackmailer. I closed my eyes.

"Who's texting you this time of night?" Fergus asked.

"Blackmailer. The one who saw me in Roberta's house. He—I—oh my God."

"What?" Fergus asked. Bharat watched me closely.

Michael Horvath is dead. I read it a few times to make sure I was seeing clearly.

Numb, I held out the phone to Bharat, who put his hand over his mouth. I aimed it at the computer screen.

"It's too small, I can't see it," Fergus said.

I couldn't speak, suddenly. "Michael Horvath—" was all I could get out.

Bharat lowered his head. "I don't know what kind of *Stranger Things* episode we're in right now, but we should get out of here."

Just what I was thinking. "The people behind this, whatever this is, are they, like, doctors, researchers, financiers? I'm trying to get the bigger picture here but I'm not seeing it. Michael Horvath has the big picture and—"

Bharat nodded. "Had."

"And look what happened to him."

Fergus' dark eyes blinked back in a fast rhythm, his brain cycling through the facts. I felt numb, too numb to speak, but I needed both he and Bharat to know what I knew for the extra backup. I rushed Fergus through the Tea Garden update, the envelope, and the email, still keeping my eyes wide open around the car. Bharat fidgeted in the front seat.

"You can't go to the Ferry Building," Fergus said. "It's too dangerous."

"I know. I'm gonna send Kit."

"T, I already told you the deal with him. You can't—"

"Fine, Fergus. I'll owe a favor to a mob guy. They ransacked my house, they fucking scared my mom, and they killed Michael Horvath because he was on to them and got too close to whatever truth they're trying to hide."

"They? You don't have a clue who that is. Do you?"

My eyes roved around the car interior, to Fergus digitized on the laptop screen, wind bending the trees sideways outside. Time slowed. Michael Horvath was dead. Something clicked inside me. "This is war."

Fergus went back to sleep. I had Bharat drive me to Linnea Caffe. He drove and I daydreamed, feeling like my world was a little smaller. Seventeen for a few more weeks, I hadn't seen much death in my life so far, except Roberta and of course my beloved Rudy. Could it be a lie? Could Horvath be still alive? Maybe someone was trying to scare me, or throw me off the path. I was onto something much bigger than an internet game or even a dead real estate agent. I felt the truth of it like a dark shadow in my bones. Something I hadn't looked for, something that didn't want to be found but had somehow found me.

I sat up.

"Hey, are you okay back there? Crawl up here to the front seat, I want to keep my eye on you."

"You're a good friend, Bharat. I'm less conspicuous back here. Besides, I'm working on something."

"I'm almost afraid to ask."

Chapter 39

Bharat dropped me off at Linnea Caffe under protest, not wanting to leave me alone. I waited until I was secure in Janelle's basement before opening the text message, re-reading the news of Michael Horvath. Enough is enough. It was time for a response. Here goes nothing.

Time to come out from the shadows, I typed in response. *Who are you?*

You'll find out soon enough.

What proof do you have that Horvath is dead? Because you killed him?

I'm no killer.

Never? Or just lately?

No response, no little typing dots.

What do you want from me, other than wasting my time, and posing as some kind of benefactor? I've had enough masks.

I know you've seen them. I know what he showed you. Believe me, it's just the tip of the iceberg.

Horvath had made that same comment. *Can we meet and talk like civilized human beings and not rely exclusively on technology to deceive each other?*

    Tomorrow. Be careful.

    Of what?

    In the shadows, you're safe from predators, but not from yourself.

    I had no idea what that meant, and I was too tired for riddles. *You still haven't told me who you are.*

    You already know.

    A metal bar from the sofa bed frame dug into my spine every time I turned. I'm not sure I slept at all. Sometime in the early morning, a text came in from Brody. No message, just a link to a Reddit page. God, not again. But something had changed, something inside me. I no longer felt afraid to look. They'd killed Michael Horvath. How much worse could it get? Half-awake, I clicked the link to a thread:

BATMAN IS DEAD

> Psychology professor, Yale graduate and noted Game Theorist, Michael Horvath found dead, shot execution-style under Golden Gate Bridge

    The Yale part didn't surprise me, neither did the psychology professor. And game theorist...that made sense only now. I shuddered at the image – his bloodied face and matted hair. Someone, presumably his killer, had photographed this man's corpse and posted it on Reddit. Maybe it was a professional hit and this photo was proof. Or maybe it was a message. What kind of a world was this?

    Hey, I wrote back to Brody. *Do you know who posted this?*

    I did. I watched it happen. You can look up the account and view the profile.

    What a lovely thing to wake up to. I'd get back to Brody later. Right now, I needed coffee. I threw on a hoodie and climbed Janelle's stairs to peer out. The place was full but no one looked suspicious. I winked at Janelle and she nodded back silently.

Meanwhile, my hair in a bun at the top of my head felt hot, and somehow heavy like it was a weight I no longer wanted to carry around anymore. Oh my God, the unthinkable realization sliced through me. Was I ready to cut my Moana hair? My mother would have a stroke. I'd only had it cut a handful times my whole life because it was my identity, my power and personality and, in some way, a link to my Pacific Islander culture. I couldn't live without it. Could I?

Back downstairs, I turned on my laptop and brought up three browser windows—Google Chrome, Chrome with an incognito window, and Duckduckgo. I'd been scheduled to meet with Michael Horvath so he could finish the rest of his story with more information I needed, but now that was no longer possible. And until I deployed Kit to retrieve whatever he'd left me, I was on my own. I had to figure all this out instead of constantly being ten steps behind. People around me were dying. I had a feeling there might be more.

Already needing a refill, I got to the top of the stairs and stood in the open doorway. Two cops in uniform by the street-facing windows, shit. I disappeared into the stairwell. Soon Janelle knocked on the door trim holding a cup.

"You're a saint," I said.

"What's going on, T?" She had taken to calling me T when she heard Fergus do the same in the café. I liked how she felt comfortable doing this, though today it came out as the third degree. Of course it would; I was living in her storeroom, attracting police like flies to sugar. I had a couple of choices: tell her everything and risk her kicking me out for safety reasons, or tell her nothing knowing she'd be assuming the worst. A compromise seemed the most sensible idea. I just couldn't think of one.

"Have you done something?" she asked.

I took the top off the coffee cup and downed a long sip, both of us standing awkwardly near the stairs. She'd crossed her arms. Now or never. "I saw something, by accident, that no one was supposed to see." I paused and she didn't move. "As if that's not a big enough problem, someone knows that I saw, and they're trying to silence me. I know who they are and I know how to stay in the shadows. I just don't know yet what it all means or why I'm such a potential threat. That's what I'm researching down here in this safe space you've made for me."

Now she shifted her feet and slid her hands into the pockets of loose, black cargo pants. "I like you, Thea," was all she said, all she had to say. Then she headed back upstairs.

In her minimalist way, she'd conveyed concern and warning. I was about to get thrown out of here. Time for Plan C.

Still feeling like all the answers were buried in the Reddit threads, I dug further and found a post on the history of the Dead Sevens game. There were references to a syndicate spelled with a capital S. Noteworthy. I searched for r/DSC/syndicate and found nothing, but when I tried r/DeadSevens/syndicate, I found an unrelated thread with references to Dead Sevens. One post, by username *rabbitrose,* asking if there could be a possible connection between the Dead Sevens Club and the Syndicate. Bingo. There were eight replies, seven of them upvoted. I zoomed in on the screen to get a better look. One comment suggested that the creators of DSC were actually members of the Syndicate, using it as a CIA or NSA recruitment exercise to cultivate a younger, more technically adept workforce. Someone else commented that it was a way the government could get away with paying their employees less. It all seemed possible now.

So, if DSC was run by this Syndicate, whoever they were, they obviously knew about Jeffrey Dade, his original group of seven, and Roberta who leased them their apartments and witnessed what happened to them. What if this Syndicate was after me because of the photograph, and what if her being dead isn't the reason why they're chasing me?

I got up to get some water. A thought flashed through my mind, something I think I'd been dreaming about for the past few nights. Something else might be in that photograph besides just Roberta. I had to see it again, and find a safe way to do it. For now—Kit.

First, I texted Fergus, to clear this perilous engagement with him. *Hi.*

Hey, he wrote back.

I'm about to text Kit about that errand I told you about. Sure you're okay with this?

Hell, no! Of course I'm not okay with it. Why don't you let me get it? Tell me the location and locker number.

I didn't even need to think about it. *Dude, no. Just...no. People have been fucking DYING around me. Have you noticed?*

I knew where Fergus' mind was right now. He would want to go with Kit. Still out of the question.

Yes, no? I pressed.

You have his phone number. I can't stop you from texting him.

I pressed Fergus' number for a call. He picked up and sighed without saying hello.

"Tell me what to do, then, if that's the wrong path. Horvath left something for me, just for me. It's related to all this shit we're going through, and the only way I can get it is by going to that locker, or sending someone else. Let's review the reason: it's because he's dead! They killed him, and it's probably because of what's in that locker."

"I think you just answered your own question," he said. Dammit.

"What options do I have? I don't know many underworld mob bosses that—"

He laughed slightly. "Kit? He'd like you to think that about him, but he's the opposite of a mob boss. He's like a mob errand boy who also runs his own scams and has his fingers in a lot of pies. The more dangerous the job, the more street cred he gets. So maybe he is the right man for the job, maybe he'd welcome the chance to do it."

"You mean without you having to owe him?"

"Yeah, just because of the stakes, and because he's hot for you."

"Gross. Should I call him or text him?"

"Text him first and tell him to call you back."

There was a silence between us that lasted more than a few seconds. I wondered if we were thinking the same thing, about me, about Officer Eve Maddox. Was the universe telling me this was the right time? No, definitely don't come out to someone on the phone.

"Okay, I'll text him and let you know what happens."

"Be safe."

"You too."

Chapter 40

I didn't text first like Fergus suggested. I hadn't even talked to Kit yet and I was already tired of his bullshit. I pressed his number. Of course he picked up on the first ring.

"Hey, Cupcake! What can Uncle Kit do for you today?"

I felt like hanging up, or maybe throwing up. But I needed him, so enduring his sexist quips was the price to pay. Hopefully the only one. I told him about the job.

"Sure, where and when?" he asked, all casual.

He hadn't mentioned price, which meant he would likely make it seem like he was doing me a solid, and I'd be off the hook. I knew what that meant. More explanation was needed.

"You're not picking up a pizza, Kit. I need you to understand that two people have died because of whatever's in that locker." I stayed quiet for two beats. He was listening and putting it together in his mind, how he could use this to his advantage.

"So, you need me to be armed? Is that what you're saying?"

"Wouldn't be a bad idea, though they're expecting me, not you."

"Who's they?" He was asking more questions than I expected. This was good. Kit was hungry for power and saw this as an opportunity to prove himself to other people in his organization.

"Yes or no. Can you do it? If not, I'll go myself."

"No, don't, it's not safe." Short pause. "I'll go."

"Good. I'll text you the details now, go as soon as you can, and let me know when you have it."

"Right."

"Thank you," I said a moment too late. So, he really did care.

Hard as it was to believe, I got an appointment at Honeycomb Salon in Noe Valley because of a last-minute cancellation, but with a different stylist than my usual one. I disguised myself with baggy, bell bottom pants, a fuchsia halter top and a long jacket. Ghetto chic? What mattered was that I don't think I was seen and I certainly didn't look like me. Time would tell.

I settled into the chair staring at my image in the mirror—of what looked like a fully grown, completely stressed-out woman rather than a carefree teenager about to start her college journey. Honestly, right now I looked forty and my hair was just unmanageable. Goodbye Moana, sniff.

"All of it?" the stylist asked, brows raised. "Really?"

"You can leave it shoulder length, but it's so thick you'll need to layer it so it doesn't look like a big ball."

They took me in the back and washed it first, which took twenty minutes. The cutting ceremony went by like nothing, my thoughts occupied by what I'd read online this morning as a sea of old, distressed, frantic hair spilled on the floor under my chair, vestiges of my old self. I'd been on the run, hiding from my mother, my tutoring students, the police, even myself. What was I doing, and how important was this truth I suddenly couldn't let go of? If I was willing to lose everything to find the truth, then why not my hair as well?

Texting covertly in the chair while my hair littered the salon floor, I asked Brody to elaborate on what he'd told me last night. He said Michael Horvath was already dead when they dumped him, shot most likely. These fucking people, the Syndicate. I had to know, and not just because of the stakes. I needed to know how their organization worked, how they had eyes on everything, people planted in cars, city streets, rooftops, standing somewhere behind two-way glass watching the pawns they're about to move, the lives they're about to destroy. I knew from my research today that these untouchable shadows were behind the Edgar Heights murders from ten years ago, and that Roberta Fenning had seen or known something that made her a loose end. I knew my path forward now. It was no longer a matter of choice.

The hair stylist was soaking up the kudos from the other stylists at my "amazing transformation", like they'd just turned a wild beast into a runway model. It surprised me how detached I was from it, this person staring back with shorter, neater-looking, tamed hair with more of my face visible. Who was this new person that I was no longer afraid to show the world?

Kit called me after I paid $90 to the salon from the last of my tutoring stash. Finished with my new look, I sat in one of the black chairs by the window to call him back.

"Hey."

"Got it."

"Thank you," I said, making sure he heard the words this time.

"What do you want me to do with it?"

"I feel like pizza tonight. Could you get one and bring it over?" I gave him the salon address assuming he'd know I meant to put the envelope in an empty pizza box. Kit could do it, he had means. And underlings.

"Be there in thirty minutes."

I hung up without saying goodbye, as Kit didn't deserve common courtesy. Noe Bagel was three doors down from the salon and my new hair style was its own disguise. I got a bagel sandwich and coffee and sat looking out at the street, unable to ignore my reflection in the glass. Who was that *woman* was staring back? A different me, a sophisticated me.

One bite into my sandwich and a man with sandy brown hair and aviator glasses walked in, turned right, and pulled out the stool beside me. "Mind if I sit here?" he asked and sat. Tall, British accent, nice sport coat.

"Apparently not." I kept chewing, eyes on the street.

"Do you know who I am?"

It's like my body knew before my mind did, the back of my

neck, back of my head, and tops of my shoulders sort of tingling. *Jeffrey Dade.* Jesus. "Yes," I managed. How else would he have known to sit right next to me? I'd ditched all the trackers and I didn't look at all like I did yesterday. What the actual fuck?

"Nice look," he said, scooting in with his elbows on the counter.

"Excuse me?"

"Your hair. Quite nice and very different. Kind of a smart thing to do, actually, under the circumstances."

"It was getting in my way."

"Ironic how things tend to do that when you don't need them anymore." He tossed a paperback book on the counter and opened it. I squinted so I could see the reflection of it in the glass. Aldous Huxley, *The Devils of Louden.*

"Enjoy your book. I'm eating lunch," I said.

The man opened the book, complete with a bookmark, though obviously just a prop. "The envelope you're waiting for from your friend Kit Fury has a tracker on it."

I set down my sandwich and wiped my mouth. Two more sips of coffee for fortification. I felt like screaming. "They'll know, what, when I open it, where I am when I open it, what color my underwear is? You people are ridiculous." I said it and exhaled.

"I'm not one of the 'people', as you say. I'm looking to take them down." He turned his head. "Same as your friend, Mr. Horvath."

I met his gaze now. Strong features, clean-shaven, slightly crooked nose and earnest eyes, one slightly lower than the other. It was my body again, not my mind, that decided he was trustworthy. "Let me guess. You need the contents of that envelope to do it."

The man puckered his lips. "No," he said after a moment. "But seeing as we seem to want the same thing, I'm proposing an alliance."

Two more bites of the bagel sandwich, reminding me that bagels were too bulky and always seemed stale. "To do what, exactly?"

"You know who they are now, yeah?"

I had to assume what I'd read on Reddit was correct. I nodded for effect, to make it seem like I knew what I was talking about. "The Syndicate."

"Sure, for lack of anything better. I can tell you a lot more than that."

"Can you tell me why Michael Horvath was shot and dumped in the water at Fort Point?"

"Certainly," he said without any reaction.

"Can you tell me what else is in that picture besides Roberta Fenning's dead body?"

"Ah. Clever girl. Not surprised you graduated first in your class."

I hadn't told anyone that. I honestly could care less, and he hadn't answered my question. My phone buzzed, Kit. I texted *Bagel place* back to him.

"My ride's two minutes away. What do I do?" I asked him, gathering what was left of my hair in a pathetic, stubby bun.

"Get in the car, the backseat, and pretend to open the pizza box but tell him you don't want to open the envelope until you get home."

"Have him drop me at the coffeeshop?"

"Yes, and get rid of him quickly. I would advise you to not touch the contents of the box. Go inside and get your things together. I'll be outside in a blue sedan after your friend Mr. Fury leaves."

How did he know about Kit? He'd never answer even if I asked him. "Do I have a choice?" I asked instead.

"Of course. A man's been sent to neutralize you. He'll be coming for you this evening at Linnea Caffe. It could be somebody you know, or not, and he'll kill you in—"

"Okay okay, fine. I believe you. Kit's here. See you in a few minutes."

Chapter 41

The morning sky was mottled gray with bits of sun struggling to push out of the thick clouds. Kit said to watch out for a white Mercedes. Of course he'd be driving a status-mobile. I wondered if he knew who I was going to meet. I stood in front of the bagel place under an awning watching him pull up to the curb a few stores down. Resisting the urge to glance left and right, I approached and pulled on the rear passenger door. Locked. I knocked twice on the window.

The lock clicked. I climbed in the back next to a large pizza box. Beautiful.

"Hey." I closed the door.

"Where we going?" No greeting. He sounded stressed. Had I finally found something Kit was afraid of?

"Mission, same place you were at before. How did it go? Any issues? See anyone?"

"Fine, no, and no." He screeched out of the alley too fast. Smoke floated up from the tires as he sped through Noe Street.

"Kit! Slow down for fuck's safe. The whole idea is to be inconspicuous. You show up here in a shiny new—"

Kit jerked his head back, lowered his sunglasses. His icy glare lasered through me. Beware, Thea. This guy's killed people. Maybe a lot of people. Don't be one of them.

I shook my head but I wasn't stupid. "Just saying," I said, more carefully. "Neither of us want to be seen with that pizza box."

I caught him watching me in the rearview. "You doing a Zoe Kravitz with that pixie haircut?"

I pulled it out of the bun so it hung near my shoulders, so obviously he had no idea what a pixie cut looked like. "Do you like it?" I asked.

It was a brilliant thing to say, and I was proud of myself for pulling that out of such a tense moment. Kit was attracted to me so I used that to my advantage. Asking him if he liked my hair was a way of asking how he felt about me. He stared at the road, silent. Gotcha, asshole.

He'd slowed to a turtle's pace through the crowded streets with constant pedestrians crossing in front of us. I stretched my left arm and used my fingertips to touch the bottom of the pizza box to gauge its weight, careful not to move it. If Jeffrey Dade was right, sensors had been implanted in the envelope's contents, so any pressure on the box could register movement.

"Linnea Coffeehouse?" he asked.

"Yes, please." Absent of any evidence to prove it, I knew Kit had been seen at the locker. I just felt it. Lately I'd trusted these feelings more than I ever had before. Grandma Irene used to talk to us about that, the whole family, about not getting pulled into the modern world, staying close to nature every day, that this was the only real way to hear your truths. My truth right now was that I was being hunted. And Jeffrey Dade might be my only means of escape.

I'd practiced my "thank you" to Kit, making sure it didn't sound either grateful or dismissive. It came out as, "Thanks, see ya." I slammed the door shut.

I stood awkwardly holding the pizza box at the back door to Janelle's little goldmine doing what I'd done so often in my life during times of fear—counting down. Twenty seemed the right number today. Nineteen, eighteen…Kit drove away thirty seconds ago and now hired Syndicate assassins were on their way to kill me. I had to trust Jeffrey Dade. I trusted Fergus, of course, and Bharat, but there was nothing either of them could do for me now. No way to protect me from this leveled-up peril. They'd already killed Horvath, and now they knew I'd picked up his envelope of forbidden secrets. Seventeen, sixteen, fifteen. Jeffrey's blue sedan, thank God. He rolled down the window.

"Pass me the box, gently," he said.

I stared, wondering.

"Do it. Then go inside and grab all your stuff. You're never coming back here."

My heart literally dropped to my stomach when he said it. He was right, it was no longer safe here - for me or for Janelle and her community. There wasn't much really—just a toothbrush, soap, lotion, my computer, some hotel-sized shampoo, and a few articles of clothing. I walked up and he exited the driver's side, opened the back door and set the box gently on the seat. I went inside and stuffed my meager belongings in my backpack and was outside in twenty seconds. Wow, I surprised myself. Maybe I would make a good operative someday.

"Good girl," he said glancing up and down the alley. "Front seat please, next to me."

I glanced at the box in the backseat as I walked around the car. "Aren't we going to open that?"

"Don't touch it. Lock your door, put your seatbelt on. Gonna be a bumpy ride from here on out."

I caught the double meaning, but it had already been way too bumpy for my taste. "Where are we going?"

"It's a lovely day for an amusement park. Don't you think?"

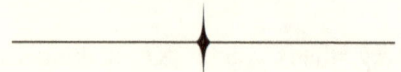

No, I didn't actually think he was bringing me to an amusement park, maybe just throwing surveillance off track if we were being recorded. But if we were being tracked, wouldn't they see where he was actually taking me? The amusement park turned out to be full circle—Seacliff, and in the same block as the Fenning estate.

"Don't even ask me to go to that house again," I said as we passed the Fenning estate.

He took the first right and parked in the third house on the left. It was one of those super-modern vertical homes that towered over the rest of the neighborhood, almost as high as a ponderosa pine on one side. We entered the driveway sliding into an empty two-car garage.

"Got a nice view from that balcony up there," I said, noting you could easily see Roberta's car going in and out.

He turned and smiled. "Well, you don't miss a trick, do you?"

Under the fluorescent lights of his garage, I caught his face in full view. I guess I expected something different from the man who had inspired such a complex web of events, someone more powerful-looking, maybe older too. Jeffrey Dade looked like a washed-up boxer who'd had his face bashed in over and over, and his features sewn haphazardly back together. His upper lip was much larger and thicker than the lower, crooked teeth, what a face. But he had runway-model sandy brown hair that, combined with his height, broad shoulders and feather voice, made for an appealing package. Not to me, certainly, but I saw how he could have transfixed someone like Roberta, especially right after her husband died. From this house, he could keep an eye on her, maybe more than just an eye. But did that mean my ex-bestie, Lise Fenning, also knew him? Last time I saw Lise, she'd used her magic locket to get me abducted. Who knows what she intended and she had a lot to answer for.

"Come in," he said. "Irene's got a room prepared for you and she's made us a proper breakfast, unlike your...bagel." He smiled in a way that told me he needed me right now as much as I needed him. I was about to find out why.

I followed him from the garage through a skylit breezeway into a great room with a grand piano and slanted eaves. Polished wood paneling lined the walls, which gave a retro balance to the sleek, modern shape. I couldn't decide whether I liked it or not. Old and new. "Irene's your wife?" I asked.

Closed eyes, lowered head. "She's eighty. My housekeeper, and an ace of a chef."

"My grandmother's name is Irene."

"Oh?"

"She's older than eighty but I don't know by how much, because she lies about her age."

"Here's to good genes then," he said, with a funny smirk. He took me down one hallway, then another, up two flights of stairs and onto a landing that led to three bedrooms. "Take your pick."

"Okay…"

"Get settled in. I'll let you try to guess the wifi password."

"Good. I like a challenge."

His face, after I said it, changed from something almost impish to life or death. He turned away toward the stairs. "Come down when you're ready. We've got a lot to talk about."

I plugged in my laptop and set it on a smooth, walnut desk in the smallest of the three upstairs bedrooms. Wifi password. Okay. I tried the obvious things first. Deadsevens, gametheory, cicada, robertafenning, blackearedrabbit. The password was likely eight characters because that convention was the most common. Then again, someone security-minded might go for a longer requirement. Most likely it was a single word, a word nobody knew about, a word significant only to my host. I took off my shoes and stepped down the wooden stairs back to the great room. The old woman had set a table for us on a terrace overlooking the most stunning, west-facing panorama. Jeffrey was seated on the piano bench facing the windows. I walked past the terrace and sagged onto the arm of a white, leather sofa with my back to the windows.

"Are you in?" he asked with a sly smile.

"Your wifi password?" I pushed air out of my lips with feigned frustration. "No, of course not. If it was easy to guess, wouldn't be much of a password, would it?"

"Touché." He leaned back and crossed his legs, then put his hands behind him on the edges of the piano bench. He looked comfortable but his face was a mess of emotions. "Go ahead," he sighed. "I can feel your questions in the air. We'll eat after."

"Good. Let's start with Michael Horvath."

Jeffrey Dade closed his eyes.

Chapter 42

All I could think about was the whereabouts and contents of the pizza box but I was prepared to play the long game. Jeffrey Dade sat in the very epicenter of the Edgar Heights killings, the Dead Sevens game, and the death of Roberta Fenning.

"What about him?"

"My ally for a total of four days, very likely dead because of me."

"And you want to know…"

"I think it's obvious who killed him, and why."

"Oh? Why do you think?" he asked.

I thought of his blog, all his writings, articles, also learning recently that he was a noted game theorist and psychologist. "He was a journalist who'd spent the past ten years, so he said, working on sussing them out, these Syndicate members. I think he acquired some sort of evidence, he was probably about to tell me what it was, and their fear of exposure made him a liability."

He examined the floor. "You seem far too sophisticated for seventeen."

I shrugged. "I read a lot of spy books."

"Is that right?"

"Look. I appreciate you giving me a place to crash, but open the damn pizza box."

He exhaled. "We can't."

"What?"

"It's too dangerous."

I got up and moved to the windows, keeping my back to him. "Then what was the point of picking it up from the locker?"

"We'll look at it eventually, but I suspect I know what's in it already. I have duplicates of almost everything there," he said, waiting.

I turned around. "So, we can examine it without letting them know we've seen it?"

"Exactly."

Okay, that was a consolation. "Well, what's in it?" I asked.

"We'll get to that later. What else do you need to know?" He moved from the piano bench to the huge, sectional sofa.

"I mostly have unanswered questions. But I suspect there was more than just Roberta Fenning in the photograph I took of her the night she died in her kitchen."

"What makes you say that?"

"If Roberta was involved with these people, and you all this time, why would evidence of her death be such a threat to them?"

He had a slight upward pull to the right side of his crooked mouth. I was on the right track. I kept going.

"I think Roberta's killer was still in the house, in the kitchen, actually. I heard him at one point, but convinced myself at the time that I was just hearing things. So, I guess I'm saying I think her killer thinks he's visible in that picture."

"You haven't checked?"

"Not yet."

"I won't ask you where the picture is, but is it safe?"

"Not really," I confessed. "I mean, it'll be hard to find but not impossible."

He moved to the windows, opened the sliding glass door, and sat at the table. I joined him as he set a glass of water next to my plate.

"I need to know what your stake in this is," I said.

"Fair question. It's no secret. These people killed my friends. Not just my friends actually. Horvath probably told you, I was orphaned very young. Those guys were my family."

His voice was solid as he mentioned what must be one of the worst traumas of his life. The old woman came to the table and spooned lettuce wraps on our plates, then handed us mini bowls of a peanut-looking dip.

"You played cards, I take it? I love cards," I added, before he could answer. "My best friend Fergus and I play cribbage almost every day. Or we used to anyway."

"Dead Sevens was our own silly version of crazy eights, maybe because we were all seven when we started playing it. Except instead of eights being wild, it's sevens. And instead of having to draw cards from the deck, when you draw a seven, you're out, or dead as we called it. Quite fun, actually." He examined the tablecloth.

I couldn't imagine growing up all the way to adulthood with six buddies and having them die, all at once. Murdered no less. It seemed unthinkable on the surface, then again so many unthinkable things had happened lately. The lettuce wraps were fresh, with a mixture of spicy pork and vegetables. I took a bite and nodded approval, still not really hungry. Would I ever be?

"Delicious."

"My guess is you haven't eaten a square meal in quite some time."

More nodding and chewing. "So, who's in charge of this shadow organization?" I asked. He glanced at the door, maybe making sure Irene was inside. "And what are they called, anyway?" After I asked the second question, I suddenly knew this would be the wifi password.

"Those are two excellent questions, to which I'll defer the answers for another time."

I stopped eating. "IG?"

He glanced at me, then down at his plate.

"Okay. Who was it who saw me in Roberta's kitchen? I guess I'm asking who killed her."

Jeffrey tipped his head sideways. "Well, those might be two different things. And to my knowledge, you've seen evidence of—"

"The videos?" I nodded. "Unfortunately, yes. Horvath sent them to me, her body being moved, though I didn't know whether she was already dead at that point."

"There's something I should explain before we go further." He paused to wipe his mouth on a linen napkin. "When you ask who killed her, there are a couple of levels of *who*—meaning an organization and a specific individual. For that, I don't know actually."

I watched his right eye twitch. "How can you not know that if you know everything else?"

He shrugged, trying to look casual. The movement didn't suit him. "One of their goons, I suspect. They've got an army of assets like that. There's really no telling."

Slight twitch of his left eye this time, movement of his brows, something with his shoulder. He was lying, but now I knew his tell. He opened his mouth to speak, then closed it.

"Why are you—" I started, but stopped as an epiphany formed in my head, not born out of any mental process but again, a truth arrived in my body; I felt its shine and vibration inside my bones. "You're lying."

"About what?"

"About who killed her." Two crows squawked over our heads, circling each other. I watched Jeffrey's every movement, tracking the depth of his breathing, the clench of his fists. I slid my chair back in a nasty screech, then stepped away from the table to get some space between us. "Did you do it?"

"For heaven's sake, Thea. I love her!" The words seemed to shake the floorboards. And he said love, not loved. "All your copious research wasn't able to discern that?"

"Don't turn it on its side." I paced in front of the table, arms crossed, like a rabid prosecutor. He was telling me this himself, his body language. All I was doing was reading it.

"Look, I'm trying to help you."

"You're trying to help yourself by using me. Confirm or deny?"

"I don't deny that, but it will also be helping you because you must admit you're in a bit of a tight spot right now. Aren't you?"

"Stop it!"

The shouting brought Irene back upstairs. I could see her shape just outside the opened door.

"You've been stringing me along for weeks now with your

cryptic little texts. Tell me the truth, Jeffrey." I sat down again, wiping my eyes on my napkin. I held it there a minute, breathing in the moment. Then, as the crows flew away, a new epiphany landed in their place. "Roberta Fenning's not really dead, is she?"

We each went away in separate directions after lunch. Hard to believe such a thing could exist anywhere within the boundaries of San Francisco, Jeffrey Dade's mansion in Seacliff had what I would call *grounds*, more typically described with an English manor. The expanse stretched to an Olympic-sized swimming pool, with walking rows between corridors of green plants, and another with large purple flowers I'd never seen before. I cooled off in these gardens for an hour with a tall glass of iced tea. Then as the sky darkened, Irene returned with a white cloth folded over her arm.

"Dinner in an hour," she said, passed me a stack of neatly folded clothes and slipped away before I could ask questions. Convenient, wasn't it? But I wasn't the least bit interested in dinner, and my host knew that well enough. I used the time to email Fergus telling him where I was. For Bharat, I sent a text telling him he was temporarily off duty from carting around Princess Thea to all of her dangerous escapades and I was okay for the moment.

I held up the folded garments after Irene disappeared: a tennis ensemble. Are you kidding me? A short, white dress, shorts, and tennis socks. I'm sure there would be shoes at some point. I surprised myself that I was able to find my way back to the bedroom where I tossed the ridiculous outfit on the floor. I was no stranger to sports, having played my share of basketball (poorly), table tennis (even worse). I was an adequate soccer player in junior high school, told I was a fast runner and a fierce competitor. Maybe that would help me for whatever was to come. In the closet was a set of clothes that looked exactly my size. I would bet my next paycheck it was no accident that I ended up here today. I needed answers and wasn't waiting any longer.

Still in my same clothes, I went downstairs following the aroma of what smelled like my mother's pork roast. Irene, apron around her waist, towel flung over her shoulder, was bent over the oven.

"Where's Jeffrey?" I asked.

"Here," he said right behind me. I sucked in a puff of air but didn't turn.

"I need some answers. I need to know what this all means."

"Would you come with me, please?"

I turned. He'd changed into tennis clothes. They looked ridiculous. "Only because you asked so nicely."

Chapter 43

The notorious Jeffrey Dade took me to a lower level in his house, through a set of double doors into a finished basement. No tennis court so far. The second door led to another section of the basement with another staircase going down. We had to be under sea level here. I stood nervously with him hovering behind me, mumbling something. Or was he chanting? Lights came up slowly, revealing what looked like a woodworking shop. Nothing would surprise me at this point.

On a long table was the pizza box, with the envelope laying on top of it. So, he'd opened the box.

"Horvath died for whatever's in that envelope. Are we really not opening it?"

"We don't need to," he said, with the crooked smile that promised mischief and deception. He pointed to an x-ray machine similar to airport security. I moved closer taking in the shapes on the screen. A long, round object, several pieces of paper, and what looked like a flash drive.

"They're all still in there?" I asked.

He pointed to a smaller table, where objects were arranged just like on the x-ray image. "Go ahead. Examine them if you wish."

One was a kind of voucher, or ticket stub, ripped on the bottom with a perforation, dark red with black letters. Then a steel tool of some kind with a flat part on one end that looked like a vaccine stamp. I'd seen this in the videos at the library.

"What do you feel right now, Thea?"

"Feel." I let out a guttural laugh, which sounded more like crying. "I don't know, so many things. Frustration, bewilderment."

He adjusted one of the machines in the lab. "What are you hiding from?" Now he turned and lowered his head so he could see my expression.

My palms went up in a typical defense move I'd used on Fergus. "What are you, my therapist? How is that even relevant?"

"You are directly relevant to everything that's been going on here, everything that's been going on lately, and more than just that."

I searched for something to sit on. There was nothing. I lowered myself to the concrete floor and sat with my legs stretched out. The cold seeped into my skin. It felt good. I leaned my head forward, holding my face in my hands.

Jeffrey sat opposite me in this creepy lair fifty feet below his house. "What are you hiding from?"

"What do you want from me? Why did you bring me here?" My voice was rock solid, insistent.

"You just seem like you're giving up."

He was baiting me. I stood, crossed my arms and leaned against the wooden counter, watching my opponent because that's what he was. My heart pounded. My breathing was ragged. Rage.

"Let it out, Thea."

My chest shook and my face felt hot. Don't cry, not here. Not now with this man. I knew what he was doing.

"Don't you feel even a little bit angry?"

"Stop it! You're manipulating me."

"That's it." He nodded. "Why are you so angry, Thea? Who are you angry with?"

Tears now, the ones I'd been suppressing, filled my eyes so I couldn't see without blinking, spilling them down my cheeks. I balled my hands into fists, digging my fingernails into the flesh of my palms to stop their flow, short circuit the emotions Jeffrey Dade seemed hellbent on releasing. It wasn't working. Fuck him.

"Your mother?"

"Stop it."

"For bringing you here thousands of miles away from the home you grew up in?" He stood, coming two steps toward me.

We were ten feet apart, the air thick between us. Why did I feel like he might attack me? I hadn't felt threatened by him before. I turned my head left and right to assess possible weapons. A vice grip, some kind of saw, and a hammer—all out of my reach.

"How about your father, Thea? Are you angry with your father?"

"Leave...me...alone." It came out as more of a moan than words.

"Is he the secret tiger you keep locked in a cage?"

"What are you doing?" I asked. "Why do you care about my father? You don't even know me."

"That's not exactly true. Do you resent your father for not coming with you to San Francisco? Do you feel abandoned by him?"

He had me, and he knew he had me. I'd just lost the game of cribbage, or chess, or whatever power struggle he'd started. "Yes," I whispered. Ninety-nine, ninety-eight...

"How about your brother, Rudy? Do you feel—"

"Don't-you-dare. You will not talk about my brother!" I think it was the loudest sound I'd ever produced. The mention of Rudy turned me into a wild animal, standing over him, finger pointed, my tears wetting the collar of my shirt. Oh my God, how could he mention Rudy? How could he even know about him?

"I'm sorry. You must understand, I'm not trying to hurt you."

"Really? What exactly are you doing? Trying to help me connect with my emotions? Yeah, two therapists tried that, elders in my family in Majuro, purification ceremonies after Rudy died. They all failed."

"So, Rudy's the tiger, then. That which you keep locked away deep in the center of your heart. The thing you can't talk about, think about, or share with anyone. Not even Fergus?"

I looked at the floor then sat on the cold concrete again. "Fergus loves me. I'm like his sister. He's never mentioned Rudy, not because he's not curious or because he doesn't care, but out of respect!" The word came out like a dagger, which was how I meant it. I felt disrespected by him. "I know what you're doing," I added, brows raised, remembering the pattern.

"What am I doing?" he asked gently.

"You're like Mazer Rackham and I'm your little Ender. Admit it. Or are you too old to know about movies like that?"

"I read the book. And yes, you're right in a way. Have you ever seen the first Terminator film, where the young Sarah Connor was confronted by a man from the future, who described her as one of the best resistance fighters he'd ever seen? He saw and he knew, and he loved actually, a future version of her that she didn't believe would ever exist. She didn't feel, at that time, like a warrior, or a fighter, or a survivalist. She was a girl working in a diner. But she was confronted by the idea of a future version of herself that was something greater, something heroic. And it scared her to death."

"That's what you see in me? A revolutionary? We're not at war, in this country anyway."

"Nothing could be farther from the truth. We're fighting dozens of wars right now. A war on racial equality. A war on gender equality. Russia and Ukraine, the Middle East. You think this country is not a part of that?"

I closed my eyes.

"There's another war, a quieter one that's been going on for fifteen years, even before the Syndicate killed my best friends in the world, my brothers. Their organizational structure was already in place five years before that, assembling, gathering resources, building their global agendas, hammering stakes in the ground. The war you're fighting within yourself, Thea, is significant and relevant to not just your future. Do you know why?"

"Good speech. You missed your calling as a politician."

"I'll tell you why *you* are important to the Syndicate. Because the war you're fighting inside of yourself right now, that tiger you've got locked in a cage *is* your power."

I was watching him now. He stopped talking for effect. I took long breaths to compose myself.

"Those emotions, your mother for bringing you here, your father for staying, your brother for dying, whatever emotions you feel as a result of those triggers are a part of you, but you can leverage them to your advantage."

"What do you mean?"

"Turn them into power. Turn them into passion."

"Passion?" I shook my head.

"For justice. For equality. You can let them out so they can mold and change you. And by doing so you can mold and change others."

I rose to stretch my legs again. "What does any of this have to do with tennis?" I asked, wondering if it had more to do with the game.

He closed his eyes and smiled a little.

Chapter 44

I followed Jeffrey Dade up a set of stairs back to the lower-level great room, or living room, or whatever billionaires called these gigantic living spaces. This one had less furniture, and the pieces were smaller. He motioned me to a sofa and turned a large, white leather chair toward it and sat, leaning forward, elbows on knees, eyeing the doorway behind me. Was he worried about Irene? She had to know all his secrets. I watched his movements, his fidgeting, assessing why I was really here and knowing, suddenly, like the truth was lingering in the air waiting for me to breathe it in. The Syndicate. My God.

"You want *me* to take them down?"

Blinking, a rise of one brow.

"Is that what Michael Horvath wanted, too?"

"I suspect so."

I shook my head out of disbelief. "I'm a seventeen-year-old girl. Honestly, I'm the best you can do? Why can't you do it? You're already involved with them. Friends close, enemies closer?" I said about the text he'd sent me.

"Well…" He sat back and crossed his arms, looking satisfied that

I'd arrived at the truth without him having to actually say it. "For clarification, I'm not an insider. Really more of an adjacent, and in many ways a victim of their methods. But you, on the other hand, are an outsider of the best kind. An informed outsider that the Syndicate knows of but who nobody's ever met. Except Horvath."

"Who's dead," I added.

"That's right. And now me."

"How would any of them even know about me?" I asked.

"Your mother," he said, after a moment of deliberation. "Horvath was shot. He almost died."

Before she was a pediatric nurse, my mother was an ER nurse. I was trying to remember if she'd ever mentioned anything about it.

"When was this?" I asked.

"Two years ago."

"Shot by who, and why?"

He breathed deep and shrugged his broad shoulders, then cracked his neck on both sides. "Because of his bloody crusade. Michael Horvath was a rabid muckraker, as they say, a diligent researcher motivated by nothing other than the truth, fearless enough to be a whistleblower and just simply not care about consequences." He rose and continued, "He'd been following the Syndicate even before they were one. So, when your mother saved his life by stopping the bleeding in time so he could be operated on, he started watching out for her, to protect her. He also studied her, learned about you, studied you, made a file on you. I think he suspected your mother was special, and so, by definition, you had to be as well."

I felt like crying, thinking of Horvath as my fallen protector. And now my mother knew him? It was all too much and I felt emotionally drained from our conversation in his basement lair. I liked it here, though, I had to admit. Upstairs in this larger room with the tall ceilings. I liked watching Jeffrey Dade pontificate like this, now with his long arms laid out down the arms of the white, leather chair. My mind was agitated, though, a new thought slowly taking root that made me feel sick. It called into question so many things I'd thought were my reality.

"He was very impressed with your ability to forge a natural friendship with someone like Lise Fenning, a billionaire's daughter, a socialite of the highest caliber."

"She's a bimbo and a spoiled brat. Yes, she was my friend, my bestie for a while there. But it's not like we had a thing in common."

"How did you meet, you two?" He asked the question nonchalantly but I suspected this too was a tactic and part of a deeper plan.

I thought back. "There was a dinner for recent clients of the real estate agent who sold us our house, my mother and I. Sort of a buffet reception at a fancy hotel. Roberta, who worked with the woman who sold us the house, was there, and…" My voice trailed off. "Had Michael Horvath introduced my mother to that real estate agent so I would meet them, she and Lise?"

Jeffrey tipped his head apologetically.

"Wa—wait a minute. So, this was all orchestrated?" I asked in slo-mo. "For what reason? And how much was orchestrated? Jesus." Rage again, rising up from the depths of my body. Another betrayal. Had my whole past been a lie? I tried to put it all together. If my mother had saved Horvath's life and it was when we first moved here, we did spend a long time looking for a house. Maybe he was trying to thank her.

"Look, there was no telling whether you and Lise would end up being friends. You seemed to just hit it off, didn't you?"

I nodded.

"Michael thought you had a quiet power about you, and powers of persuasion. I think he thought of you as a potential protégé."

"Fergus? Did he fucking orchestrate that, too? So, I'm guessing it's no coincidence he delivers documents to a medical supply company?" I got up and walked to the large, picture window, exhaling long breaths out my mouth. "Is there anything in my life that's fucking real?" I turned. "Is this rage enough for you, Jeffrey? You want more?"

"Oh, yeah," he said. "I want all of it. Everything you've got."

Irene prepared a candlelit dinner at a table intended for twenty.

"Should we sit at each end and yell to each other?"

He took two plates from the center and set them across from each other on one end. Irene brought out silverware, then served us from nice looking, plain white bowls. Chicken, potatoes, asparagus. I stared down at the plate.

"You're not hungry?"

"Overwhelmed is too small a word."

He ate in silence, after which he informed me the tennis game would be after dinner. I took a few bites. Expertly prepared, delicious. So much for digestion.

"Why did they kill Horvath? I know he set out to expose them, but he had to have envisioned that as a possible outcome. He also had to have some sort of evidence, at least the kind that would be meaningful to law enforcement."

"You know, you really are far above your years." He shook his head and smiled. "You're right of course with that last part. Evidence is one thing, but evidence a police detective would likely use to start building a case is something else entirely." He took a bite and Irene was back with her serving bowls. I'd barely taken three bites.

"Not hungry, dear?" she asked.

"It's delicious," I said. The thought of eating when the ground had been removed seemed so pointless. She disappeared a moment later. Jeffrey put his arms on the table.

"The pizza box?"

"Mmm." He nodded, again eyeing the door. So apparently Irene wasn't privy to everything.

"It looks like a medical device. One of the videos Horvath sent me had a closeup of one edge of it."

He wiped his mouth and sat back. "You've seen the insignia."

"IG."

"Do you know what it means?"

"We think, Fergus and I, that it might be the parent company of a medical supply company he delivers documents to. He's a bike courier."

More chewing, more nodding. He set down his fork and stared at my plate.

"Jeffrey, try to imagine how this all feels in my eyes, that my life has been orchestrated and manipulated to lure me into some global plot. Yes, the chicken's delicious, and the sky is blue. What do either of those things have to do with the crumbling foundation of my life?"

"I understand," he said, but he didn't. He was a billionaire socialite who came from nothing, no parents, and worked his way up. To this.

"Can I ask you something now?"

"Anything." He seemed to like the question.

"How do you afford this estate? Do you own it, are you renting it, how do you make money? I don't even know your profession."

He looked around with a self-satisfied smirk. "I designed this place myself."

"You're an architect?"

"Of sorts, not really residential though. More like commercial buildings. I've designed a few hospital wards, a city hall building, and a few parking garages earlier on. When magazines feature your work, the jobs get better."

"I'm seeing the connection now. Roberta, a real estate agent. Did she sell lots and hire you to design the homes built on them?"

"A few times, yes." He lowered his face to the table and played with his fork. He didn't want to talk about Roberta. She was one of his triggers. This might come in handy later.

"IG?" I asked.

"Oh yes. It stands for Interessen Group. German for interests."

"Are you a member?" I asked, more interested in that than their mission.

"No. A consultant, and before you ask, yes there's a difference," he shot back.

"So, IG makes medical devices?"

"I'll tell you everything you want to know about them." Slight grin. "Over tennis."

I shook my head.

"Everything has a reason, Thea."

"Can't wait to hear this one."

"We're practicing for the real thing."

Chapter 45

First impressions: I hate tennis. It's too slow, the racquets are too big, the games too short, and this dress, seriously? It barely even covered my hips. Why bother? He made me change into the exact clothes he set out, which also included a pair of brand new white tennis shoes, my size no less.

The tennis courts were a five-minute walk from the house under a bed of stars. I could hardly believe how many more were visible here compared to the Mission. This barely seemed part of the same world, let alone city. I knew how the game was played of course. I'd played before at a friend's birthday party, where everyone got a twenty-minute private lesson. I'd even watched Wimbledon once with my mother. I never understood how or why she liked tennis so much. In Majuro, it's all wrestling and baseball.

I went through the motions. Every time it was my serve, I gave a theatrical eyeroll combined with shoulders and head slumping forward. We volleyed back and forth, Jeffrey won every game, mostly because I just didn't give a shit.

"IG?" I asked, after I served for the second time into the net. Jeffrey jogged towards my side of the court, no doubt to give me some tennis pointers.

"They're a global consortium of elite world leaders who fund projects that are in the best interest of evolving humanity."

"What a crock. Where'd you read that, Wikipedia? The best interest of humanity. I'll bet."

We didn't keep score for the last two games, just volleying back and forth in this pointless exercise. I was trying to understand what tennis had to do with the secret agendas of an elite, global shadow organization. I asked him as much on our way back to the house.

"It's where all the magic happens," he said, finally. We went in the back door and cut through the largest of his three living rooms. "Come on," he said, again heading toward the creepy basement dungeon. What could go wrong?

"I'm gonna change first," I said. "If I don't get lost, I'll be back in five minutes."

"Very well."

It was strange not having spoken with Fergus in half a day, not even texting, and even stranger to think of myself walking away from him and my mother. Unthinkable, really. Then again, the unthinkable was beginning to feel commonplace. As I climbed the stairs, I thought of two things: I needed a shower. I'd also just created an interesting opportunity for myself.

Would Jeffrey know what I was thinking? Of course he would, probably before I even thought of it. Question was, would he try to stop me?

Miraculous as it felt to think it, I'd just had physical exercise, a square meal, and I had an actual bed to sleep in tonight without the threat of catastrophe. I thought of Janelle, my protector, and hoped to God she was okay. It's true, I did feel safe in this fortress, here with Jeffrey. What he might be planning in the dungeon would give me more of the answers I needed. I probably could have escaped, but truth be told, I think I needed him right now as much as he needed me.

The door to his basement was closed this time. I knocked three times and opened it, poking my head down the stairs. "Hello?"

"Yes, yes, join me. Show and tell."

"That's not creepy at all."

His forehead was high, eyes wide when I got to the bottom of the stairs. I'd changed; my hair was down now, what was left of it. Was he noticing? "What?" I asked.

"You didn't run."

"Is that what you thought I'd do?"

"I might have, or certainly would have considered it."

"The deeper I go, the more questions I have. You seem to be holding all the cards, so to speak." I settled on a hard, wooden stool, ready.

"But it's you who's holding the trump card."

I pointed at the pizza box, unsure what he meant.

He nodded and ran up the stairs to close the door. I heard a loud, metal click and three beeps. "Now we can talk."

"Without Irene hearing us?" I asked, then realized how stupid that must have sounded.

"Irene knows enough about what I do to not ask questions. This system—" he waved his index finger in a circle while he looked around the room— "is a sort of DMZ or buffer zone, where surveillance won't work." He was proud of it. He'd probably designed it himself.

"Like a Star Trek forcefield or something?"

"It's totally possible. Now," he said and opened the pizza box, "we can touch these objects without getting detected." I sat back while he took the flash drive from the box and plugged it into one of his laptops. He looked up. "Let's talk about the videos Horvath sent you."

"I've tried to put them out of my mind."

"Sorry." He motioned me to the laptop, where we stood side-by-side in front of a screen positioned on a high table. He touched the play button and a video showed up in full spectrum, a much larger form than the ones I'd seen in the library. A line of black-robed figures in surreal masks seemed barely human, one-by-one shuffling forward to present a bare hand where a metal device stamped down on the skin. Each time, the metal device was replaced by a paper voucher.

I pointed. "That, I've seen that before. What are they being injected with?"

"Not injected. It's a DNA sampling device."

I knew it. "DNA, they're taking their DNA? For what? And

what's the voucher for?"

He looked at me, my arrogant mentor, waiting for me to arrive at the truth on my own.

"Money?"

"Yes," he said.

"They hand in their DNA voucher and receive, what, a hundred thousand dollars? What the hell for, and who would pay people that much for their DNA? I would think it would be easier to just take it, you know, surreptitiously."

That look again.

"Jeffrey, for fuck's sake. A conversation is when people talk back and forth. So, I'm asking and answering my own questions now?"

"You don't seem to need much help figuring things out."

I moved around the space, touching things like a restless teenager. "So, the hundred-thousand-dollar question, then, is what are they using the DNA for?"

"Exactly. I'll tell you all about that, but first," he said, picked up a folded page from the counter and held it out.

"What is this?" I opened it, a printout of a note Michael Horvath wrote me before he died. Classy of Jeffrey to print it out for me instead of making me stand awkwardly leaning over his desk. "Thank you." I returned to the stool across the room.

> Thea, if you're reading this now, they've gotten to me before I had a chance to tell you everything I wanted to. There's so much, and it goes so deep. I wish I'd met you earlier. I mean, I knew you for a long time now, have watched you and studied you, but it was never safe to come forward. I'm surprised I took the chance I did at the library. Your safety, and your mother's safety has always been of paramount importance. But things escalated, and time ran out. I had to make contact, despite the risks. I'm sorry, Thea, sorry for everything, for mismanaging the information I had, probably mismanaging our communications. Look what happened? You're in hiding now. The fact is, I need someone to continue my work. Why? Because I'm

the only one who knows the truth and has the ability to expose them. If you're reading this, they've figured out what I was preparing to do and eliminated me. You're the only one left, the only one strong enough to do it, who can expose the ugly truth of their "humanitarian projects" to the world so they can be stopped. And they can—with the right evidence, the right law enforcement support, and a little luck. On this same flash drive are two videos, and a folder of several other documents with pictures, names, positions, even Interpol identity numbers for some of them. Jeffrey knows the rest, but he can't move forward with anything because he's too close. You're an outsider, so you have the best chance of anyone to penetrate them and expose the truth, and the man behind it all. I hope someday you believe in yourself as much as I believe in you.

Ever your ally,
Michael

Chapter 46

The darkness of Jeffrey Dade's basement felt like good protection right now—and so silent. Too much so.

"Have you read this?" I asked, as if my heart wasn't breaking.

"No."

I handed him the sheet then looked through the other files on the drive. I waited long enough for him to finish, because I felt that the gravity of Michael's death registered for both of us. "You said this group, the Syndicate, funds projects that evolve humanity."

He glanced up from the page.

"What the hell does that even mean?" I asked.

He opened his hands and then folded them. "IG are futurists, or that's what they like to call themselves. They have a lot of code words they use to describe their operations, highly classified—"

I smirked. "Obviously one of those code words is your wifi password."

His lips formed into a partial smile, but he didn't confirm or answer. "They're a global enterprise of technology and media influencers, futurists if you like, with unthinkably vast financial resources, who use their collective talents and assets to impact the global balance of power and direction of civilization's evolution."

It still sounded like scifi. "How? How do they do this?"

"Three ways," he said, though I hadn't expected him to actually answer the question. "Deep fakes, counterfeit diamonds, and organ cloning."

Neither of us spoke or moved. I replayed his words in my head. "That's what the DNA is being used for," I whispered. "Oh my God."

He moved to the empty space at the bottom of the stairs, in full classroom teacher mode. "Deep fakes. Do you know what that is?"

"Fake news, right?"

"More than just fake news. Here, I'll show you an example." He moved to the computer screen, opened a browser window, went to YouTube, and found a saved video from his library. He brought the machine over to me and held it up while I watched.

"What am I looking at?"

"Doesn't matter. What matters is that it absolutely looks real, doesn't it?"

"Looks like a news story, something like what I'd see on BBC news or something. Why, though?"

"Deep fakes are used for political impact and to influence sentiment, social media trending, government, the stock market, consumer spending. They're terribly powerful if used the right way at the right time."

"How do they get away with it? What about Snopes?" I asked of the debunker of urban myths and fake news.

He smiled and tilted his head.

"God, let me guess. One of them works for Snopes?"

He shrugged.

"So unethical. I still don't understand why they'd go through all that planning and expense."

"Political equity and financial gain. As to the ethical question, the Syndicate formed because a top-tier of elite technology leaders was fed up with unchecked corruption, fake news, and conspiracy theories becoming fact. The distribution of power was all wrong. There was no retribution for anything. People were vulnerable and needed leadership." He nodded. "A lot of money could be made in the process. With me so far?"

"Unfortunately, yes." I felt queasy. Maybe it was this room.

"Okay. Pivoting to another topic, gemstone reproductions are sold as real diamonds for a massive profit. The Syndicate manufactures them."

"How the fuck do they get away with this? Let me guess—one of their operatives—"

"Right again, works for GSI, the premiere authority of gemstone valuation and authentication. They have operations in South Africa and Argentina running distribution in diamond mines, to get sourced the highest quality original gems on which to base their manufactured versions."

"Glass, or crystal? How do they do it?" I asked, perched on the edge of a stool.

"They're cloning them."

Cloning diamonds. Deep fakes. So far I was only listening, not necessarily buying it. "Let's say for a minute that I believe you. Where does all this happen?"

He waved his hand left to right. "Various strategically-placed locations. Here in San Francisco, all over the world."

"San Francisco? Where?"

"You've been to the Cobaltic office."

I nodded, remembering how Bharat saw Lise working there. A tiny icicle in my heart froze a few degrees colder every time I thought of her. "That's a legitimate consulting firm, though. Probably not enough space for an operation like this."

"You'd be surprised what can be developed in small spaces when you know people on the zoning commission."

"Unbelievable."

"Do you know about the diamond exchange below Brannan Street?"

I knew where Brannan Street was but I shook my head.

"It's a subterranean labyrinth of underground offices. A fine jewelry wholesale marketplace."

I was picturing large buildings on Brannan. "For fake and cloned gemstones, you're saying?"

"No. The Syndicate's diamonds are not sold in any public market. But some of the manufacturing operations are done in offices in that location. Same with Cobaltic. You're right, they're a consulting firm. But not every inch of their office space is utilized for tech consulting."

Jeffrey walked around the space with his hands clasped behind him, giving me time to digest this wild story.

"What I don't understand is why go through all the trouble of diamond cloning. It sounds complex, expensive, and risky. Aren't there easier ways to make money?" I felt naïve asking this.

"Sure. Organized crime makes money through layers and layers of kickbacks from transactions related to waste management, contraband smuggling. We're talking about a very different level of commerce here. The financial gains, the new revenue streams and margins are unthinkably high."

There was that word again, unthinkable. Understatement.

"Get to the DNA part," I said. "I'm tired."

"Quite right." He came to the workbench, pulled out the other stool and sat beside me. "That's the most controversial one. Organ cloning and trafficking is a highly profitable, international black-market trade."

"I'm almost afraid to ask," I said. And the idea that Jeffrey—and Michael Horvath—were expecting me to take down this crime syndicate seemed surreal.

"Their operatives are geneticists and molecular biologists already in position at major pharma corporations with access to the latest technologies and test labs. They have expertise in DNA cloning, DNA genotyping, and are working on cloning organs."

"They're doing this now?"

"Oh yes. We've, they've had about eighteen successful placements so far."

"Placements. That means what exactly?"

"They passed these cloned organs off as originals to hospitals and other entities, and received a million dollars for them. Each."

I'd watched all but the last season of Orphan Black and Clone Wars, but outside of TV, I knew nothing factual about it. "Doesn't a donor and recipient need to be a DNA match?" I asked.

"Not DNA, no. You need compatible blood type as well as something called HLA matching. HLAs are essentially protein molecules, and though it's tricky with cloned organs, it can be done. They've sunk decades of research into this science."

"More like science fiction I think." I watched him as he spoke, deciding where he was on my bullshit meter. He seemed to know what he was talking about. "If they implant a cloned organ in someone, and it's not a match and the person dies, how is that a success?"

Jeffrey shook his head. "I'm not a part of their operations, Thea. I want you to understand that. But as our friend Michael said, I'm close enough to know what they're doing, how they're doing it, and why. The Syndicate has operatives who live on the black-market trading sites every day and understand those unique and highly variable supply chain logistics. They're skilled in running black-market financial transactions and have relationships with whitelisted legitimate vendors for distribution."

"Why not something easier and less expensive? Not to mention less unethical."

"Money." He shrugged. "When organs aren't naturally available, it creates a supply chain disruption and a lag in financial revenue streams. Manufacturing the desired organs through cloning is a supply chain solution that brings potentially outrageous profits, because in a dire situation when nothing else is available, families will pay literally anything."

I felt nauseous. "I wish I'd never come here."

"I'm sorry. I can imagine how this all sounds."

"Can you? Really? I doubt it."

"You're strong, good. You're gonna need to be stronger."

"Just a minute! I'm not agreeing to anything."

"Listen to me. The strongest people don't find ways to compartmentalize their feelings or push them down, pretending they're not wounded by them. They let themselves be cut, let themselves be wounded…and they use it. That's exactly what I want you to do."

I was only half listening at this point, checking out in the way I do, twisting my hair, counting back from a hundred, eyes gazing at a blurry spot on the ceiling.

"We're going to play tennis tomorrow morning, and practice."

"What is the fucking deal with tennis? I don't even like tennis."

He rose from the stool and leaned against the counter. "Michael Horvath has passed you the baton and given you the evidence you need to see it through. You need to decide whether you're gonna walk through that door."

"Cut the sales pitch," I sniped back. "Horvath gave me scraps of evidence, literally crumbs. He gave me no resources for law enforcement support, no indication that there was anyone even warm to the idea of pressing charges against these people. He's sending me on a trip to the woods blindfolded. What's my incentive for moving forward? I've already risked and lost so much." I paused and took a long breath. "Besides, I don't even have a way in."

"Oh, but you do."

"What?"

"Tennis is where they do all their negotiations, all their dirty dealings, out in the wide-open air for everyone to see."

"Hiding in plain sight," I mumbled. "Still doesn't tell me the way in."

"They play doubles every Saturday, all day Saturday, every weekend. It's a wellness ritual because it's good exercise for old men, and a socialization opportunity. Every weekend there's a sub on call to stand in if somebody can't make it. No one cares how good or bad the sub is because they're a sub. These people aren't competitive and they aren't there to win. They don't even keep score, really. They're doing business. They just want to run around and sweat and burn calories."

"You're grooming me to be a tennis sub? That's funny. But they won't talk business while I'm there, will they? I'm a stranger, a teenager."

"They'll see you around, they'll see you play, see how young you are—"

"Gross, a bunch of old men hitting on me? Is that what this is about?"

"For God's sake." He sighed and looked at the floor. "They're going to want to recruit you. When they talk to you, hear how smart and insightful you are, see that you have your own mind, a backbone, and a conscience, they'll be fighting over you like jackals with a rabbit."

"Lovely. And then what?"

"One thing at a time."

No wonder Michael was trying to stop them. If ever there was a reason to be a whistleblower, he'd found it. Jeffrey mentioned the pharmaceutical industry. Fergus and I watched a documentary on YouTube once about criminals posing as pharma employees and influencing drug trials to make them go faster. What if there was something even more sinister going on? What if the cloned organs were being traded in exchange for influencing drug trial results? I'd save that question for another day.

"Just one more question before my brain completely explodes. Where does all this happen?"

"The tennis matches, you mean?"

"No. You told me about their gemstone operations. What about the rest, the cloning operations and the deepfake videos?"

"I'll show you. Tomorrow. Now go get some sleep."

Chapter 47

Half of me was too agitated to sleep. The other half saw that king-sized, four-poster bed with its fluffy comforter and pillow-top mattress. I floated through this exhausted seesaw all night, remembering scraps of masked faces, syringes, gunned hands, bodies slathered with oil and robes with blood dripping from the bottoms. It was all so sickening and, yet, in a dream it felt safe, insulated from the reality of this dangerous new life. High school and innocence felt lost forever.

I lay there thinking about Eve Maddox, wondering what she might be doing right now, wondering if she wore silk pajamas to bed, what she ate for breakfast. Maybe she was thinking about me. More likely thinking about arresting me.

At some point, I got up to snoop around Jeffrey's house, happy that the floors were tile instead of creaky wooden boards. In my bare feet, I could almost run down a corridor without a sound. Doors were a problem, of course. In a mansion like this, a door could have cost twenty thousand dollars and been made of solid, polished teak. I found one I'd never seen before. It opened with a silent, liquid glide. Pitch darkness, exhaustion, I had no idea where I was in the house.

Just that I knew for sure I shouldn't be there.

I eased the door closed behind me and stood against a wall looking out at the twinkling night through long, vertical windows. What it must be like to be an architect and have enough money to design and build your own dream fortress. Beautiful, elegant, but was still jail. There had to be a way to contact Fergus, to let him know I was okay and ask him to go see my mom. I can't contact him, according to Jeffrey, or anyone from the life I've known since arriving in San Francisco, ever again. So they say. Still, I knew things. Secret things. Things about myself that others might now know, that I was more than just smart. I was wily, crafty, able to think of sneaky solutions to problems that no one else dared to because they involved risk. So, use it, I told myself in the dark room, told the bright stars twinkling back at me like silent cheerleaders.

Somehow I'd thought to bring my phone with me while roaming around the strange mansion. I texted Janelle, poor Janelle bothering her at this hour. But she'd told me once that her boyfriend insisted they keep phones out of the bedroom. *Fergus came to the shop yesterday and left his phone there,* I wrote. *Could you call him tomorrow morning and let me know if you found it or not?* I added gratitude-hands and heart emojis. At least now he'd know I was still alive, if she called him.

My eyes adjusted to the darkness. By the shape of the furniture, this was some sort of den probably used for cigars and brandy after dinner down the hall from the formal dining room. I was looking for a secret room, though, and of course there was one. There had to be. Why else would an architect design his own house if not to install secret rooms and passageways? The middle of the room had one of those tufted, leather sofas and two matching dark leather chairs with a heavy table in the middle. A long, narrow table lined the back wall against the windows. On the sides it looked like wood paneling. I nodded and smiled in the dark. This was an architect's house.

When Jeffrey told me about how he'd designed it himself, I swear his face looked like he was hiding a spectacular secret, one he was dying to tell someone but wouldn't dare. Irene might not even know about his secret room. I knew because it was just logical that he would have one. I loved how he'd passed off his basement fortress with its loud click and beeping mechanism as the place where he did all his secret work. Yeah, right. I knew enough now to rely on my instincts. Jeffrey Dade was trying hard to be trustworthy, but it wasn't working. Maybe my suspicion would help me stay alive a little longer, maybe long enough to do what Michael Horvath couldn't. It still hurt when I thought of him. Like Jeffrey said tonight, maybe I could use that pain, tap into it, to move me closer.

I'd kept track of the number of steps down the hallway that led to this room—twenty-five. If the next room was the dining room, theoretically there could be twenty-five feet of space hidden within the walls. An undeclared, unpermitted space. I resisted the urge to use the light from my phone, not wanting to betray my presence. Then again, I was certain he had cameras all over the house so he could be watching me right now, maybe expecting me to be doing exactly this. I started by walking left, feeling with my palms on the wood paneling, pushing with my fingers to see if anything popped open or if a lock had been installed. No. A lock would be visible to the naked eye and the whole point was for the opening to be invisible. I made my way to the back windows feeling nothing but smooth, polished wood. I didn't touch the back counter because it was glass and my fingerprints would be more visible there in daylight.

Now in the far-right corner of the room, I touched the wood, this time higher and lower as well as in the center, moving from the corner to the right wall. Wait. This corner of the room was just floor and walls, but the other corner had a tall plant. I'd brushed past the cool leaves on the way to the back windows. Wouldn't the symmetry of two plants be a better design balance in the room? Why only one plant?

Gotcha.

Quickly, I moved back to the other corner. The plant was fake, light enough to lift from the center trunk and set behind me. My open palm scanned the wood behind where the plant had stood for anything that felt out of place. No locks, no metal. Wait, I felt something. My right index finger touched a tiny cutout in the wood, like an indentation or small ledge had been installed. I groped above and below the ledge first. My hands picked up something that didn't feel like the rest of the wood panel. I made sure the flash was off, snapped a picture of that area with my phone, then moved behind the couch and crawled under it to check the image. Only when I was flattened under the couch did I raise the brightness 10% in my phone settings. I opened the image. Yes! I could see it was a slightly different color wood just under the little ledge I'd felt. I knew what to do. Phone off, back in the corner, I pulled down on the ledge. A 12 x 12-inch panel popped open to reveal a keypad. I stopped breathing, listening behind me. I looked closer; it was a typical alpha-numeric keypad. I typed in the numbers corresponding to the word Syndicate, without success, then added an asterisk in the beginning and end. Still no.

I'd had Michael Horvath on my mind all day, passively lurking in the back of my thoughts. It was the way his face looked, I still remembered it exactly when he said Jeffrey Dade was an interesting...and then he paused and said the word specimen in a Voldemort sort of way, like he might be struck down by lightning for saying it out loud. I typed the numbers for that word into the keypad and stood back. Nothing happened. Then without the slightest noise, that whole wall panel, top to bottom, glided open two inches. A noise from behind startled me. My head...

Chapter 48

I always know I'm dreaming because of how things sound. In this place, I was back in that ridiculous tennis dress and uncomfortable shoes moving toward a large fountain in the middle of Jeffrey's garden. But he didn't have a fountain; I'd been there twice already. In the dream it was sunrise, so there was a slight glow to everything around me—trees, flowers. I saw my face reflected in the water that pooled in the bottom of the dream-fountain—a shimmering, bubbly version of my face. What could be hidden in those bubbles, in the ripples in the water? A dark shape clouded the sky over my head but only in my reflection. The shape moved closer to me, then thinned out at the top showing jagged points that resembled the angles in a man's face.

"Hello, Thea."

Left thigh and butt cheek numb, an ache in my lower back. The front part of my head felt fuzzy and throbbed at the temples. Who is this man?

I woke on a rigid, upholstered bench against the wall of what looked like the inside of a trailer. The ceiling was low with the same tile floors as Jeffrey's den. This had to be it—the hidden room I knew was here. I jerked upright and my eyes searched for a fountain. There was no fountain, nor was there any reflection of me or my assailant in the water. But someone hit my head to slow me down. My weight wobbled on my bare feet when I stood. I walked slowly, moving to an open doorway. It led down a long passage the exact shape of the hallway on the other side of the wall. Good trick.

"You're awake," someone said from a room ten feet ahead, which made me suddenly aware of my attire—long t-shirt and no pants. Great. The room must be on the other side of the dining room. There were tiny lights embedded in the floor like an airport runway. I followed them into an expansive office with a huge, glass desk, glass tables, crystal lamps, and a scratchy wool rug. The desk was in the far-right corner; the man from the fountain was leaning against a wooden credenza in the middle of the room. He was old but still handsome, with a long face and sculpted features, clean-shaven, expensive clothes. Dark pants, white shirt, and gray vest. He was over six feet tall, taller than Jeffrey, with his hands knotted in front of him.

"Sorry about your head," the man said. His voice wasn't familiar; he sounded English, like Jeffrey.

"What was the point of knocking me out? You obviously know who I am and know I'm not an intruder. I'm an invited guest."

"Oh, you're an intruder alright," the man countered. "Of the worst kind."

"Really?" I was embarrassed talking to an English gentleman in a t-shirt with my bare legs showing, though he made no indication that he cared one way the other. Still, it felt awkward. I'd learned enough in seventeen years to understand power struggles. My inappropriate attire made me feel self-conscious and vulnerable. Jeffrey would tell me to use that to my advantage. "Does Jeffrey know you're here?" I asked.

The man pinched his lips together, drew in a long, slow breath while he ignored the question. Fine. I'd launch another one.

"How about telling me what you injected me with, when I was

climbing down from a garbage can behind my house."

"What in God's name are you talking about?" he asked, his words jumbling together.

"Stop pretending, you know it was you. Or someone who probably works for you."

"Cheeky, aren't you? They warned me. I think what you really want to know is if Jeffrey knows you found this place."

"Well, does he?" I asked.

"Nobody's up right now but us."

I looked around the room trying to recall whether the secret door was still open. The man got a smarmy smile on his face, brows knitted. "How did you know to even look for it?"

I shrugged. "Seemed obvious. Jeffrey showed me his secret room in the basement."

"I should think that would have been enough to satisfy the curiosity of an average teenager," he said.

I knew what he was doing. I let him proceed with his ingratiating words for a while; it was an opportunity for me to observe him.

"He's an architect. What's the fun in being an architect if you can't design secret rooms in your house?"

He blinked back, nodded to himself. "So, you suspected there was another secret room and went looking for it."

Wasn't he curious how I knew the correct code word to access this part of the fortress? "It wasn't a conscious decision, really. I couldn't sleep. I just sort of found myself wandering around the house and ended up lost and in his den by accident." I sighed, letting the seventeen-year-old me take over for a while. "Can I, like, go? I'd like to get dressed if you don't mind. Or had you planned to torture me here?"

He wasn't fazed by my sarcasm. "I've been hearing about you and wanted to meet you myself."

"How did you know I was here?" It was a great question. Great questions could be useful equalizers in the realm of high stakes negotiations. I'd seen enough movies in my life to know how they usually ended up, but I could be the exception to the rule. He didn't answer so I kept talking. "Are you an associate of Jeffrey's?"

"Thea...you have something in your possession that is...of immense value." He talked with long spaces between his words, this handsome English gent with fine clothing and sleeves neatly rolled up.

"Yeah, so I've been told."

"Do you know what it is?"

I shook my head quickly so he'd think it was an honest answer. I knew, though, didn't I? It had to be the picture I'd taken of Roberta that night, the one I'd hidden so skillfully.

"I don't know exactly what Jeffrey told you, but this is an important opportunity for you, an opportunity of a lifetime, really. For you to see, experience, influence some of the most significant levers that balance power across the globe. You, Thea Riggs, have the power to change the world."

"Really?" I felt sickened by his display. "The way you people are changing the world?"

"Listen to me carefully. I want to tell you a story."

"You like stories?" I cut in. "I've got a story." I cleared my throat. "How about the story of Roberta Fenning, who you and your associates pretended to kill so no one would go looking for her, and now you've been experimenting on her for your organ cloning business, where you sell the cloned versions for a million bucks each."

The man's face looked like chalk. I kept going, the idea of Roberta being alive only an unproven theory at this point. Wow. He wasn't refuting it so far.

"Let me ask you something. What do you see when you look in the mirror?" I honestly didn't know where that voice came from, this new voice, or a new version of me, a super badass version. I liked it.

The man tried to be smooth but his forehead was sweating. So maybe he wasn't Jeffrey's associate, maybe he wasn't part of the Syndicate. So, who was he and what was he doing in Jeffrey's house so early in the morning?

"I see a problem solver. A revolutionary. And what about you, Ms. Riggs? What do you see in that mirror?"

"The same."

I heard noises behind me, a door and footsteps. I turned and never thought I'd be relieved to see someone like Jeffrey Dade.

"Hope I'm not interrupting the party," Jeffrey said, clad in sleep pants and no shirt. Nice body. There had to be a gym in here somewhere.

"Come now, Jeffrey," the older man said. "Let's not be the creepy old men fighting over a young girl."

Jeffrey hovered in the doorway assessing the situation, our body language, the vibe. I read his entire relationship with the man by his contracted features.

"You were right," the older man said.

"About?" Jeffrey asked.

"She found it, just like you said she would. Your own little Hermione Grainger, the smartest witch of her time."

A Harry Potter reference, interesting. I stood off to the side, allowing them to spar uninterrupted.

"I see you've met my brother," Jeffrey said, his eyes fixed on the man.

"Don't you mean my older half-brother? It's how he always introduces me," the man replied with a strained smile.

"Thea Riggs, meet Dr. Axel Dade."

"Axel?" I tried not to laugh.

"It's a very old name from the English aristocracy," the man replied.

"Whatever."

"Are you quite alright?" Jeffrey asked me with searching eyes, but I knew he was asking about the code. What else would that word unlock?

"You've told her too much, brother. And isn't that typical? Always taking liberties you shouldn't, taking risks that affect more than just yourself."

"On the contrary," Jeffrey said, still in the doorway but taking one step towards me. "She worked it out for herself. I merely confirmed her theories."

"Any other theories, Miss Riggs? Or questions, while we're both here?" the older man asked. Axel Dade.

"What kind of doctor are you, exactly? Another Dr. Mengele?" I asked, hoping they'd be impressed by my historical knowledge. "Are you also working on cloning human embryos, not just organs? Why not, right? Not like there's any risk or ethical considerations."

"You're appalled, Miss Riggs, I can see that," older Dade said. "I'm primarily a geneticist, but I have considerable research experience in a number of adjacent fields. To answer your question, organs are a bit of a no-brainer, as you Americans say. But how genetic code would behave in an entire organism is still theoretical at this point. And way too risky a proposition without the right controls in place."

"And not at all part of Syndicate's future activities," Jeffrey added, taking a seat beside me, which changed the dynamic of the room. Jeffrey and I a unified front against his evil brother. They were both very likely just as evil as each other.

"I do have another question," I said. "Why Roberta?"

"Why not?" Axel answered, then shot a nervous glance at Jeffrey.

"I don't think for a minute that you choose just anybody for your organ clone DNA donors." I heard Jeffrey draw a deep breath beside me. "She was, or maybe still is, a relatively young woman, beautiful, widow of a billionaire. But besides being young, healthy and rich…" My voice trailed as I continued thinking. "There's got to be more to the story." I watched both their faces as I asked my controversial, maybe even divisive, question. Jeffrey looked satisfied, Axel nauseous.

"Do you see now?" Jeffrey asked his brother. "All the fuss you've been making about a seventeen-year-old girl. Now you know. She's not just bright, she's insightful, fearless, and all on her own she became connected with an elite, powerful family."

I knew, hearing Jeffrey just now, that what he'd told me last night had to be true. He was confirming his support for Michael Horvath's challenge that I somehow penetrate and expose the activities of this underworld alliance. Me. Jeffrey was promoting me to point man in the operation, and Axel was going to do everything in his power to stop me.

Chapter 49

Our house in the Mission had a secret—an illegal basement, a rarified space underground with a window that peeked onto Lexington between the magnolia leaves in our front yard. I knew now that this was my path forward—out of the spotlight, and instead seeking clandestine spaces like this from which to watch the tangled war of highs and lows, saviors and predators, while feeling my way to the right side of truth.

My reality check with Jeffrey Dade had left my chest heavy and mind dark. And I desperately missed my mom, though what would I even tell her at this point? Taking a tally of what I'd lost and gained in the span of one summer, I wondered how this path was supposed to be traveled. There had to be better ways of monitoring these monsters, checks and balances. But if the last three months were a glimpse of adulthood, I'd be better off locked in my room.

I never got an answer to my question about Roberta, which was answer enough. Roberta Fenning was more than just a billionaire's wife, more than a real estate agent, and by no means an average forty-year-old woman. I left the secret room without another word, knowing they wouldn't stop me. Back in the bedroom, I climbed onto the soft mattress. Axel Dade had hit me on the head to knock me out, but all that remained was a soft, dull ache in the left side of my skull and a deeper pain in my heart. What if while I was unconscious he'd injected me with something? It reminded me of the ankle shot I sustained, and I had no reaction to whatever they'd injected. Why did I think that was a bad sign?

Out of bed again, I stood in the bathroom and stripped down to examine my body under the overhead light. My skin looked dry and flaky, my breasts even smaller than the last time I'd seen them, if that was possible, and I could see my ribs sticking out more than before. I'd been skimping on meals and not working out. I looked thin and frail. I didn't like that. There were no obvious marks on my body, no pinpricks or red spots or areas that felt tampered with, or not that I could see in the medicine cabinet mirror, or with my own eyes. I returned to the bed telling myself to calm down and relax. These men weren't looking to kill or harm me. They needed me. And now I knew what that meant for me, too.

The windows in this room had no curtains and looked out over the back gardens. I remembered I'd grabbed my other burner phone and stuck it in a part of my backpack no one would ever look—at the bottom of the water bottle compartment. I pulled it out. Half-charged.

I made sure the bedroom door was locked and climbed back under the covers. "Hey," I said to Kit Fury hoping he could hear me. "It's Thea," I added, knowing he wouldn't recognize the number.

"Hey, Cupcake. I can barely hear you."

"Well, try because I can't talk louder. I need help."

The pause, always the pause with Kit, his mind working through personal gain opportunities. "I'm driving back from Sacramento. Where are you? Never mind, you probably can't say. What do you need?"

"A surveillance device. I'm staying in a house and I need to monitor their conversations."

"Well, there are lots of kinds of surveillance. You looking for just audio, video, a bug, a dot, coin, jewelry?"

I flipped over the top of the comforter to look out into the bedroom. Of course, no one was here. And of course they were surveilling this room with a hidden camera. Even so, they'd never hear me or even know I was on the phone. You're safe right now,

Thea, chill. "Something small and preferably sticky on one side. I want to stick it under a desk or something."

Another pause. "If these are the people who were tracking you, they're gonna have devices that constantly sweep their environment and detect devices like that."

Lord. He was right. "Any ideas?"

"I could put a car outside with monitoring equipment. Be easier to hear what they're saying. The range for reasonable audio coverage is about a half a block. We can install devices on the outside of the house so you won't need to do anything."

"Perfect. How do I, like, engage you to do this work for me? And what will this cost me?"

"Dinner," he said, no pause this time.

I sighed a little too loud. The last thing I wanted to do right now was piss him off. "With you?" I asked, just to clarify that's what he meant.

"Yes, Thea, dinner with me. No charge for the device, or to put a team of two people on the property for however many hours of service you need, wherever you're staying. Just dinner."

"I'd like Fergus to be there."

Long pause this time. He was trying to make it into a date, probably hoping I'd wear a dress and drink too many glasses of wine...I'd better stop there before I literally got sick.

"Alright, deal. Where are you?"

"Seacliff."

"Whoa."

"No, not the Fenning estate," I said. "It's a block away from there, I think at Sea Cliff and 27th Ave. Can you use my phone signal to find my location?"

"Yep, I got it."

I think I finally passed out around 4:00 a.m. waking with the same headache and someone's hands on my shoulders.

"Miss Riggs, the younger Mr. Dade would like to see you once you've woken properly."

It was Irene. I was surprised to hear that she too was English. I hadn't heard an accent yesterday. I took a quick shower and dressed in some of the nondescript clothes in the closet—loose sweat pants and a matching cropped top. I wore my own sneakers.

Sunlight seeped in through the tall windows, high in the sky so it had to be late morning. My phone read 10:50 a.m. Could that be possible? Amazing how comfortable I was becoming living out of a stranger's house, wearing clothes I hadn't bought, dodging one challenge after another and no longer requiring sleep. Was I getting used to this life on the edge, or had I sufficiently numbed my emotions so I was unable to feel anything at all? The thought scared me, this new and different Thea, because I knew my mother would be so disappointed in me right now. All she wanted in the world was to send her only daughter to college in the US. That dream, of hers anyway, felt a million miles away.

An urge to look out the windows to spot Kit and his goons stopped me at the door. No, forget about Kit; let him and his team do what they do. Downstairs, Irene had set two places at the outdoor table where I'd eaten with Jeffrey yesterday. There was no sign of either Dade, but I found her standing over the stove in a different apron today.

"Morning," I said.

She turned. "How are you feeling?"

"Why do you ask?"

"When I woke you earlier, you felt warm to my touch."

A devious plan hatched in my head as she said the words. I would, after all, need an opportunity to hear Jeffrey and his brother talking before I knew what they really had planned for me. Jeffrey's idea of them wanting to recruit me had a sort of egotistical appeal, thinking these powerful players might value a skillset I didn't know I had. But I suspected, even if that were true, this was only part of the plan. They needed willing volunteers to submit to their medical testing. I now knew that's what they'd been doing to Roberta. I saw her the night they faked her death—probably fake blood under her head on the white tiles, some kind of makeup to make her skin blueish. At that moment, she was obviously ill, near death, maybe just minutes away.

It was all forming in my head as I stared back at Irene and her look of feigned concern. Okay sure, I was paranoid, I had reason to be. They'd been experimenting on Roberta Fenning, though I still hadn't figured out why they chose her specifically. Did they remove one of her organs and implant one of their cloned organs to see if her body would accept it? Or worse, more than one organ? Jesus. If this proved to be more than just another of my theories, that seemed enough to explain how she looked on the floor of her kitchen. Something about her skin color made her look not just sick but almost…wrong. As if her body had been violated by something that shouldn't be there. Cloned organs. It still seemed like a bad movie.

"I hardly slept last night and I feel sort of nauseous," I lied, watching her deep, blue eyes stare back under a coiffed, blonde bob.

She nodded. "Let's have you go straight back upstairs, then, and get back in bed. I'll bring you up some tea after they've eaten. I'll let them know you won't be joining them today."

"Joining them where?" I asked.

"The tennis match."

I did what she asked, walking slowly and stopping to rub my face in case she was watching me and didn't buy my story. I pulled my burner phone, the second of my cheap, prepaid burner cells, out of the drink compartment of my backpack again. There was a new text from a 415 number. It was from Kit. He'd sent a single green checkmark with no text. That meant he and his team were in place with the audio surveillance. I exhaled.

Great, I typed back. *House?*

Y, three locations.

What if they leave?

We're on it.

How can I hear them?

Open your laptop.

How in the fuck did Kit get in this house and access my laptop? My room's on the second floor. I ran to the window. There were no trees tall enough to be climbed. Had he walked in the front door, posed as an electrician or delivery worker? I was almost afraid to look. I'd tucked the laptop in my backpack before going downstairs. I pulled it out, set it on a small desk and opened the lid. Sure enough, on the keyboard was a pair of ear buds beside Kit's business card that read, "Karl Fury, Business Innovations." Funny. Karl? I couldn't help but smile as I turned over the card. He'd written a URL in blue pen. Apparently I'd log onto this site to bring up an online player window, where I could tune into the audio of the oncoming Dade apocalypse. Hopefully I'd live through the experience.

Chapter 50

I stayed in my clothes and crawled back under the quilt again, dying for a cup of strong coffee. I felt proud of myself for creating a near-perfect scenario. Of course, waiting till they left for tennis was the right choice, because no doubt one of them would come up here to: a) make sure I was still here, b) verify that I was actually sick, and c) vibe me out with a menacing glare in case I had a mind to run. I didn't, because that would be too obvious. Our power struggle, so far, had been an interesting dance—me with my big theories and what Axel described as impressive insight, counterbalanced by the trauma of the past few weeks and my bottomless sense of dread. They could feel this, too, my well-mannered captors. I knew in my bones that they would likely try to kill me. Probably soon.

Kit again with a text. *Log on, they're leaving.*

Wait, so they hadn't come upstairs to check on me? Nothing? Just left with only Irene's report that I wasn't feeling well? These were not men who left anything to chance. So that meant there were cameras in the room. Without looking for them, I got out of bed, wrapped the laptop in a bathrobe, and slid it under the covers. I'd look for the camera later when it was darker. I pulled the quilt over my head and rolled to the side, adjusted the pillows and, in so doing, set the laptop on the bedside table with the headphones plugged in. From the doorway or surveillance cameras, you'd never see anything but a girl lying in bed. Perfect.

Getting set up now, I wrote to Kit.

Text me back when you're on the site and jacked in. I'll do an audio check.

I'm in, I typed, having logged onto the site, which was a radio broadcast showing an audio signal and frequency bands responding to sounds.

"Check check," Kit's voice. "This is for Thea. We can't hear you but text me if you can hear this."

Loud and clear, I wrote.

"Okay, changing the channel now. You should start hearing voices as soon as they talk," Kit said. "We're tailing two men, one middle-aged, one older, in the backseat of a black Lexus with someone else driving."

That's them, I wrote. *How far back is your team? They'll be onto you pretty quick, so be ready for anything.*

"We're about six cars behind him, getting on the freeway right now. Keep this channel open if you can do it safely and keep listening," he added.

He couldn't hear me, but how could he hear Jeffrey and Axel? Maybe for the same reason he was able to make it undetected up to this room to put his business card on my laptop. Kit's team had installed a tracker and listening device on their car. Maybe he wasn't so bad after all.

Plate number? I typed.

"Nada," Kit replied. "Government plates, which won't bring back anything. Stay tuned, I've just heard something. While you're listening to them, you won't be able to also hear me. I'll go to text communication till I say otherwise."

Okay, I wrote, and couldn't help feeling impressed by the velocity with which Kit had mobilized his team.

What about dinner? he shot back before I put down my phone. *That was the deal.*

Happily, I'd almost forgotten. *As soon as both you and Fergus are available, let me know and I'll be there.* Sure. I'd go out to dinner with Fergus and Kit. Two beers in, they'd start talking about Game of Thrones, and it would be like I wasn't even there. I'd slip out to the ladies room…and leave. There, a plan.

Kit hooked me in but all I heard so far was a car motor and muffed voices. This was never gonna work.

Knock knock knock. Shit. Someone at the bedroom door. That someone had to be Irene. Like the practiced little faker I had become, I slipped my phone, volume off, into the tissue box on the bedside table, a highly underrated hiding spot, pulled down the cover on the laptop, slid it all the way under the covers, and rolled over facing the door.

"Come in," I said, softly, like I'd been dozing.

Irene pushed open the door with one hand, balancing a tray with the other. A pot of tea, plate of buttered toast, and a tiny bowl of fresh raspberries, which actually looked appetizing. I sat up. "Thank you so much; you shouldn't have gone through the trouble."

"I'm the chef," she said, without any eye contact. She handed me the tray and I set it on my lap over the comforter.

I smelled it now—coffee, not tea, thank God. Miracle. Next, she placed her hand on my forehead and touched a thermometer to it without asking first. The thermometer beeped.

"One hundred point six, slight fever. How are you feeling?" Arms crossed now, standing at the bed. Up close like this, Irene looked about sixty, not eighty like Jeffrey said. She knew how to maximize her best features with makeup. Pearl stud earrings, single strand of small pearls, yellow button-down blouse, gray skirt, white apron. Sturdy and stocky without looking the least bit fat. I watched her face, the distinctive shape of her nose, and wondered what she was really doing here.

I knew she'd be back soon to make sure I'd eaten, and to pick up the tray, probably ultimately to spy on me and make sure I hadn't left. And no doubt my captors would be watching. I could certainly leave if I wanted to, just walk out the front door. I mean, how could she stop me? But then how would I get answers to the burning questions in my head, questions people had already died for? No. That's not who I am. I'm not running anymore. I'm in the lion's den right now and that's exactly where I should be. I believe in my heart that Roberta Fenning is still alive, and I might be her only advocate alive in the world. So, it was my job to find her. Michael Horvath trusted me with the task of taking down this corporate cancer, this Syndicate of destruction, but that wasn't the only reason. I'd found her, I'd seen her sickly, discarded body on the floor of her kitchen, maybe because I was meant to see her, or maybe it was an accident. I might never know. Right now, I had a choice. All in, or nothing? All in.

Oh my God, that was good coffee. I realized I hadn't had any in days, not enough hydration, which of course accounted for my headaches. I ate all the toast, every last berry, and most of the coffee before returning the earbuds to my ears. I felt suddenly drowsy, drowsier than I should be this time of day especially after two cups of coffee. Maybe I really was sick. Would serve me right for lying. I logged onto Kit's URL from my phone, so the next time Irene came in, I could show I was lying down listening to music. The sound of the car motor reduced to a low drone, the voices a little louder. I recognized Axel's stronger British accent, two different voices though; they were muffled so I couldn't tell them apart. They were arguing, one voice low and compliant, the other insistent and clipped.

"Well, what do you suggest, then?" one of them asked.

"I don't know but it's too dangerous. Horvath showed her the holy grail. She's seen everything, and who knows who she's told. She cannot be harmed. It's too dangerous."

"For God's sake, life is not a fairy tale. You know they'll come for her. And when they don't find her, they will come for you."

I texted Kit. *Where are they now? They're not playing tennis yet, right?*

I saw the status dots right away. *Parked.*

Where?

Cliff House parking lot, he wrote of the historic, ocean view restaurant up near the Sutro baths. I still couldn't believe it closed after over a century.

I sent back a thumbs-up to thank Kit for the status, sipped the last of Irene's coffee, and my lids clamped shut.

Chapter 51

I can't see but I can feel that I'm on a smooth surface. Oh God, it's that long table in the black robe mansion in Michael Horvath's video. I reach down and touch the soft cotton of a white nightgown over my naked body. Who put this on me? Where am I? How did I get here? Wait, no. I feel something cold under me, a floor. I'm on the floor. A white floor. A white, tiled…I'm lying on Roberta Fenning's white tiled kitchen floor next to the island, just like I'd seen her in that picture. My frantic fingers reach down, testing the fabric to see if it's wet with my blood, pushing on my skin to check for wounds. But nothing hurts. I'm not injured. Wait, now I'm back in Jeffrey's upstairs bedroom again. And now I'm on a table in the middle of a drafty room. What the hell is going on here?

It was morning before; now it was night. My gums hurt and my head felt fuzzy. Those unblinking blue eyes. Irene drugged me with a pot of strong coffee, and now I had no idea what time it was or how long I'd been out. My lower back was sore when I tried to turn over. I looked at my phone. It couldn't be.

I'd been out for…almost two days??

Someone must have given me water because I didn't feel dehydrated, but there was no IV in my arm, and no medical tape on my inner elbow where it would have been connected. Testing my mettle, I see. Fine, assholes. Bring it.

"Hello? Hello??" I shouted louder this time. I should have been afraid, of course. Anyone would in this situation. But looking around this large, dark, empty hall, fear was not what I felt. It was my tiger, pushing his nose between the bars on his pen. It was my rage waking from its slumber.

First, I sat up and looked under the white, cotton nightgown. For what? I laughed out loud at the absurdity. Was I looking for gunshot wounds, surgical scars? Just the shock of my naked skin, hip bones sticking out higher than usual, and the horrific truth that wrinkled hands had removed my underwear and pulled this ceremonial white lace over me like a sacrifice to the gods. I felt groggy but knew I'd have to work fast. They'd be coming back soon.

Growing up, *The Princess and the Goblin* had always been one of my mother's favorite stories. She read it to me in the little nook in my bedroom in Majuro, Grandma Irene lurking in the doorway listening, my father snoring in the rocking chair two rooms away. I was dressed now like Lottie, the little princess roaming through her vast castle. I needed to find my clothes and figure out where I was. I left the drafty hall and went looking through rooms one after the other, opening doors, seeing nothing but covered furniture and long drapes. I picked one random room and walked in, closing the door quietly behind me, staying close enough to the hall that I'd be able to hear footsteps. I opened the curtains, which lit up a den similar to Jeffrey's den with the secret room. But this room—I stopped, mouth gaping. I stared out the window at, how could this be? It was a view of the Eiffel Tower.

I think I'd heard one of them mention Paris before I passed out from Evil Irene's spiked coffee. The party they spoke of—the next DNA-collection depravity ball, was to be held in Paris. Why there? Right now, I needed clothes.

"Thea."

Jeffrey's voice echoed from the narrow corridor connecting the hall to this wing of bedrooms. I opened the door and went toward him. What choice did I have?

"Thank God you're alright," he said. His face looked anguished, as he stood tall in a beautiful, dark brown suit like he was ready to address Parliament. He made a *follow me* motion and took off toward an open doorway on the other side. The floor was cold and my feet were freezing. This wasn't a mansion like the Fenning Estate. This really was a freaking castle.

Jeffrey stood outside an open doorway pointing in. Okay, sure. I'd follow you, sick bastards. What else did you have planned?

"Your clothes," he said, motioning to the bed, where my sweater, undershirt, bra, underpants, and jeans were neatly folded.

I dressed right in front of him, whipping the nightgown over my head, uncaring that he saw me. "Who took those clothes off me?" I asked. "Irene, or was her job just to drug me?"

"None of that was my idea," Jeffrey said, standing watch.

"No, of course it wasn't." But I believed him.

"They needed you at this party tonight and had to find a way to get you here." He gave a small shrug. "It was obvious you weren't going to come quietly."

Fully dressed, I moved to within a few inches of him. "Who took my clothes off?" I repeated. "You? Did you like what you see? How many other girls like me have ended up here, hmm?"

"Axel wants to see you now," he said, ignoring my taunting.

"Well, by all means, let's not keep his highness waiting."

"Thea, listen to me. It wasn't—"

I waved him off, waiting to see which direction he led me to next. "Why is my presence needed at this fucking party? You put me out for almost two days." That reality sank in deeper after I said it. "Two days, Jeffrey. So, you had plenty of opportunity to take a sample of my DNA. What else did you do? Impregnate me with an alien human hybrid embryo?"

"Nothing was done to you," he said, and leaned his head towards my ear. "Yet. You were brought here and put into that ceremonial gown because, yes, you were intended to be, how shall I say, presented in a ritual purification process tonight."

I shuddered. I'd seen that video. I'd jump out the window before

I let anyone touch me. There was no way.

"But I'm gonna get you out of here."

I stopped to look at him again, Jeffrey Dade posing as my ally. "I don't—"

"Just come with me. There's no time. Now, Thea."

At the end of one hallway, we turned right to enter another, and another, which led to a rotunda with a spiral staircase. "Down there?" I asked.

"No. Here." He pointed, running now through the next hallway and across a large, empty expanse. I struggled to keep up with him, remembering that I'd been drugged and needed food and water badly.

"Jeffrey—" I called after him, now hearing footsteps behind me. Shit. I moved faster down a straight staircase with, I counted, forty-seven steps, remembering how I'd used numbers to calm myself during times of anxiety. Almost to the bottom, I checked in with myself. No, I didn't feel any of that anxiety, even now. I was closer than ever to seeing the truth with my own eyes.

I was absolutely going to that party tonight, for Michael Horvath's sake.

I just had to figure out a way to leave that didn't involve a gurney.

Chapter 52

I followed Jeffrey into another room, where he closed and locked the door behind us. It looked different than the others—larger, brighter, modern furniture, whites and grays, with a black carpet. Interesting design choice. Maybe black concealed stains, like blood?

Axel sat at one end of a rectangular table, flanked by two men I didn't recognize, Jeffrey standing at the other end looking like he was awaiting instructions, me ready to run.

"Oh good," Axel said, clapping his hands when he saw me. What theater. "Lovely to see you again, Miss Riggs. Glad to see you've found your clothes. My two associates..." He stretched his arm toward one man. "We were just meeting—"

"About world domination? Assassinating the President? Designing a new version of Ebola?"

The other two men looked uncomfortable. Axel lowered his eyes and smiled, apologizing to his associates for my rudeness.

"How do you test your cloned organs before implanting them in a dying person's body?" I'd found my voice again.

No answer, just three men constructing a tacit plan for my demise. Axel kept a close eye on Jeffrey, who stood with his hands at his sides.

"I think Roberta Fenning's been your test subject, maybe your entire control group. How many of her organs have you replaced so far?" I remembered her ghastly skin tone. "One, two? More?"

"Four, actually," Axel said, watching me closely now. "And happy to report she's coming along beautifully."

"Really? Can I see her?" I asked, remembering how she looked that night.

The man to Axel's left raised his hand. Axel gave his head a single shake. "No, my dear. I'm afraid that might pose some security risks."

"Of course it would," I replied, hoping Kit and his team were somehow recording this conversation through their surveillance equipment, though we were in Paris thousands of miles from home. I walked along the far end of the room by the door, pacing in long lines, wondering about the game, the Dead Sevens game, how many clues had been dropped, how many more lives were interrupted by it. "I'd like to actually play Dead Sevens sometime."

It suddenly felt like all the oxygen had been sucked out of the room, or the world. For a few seconds, I couldn't detect a single sound anywhere. One…two…

"What did you say?" Axel stood, finger tips on the table. And Jeffrey's hands were out of his pockets clenching into fists. I moved further into the room, walking along the right side towards the back windows, closer to one of Axel's men. Now I also had a view of Jeffrey as well. Axel's face looked as if I'd asked him to take off his clothes and mount one of the other men. I shrugged. "Just wondering if anyone fancied a game of Dead Sevens."

Axel and his two associates held their mouths open, eyes wide with blank, horrified stares. Meanwhile Jeffrey, at the other end of the table, stood soldier-stiff, eyes on the back window, face frozen. I looked at Axel for guidance. What just happened? I asked a simple question, absurd yes, but still an innocent question about a card game. Jeffrey looked not just at-attention but strange, like he was suddenly no longer himself.

Oh my God.

"What the bloody hell have you done?" one of Axel's men's shrieked, face posed in horror.

"I've done nothing," Axel replied calmly.

"Then how do you explain—"

"I told you."

A new thought cracked through me as I remembered a movie I'd seen as a child, a grown-up movie my parents never knew I was watching from the staircase, Rudy and me. It was a movie about subliminal mind control and a soldier was being activated, triggered they called it, by a question. I think the trigger, in that movie, was about going swimming in a pool; any mention of it put the soldier in a sort of trance, where he could be programmed to do anything they asked. I bent forward and lowered my head, afraid I might get sick. How could I have known this?

Still stiff as a board, Jeffrey's face told me everything, what they'd done to him, how they'd used him, this Syndicate of terror. Oh my God, Jeffrey, I had no idea. I wanted to run to him. Time clicked at half pace. My face felt cold, sweating, as my adrenaline-soaked brain climbed through the tangled threads. It was Jeffrey who had killed his own circle of friends that night, after he'd committed the violation of telling them what he saw at one of the Syndicate's surreal parties, threatening exposure of one of the world's most secretive and dangerous alliances.

I don't know how I knew this, suddenly. I just knew.

They'd programmed him, triggered him like I'd just done accidentally, to kill all of his friends to prevent any security leaks. All this time, I'd wondered why they never killed Jeffrey back then, why they let him escape. And of course, now it seemed so obvious. He's their secret weapon. My legs wobbled and my weight felt shaky. Hold it together, Thea. No sudden moves. Focus.

First things first, I remembered what Jeffrey had told me about deep fakes. What if I was in the middle of one right now? I moved to the back windows and tore open the curtains...and saw a perfect view of the Golden Gate Bridge. I shot a look back at Axel, shaking my head in disgust.

"So, your Eiffel Tower's a simulation. Not sure I understand the point, but nice gag." We were still in California, thank God, probably Belvedere by the angle of the bridge view. I exhaled a deep breath of relief. So that meant it was at least possible Kit was still monitoring and recording the conversation. I had to get a message to him somehow. But right now, I had a bigger job than that. Right now I had a highly trained assassin awaiting instruction.

If my crazed theory was right and Jeffrey's mind had been programmed to respond to specific triggers, my asking about a game of Dead Sevens had just prompted him into a highly suggestible state, where he could be ordered, or programmed—maybe by me—to do anything.

"Specimen," I said in a clear voice, looking directly into Jeffrey's eyes.

Axel's other soldier jumped up from his chair.

"This is outrageous," the man said. "She's just a girl. How could —"

Axel stretched out his arms to restrain them.

"Acknowledged," Jeffrey answered directly to me, not looking in my eyes but in my direction. He'd heard me. I had him now, the Syndicate's weapon; their biggest secret of all. Now or never, Thea. Deep breath.

"Roberta Fenning is here on-site," I said to Jeffrey. "True or false?"

"True."

"She's alive, correct?"

"Yes, Sir," Jeffrey answered me. Sir...interesting.

One of Axel's men retrieved a gun and trained it on Jeffrey's forehead.

"Don't shoot him," Axel shouted. "You can't take him out. He's my—"

"Brother?" I interrupted him, repeating what Jeffrey told me about Axel, which I realized only now was another cover up. I looked at their two faces, Jeffrey and Axel, back and forth. Of course. "He's your son," I said. "Isn't he? Jeffrey's parents didn't die in a car crash, that's the story I was told. It was another lie, wasn't it? His parents didn't die at all. You're his father." I turned to face Jeffrey again, whose face was still stone. "And Roberta Fenning's his mother."

Axel hung his head and covered his face with his hands.

"Why is Roberta here, Jeffrey?" I asked.

"She's a test subject for genetic research," he answered, as mechanically as the rest of his answers. I wondered how long this could go on, but more than that I wondered if he knew, before now, the truth about his parents. He didn't react. Not sure what that meant.

"Cloning research?" I asked him, taking a step toward him.

"Yes, Sir," he said.

"Take me to her, Jeffrey."

"Yes, Sir. Follow me please."

The fact that he was calling me sir had to mean that he'd been programmed to take orders from a man, probably only Axel. I followed him out of the room closing the door behind me, expecting to hear Axel's thugs chasing us through the house. They didn't.

"Jeffrey, run. There's not much time. We need to save her."

"Yes, Sir," Jeffrey said and broke into a sprint, obviously knowing exactly where he was going in the house. We took what looked like a servant's quarters staircase, a smarter idea than a closed compartment like an elevator. Three floors, four, how many were there in this place?

"Find my phone, Jeffrey," I said. It felt so odd to be giving him commands, and so wrong to be taking advantage of how they'd manipulated his brain, weaponized him. How many people had he been ordered to kill over the years? I felt sick.

Jeffrey reached into his jacket pocket and pulled out something. "Here, Sir." He handed me my phone, meaning my most recent burner phone. I slowed my walking pace to text Kit. *Transcript?? Are you still recording? Please I beg you say yes.*

Yes.

You followed us here? I think we're in Belvedere.

Tiburon, he wrote back. *We're right outside. Tell me how you want to play it.*

If Kit were here now, I swear I'd hug him.

Jeffrey stopped ahead at a closed door. A suited man stood in front of it. He saw Jeffrey and looked up as if waiting for instructions. Jeffrey looked at me.

"Remove the obstacle," I said.

With neither greeting nor hesitation, Jeffrey pulled a pistol out of the back of his waistband, lifted it, and shot the man in the forehead.

I held my hand over my mouth to keep from screaming.

The man's blood splattered over both of us as his body crumbled in the doorway. Jeffrey stepped over it and opened the door.

Chapter 53

The makeshift hospital room had the wrong smell but was equipped with a hanging IV and monitoring equipment in the far corner. Tears sprang from my eyes when I saw Roberta's lush mane of long hair, previously dark, now thin with streaks of gray. Could it be real? Her eyes, her face looked like the Roberta I knew. Her skin looked more normal than the last time I saw her. Seeing us, she reached out her hand. I went to her, Jeffrey standing at attention inside the door, which he'd closed behind me to conceal the body now littering the corridor. Roberta Fenning had always been smart, more than your average high school friend's mother at least. Her eyes took it all in, but I honestly didn't know how much of her was left at this point.

"Has he been…"

I nodded slowly, assuming she was asking if he'd been activated.

"Hello, Sweetheart," she said, to which Jeffrey replied "Hello, Mother," without looking at her. So he knew that, at least. Had I been the one to spill the truth about Axel? I almost felt bad in a way. I rubbed my weary eyes, reminding myself to stay focused.

I leaned down toward her face. "Does the untriggered Jeffrey know and respond to what happens with the triggered version?"

Roberta shook her head. "They're two separate regions of his personality." Her eyes glazed over, retreating into her head somewhere. "They did that on purpose, constructing their weapon very carefully." Her eyes met mine again, searching my face. "If you're here, and you know all this, that means they've severely underestimated you." She smiled. "I suspect most people do." She took my hand. "I didn't."

"I need to ask you this, because I just watched Jeffrey take out a guard in the hallway with no effort. Did he kill the original members of his childhood Dead Sevens Club?"

Roberta looked at Jeffrey's stone-still face. So did I. The eyes were open, but it looked like nobody was home. She nodded slowly. "They made him do it."

"That's what kept the Syndicate from killing him a long time ago?" I asked, trying to put the pieces together in my head.

"They have me, my compliance, my agreement to let myself continue to be tested, operated on, surgically…" Her voice cracked and she stopped, wiped a single tear. Wow, that strength. "Surgically improved, as they call it. I do that so Jeffrey can live in his nice house, play tennis, and feel like at least one part of him is living a normal life." Her head and trunk shook with sobs. "Other than Lise, he's all I have now."

"Does Jeffrey know Axel's his father?"

No answer. I knew what that meant. "They've used Jeffrey to test memory-wipe procedures. It's happened so many times, I'm surprised he can even find his way home anymore. And, like I said, the separateness of the two sides of his brain is what allows him to emotionally survive."

"We have little time," I said. "Can you walk?"

"Slowly, but I've been practicing walking around the room." She cleared her throat and used my hand to balance as her feet touched the floor. "I knew you were coming. I knew it would be you, Thea. I always knew."

Did she mean instead of Lise?

"We need to find a way out of here," she said.

"Can I assume the weapon gets turned off the same way it's turned on?"

"Yes."

"Same word?" I asked. *Specimen.*

She nodded.

"Then we'll use him to help us get out. He's still activated."

"If we don't have evidence, there's no point."

I remembered the text from Kit. "I might have that covered, too." It was so odd that of all people Kit was my lifeline right now, outside on the street doing his underworld magic, gathering evidence that would probably never be admissible in court.

"Jeffrey," I said. "Get us out of here safely and back to your house. Can you do that?"

Just then, a door slammed closed, a raised voice somewhere in the house. Shit. They know.

"Yes, Sir," Jeffrey said. "This way. Quickly."

"They're following us."

"They know nothing about this house."

With a strength I wouldn't have guessed she had, Roberta pulled the blue hospital gown over her head. She was fully dressed in the same clothing she'd had on the night I saw her. Dead, or so it seemed, in her kitchen. The second worst night of my life.

Roberta trailed after us with Jeffrey in the lead down the polished hallways of the Tiberon mansion. First a staircase, down one floor, then to a freight elevator that smelled of laundry detergent and cigarette smoke. Jeffrey pushed the letter B. With a hard thunk, the oversized elevator car glided down five levels and stopped.

The doors didn't open right away.

From somewhere above us, I heard a loud screech and another slamming door. They're never going to let us out of here.

My heart, already in overdrive, thumped in my bony chest. Jeffrey calmly withdrew a set of keys from his pants pocket then stuck one of them in a lock on the elevator console pad, rotating it to the left. The doors opened to darkness.

"Follow me," he instructed in a cold monotone. "Wait in here by the windows. They're unlocked. When you see the lights, climb out."

"Where will you be?" I asked him.

"Standing guard outside the door."

I thought about the code word, then, wondering if now was the right time to re-trigger the man I otherwise knew as Jeffrey Dade. If I did, there seemed less chance that he would make it out alive. Would normal-Jeffrey be willing to kill anyone in his path for our freedom? Or would he end up as another of their research subjects? I already knew the answer.

With one arm around her waist, I helped Roberta to the far windows checking to make sure they opened. One was locked, the other unlocked. Hopefully it would be low enough for us to climb out and reach the ground without injury.

"Why don't you sit here and rest." I lowered her to the floor just under the windows. Next, I texted Kit. *Can I call you?*

N, he wrote back. *What's your status?*

Extraction needed. Someone's helping us and is supposed to be bringing a car around to the basement windows of this Tiburon mansion. I'm here with one person waiting. Can you monitor the situation?

Yeah, sit tight. Lemme find you first.

Hey, listen to me. The person helping us is very dangerous. He'll shoot you without a second's thought, Kit. You can't talk to him. Don't bother telling him who you are. I'll explain later.

Short pause. *Roger that.*

"Help is coming," I said to Roberta, who'd closed her eyes. I sat beside her with my arm around her, pulsing my hand on her arm to help keep her awake. Her skin felt cool. Too cool. "Stay with me," I whispered.

"I'm surprised I've lived this long," she said. "Live—" She exhaled.

"How long have they been doing this, you know—"

"Organ cloning's big business," she said, her eyes open again. "It's an international black-market trade going back decades. Only difference is that transactions now involve online commerce, like crypto."

"How is the Syndicate involved?" I asked her.

She sat up straighter, her eyes glassing the room, seeming to come alive from the possibility of escape. "They monitor black-market trading sites, which means alternative supply chain channels," she began. "They have relationships with approved, vetted, legitimate distribution vendors. The same people that run these black ops are CEOs of major corporations. It's inside-outside all the way." I had no idea what any of that meant. She turned to look into my eyes. "You can't imagine the scale of this, Thea. They've got an army of doctors, scientists, skilled operatives on every content."

"Politicians?" I asked.

"Hell, yes."

"What about the parties? Isn't there another one soon?"

"Tomorrow night," she said. "You—know about those?"

"Sorry to say, yes. So, all the people who give their DNA samples—"

She nodded. "All Syndicate operatives. Some are medical workers who use those samples to perform a complex set of tests to determine compatible blood types. Kidney, liver, thyroid, HLA typing."

I watched her eyes blinking, coming back to life as she rattled off the list. Another thud sounded from upstairs, creating a vibration on the floor. My eyes and ears were on red alert for the sound of that elevator. Supposedly Jeffrey was outside the door, but we were still sitting ducks down here. I stayed poised at the window monitoring sights and sounds.

"Then the usual EKG, chest x-ray. I'm a goddamn expert." Roberta shook her head.

Her hair was dirty, oily and matted. I still remembered the image of her in an emerald green evening gown once, going to a gala dressed in sequins like the starlet she was bred to be. I pulled that image into the secret box in my heart, where I'd keep it forever.

"There's a lot that happens behind the scenes even before they get to me, and the others, to start testing."

"How many other cloning test subjects are there?" I saw something outside the basement, a flash of something – not light but movement. I positioned my ear to the ground to listen, but there was no sound. I looked back at Roberta for the answer to my question.

"Hundreds now," she shrugged. "I was the first."

My God. All this going on in San Francisco right under our noses. "How many cloned organs do you have in your body right now?" I asked in a meek voice.

"Four," she said like she was counting pieces of fruit. "They're clones of my own organs so you'd think there'd be no compatibility issues. But there are, well...unforeseen issues no one ever planned for."

"Do you even realize how many lives you might be saving by your sacrifice?"

Three knocks from the window over our heads interrupted the moment. Show time.

Chapter 54

As my eyes had adjusted further to the darkness in the room, I could see something long, slim and gold with an odd-shaped handle ten feet in front of us. A fireplace poker on a stand with three other tools—a long-handled clamp and a mini-shovel. Someone somewhere was looking out for me. I grabbed the poker and returned to Roberta, whose eyes were closing. She was weakening.

Three more knocks, open palm this time, more insistent. I peered out but couldn't see the face.

Kit, is that you at the window? I texted.

No answer.

"What do we do about Jeffrey?" I asked Roberta.

"You mean if that's not him at the window?"

That wasn't what I meant. "Who's going to, you know, deactivate him?"

"Too late for that. Maybe it's for the best." She looked right at me. "He's a weapon now. And he'll need to be."

I crawled a little further under the window, behind some stacked wooden crates, the very crates we'd need to stand on to get out through the window. Then I saw a face that melted my heart.

"Fergus thank God," I said aloud. An instant warmth bloomed in the center of my chest. "We're safe," I said to Roberta. "Try to get up." I reached down, held Roberta by the elbow, and hoisted her up onto the first crate.

"Ooohh."

I grabbed her. "Come on, a little higher," I said, knowing her pain was less important than our escape. I placed my palm on the window exactly opposite Fergus's hand. My heart exploded with relief.

"Open the window," Fergus said. My fingers found the latch eight inches up from his hand. I rotated it toward me; it finished the cycle in a sort of pop. I pulled it open and stuck my head through.

"Oh my God you have no idea..." My voice trailed. I grabbed his face and touched foreheads. "Where's Kit?"

He backed away and stared, mouth closed. Shit.

"No."

"Over there." He pointed. "He's been shot."

"We didn't hear anything." I lifted Roberta by the hips. He grabbed her under her shoulders and pulled forward while I pushed her legs through. I was deciding whether to take the fire poker with me when I heard the familiar clunk of the elevator. God, no. I scrambled out the window pulling it shut as best I could from the bottom, fire poker in-hand.

Roberta sat panting on a mound of grass outside the window, Fergus beside her wearing a wool cap and dark hoodie. "Silencer, maybe? You can see the bullet hole."

I whispered to Fergus about the elevator, not wanting to alarm Roberta. Then again, what that woman had lived through, there was probably little that would surprise her. We headed out to the left. Fergus pointed to a body on the ground. "Oh no, Kit." Hand on my mouth, I was muffling emotion that couldn't have formed for Kit Fury. But it did. He was here for me. I leaned down and touched his neck. "There's a pulse, barely. We've got to take him with us."

"You take Roberta," he said. "I'll get Kit."

Crickets, low clouds over a dark sky, and a damp smell in the air. Fergus and I used to love camping out on nights like this in our backyard, freezing on the cold ground and not caring because that's what you do during summer, during your glorious two months off

275

from school. Was it still even summer anymore? Was this even California? When had I last seen the sea?

"What are you doing here?" I asked Fergus. "I mean—"

"Kit called and told me to contact the PD and ask for Officer Maddox. I got here a while ago, and he told me everything."

"The recordings?" I asked, frantic that our evidence be preserved.

He was ahead of us but I saw his head nod up and down. "We've got everything recorded. I've got something else, too."

"You okay?" I'd been holding Roberta around the waist but by now she was walking okay, almost on her own.

"Where are we going? The road's in the other direction," she said.

"Right up here," Fergus answered her. "Kit's van is parked under some trees."

The van was huge, almost double the normal size. The door was open on one side. A blocky, military-looking dude reached down to grab Kit. Fergus told him he'd been shot. I touched Kit's neck again. No pulse this time. My God. I helped stretch out his body straddling him, opening his mouth with my fingers. I breathed two large exhalations down his throat, then sat back and pumped his chest, was it twenty-five or thirty times? Or did it depend on the person's body weight? I'd taken CPR two summers ago and never had to use it.

"Wake up, Kit. Kitty, come on, we need you!" I repeated the process, this time thirty chest pumps, careful with the placement of my hands to properly massage his heart. Oh my God, Kit, if you don't die I swear I'll go on that date with you, even without Fergus. I leaned down to give him mouth to mouth again and I saw his eyes move under his lids. "Kit." I tapped his cheeks. "Kitty. Wake up."

He coughed.

"Oh, thank God." I grabbed his head and wrapped my arms around him. Fergus hugged him awkwardly from above.

"Yo, you got water up there?" Fergus asked the driver, who passed back a Hydro Flask. Fergus lifted Kit's head and gently poured two small sips of water into his mouth. What an expert. Kit's eyes were barely open, but he swallowed the water and laid down again.

I grabbed his hand and squeezed it. "Stay with us." He squeezed back with a single pulse.

"Where's the nearest hospital?" I asked.

"Marin Health Medical Center," someone said from the back. I knew that voice.

"Mr. Wilde?" What was Fergus' father doing here?

"Roberta, back here." Fergus positioned her in one of the only actual bucket seats in the van; the rest had been removed for equipment. He strapped her in.

"Thank you," I heard her say to Fergus. "All of you. Hurry. They're coming."

The military dude, named Hansen, drove out through thick trees, jostling us in the backseat. Kit was lying flat while Fergus and I tried to hold him down. Mr. Wilde stayed in the furthest backseat with headphones on, monitoring something on a computer.

"Kit saved your life, you know," the driver said, looking back at me specifically.

"I know," I said.

"I mean, he shot the guy who was coming for you. I found him in the woods."

I had no words.

"What's your dad doing here?" I asked Fergus, though having a lawyer around was not necessarily a bad thing.

"He's compiling data and preparing a report, which you'll need to help him with, to give to a federal judge to get a search warrant for this place."

If Kit and Mr. Hansen had recordings of all the conversations that took place in that house, and in Jeffrey Dade's house, that was powerful evidence, the kind of evidence for which Michael Horvath died. The kind of evidence that would be hard to ignore, unless of course the Syndicate owned every federal district court judge in California.

I recognized the road when we got onto the freeway. Route 131 went right into Marin General Hospital where it met Highway 101. It was late. We'd be there in ten minutes. Still, I kept my head turned back looking out the rear window, paranoia well intact. Why wouldn't they be following us? Roberta and I were both powerful witnesses, adversaries, and liabilities that threatened exposure of their operation. We knew their identities, but more than that, we both understood the larger scope of their agenda, and their motives. Of course I'd help Mr. Wilde with that report, unless it was already too late. Bright lights shined in my eyes.

"They're right behind us."

"Kit's stopped breathing."

I felt disconnected, maybe due to adrenaline overload, like I was watching myself give Kit CPR with our bodies bobbing up and down in the back of a massive van with no seats, tearing down the freeway at ninety miles an hour. The car pursuing us was no doubt driven by a Syndicate driver, or maybe Axel himself.

Another possibility was that Jeffrey could be programmed by more than one person and maybe Axel had coded him to kill me.

Could he do that, though? Was there enough of original Jeffrey Dade left in there to resist their commands? Only Roberta would know that but right now she was sleeping through the drama. Lucky her.

I called Marin General to let them know we were two minutes away. I should have phoned 911. There was no time to wait on hold. Kit wasn't waking up now.

Fergus was holding Kit, rocking him back and forth. My God.

Fergus' father had taken off the headphones and closed up his computer in a backpack. He looked at me and nodded, conspiratorially. Maybe that meant he'd just emailed me the transcript, or emailed it to himself for safety. Michael Horvath died for that transcript. Now Kit's died for it too, died saving my life. Saving all of us.

I checked Waze. We were two exits from Marin General.

"It's up here on the right," the driver said. "Hold on, I'm gonna make a quick exit."

The driver screeched into the right lane, not losing any speed. He veered off the exit ramp, no doubt still visible to our pursuers.

Hansen, the driver, pulled up to the ER entrance, parked, and dragged open the side door.

With Kit and Roberta attended to by medical staff, I led Fergus and his dad to a Family Lounge on the second floor. All hospitals had them. When Rudy died, I'd found one for my mother and me. My dad had been parking the car that day and he couldn't find us for an hour. Worst day of my life.

Chapter 55

I smiled at Fergus over the cribbage board on the floor of my room. We'd spent the past twenty-four hours sleeping, eating, and explaining things to my mother until I ran out of words. She kept bringing in trays of food, even when we were already eating. I knew she was a trainwreck. I'd been MIA for way too long.

"So, what's this I hear about a date we're going on, with Kitty?"

Teflon Kit had survived a close-range gunshot wound, and was moved this morning from ICU to a regular room.

Roberta had been admitted. She was still undergoing tests while struggling to get her medical team to believe her claims of cloned organs.

No one had heard anything from Jeffrey.

"Kit said he'd help me with audio surveillance of Jeffrey and his brother if I went on a date with him."

Big smile. "I can't believe you said yes, for one thing. But—"

"I only said yes if you could come with us, and he agreed."

"Okay."

"What?"

"Does he know you have a crush on a police officer?"

It felt like my heart dropped into my stomach. I didn't move, then turned my head to see if my mom had heard the question.

"A female police officer?" he added.

"You know?" I whispered. "How do you, how long have you—"

"I'm your best friend, right? It's my job to understand you."

I saw him but my vision was blurred by tears. He knew? How long had he known, how long had I agonized in my isolation that no one knew this formidable detail about me? More importantly, did this mean I was out, as in out-out? Still locked in Fergus' dark eyes, no. Nothing felt real unless my mother knew about it. But now I was one step closer.

My mother looked sullen this morning, like she'd given up on something. Hopefully not me. I felt the vibe and found her in her room laying out a clean pair of scrubs for work.

"Aren't you off today?" I asked, careful, still knowing she was fragile right now, that my sudden disappearance had scared her to death and that I'd probably lost her trust.

She turned, wrapped her arms around me, and pulled me close to her, close enough to hear her heartbeat. "I'm just going in to check on a patient, no duty shift. Thirty minutes at most."

"That's fine," I said. "Fergus and I are going to check on Kit and Roberta. Can we ride in with you?"

"I'm leaving in five so if you're ready, sure."

A nurse was bringing Roberta back to her room after helping her walk around the floor. She smiled and reached for my hand when she saw me in the doorway.

"You look stronger today."

"I feel okay," she said, then closed her eyes a moment.

"What is it?"

"Lise was here. Earlier."

My face hardened. "She knew everything. Didn't she?"

Roberta thanked the nurse and I helped her back into bed. She didn't need to answer me, I already knew. Maybe the night I found her, Lise ran out to escape the horror of what they were doing to her mother. And maybe when she said she'd be better off dead, she was right.

"I haven't heard from her," I said.

"You will. She told me. Soon."

Kit was out of ICU but looked like he was let out prematurely. His color looked patchy, reddish stubble on his neck and chin, eyes closed, his lids were red. Fergus and I stood in awe in the doorway, then moved quietly to each side of his bed.

"He's probably faking," Fergus said, purposely too loud. "Such an ego. He's just trying to get attention."

A low tone emerged from Kit's throat. He turned his head toward Fergus. "Water," he said.

We stayed with him like that, letting him communicate with just nods to not drain his energy. Then, when we were about to leave, his hand surprised me by grabbing my wrist. I jumped back an inch; my sneaker squeaked on the floor. Fergus turned.

"Hey, I'm right here. We'll be back tomorrow, don't worry. They said you need to rest."

"When's our date?" Kit asked, his voice raspy from intubation.

I flashed my eyes at Fergus and smiled.

Out in the hallway again, there was so much I'd wanted, and still needed, to say to Kit Fury, to thank him for responding so quickly to my SOS, for the van, the equipment, his associates. I was dying to know how he got in and out of Jeffrey's house. But most of all for saving my life. My phone, my real phone now, buzzed with a text from Janelle. I told Fergus.

"Does she know where you've been? She's probably worried."

"I told her I was working out of town."

"Nice."

I checked the text. "She said, um…"

"What?"

"She said there's a guy asking for me at the shop." I wrote back to her. *Cop?* I asked her.

He says he's your dad.

I showed the text to Fergus.

"Your face," he sort of laughed. "Total deer in headlights."

"What do I do?"

"No problem," he said. "You got this. Come on."

"Where are we going?" I asked, panicking. Was he coming with me?

"To see your mom."

Right. I followed him down a hallway and one floor. The nurse's station said she was in a room around the corner. We found her behind one of the nurse's station reception desks sorting through a file. Fergus took my phone from my hands and held it out to my mother.

"Oh. Fergus," she said. "How are you? What's that?"

"A text Thea just got."

I stood beside Fergus on the other side of the desk from my mother and another nurse talking on the phone. My mother's face hardened into an odd shape.

She passed the phone to me. "I'm working," she said.

"Wow, Mom. Really? You're not gonna see him?"

"What's he even doing here? He hates to fly, and that's a really long trip."

She was right. Majuro was a fourteen-hour flight across the Pacific. "That's fine," I said without answering her. "I'll go."

Fergus grabbed my hand. "I'm going with you."

My mother pinched her lips and sighed. I always loved Fergus' quiet manipulation techniques. He successfully guilted my mother into going to see the husband she'd abandoned. I rode with her. Fergus left for work, vowing to meet me later to check on Kit and Roberta.

I hadn't seen Janelle in a week. The fact that she hadn't texted me till now told me she was probably relieved to see me move on. Still, I owed her an explanation, since she'd probably saved my life.

I hadn't seen my father in almost five years. Funny how the human heart has the ability to surprise you. Before my mom had even turned off the engine, I bolted out of the car, running down the street towards the café, leaving her to deal with the parking meter. I saw him through the glass, standing by the window awkwardly between two small, round tables. My mom, now, was behind me twenty paces watching him through the other window, our fractured little family once again co-existing in the same zip code, triangulated through time and two pieces of glass.

My heart caved at the sight of him like I was seven again, running toward him from the far end of Laura Beach, past the large kukui tree, past the rock wall remnant jutting out into the water. "Pick me up, pick me up," I used to say, then when I got to him I'd say, "Carry me."

Yet somehow, since then, I'd learned to carry myself.

Chapter 56

Grandma Irene was dying, he told us. We sat there at one of those small, round tables drinking Janelle's damn fine coffee till dinnertime. He wanted to visit us for the entire month of November but, for now, he was petitioning us to go *home*, as he called it, back with him to Majuro to say our goodbyes.

He was staying at a hotel instead of our house, which I could tell my mother found insulting. Though I knew she'd act put out if he asked to stay with us. I was supposed to start school in two weeks. I hadn't told my mother yet whether I was going or not. Aside from how wild horses couldn't drag her there, I suspected she wouldn't be able to take the time off of work anyway, and would rely on my pre-college freedom to return with him to Majuro.

The next day, I let my dad drive me to Berkeley, where I met with three of my tutoring students wanting to bolster their math skills and confidence before starting high school. I owed it to them.

"Do you like tutoring?" my dad asked me.

"I love it." The words came out before I had a chance to review them.

"Look at you, Thea," he said beside me in his rental car, his eyes narrow and searching. "I can hardly believe it. You're a young woman now."

It was true, I loved teaching. But I now understood that I was destined for something very different. After the events of the past few months, I'd developed an unhealthy shoe-drop habit of expecting catastrophes. It wasn't anxiety and I wasn't scared, but more like expectation. I still didn't know why no one from the Syndicate had contacted me, why they'd let us go. Of course they were paranoid about exposure and maybe taking me down would be too obvious, and damaging to their enterprise. By now the Justice Department had to have reviewed the documentation package we helped Fergus's father write. Tonight, I would ask him for an update.

My dad dropped me off in front of the student's house, and leaned over to hug me and kiss my cheek before I got out. He'd always been a man of few words. This time, he was on a mission.

"So?" he asked looking out the opened passenger window.

"So what?"

"Are you coming or not?"

I loved my father's deep set, soulful eyes. They were the eyes of a watcher, a dreamer, like me. He had the traditional Marshallese *eeon-maj* tattoos of vertical lines going down the right side of his face. He told us, Rudy and me, about his tattoos when we were little, about our *jowi,* our family's clan, called *Irooj Rik.* He watched his controversial question wrestle its way through my body because I hadn't answered.

"She has a message for you."

My heart sank. Really? He was pulling this out now? Obviously a planned manipulation to try to get me to go there. "I'm listening."

"Grandma Irene has something she wants to give you, and she'll only give it directly to you. After she's gone, no one will ever know what it is."

"Sounds like her," I sighed and got out of the car at my student's house, then texted him a few minutes later. I guess I felt a little played and needed him to suffer about it. I agreed to go, fly all the way across the open ocean to see my magical grandmother before she became part of the sky.

My father had some people to see, so, after tutoring, I took an Uber home. Alone in the house, my mother at work, I picked up

Sasha and held her in my lap, stroking her long, luxurious coat. There it was again, listening in the darkness. Just crickets, the next-door neighbor's too-loud TV. I showered, put on a long t-shirt and leggings, and—a noise on the front porch that sounded like the shuffling of feet on the slate steps. Were they coming for me finally? I no longer cared about the Syndicate's cloak and dagger bullshit. I walked to the front door and opened it wide without looking out the peek hole.

It was Kit.

I opened the door wider, wrapped my arms around his neck and made him come in. He was actually walking okay, but I deposited him on the couch to be safe.

"You don't look that terrible, actually."

"Gee, thanks," he said.

"Dude, you were shot two days ago. You're lucky to be breathing."

"The bullet hit my shoulder and grazed my skull," he said, with a sly smile. Kit could be cute sometimes, shocking as it was to realize.

"Did you drive here?"

"I live-parked out front so I can't stay long."

"Dinner whenever you want," I said. "No Fergus, and I'll even wear a dress."

He lowered his gaze to the floor.

"There's this math lecture I was thinking of going to, on number theory. I mean, if you want to see something I'm really interested in. Then we could go to dinner after?" He wasn't talking. "What is it?" I asked. "Something about the case?"

He shook his head, leaned forward, and slowly pulled out some folded sheets of white paper he'd stuck in his back pocket under his shirt. I could tell he was in pain. He handed them to me.

"What's this?"

He set his hand on the paper so I couldn't unfold them. "Let me tell you about them before you look. This is a partial transcript from the other day, from the house in Sea Cliff. I followed the two guys and their driver to a tennis court, like you expected. But they didn't play—they just sat there talking for an hour."

"About...Roberta?"

He shook his head.

"About me?"

"At some point, did they drug you?"

"Yeah, twice. Why?"

"Because they took a sample of your DNA."

Oh my God, the ankle prick. This wasn't happening.

"They sampled your DNA and they were talking about what they found. When you read this transcript, you're gonna read about how you apparently share several genetic markers, they called them," he exhaled. "With Jeffrey Dade." Kit paused. "Do you know what that means?"

It seemed like I was thinking, it must have looked like I was thinking, but my mind was a complete blank.

"They think you and Jeffrey Dade are, somehow…siblings. They talked about it for a long time, argued about it."

"Axel and Jeffrey?"

"I don't know their names. The tall older fellow and the younger thirty-something guy. I don't know who was talking, just that it was those two."

I drew a quick breath and nodded, poised for battle. "Keep going. Tell me what you know."

Kit put his hand on mine. It was cool and clammy. Clearly he was still in danger, medically speaking. "Apparently your mother, when she was putting herself through nursing school, was cleaning houses to earn extra money."

"I know. She did."

"Well, she was cleaning the Fenning Estate at one point, working for Roberta, while Roberta was dating the older guy. Roberta went on a weekend trip for work, and—" Kit closed his eyes. "I'm sorry, Thea."

"What?" I was thinking the worst. "My mom? Fucking Axel? Did he rape her or something?"

"He said, the older guy, that they had relations twice that weekend. They also talked about how your parents, your mom and your dad, weren't married yet and had broken up for a few months, but after that affair they got back together and your mom moved to the Marshall Islands and married your father. Because of the timing, your mom always assumed you were your father's child."

At some point I'd sat on the floor, though I didn't remember moving. I was holding onto my shins, rocking back and forth. "So, are you telling me my father isn't my father after all, Axel Dade is my father and Jeffrey Dade my half-brother?"

"Just read the transcript."

I swallowed the lump in my throat. How could this even be possible? And what was I supposed to do with this information now?

I didn't sleep at all. The next morning, while my mother was still in bed, I opened the front door to bring in the newspaper and found Eve Maddox sitting on the bottom step. Almost not recognizing her out of uniform, I stopped breathing for a second.

"Officer? Is that you?"

"Good morning." She got up and stood facing me, dressed in jeans and a tight t-shirt, tucked in. Her hair was pulled back, like always, and she wore no makeup today. My heart pounded as I considered all the possible reasons for her visit. I went out and closed the door behind me.

"Shit." I closed my eyes.

"What, did you just lock yourself out?" she asked, laughing at me.

"Yeah, but..." I reached down and pulled the key from under the doormat. I held it out to her.

"I'd strongly advise against putting your key under the mat, from a personal safety standpoint."

"But you're not on duty right now, are you?"

"No, I'm not. I'm not here as a cop."

Gulp.

"Your friend Fergus must really love you," she said, emphasizing the word you.

OMG, Fergus, what did you do? "Love? Sure, friendship-love. Family-love," I clarified. Was she fishing for something? I couldn't get a read on her.

"He seems to think you've developed some sort of attachment to me."

My forehead was sweating, and my mouth went completely dry.

Just kill me now. "Um…I'm sorry. You're making me really nervous."

"How do you know I'm not straight?" she asked, of course the million-dollar question. She tilted her head when she said it. That had to mean something.

"I don't know. Because I feel it."

"You're right, I'm not," big smile now. "But I'm partnered. She's actually moving in with me end of this month."

I said nothing, which seemed like the safest thing to do. I looked at the trees off in the distance, the sidewalk across the street.

"Are you even out yet, Thea?"

I looked down. "Other than Fergus?"

"Well, you told him, obviously."

I exhaled. "I can't even take credit for that. He guessed."

"So, you haven't told anyone, not even your mom?"

Especially not her. "Not yet. I've been a little busy lately."

"I guess so." I knew she'd been copied on all the correspondence going back and forth from Fergus's father to the feds about the evidence we'd compiled.

I was barely awake and forced into an encounter with someone I so badly wanted to impress. "Am I under arrest?"

"I'm here as a friend, because I think you might need help right now. I'm a sworn officer of the law, and at the beginning and end of each day, that's what we're supposed to do. Help people."

I invited her in for coffee, she declined. I still didn't know the purpose of her ambush, other than to tell me that a) she was gay, b) she knew I was gay, and c) she was unavailable. I'd add it to my long list of disappointments.

Chapter 57

There's something inherently naughty about grandmothers. It's not that I thought my father was lying when he told me Tata was dying. Or maybe she was lying—to him, to everyone, just to lure me back to my roots.

It worked. I flew with my father, while my mother stayed home brooding, taking on additional shifts so she could avoid how she felt about my father's unexpected visit, how he suddenly gave a shit about us after seven years. I knew how she felt because I felt it too. But when I took in his face, the sad look in his eyes and the slight downturn on the right side of his mouth, like Rudy's, I was defenseless because it touched the most vulnerable part of my heart. The hollow part that I still don't think anything will ever fill. It's this room, no, more like a sacred chamber—dark with tons of tiny candles, incense, where Rudy lives inside me, playing guitar in cutoff shorts and bare feet, always knowing what I was thinking…hiding. Even now, Rudy would know that I was completely avoiding the conversation with Kit and had no intention of actually reading the transcript he'd left with me about my real, biological father, Axel Dade. I hadn't seen the test results myself, but Kit said the printout of the results showing the genetic markers in common with Jeffrey were on the last page. I wasn't sure this was enough to constitute conclusive medical evidence of paternity. It was a theory and nothing more at this point.

We waited at Amata Kabua International Airport after an exhausting, bumpy flight from San Francisco. My legs were sore and cramped as we walked into the terminal. My cousin Darius, who'd never cut his hair, met us in a new pickup, tossing our heavy bags in the open bed like they were made of feathers. I sat in the back letting him catch up with my father. My heart felt heavy and I needed the solitude. Today was my eighteenth birthday and my father hadn't mentioned it. I suspected he probably didn't know. My mother would be all the more depressed having me away from home today.

Around me were healthy, green trees, aqua sea, and wide, smiling faces unburdened from the speed and complexity of life on the mainland. I was definitely not in San Francisco anymore. I sort of laughed inside considering how this all might be a big fake. She would do that, too, Grandma Irene. I remembered the Betty White fake death scene in that movie "The Proposal" where she didn't fess up until they were all on a plane and it was too late to turn back. Rabid. Irene would definitely do this because she was funny, light-hearted, and at her core didn't give a rat's ass what anybody thought. A true matriarch thriving in her power.

We stopped at home, meaning the home I grew up in, to drop off our bags and let me change clothes for a swim. Oh my God, that water had been beckoning me, so warm and clean you could drink it. I'd never swam in San Francisco because, seriously, who could do that without a wetsuit, and why would I want to cover myself up to swim in the sea? I knew about surf culture, I watched Fergus, I'd done it myself. But that was surfing. Swimming—that was a special, immersive, almost spiritual experience. Wetsuit? No way. Just go where the water's warm, right? But I didn't swim after all—just floated there with the sun on my face, seaweed touching my fingers as I stretched my arms in and out to feel the viscosity of the water. My father sat holding his knees on the sand. In the same way his crooked mouth reminded me of my brother, I must be reminding him of the same thing.

No, for the hundredth time, Dad, I wasn't hungry, even though the breadfruit and fish he'd prepared looked amazing. He put up his palms and backed away. Of course, we didn't know how to deal with each other. I was a baby, just about, the last time he saw me, a gawky ten-year-old. And now, I'd just set the stage for a take-down of a corrupt, global crime syndicate. Hard to believe, especially for me.

I finally got to Tata's by 6:00 p.m. One of my aunties had done up the room to make it look like a hospital room. I say "done up" because I knew in my bones that they were all full of shit. Irene looked pale, laying on her side pretending to sleep. Yeah, right.

"Baba says you're not well." I closed the bedroom door behind me. Her bedroom always smelled like her favorite perfume, Elizabeth Taylor Passion. I think she just liked it because of the pretty purple bottles, since purple was her favorite color. I rubbed her shoulder, pretending to rouse her from her fake nap. That's when I realized she could actually be dying. Her cheek felt clammy, but it was always humid here, so hard to tell.

"Grandma, are you awake?" I said now in a meeker, younger voice. Maybe she was really sleeping. Maybe cancer was working its way through her body. I stepped away and stood at the south facing window.

"It's on the dresser," she said, and coughed. Well, that cough didn't sound good at all. Maybe the joke was on me.

Some folded papers with something hard in the middle reminded me of the transcript from Kit, which I still hadn't read. I plopped down in the white, ratan chair by the window crossing my legs. The pages were empty but two, 3 x 5-inch pictures dropped onto my lap —one of Rudy and me when we were little, and another of both of us on each side of Irene's lap. Outside in that very yard behind me right now. My composure surprised me as I held them in my fingers, remembering Rudy's joy, and knowing he had demons that he never wanted me to know about. I knew he was using drugs before anyone else did, because his eyes didn't look like his.

I set down the pictures and emptied something from the folded, white pages—a jade pendant of a fishing rope on a black, leather twine, crudely knotted on the end. Rudy had worn this all his life; he was wearing it in both of these pictures. Before I knew what happened, I was sobbing in a heap on the white carpet of Tata's room, sobs convulsing out of me leftover from all the unchecked emotional baggage of the past two months, from the worst summer of my life, and probably the most important. I pictured my father and auntie on the other side of the door, deciding what to do with me. I stayed there like that, coiled in a fetal position, face pressed into the shag rug, knowing Tata was with me in this moment a few feet away.

I felt her hoist me up into her arms and she held me there, standing up by the window in her room.

"You know you're not sick, Tata. Stop pretending."

"We're talking about you right now. What's going on inside that head of yours?"

It wasn't my head; it was my heart. But maybe she was right, I too often let my head guide me instead of my inner compass, like she'd taught me. "I don't know what I'm doing."

"Oh, yes you do," she said, gently. How I loved her voice.

The family perpetuated the Tata game for a few more hours as they prepared a big feast. I told them all lies about how I'd spent my summer, playing cards with Fergus—whom they were sure was actually my boyfriend—tutoring math students, and taking college prep courses for San Francisco State. Tata always said I had an affinity for herbal medicine; she was the Majuro Atoll's most revered herbal healer. I shook my head at the dinner table when she mentioned it, not to scoff or disrespect, but because I knew I had another life waiting for me on the other side of the world.

"What will you major in?" Tata asked, as if I'd already agreed to go, confirming this next phase of my life.

"Criminal justice." Those two words tumbled out before I'd even had a chance to review them. Hearing them spoken vibrated something in the center of my chest, maybe that secret room where Rudy lived. I felt a light turn on in there just now. Father or not, Axel Dades of the world—beware. Thea Riggs is coming for you.

About the Author

Lisa Towles is an Amazon bestselling and award-winning crime novelist, and a passionate speaker on the topics of fiction writing, creativity, and self-care. *Specimen* is her thirteenth published book with a new thriller, *Lineage*, planned for 2025 release. Her 2023 thriller, *Terror Bay*, won a NYC Big Book Award, Literary Titan Award, and is a Crimson Quill Awardee from Book Viral. Her 2022 thriller *Salt Island* won five literary awards and is the second book in her E&A Investigations Series. Lisa's deep commitment to helping other authors led her to develop her YouTube author interview series, Story Impact, which gives authors a powerful medium for promoting themselves as speakers and discussing the meaning and impact of their books to readers. Lisa has an MBA in IT Management, is a communications and marketing advisor, and is a member of Mystery Writers of America, Sisters in Crime, and International Thriller Writers.

Follow Lisa at linktr.ee/authortowles and subscribe to her monthly newsletter:
https://tinyurl.com/4a3bvdpn

Acknowledgments

Writing a book and bringing it to readers is a messy, convoluted process that requires equal parts inspiration, perspiration, discipline, and recklessness. For every book you see in a bookstore, there are a multitude of hands that helped shape, strengthen, beautify, and refine that story to make it worthy of you. I loved writing *Specimen*– Thea Riggs never stopped surprising me by her strength and grit. If you enjoyed her journey and story, it's largely because of the kind souls below who helped keep me sane during the writing process, pushed me to improve my craft and inspired me to reach the finish line.

To my husband Lee - thank you for understanding, supporting, and encouraging me to continue to grow. Your love makes literally everything possible.

To my parents, who continue to inspire me by their agility, resilience, adaptability, and talent. You're my guiding light.

To my sister, who's such an amazing mother, business leader, companion and supporter. You're the wisest person I know.

To my nieces, who are growing into such amazing young women.

To my publisher, Lisa, for your wit, wisdom, guidance, and patience.

To my editor, Cindy - without you this book wouldn't have been publishable. Thank you for all you do.

To my kind and generous beta readers – Lee, Missy, Kat, Max, Ron, Ben, and Ana. Your feedback and attention to detail are helpful and precious gifts.

To my cover designer Tatiana, for once again doing your magic!

To my cherished writing companions, for your inspiration, guidance, and companionship. I'm a better and happier writer because of you.

And to the wonderfully supportive readers of this book and my other books – THANK YOU from the bottom of my heart for your honest feedback, comments, support, and love.

Thank You for being on this journey with me

The Ridders

Political Thriller
Indies United Publishing House (2022)

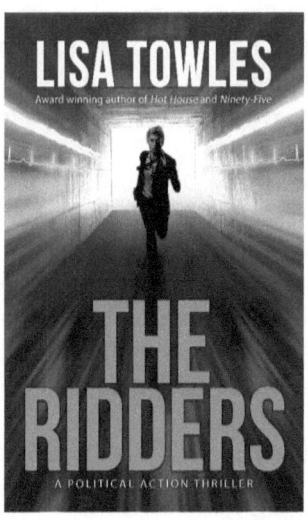

Young PI, BJ Janoff is randomly approached by a stranger with a proposition he can't refuse – a million dollars to deliver an envelope to a hotel lobby. The pusher forces him to accept the money upfront and threatens to kill him if he doesn't deliver the envelope in three days. BJ's growing obsession leads him down a treacherous path toward the orchestrators of the game, where he discovers a large-scale political controversy, a treasure hunt for a priceless sword, and a global crime ring linked to a WWII-era secret society. When an act of brilliance changes the balance of power, the safety of everyone he loves is in jeopardy. And the more he digs, the closer he comes to truths he can't bear to face – about his missing father and the elusive Bilderberg Group.

Chapter One

What would you do if someone offered you a million dollars to bring an envelope to the reception desk of a luxury hotel? That's it. Sure, a no-brainer. A relatively inconsequential risk, easy money, right? Trouble is, anything involving a million dollars might not be what it seems. So many questions. Namely why me, BJ Janoff, should be offered this seemingly innocuous task. There were no answers available, no consultants waiting with details or clarifications. One million dollars in cash to perform this social experiment. Right now. Yes or no?

I know what my older brother Jonas would do. He'd say no because of the multitude of potential hazards his paranoid mind would concoct, keeping him tied to the past, still wearing the same ugly khakis from ten years ago, stuck in the protective bubble of his big house in Ladera Heights and his geriatric Mercedes. So, of course I didn't tell him. Yet.

Then there was Lacy Diaz, the girl-next-door-turned-lawyer, who drives a car flashy enough to get a speeding ticket if she goes over fifty on the freeway.

"Hell, yeah, I'd take it," she said, with about a hundred caveats. What do you expect; she's a lawyer. "Wear rubber gloves," she said. "Ask to see the contents of the envelope first. If it's money, fan it out so you can see the bill denominations. Take photos of the payor."

"Photos of the payor?" I laughed and closed my eyes, a response Lacy inspired by pretty much everything she did. "Excuse me sir, would you mind if—"

"I'm just trying to protect you from potential—"

"Potential. Now you sound like Jonas. His whole world is so much potential there's no room for now."

"He's your brother. You can't choose your family so get over it."

So be it. A million dollars? Hell yeah, of course I said yes, I'm not stupid. Luckily, the task was intended for not only the most beautiful hotel in LA but the one I went to almost every morning. Sure, the cappuccinos were okay at the Peets counter, but the staff was even more noteworthy.

"Good morning," I said, loping up to the counter.

"Is it?"

"Pretty sure." I didn't let my eyes fall below Raquel's neck, given her choice of a low-cut blouse.

"Usual?"

"Yeah." I watched the Westin Bonaventure Hotel staff moving wordlessly through their tasks today. A keen observer of human behavior, I knew something was going down when Mario the bellhop pushed an empty cart past me and lowered his eyes to the floor. No banter, humming, rapping, high fiving me. No smile. "Hey?" I called after him. "What am I, invisible?" Alena, who managed the daytime housekeeping staff, hurried after him toward the elevators. Her face looked like she'd been crying all morning. No makeup and she was buttoning her uniform top while she walked. Maybe I'm paranoid.

Raquel was moving slowly and clearly not interested in talking. So I took three steps to the left to get a view of the reception desk. The typical chorus line of coiffed, perky concierges today included a confused, twenty-year-old in a wrinkled t-shirt. Something, no doubt related to the FedEx envelope I'd tucked into the back of my pants, was afoot. Out of coffee sleeves, I burned my fingers on Raquel's cappuccino and hunkered low on a lobby sofa watching and sipping. A cadre of men in identical black suits marched to the reception desk. Here we go.

I calculated my distance to be roughly fifty feet from the polished, walnut counter, maybe forty-five. Lucky for me, the acoustics in here rivaled the Guggenheim and I could hear everything. One suited man in front, nine underlings huddled behind awaiting instructions. I heard the word envelope posed as a question. The misplaced pothead behind the counter looked like he might start crying any moment. He gazed through the suits into the cavernous lobby space. Don't look at me, buddy, I don't exist right now. I took three more sips of coffee then back to my morning theater.

My phone buzzed with an incoming call. Jonas, who I suppose qualified as my business partner even though I wasn't paid an equal salary, and there was no legal agreement in place that formalized our working arrangement. "Hey, bro," I whispered.

"Hey, bro?" Repeating was one of his annoying traits. He had so many.

"What?"

"Where the fuck are you?"

"On a job," I lied. "Where are you?" I laughed inside, knowing this would unglue him. He hated the idea of my taking side jobs because he felt I was unqualified to be a private investigator. When our partner Archie Dax was still around, we used to laugh about this. He and I were so similar. He understood me almost better than anyone. I'd only had my investigator's license for less than a year when he died, but he never thought that mattered. Said I had the right head for PI work. Aww, Arch. My world's not the same without you.

"Job? What job?"

Poor Jonas. I still hadn't told him.

"Okay look, we've got the Bergman family coming in at nine tomorrow morning and I need the…" He exhaled long and hard, specifically to relay his frustration and inspire guilt. That ploy never worked with me.

"What, Jonas—WiFi? Maybe you've heard of something called the internet. Yes, I know, and we're good."

"Router, that's it."

Lord. "It's not the router, it's the modem speed and the unit will be upgraded within the hour. We're fine. Just let them in when they arrive."

No response.

"Are you crying?" I asked. "Pacing? Take your pill, Jonas."

"Fuck off. Say hi to Raquel for me."

I hung up and the phone rang again. "Dude, what?"

"And please don't wear your stupid backwards baseball hat. Please? I beg you. The Bergmans have money, a lot of it. We need that right now."

"Okay Jonas, no hat. Happy now?"

"We'll see."

Okay, so about the Bergmans. Jonas had been talking with them, Sten and Estelle, for the past two days about their vanished eighteen-year-old daughter, Anastasia, heir to their multi-billion-dollar estate, and how her net worth made her an especially enticing ransom target to what they described as "the underworld". LA's not utopia but not sure I'd call it an underworld.

Just two more errands today. First, I put a five-dollar bill in Raquel's tip vase even though she didn't see me. She still deserved it for being open at 6 a.m. and for looking so goddamn beautiful first thing in the morning. Then I held a small, black plastic ball in my hands and set it on a side table with a perfect view of the hotel's reception area. The table was on the other side of the seating area so that meant roughly thirty feet from the front desk. The plastic ball, a nanny cam designed to look like an air filter, was partially concealed by the fat leaves on a fake rubber tree plant. Unless someone moved that plant, or the filter for that matter, I'd be able to see the front desk of the Bonaventure Hotel for the next twenty-four hours via an iPhone app, which I suspect would be time enough to see why someone would pay a stranger a million bucks to deliver a stupid envelope.

"A fast-paced, tense and gripping murder mystery" - *Readers' Choice*

"A captivating tale that engrosses on many levels" - *Midwest Book Review*

"A must-read for fans of suspense thrillers" - *Book Viral Reviews*

Awards: BookFest Award (1st Place), American Fiction Award (1st Place), Millennium Book Award (Longlisted), Literary Titan Award (Gold)

Ninety-Five

A Young Adult Thriller
Indies United Publishing House (2021)

Troubled University of Chicago student, Zak Skinner, accidentally uncovers evidence of an on-campus, organized crime scam involving drugging students, getting them to commit crimes on camera, and blackmailing them to continue under the threat of expulsion. Digging deeper, Zak discovers that the university scam is just the tip of the iceberg, as it's connected to a broader ring of crimes linked to a darkweb underworld. Following clues, Zak is led to a compound within Chicago's abandoned Steelworker Park, only to discover that he's being hunted. While trying to find his way out alive, Zak discovers there's something much more personal he's been running from – his past. And now there's nowhere to hide.

Prologue

"Ten dollars...each."

I reached for my wallet. Riley put up his palm. "We're guests of a member."

The bouncer eyerolled. "Who?"

"David Wade," Riley said.

"We're both students here. Asshole." I held out my ID.

"Wade's not here and I'm not going looking for him. Twenty dollars or leave."

I handed the guy two tens, then he stamped both our wrists. The entry doors opened with David Wade on the other side, hair styled like a teen magazine cover. Typical.

"Hope you didn't pay," he laughed. "You're my guests."

"Wade." I had a feeling I'd be doing that a lot this year. We followed him back to a booth by the pool tables.

"I've set up two meetings," Wade explained. "For each of you, and they'll be conducted separately."

"Why? Divide and conquer?" Riley asked.

"I shouldn't even be here," I said eyeing the door. "Riley's way more desirable to a fraternity. He graduated third in our high school class." I was in the top thirty percent, if that.

"Dude, you are not leaving me here alone. This was your idea," Riley reminded me.

"Listen up. Sigma Chi's first, then Phi Gamma Delta." Wade with his frat salesman flair. Fine, I'd give them five minutes.

"What's your finder's fee?" Riley asked the most important question of the night.

A pitcher and three glasses appeared on the table. Funny how I never knew what I was drinking in this place. Just beer. Not IPA, Pilsner, Belgian. We were college students; we'd drink anything, right?

"You mean if you're selected? Less than forty-percent of frat recruits actually make it in." Wade lowered his head. "Even lower for enlistees."

I repeated Riley's valid question. "What do you get out of this? For some of these elitist Republican machines, the dues are like three hundred bucks a month."

"What?" Riley snapped his head toward me. "You're right. What are we doing here?"

"We're socializing, remember?" I said. "We just transferred two months ago. We hardly know anyone." I could barely remember NYU at this point. Chicago's a long way from home.

Wade smiled his smooth, snaky grin, enjoying the logic of my statement. He raised his glass. "Well, here's to new beginnings."

"Choke on it." Riley clocked Wade's glass. He glared at me while he guzzled the entire contents.

Wade refilled Riley's glass and disappeared with the empty

pitcher. Now that the pool tables were filled, the noise had doubled, probably because we were getting drunker. Riley hated to drink. In fact, I was surprised he agreed to come in the first place. But it was on campus, just a short walk from Granville West, our home away from home.

"Hey." A new guy shoved into Wade's side of the empty booth. "Sigma Chi, how's it going? Which one of you is Zak?"

Riley and I pointed to each other. The guy had a peach fuzz crew cut. His face looked like it was scrubbed every thirty minutes.

"I can't imagine why you'd be even remotely interested in me," I admitted. "Riley's got a 4.0 GPA and a way better pedigree."

"Yeah, but you have lawyers in your family," Riley shouted in his bar voice. He leaned in and smiled in a way that revealed rising blood alcohol level. "More likely you'd be able to afford the fees."

The frat salesman shifted on the bench, sizing us up. He turned his head back toward the bar, probably looking for Wade, the eternal icebreaker.

"Fees are optional," he said in a bitchy tone.

I peeked one eye at the door, making sure we had a path of egress. Wade was naturally nowhere in sight.

How could Riley bring up my family like that? So crude and indifferent. He never could hold his liquor. I didn't mind paying to get in here, or even sitting through this ridiculous formality. It beat the monotony of hanging out in our dorm waiting for life to happen. But Wade had showed up at the door, vanished, and now I just felt played.

"Oh, I see," Riley broke in. "You only charge them to offset your legal fees resulting from discrimination, rape, and aggravated assault lawsuits? I get it. That must be really expensive. You know, hard to plan when all your Daddy's money's going to—"

"Riley," I clipped. "Shut it. Let's get out of here."

I scanned the interior. Pool tables, dart boards, wood paneled walls; I remembered reading that The Pub in the basement of University of Chicago's Ida Noyes' Hall had been run by descendants of the Medici's. The only thing missing in here was Sherlock Holmes. Raised voices caught my attention from the opposite corner, then the sound of a beer bottle breaking. Ah, the perfect diversion.

I yanked Riley's elbow and we headed for the entrance. Five seconds later, I looked back still plowing through the crowd.

"Where are they?" Riley asked.

I pulled open the door and we slipped out.

Two guys followed. One from Sigma Chi and another I didn't recognize. They were all the same to me.

"Walk faster," I said. "Follow the path, straight ahead." Sure, we needed to get away from these people, but the more important question nagging me was why we would be of interest in the first place. New to campus, barely social, not wealthy. What attributes would be of value to them?

"The Fountain of Time's up ahead," Riley said, speeding up. "Are they behind us?"

As I was about to answer him, two different guys cut through the evergreens to our left and blocked us.

"Hey guys," one of them said, palms up, toothy grin. "Look, Damen got us off to a bad start. Let's start over. I'm from Sigma Chi."

"And I'm from Phi Gamma," the other said. "Please, come with us so we can talk. That's all we want."

"We're not interested in you frat clowns, the world's fucked up enough already."

Riley drunk always cracked me up.

"We're all here because you think we might have the money to pay your dues so you can maintain your alcohol supply," he added.

The thugs squared off in front of us. Riley stepped back. When he crossed his arms, he lost his balance and fell back on the grass. Nice.

Phi Gamma dragged him off with an arm around his shoulders. Sigma Chi stayed with me, waiting. Watching. He sat on the grass and pulled out a flask. I kept my eyes on Riley, now twenty feet away.

"Liquid courage?" I crouched on the ground across from him, knowing at this point we'd need to listen to the pitch before they let us go. If.

Riley and Phi Gamma were no longer visible. Fine. I'd give this freak five minutes of my life, then I'd go find him. I had no fear of him at this point, just irritation. I watched the guy pour something into two little silver cups—one the lid of the shiny flask, the other from his pocket. What else had been in that pocket?

"Absinthe," the guy said with conspiratorial pride.

I raised an eyebrow. More impressive than Budweiser.

"With or without *thujone*?" I asked of the historical wormwood hallucinogenic constituent.

"You know your poisons," he replied. "Without." He handed me a cup and tapped it, then swigged his down in one gulp.

Where was Riley? What the fuck were we doing out here? I came to this school for a fresh start, as my mother put it, and somehow I didn't think this was what she, or even I, had in mind. Sigma Chi, my salesman, held out the shiny silver cup with a wet smirk on his lips. Was I about to end up in Mexico or as somebody's bitch in Danville Prison?

"Riley, you alright?" I shouted behind me.

No answer. Sigma Chi stared, wiggling the cup. At this point I was more annoyed than afraid. I wasn't happy at this place yet, at this University. Riley wasn't either. But I wasn't ready to throw it all in either. Had anyone ever died from absinthe? I grabbed the cup, swiveled it around a bit, smelled it, then chucked it back in my throat. Like sophisticated licorice. God help me.

"A dazzling trip into a dystopian techno-nightmare" – *David Prestidge*

"A riveting thriller" – *San Francisco Book Review*

"Marked by its striking execution and razor-sharp dialogue, this places Towles among the best of the genre" – *Prairies Book Review*

Awards: Readers Favorite Award (Winner), Literary Titan Award (Silver), Clue Award (Finalist), Indies Today Award (Semi-Finalist)

Stay Updated on Lisa Towles' Releases:

https://tinyurl.com/2rscr38y

Stay Connected:

https://linktree.com/authortowles

LINKTREE

NEWSLETTER